OUTCAST NEW BEGINNINGS

A WORLD OF ZENTOS STORY

OUTCAST
NEW
BEGINNINGS

Book 2
Tarrenfall Chronicles

AJ Ashton

First published through Amazon 4 May 2023

My Awesome Editor: Yvonne Davis, whysewordswork@gmail.com

Formatting and cover design by AJ Formatting

Outcast New Beginnings

AJ Ashton

Second edition 2025

AJ Ashton

ISBN - 978-1-916969-06-3

DEDICATION

To my parents and my son for always listening to my ideas and giving me the encouragement to publish my books out into the world.

Also, to Kate and Howard for being my number one fans. Both have always given me such positive support. Hope you enjoy this one as much as Book 1.

WORLD OF ZENTOS BOOKS
IN TIMELINE ORDER

Outcast Origins Book 1 Tarrenfall Chronicles

Outcast New Beginnings Book 2 Tarrenfall Chronicles

Quest of the Stone Book 1 Ranger Chronicles

Quest of the Broken Stone Book 2 Ranger Chronicles

Outcast The Return Book 3 Tarrenfall Chronicles

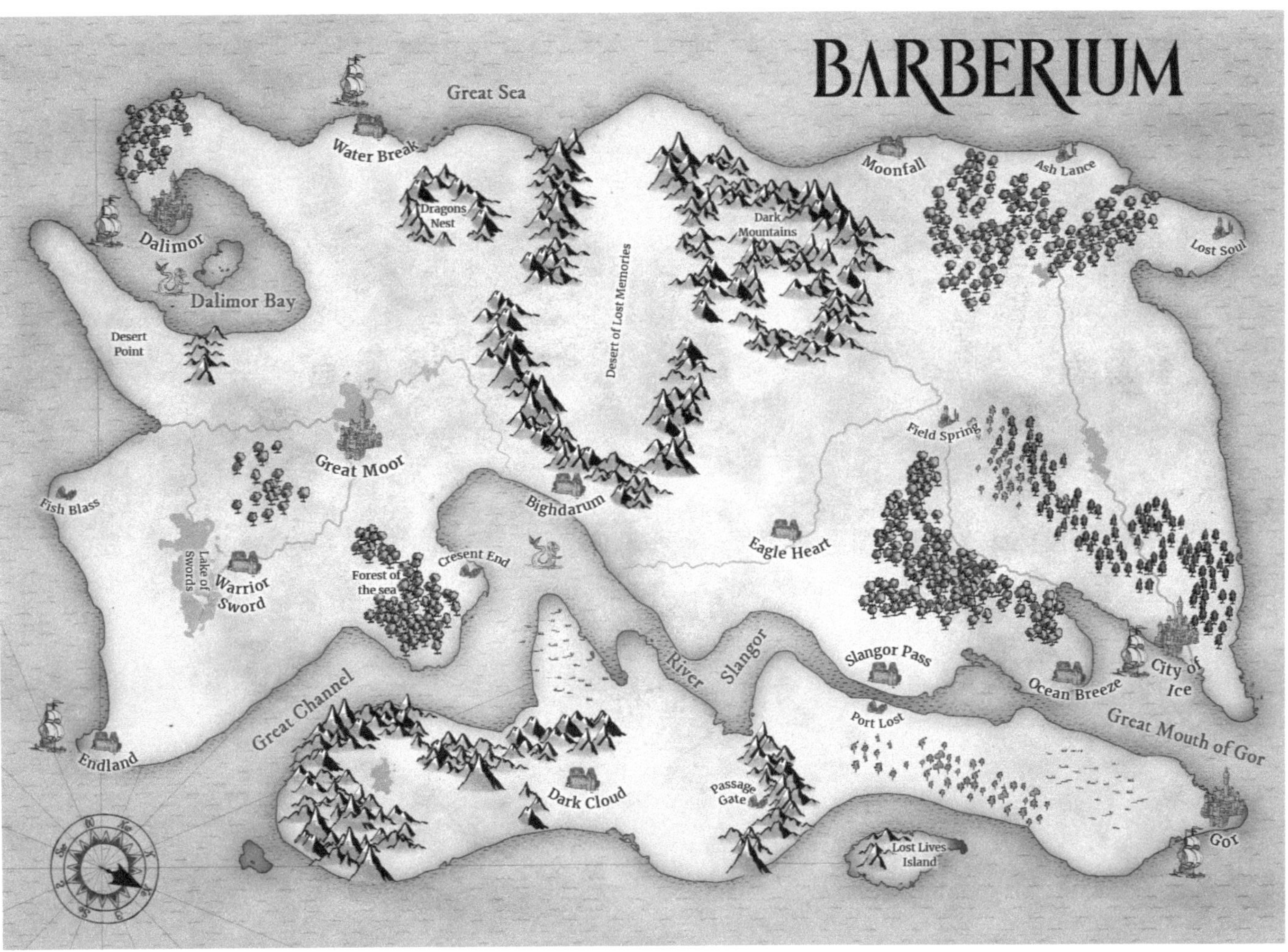

BARBERIUM
Great Sea
Water Break
Moonfall
Ash Lance
Dragons Nest
Dark Mountains
Lost Soul
Dalimor
Desert of Lost Memories
Dalimor Bay
Desert Point
Field Spring
Great Moor
Fish Blass
Bighdarum
Eagle Heart
Lake of Swords
Forest of the sea
Cresent End
Warrior Sword
Slangor Pass
River Slangor
Endland
Great Channel
Ocean Breeze
City of Ice
Port Lost
Great Mouth of Gor
Dark Cloud
Passage Gate
Lost Lives Island
Gor

LOST ISLAND
The Great Sea
Silver Wood
Derlin
Ra
Fish Hole
Diran
Shadefall
Ore
Tenrena Cove
Spirit Cove
Tenrena
Nameless
Diamond Sea

PROLOGUE

A BLACK RAVEN drifted across the calm ocean, the moon hung high in the sky illuminating the white sails that billowed with the gentle sea breeze. The evening crew went about their duties, while the rest slept or rested below deck. Next to the captain's quarters was a comfortable guest cabin for the ship's only paying passengers; the lycan siblings, Lara and Derwyn. A lamp suspended from the ceiling of the cabin cast eerie shadows on the walls, indicating the large vessel was in motion. There were sleeping cots against the walls and positioned between them was a small desk with a porthole above it.

Lara sat at the desk, writing in the leather-bound book she always carried with her, as Derwyn reclined on his cot, reading a book about Barberium that he had purchased in Palasses. They had been sailing for a couple of weeks and had kept to themselves for most of it. Both had been sad about leaving their home during the first week. Lara even more so with missing Carn. She had been quiet for days. Derwyn had tried to get her to talk, but in the end, he left his sister to work out her feelings. Lara had known that leaving Moonstar behind was the best thing to do, but still, she felt lost without Carn by her side. Carn, the boy she briefly met, then crossed paths with again as a man. Even with a decade between meeting, the attraction was still there and they fell in love. In those first few days on the ship, Lara had meditated and focused on her wolf self, her alter ego giving her the comfort she needed. Finally, she was able to look ahead, excited and curious of what the possibilities would be for their new adventure.

Derwyn looked up from his book and asked, "So, when we get to Barberium, what's the plan?"

She looked over at him, pen poised mid-sentence, her green eyes focusing on his handsome features. "I thought we would explore, see what's out there. But the coin we have will not last long. So I was hoping, when we get to Gor, I could look at getting a Sword contract."

Derwyn snapped the book shut, swinging his long legs off the cot and sitting on the edge. "Sounds like a good idea. Think I will ask about getting one, too."

Lara raised an eyebrow, putting down her pen and rubbing her hand on her dark grey trousers to remove the ink on her fingertips. "What? *You* look at getting a Sword contract?"

Derwyn smirked from where he sat leaning on his knees, and looked up at her through his eyelashes. "Aye. Why not?"

Lara scrutinised her younger brother. "But you have always disliked Swords. Carn is the prime example. You hated him. You even complained when I took up a few contracts when we left Naverac."

Her brother got to his feet, his black trousers and white shirt showing off his athletic frame. As he strolled over, the ship dipped, but Derwyn adjusted his step to keep his balance. He stopped next to the desk and responded, "Aye, but I've had a change of heart."

Lara gazed up at him. Every time she looked at her brother, his dark hair and hazel eyes reminded her of their father. He was the lycan alpha who protected the town of Lake Wood with some help from a human and a witch. He was strong and strict, but gentle and caring. He loved his children and reared them with a firm hand. Lara was told she looked a lot like her mother, but she died when Derwyn was just a babe. Lara, having only fleeting memories of the woman who birthed her, had only learned more of her when she found the journal her father was always writing in.

"It was Carn, wasn't it? You had warmed to him by the time we left. I think that was what did it."

He shrugged. "Nay . . . Well." He paused regarding his sister. "Alright, aye, it was Carn that changed my mind. He had good ethics."

"What about mine?" asked Lara, an undertone of hurt in her voice.

He squeezed her shoulder, the cotton of her brown shirt soft to the touch. He gazed at her features, accentuated by her long brown hair pulled up in a soft bun. "Well, of course yours."

Lara smirked and leaned back in the old, battered chair to look up at her brother from her seated position. "If we both go for contracts, we can take joint work or separate ones. You are an excellent Sword, and it won't take long before you can set your fees."

He shrugged. "Well, I'm not at your standard."

"Aye, you are."

He gazed at her. "I had a talented trainer."

His eyes focused on the leather-bound notebook and what Lara was writing. She had been filling it in over the years and it amazed him at what she had remembered from their adventures. He nodded toward it. "So, who's going to be reading this?"

She glanced at the account she had written of them leaving Moonstar and smiled. "Your children, I hope."

Derwyn suddenly became uncomfortable and shifted his booted feet. "Well, I don't know about that."

Lara grabbed his arm. "Oh, come on Derwyn. I have a feeling you'll find someone."

He regarded his sister. "Well, we'll just have to see, won't we? I think we'll be too busy travelling. And anyway, after Iowyn, I think girls are the last thing on my mind."

Lara smirked again. "We shall see."

Derwyn shook his head slowly, strolling back over to his cot. He glanced back. "Pig will be this evening's meal. You should ensure you get some early on."

Lara sighed. "Stop trying to change the subject."

Derwyn had been looking out for her since he was eleven years old. He was the only person who knew she was a hybrid of both lycan and vampire. In spite of their age difference, he was often the voice of reason; and the only one that could calm her, talk her down when her vampire side surged to the front.

Her brother chuckled, slumping back down on the cot. Yet, Lara was aware her brother was right. If the cook was slaughtering a pig, that would be the time to get some fresh meat. She had not fed since they had boarded the ship and she would need to soon. A talisman had lessened her hunger, but she knew it would be best to ensure she did not push her luck too far.

From their cabin, it was a straightforward route down to the galley. Lara had practised getting there without being detected and had learned the cook's routine. She knew she could sneak in and get something to keep her thirst under control. She pushed the cork back into the ink pot and placed it in the desk drawer with her pen and notebook. She looked across at her brother. "Did you want me to ask the cook about eating in the cabin again?"

He glanced up at her. "Unless we take up the offer from the captain."

"Up to you. I just need an excuse in case he sees me."

Derwyn smiled. "You will be far too fast."

She shrugged. "True."

"Anyway, I think we should dine with the captain. He seemed a little sad that we've been staying in the cabin when I saw him last eve."

Lara sighed. "Alright. He seems a good man, so if he insisted, then we should. I just don't want to be in the way."

Derwyn grinned. He had taken a stroll on deck the evening before to get some fresh air, and had spoken with the captain. He was out for quite some time and Lara realised her brother had wanted to interact with the crew more than she had thought. When they had boarded, she had informed the captain that they would stay out of the crew's way while they sailed with them, but it was going to be a long voyage. Lara had to admit, it would seem odd if they stayed in the cabin all the time. She got to her feet. "Well, I'm going down to the galley. Want anything?"

He glanced at her. "Just don't get caught."

Lara smiled and opened the cabin door. She used her extraordinary hearing to locate the crew as she glanced both ways along the narrow corridor. There were a few on deck and she heard a faint cheering coming from the crew's quarters, but few were meandering about the ship. It seemed she could get to the galley unseen. She left the cabin and with vampire speed, Lara whooshed through the lower decks, avoiding any crew, and made it to her objective unnoticed. As she got closer, she could smell the fresh blood.

The cook had already slaughtered the pig. She snuck in and kept out of sight behind some barrels of rum. The cook stood at the counter with a large cleaver he used to chop up the animal. The smell was intoxicating. Lara licked her lips, feeling the first pangs of hunger. She picked up an apple from the crate next to her and threw it across the galley, knocking something over at the back of the room. While the cook went to investigate, Lara took a large section of bloody meat and devoured it from where she hid. Licking her fingers clean, she then ran back to the cabin.

Derwyn looked up as she quietly came back in. "Better?"

"Aye. Not sure what it would have been like if I hadn't got this talisman."

Derwyn glanced at the pendant around her neck and responded, "I think it would have been more challenging." He looked towards the small window to see the evening sky. "So, shall we take a stroll on deck? Find the captain?"

Lara eyed her brother. "You seem rather keen on having dinner with him."

"Well, he's an interesting man."

She regarded her brother, wondering what he and the captain had been talking about that made having dinner tonight seem so important. She sighed, realising he was doing it for her. She had not felt so lost these past few days, but her brother was right: an evening talking to someone and not sitting in their room dwelling on the past would do them both some good.

Captain Raven's cabin was larger than theirs, with a cot at one end and a desk on the opposite side covered in rolled-up charts. They sat at the large table in the centre and Lara realised that the charts had probably been spread out there, so the captain would have been able to plot courses with ease. A large oil lamp above slowly swayed with the movement of the ship, illuminating the strange trinkets the captain had collected over the years that were scattered around the room.

The man's dark, leathery features regarded them both, his eyes focused on Lara's untouched plate, as she took a big gulp of her rum. "Not hungry?"

Lara glanced at the plate. "Still a little seasick."

The man chuckled, glancing at Derwyn as he devoured his food. "Seems ya brother has got his sea legs."

Lara took another sip of the rum, she really liked the flavour of the drink. She eyed her brother. "Aye, he seems to have."

Derwyn looked at her and dragged her plate towards him. Captain Raven raised an eyebrow, then turned back to Lara. "I have been talking to the crew, and they'd like to meet ya both. It's a long trip to Barberium, and think it will do ya both good to mingle with the crew now and then."

She responded, leaning back in her chair and crossing her arms, "We don't want to cause issues."

The older man laughed. "Nay worry, lass. They'll stare, but otherwise will leave ya be."

Lara eyed him and smiled, taking a sip of her drink. Little did he realise she was far more dangerous than any of his crew.

Lara eyed the bald crewman as he slowly gulped down the rum. He swayed and slammed the empty mug on the table, and gave her a big toothless grin. Lara glanced round at the rest of the crew, all of them leaning forward with anticipation. She took hold of her newly filled mug and gulped down the strong rum. Then placed it back on the table, empty. She had lost count of how many they had had, but by the looks of the man opposite, he would not last much longer. Another crew member eagerly refilled the mugs and stepped back, waiting. The bald man went to grab the mug in front of him and missed. He gazed back at her, smiled, belched, and then passed out, his face slamming down into the table. Derwyn cheered and laughed, as the crewmen all threw their coins onto the table.

A large, burly bosun who stood off to the side shook his head and regarded Lara. "Ya 'ave a stomach made of iron, lass. How, on Aquasious, are ya still standin'? To be 'onest, I expected Derwyn to hold his drink. But you lass, not in all me years 'ave I seen such a wisp of a thing drink a sailor under the table."

Derwyn smiled as he gathered the coins. Lara smirked and faked a sway as she got to her feet, then slurred, "We ken juss hol' our dreenks."

The bosun laughed and patted Derwyn on the back. "Well, ya both won again."

Lara regarded him and stated, "It's been a lon' night, lads. I'm headin' ta bed."

She faked another stagger, Derwyn grabbed her arm, joining the farce. He looked back at the crew. "Think she'll sleep well tonight."

The crew all laughed. One man went to move the table back and winced, cutting his hand. Lara instantly turned around, her senses picking up the blood, her body aching to taste it.

They had been on the ship for nearly three months and the voyage was nearing its end. The blood tempted her more than ever before. She had noticed the last few days that the talisman seemed weaker and found it hard to keep her cravings under control. The witch at Palasses had warned her of its time limit, but Lara had hoped it would have lasted till the ship had docked. She would have to be careful for the remaining few days. The fact that she had not been able to hunt for months did not help, and it was beginning to take its toll. Lara was still stronger than a human, but she was beginning to feel weaker and the last few nights had been difficult. She had tried to meditate with her wolf self to keep some control, but had found it was having little effect.

She froze, staring at the man's bloody hand. Pain filled her gums as her fangs began to grow. The smell of the blood was becoming intoxicating. Lara's features paled and she spun away, feeling her vampire side trying to come forth. She clenched her fists and took some slow breaths.

The bosun stepped towards her. "Ya alright lass."

Derwyn quickly stepped in front of his sister, blocking her from view. The last thing they needed was a human getting too close if her vampire side was trying to take hold. The young man chuckled, trying to seem relaxed, patting the bosun's shoulder. "I think the rum is taking its toll. I best get her up on deck for some air quickly."

The crewman nodded, genuine concern on his features. The crew had grown close to the siblings over the weeks, and they had all become firm friends. Lara clenched her fists, trying to keep control. She could not weaken so close to the end of their journey, but the blood still pulled at her. She quickly pushed past everyone and staggered down the corridor to get up on deck. At this time of night, it would be the quietest place. An ideal location to regain control.

When Lara was twenty-one years old, their home was attacked by rogue vampires. Their father did his best to keep the vampires out of the house, but died of his brutal wounds. Two vampires got inside, determined to kill everyone. But Lara knew that a lycan's bite was deadly for them. In her wolf form, she ambushed the vampires, and tore open the arm of one, filling her mouth with its blood. Although she was mortally wounded fighting the last vampire, she survived with the help of her father's best friend and his wife. She had become a lycan just three years before, and the vampire blood somehow, with the help of a potion, mingled with her own without killing her. Through sheer willpower, she overcame the odds and forced the vampire side of her back, staying true to her wolf self.

Lara leaned against the side, staring out at the ocean. The ship dipped up and down with the waves. Derwyn came up beside her. "Sis?"

She glanced at him. "I'll be alright. I just needed air."

He regarded her. Her features had returned to normal once more, but he could also see the talisman was slowly taking effect. "You haven't reacted to blood like that in some time."

She glanced at him. "Nay. I think the talisman is losing its power. And I feel weak too. When we get to port, I'll need to hunt straight away."

He nodded. "Understood. Till then, shall I get a few rats?"

She sighed, her features looking pale and drawn. "I hate rats."

"I can see if the cook has anything."

She shook her head. "Nay, rats will do. But I'm going to stay up here a bit. The cool air seems to help."

He nodded, regarding her with concern. "I'll get those rats."

She smiled at him and squeezed his arm. "Thank you."

Derwyn gazed at her. "We stick together, nay matter what."

Lara leant against the side and watched him head back down below. Derwyn had helped her with her cravings over the years, even when she could have easily lost control, and fed off him. But Derwyn kept calm. He always got her focused and pulled her through it. With a sigh, she gazed back out across the ocean and then up at the stars in the clear night sky. She closed her eyes, feeling the salty air caressing her face. She so wanted to run; her wolf self ached to be free once more. Only another week, and then she would be back on land. Lara focused on her wolf; promising she would run for miles and hunt till she could not eat any more.

"Seas have been calm lately."

Lara froze and turned to see the captain. She smiled softly. "Aye."

He regarded her. "You seem to have got some of your sea legs at last."

Lara nodded, gripping the edge of the deck, her vampire side trying to claw its way to the surface again. "That I do. But think I will be happier once back on dry land."

He replied, "Aye, the sea isn't for everyone." He raised an eyebrow. "I hear ya have been drinking me men under the table."

Lara smirked. "Well, I wouldn't say that much."

"From what me bosun says, you and your brother win every time."

Lara regarded the man's leathery features, wondering how many years he had been at sea. "I know I have thanked you before, but again, thank you for letting us take passage on your ship."

He smiled. "Lass, I'll never ask the reasons ya needed to leave Moonstar, but I do hope you and your brother find a good life in Barberium."

She regarded him. "We will."

He nodded and strolled further up the deck, barking orders to his crew. Lara glanced out at the ocean again and wondered what her and Derwyn's life would be like in a new land.

Lara took a deep breath and walked back down to the cabin, her vampire side back under control. Fresh meat from the galley had been sustaining her for over two months, but these last few weeks, she had found that she had been needing more. The small rat population on board the ship had been an advantage. She bit her lip. It was not the best diet for a hybrid, but it had to do. Derwyn had got pretty good at being a ratcatcher, and there would be at least a couple waiting for her in the cabin.

The ship glided slowly into the docks at Gor, its sails folded away by the crew as Captain Raven barked orders. Two large rowing boats pulled the ship effortlessly towards the main dock to ensure it moored in the right area. Once close enough, the crew pulled their ropes free, and the ship came to a stop, the anchor dropping in the still waters.

Lara and Derwyn had been standing on deck since the captain informed them they were coming to land. They had watched the large, impressive city of Gor come into view. As they entered the harbour, they could see it was far larger than the one at Palasses. It seemed to be a major port for ships from all over Zentos. Derwyn gazed at the city, seeing the impressive walls and watchtowers placed at relevant points. Blue and green flags waved from the tower roof tops, adding to the city skyline's grandeur.

He glanced at his sister. "Looks an impressive place."

She stared straight ahead without her eyes focusing on anything. Her mind concentrating on her body which was feeling even weaker. Lara glanced at him. "As soon as we dock, I need to feed."

She gripped the side; her knuckles were white. Derwyn looked at her with concern. "You alright?"

She shook her head. "Nay, these last few hours I have found it hard to focus and now I am hearing heartbeats. If I don't get off here soon, I may not curb the thirst."

"Feck."

Lara smirked. "Aye."

Derwyn pursed his lips. "Alright as soon as you can, I want you to get off the ship. I can distract the crew if need be. Then tell them you're below decks or something."

She smiled at her brother. "Thank you. Once I've eaten, I'll come back here. Are we still meeting the crew at the tavern?"

"If you're up to it."

Lara eyed her brother. "Aye, I will be. Once I've had a decent hunt, I'll be back to normal."

Derwyn nodded, seeing the gangplank being lowered. "I'll get rooms at an inn, and get our belongings stored." He nodded towards the dock. "Think it's as good a time as any to go."

Lara smiled and with a vampire speed ran off the ship before the crew even noticed. She hid behind some crates to regain some strength and then dashed through the docks. She soon found a side gate and was out into the lands of Barberium. To Lara's relief, there was a wood not far away. Once she was in the trees, she stripped. It was painful turning, her joints popping, her limbs snapping backwards on themselves. She fell on her knees, crying out in pain as her body changed, her jaw elongating, taking her wolf's teeth. Being so weak from the talisman, she had not felt this much pain in turning since her initial transformation all those years before. Yet once in her wolf form, the pain vanished, and it was a relief to be on all fours again.

She looked up at the trees with her wolf eyes and took a deep breath. She picked up the scent of a deer and followed it. It felt good to be running again after so long, her wolf self happy to be having a good stretch. She saw the deer ahead and ran towards it. She jumped and clamped her jaw down on the animal's neck, breaking it. Lara kept her jaw on the deer's neck, the warm blood running down her throat, her body tingling with delight. She slowly released the animal and then devoured it all.

Lara strolled back through the main gate in the late afternoon sun. She had been running and hunting for hours. It felt good to be back to her full strength once more. She regarded the busy city of Gor and walked back towards the docks. It reminded her of Palasses, but on a far larger scale. Reaching the massive docks, she soon picked up Derwyn's scent and saw him leaning against one of the cargo crates. He was chatting with some of the crew of the Black Raven. The men were laughing and joking. He picked up her scent as the breeze blew his way. He looked up and smiled warmly.

She came up to them and nodded a greeting to the large bosun as he said, "Ya looking well, lass. Got some colour back in ya cheeks. Think solid ground agrees with ya."

Lara smirked and nodded, glancing at Derwyn. Her brother turned to the men. "So, a farewell drink?"

They all nodded, and the group walked into the city to a tavern not too far from the port. It was popular with dock hands and had a loud, boisterous atmosphere. They found a table near the back.

The bosun went to the counter to order ale and food. He joined them at the table and said, "I ordered meat and potatoes for everyone."

Derwyn grinned, Lara leaned towards her brother and whispered, "Like old times, you'll eat for two."

He glanced at her and chuckled. The bosun passed them an ale each and raised his own. "To new beginnings."

The two raised the ales and repeated the toast, "New beginnings."

The large man took a big gulp and regarded the two. "So, what're ya plans?"

Lara took a sip of her ale and responded, "Explore. See what Barberium has to offer."

The large man eyed them. "I saw ya swords, so guessing you will take up contracts?"

Derwyn glanced at his sister and said, "Aye, that's the plan."

The large man started eating his food. Speaking with his mouth full. "Well, ya both will make a fine lot of coin."

The siblings nodded, then Derwyn turned his attention to his food. Lara leant back, regarding the crew as they ate, and looked over at Derwyn as he devoured his food. Lara smiled softly. She was looking forward to exploring the land, and with Derwyn by her side, it felt like old times. She took a sip of her ale, she had a good feeling about being there. Her eyes focused on her brother. He felt awkward when she mentioned a family, but she had a feeling he would find someone. She swirled her drink and gazed at the amber liquid. *What will I do then?* Lara looked back up and smiled when one of the crew said something funny. She was going to be on Zentos for a very long time. Lara planned to savour the years she will have with her brother, but when they went their separate ways, she would explore as far as she could.

CHAPTER 1

FIFTEEN YEARS LATER

LARA TURNED HER green eyes back to the busy inn when the group of Swords made a loud cheer, breaking her train of thought. She looked across at them. They had seated themselves around a large table near the fireplace at one end. All were cheering for one of their companions when the barmaid smiled at him. Lara sighed. The inn, like others in Eagle Heart, was always busy and a popular spot for Swords and travellers alike. The town used that popularity to its advantage and prospered well from it. Leaning back, savouring her drink, Lara placed her feet on the chair across from her under the table. From where she sat at the back of the inn, she could watch most of the activity in the large open room. Several barmaids were weaving between tables, carrying trays of food or tankards of ale while tactfully taking rowdy comments from customers, and keeping away from any stray hands.

Her attention soon turned back to the group of men. They were all trying to outdo one another with tales of their antics with contracts they had taken over the years. Lara found their drunken conversations rather entertaining. One looked her way, his handsome features flushed from alcohol, and gave her a big smile, flashing his crooked teeth. His eyes wandered down her grey shirt, black trousers, and wide brown belt that accentuated her slender figure. Yet when his eyes focused on the sword leaning on the chair by her side, it was made clear; look, but do not touch. She nodded to him; they had been close a few times over the years, but it had never been serious. He gave her a wink, gazing at her slender features, which were enhanced by her long brown hair being pulled up in a soft bun. Lara smiled at him. She felt tempted, but then shook her head. She was there for business, not pleasure. He gave her a sad look, accentuating his disappointment. He then nodded and turned back to his companions. Lara liked the fellow. He never pushed, but if they were in the same place and both agreed, they usually ended up having a good night together. She had seen some of the men around, and knew of others just from their reputation. Little did any of them know she could beat all of them if needed. But it seemed there was an unwritten code with the Swords here, and no one ever crossed it.

She turned her attention to the other customers in the large open area. Some of them, she realised, were locals, having stayed at the inn for a few days. They seemed a little annoyed at the group's brashness, but no one would dare tell them to quiet down. As she looked around, she could spot the odd lone Sword and many traders. Most would stop in for a night or two before continuing north. The route south from Eagle Heart was harder, as part of the journey skimmed the outlands of a large desert and mountain range that almost split Barberium in two. There were several rough mining outposts in the surrounding mountains, and not always known for their welcoming hospitality. Rumours abound of shorter routes through the mountains or the desert itself, but any seasoned traveller knew they were just rumours. The primary route was always the safest option, but it passed through Bighdarum, the largest mining outpost. It was popular and had a reputation for being welcoming, if your purse was heavy. Some travellers tried to just pass through, but there would always be some way of luring them to stop for a while.

The main entrance suddenly opened; rain, and the cold evening air, rushed in along with a lone traveller. She watched for a few moments, but it was not who she was waiting for. Lara sighed, taking a swig of her drink. She should know by now that Kayd was not reliable on his promptness and the message had been vague. They had arranged to meet at the inn two months after she picked up her last contract from him. She had finished the contract weeks ago, and when she arrived, Lara had not expected to be there more than the two nights that had already passed. Then again, it was better to wait a few more days than to travel south to the city of Dalimor if she did not need to. Kayd may have had bad timekeeping skills, but he was still an expert handler of contracts.

The siblings had learned early on that if one wanted to make good coin, it was as a Sword. After asking around over the years, they tried a couple of Sword handlers in Gor and the City of Ice. But they found that Kayd, who was located in the south, had an excellent reputation. Lara smiled, remembering teasing Derwyn when he became a Sword. It seemed Carn had more of an effect on him than he had realised. It felt good working together as a brother and sister. They even built up an excellent reputation over the years.

The door opened again, and a big gust of cold air blew in with the traveller, who fumbled with the door to close it. Everyone in the draft started moaning, telling the wet, hooded traveller to stop delaying in closing the door. But his cloak had hooked on the handle, taking him longer to detangle. The hooded figure kept apologising as he fumbled to get the door closed. Lara smiled and sighed, knowing the inept, clumsy traveller had to be Kayd. Only he could have made such an entrance, and that was without his familiar scent invading her nostrils.

Kayd apologised again as he looked around the inn. He pulled down his rain-soaked hood to reveal a middle-aged man with a thick, greying beard, and a jagged scar that crossed over a clouded left eye and down his cheek. When his good eye focused on Lara, he gave a big grin, exposing his broken yellow teeth. He weaved his way through the inn towards her, nodding a quick good evening to the Swords at the large table. Lara signalled to the barmaid, who nodded and started weaving her way over with a tankard of ale and a large bowl of stew. Kayd had been to the inn so often that they knew exactly what he wanted without him having to order. He was also very fussy, and it had to be fresh stew, and ale that was locally brewed. The last barmaid, who thought Kayd would like to try something new, had run from his table, crying from his harsh words. The innkeeper had then made sure all his staff never wavered from Kayd's usual order.

Kayd stopped at Lara's table and sat with a 'humph' opposite her, just as the barmaid placed down his order. He smiled up at the girl, his good eye lingering on her ample bosom. "Thank ya, love." He then turned to Lara. "It's fecking cold out there!"

Lara smiled. "It's good to see you too, Kayd."

He pulled off his wet cloak and looked a little sheepish. "Oh sorry. Aye, good to see ya too, Lara."

She took a sip of her drink and studied the seasoned Sword. "So, how are you?"

Kayd took a big sip of his ale and, as he wiped the froth from his beard, he took a big, deep breath, taking in the aroma of his stew. He looked up, his hazel eye focused on her, while his clouded one seemed to be focused off to the left, at the wall behind her. The brutal injury was the main reason he was no longer a Sword and had turned to the paperwork side of the job. But even with the loss of vision, he was still a hard Sword to beat.

Kayd smiled. "Good, good. Just travelled from Slanglar Pass. It wasn't too bad till this fecking storm came in." He took another sniff of his stew. "I'm *ravenous!*"

Lara nodded, leaning back, and letting the older man eat his stew before it got too cold. Kayd shovelled down the food, bits dripping into his greying beard, from his overfilled spoon. It was not a pretty sight, but then again, Kayd was not one for manners, anyway.

He looked up after devouring half of it, then he wiped his bearded chin and studied her. "So, me girl, how are ya? I 'ave had excellent reports yet again. It seems the client was incredibly pleased with ya results over the last job."

Lara smiled. "It was easy enough. To be honest, it wasn't as bad as the client led us to believe. It was a ghoul hive. But only a small one."

Kayd laughed, taking another big sip of his ale, belching slightly. "Ahhh, but ya know how to deal with those pesky demons more than other Swords round 'ere." He raised an eyebrow, glancing towards the table with the Swords that were now even drunker, their tall tales getting taller.

Lara smiled, studying Kayd. She wondered what he would think if he knew she was a demon herself. "Well, let's say I've had the experience."

He nodded. "Aye, ya do girl." He leant forward, tapping his finger on the thick book placed near the centre of the table. "See ya studying up."

She glanced at the book on demonology she had been reading earlier. "Well, you know me and a good book."

"Aye, that I do." He peered at the open notebook that was by the book in front of Lara. His eyes focused on her drawing of a ghoul. "Didn't think ya was an artist."

Lara glanced down at the leather-bound notebook, gazing at her sketch and her jottings to the side of it. She looked back up at him as she closed it. "Oh, just notes I made after dealing with the hive."

Kayd arched his eyebrow. "Well, you pretty much got the ghoul. I don't think many could. So ya make notes?"

She nodded, placing her hand on the leather cover. "I like to make records of every demon I come across and update when I find out more."

"Useful to have."

"Aye, it helps, especially when I come across them again."

"Ya always have ya nose in a book, so making ya own doesn't surprise me."

Kayd took another big sip of his ale and then bent down, pulling up the satchel he had placed by his feet when he joined Lara at the table. He started rummaging in it, muttering to himself.

Lara sat back, slightly amused. Kayd looked and gave the impression of a disorganised, half-blind, retired Sword, but he was a very shrewd and well-organised businessman. Lara had found out early on that he played that persona to his advantage, knowing most would not give him a second glance. But anyone who truly knew him was aware to keep their wits about them, as he would always make sure he weighed every deal in his favour. Even though he would short cut his Swords, he would defend them to the death. Compared to other Sword handlers, he was still the most trustworthy. Though Lara had not been working with him for years, she knew how to play him at his own game. Kayd thought she had a soft spot for him, and part of her did, but she was also wise to his games.

Kayd stopped rummaging in his bag and pulled out a folded piece of paper. "'Ere it is." Lara leant forward when Kayd passed it to her as he continued, "It's an interesting one. It *appeared* in me bag this morn. Not much detail, but I know ya will be interested in it."

Lara looked at him, knowing how sorcerers could send messages magically to recipients. She opened the piece of paper and read it:

I, Malaki, Sorcerer of Great Moor

require a Sword with demon knowledge, along with exceptional

abilities with sword, and mind, for a quest of great secrecy.

Meet me at my tower.

I will pay 500 gold coins.

Lara raised her eyebrow, checking the back of the paper, expecting more info. Kayd chuckled. "I knew ya'd want it."

Lara nodded, studying the elegantly written text again. "I am intrigued. This Malaki, have you heard of him?"

Kayd laughed. "'E's a little old now, but was quite a famous sorcerer in 'is youth. It is said he killed a dragon on the Black Mountains east of 'ere."

Lara pursed her lips. "I see. My curiosity has increased even further. I've always wanted to know what a dragon looks like up close."

Kayd leaned forward. "Well, ya can ask 'im when ya get to Great Moor."

Lara leaned back, taking a swig of her drink. "I think I will." She glanced across at the group of very drunk Swords. They had all become louder as the night progressed. "Any of them on your books?"

Kayd squinted across at them while taking a big gulp of his ale. He turned back. "Aye," he said as he put his ale down. "Three of 'em. One of 'em I need to see," he paused, wiping his lips. "Think I'll wait till the morn."

Lara smirked. "You won't get much sense out of them this eve."

He leant forward a little. "Well, speaking of Swords, just picked up a new one. Ya may see 'im when ya get to Great Moor. I've told 'im to base 'isself there between contracts till 'e gets the lay of the land."

Lara looked up at him. "I'm not training him for you."

Kayd chuckled, taking a swig of his ale. "Nay, he's an excellent Sword, as good as ya. He came across from some distant land like ya self. He has a similar accent. Think he's after a new start. Bit of a moody fella, but he won't take contracts that need more skill, like yas. Was wonderin', if ya cross paths with 'im at Great Moor, could ya, ya know, convince 'im?"

Lara regarded Kayd, knowing there was some ulterior motive. The demon contracts she dealt with offered much more money, which meant more to line Kayd's pockets. As she was established enough to set her fees, he always got a little less from hers. It seemed the new Sword was good, and if he could get him on his books, then he could take the more dangerous contracts. Kayd was aware that another excellent Sword who would pick up the ones she refused, or was too busy to take, would make him rich.

She sighed. "Alright. If I cross paths with him, I will try to convince him. Does he have a name?"

"Erm, it's Larn." He paused, thinking for a second. "Aye, Larn. Not a bad looking fella." Kayd winked and chuckled. "Just like ya self."

Lara looked at him. "Let's just stick to business, Kayd."

Kayd studied her. "Of course. So, how's ya brother? 'E was as good as ya with the sword. I missed 'im when he left."

Lara smiled. "He's well. Not seen him for a while."

"Well, ya could always pay a visit when ya down that end. 'E's in Warrior Sword, isn't 'e?" Lara smiled, and Kayd continued, "Check on 'im and 'is wee ones. Also, that fine lass of 'is, Skylar, isn't it?"

Her brother settled down with a family of his own after they crossed paths with a lycan pack over seven years ago. To her surprise, they had been welcoming to them both. While there, a young woman named Skylar had captured her brother's heart. He had stayed and eventually married her. That was the first time a pack accepted Lara as a hybrid. Most tried to run her out of town once they realised what she was. They called her an aberration; but she knew they were citing 'keeping the lycan lines pure' to keep their self-perceived entitlement.

Lara nodded. "I may. I need to see what this Malaki has for me first."

"Tell that brother of yours, 'e's welcome to be back on me books any time. But don't *ya* start living that way again, it was hard for business."

Lara smiled. She had tried to stay in one place when Derwyn had settled down and had narrowed her contracts to the local area. But after a while, her vampire blood wanted to be on the move again. It had been hard leaving Derwyn, but she was happier when she kept moving. Even though she was taking contracts all over Barberium on her own, whenever she could, she would stop by to see him, Skylar, and her niece and nephew.

She gazed at Kayd, knowing that he would never say it, but he had a soft spot for Derwyn. One drunken night he had told her how Derwyn had reminded him of his son, whom Kayd had sadly lost at a young age.

Lara said, "I will."

Kayd nodded and returned to his stew. Lara looked at the brief note again and wondered what the sorcerer would be like. She studied the parchment and noticed there was a sizeable gap below the text, like there should have been more. She looked at it closely, then gasped when more letters developed before her eyes.

Kayd looked up, his spoon of stew paused in mid-air. "What?"

Lara looked up at him. "There seems to be more of the message."

Kayd put down the spoon and focused on the parchment when Lara turned it towards him. The words slowly developed, the paper shimmering slightly from a spell being activated. It was in the same handwriting as the message above it:

For the rest of this message to reveal itself, you are indeed worthy, but beware.

This is not for the uneducated, as you will be tested. Only the true of heart will be able to complete this request.

Once on the path, there will be no straying from it. You must push aside any doubt in your mind. A young mind with an old soul can break the barriers needed to see.

Take heed before venturing into this quest.

I will see you at my tower at dawn.

Malaki

Kayd snatched the piece of paper and sniffed. "Now that's a bit cryptic. But wouldn't have expected anything less with a sorcerer involved."

Lara studied him. "Should I be worried?"

Kayd laughed. "Nay, it's a sorcerer's big words. They always want to look mysterious. Ya will be fine." He gave her a big wide grin, then leant forward, passing the piece of parchment back. "But best be on ya guard, just in case."

Lara regarded him, then the note again. It only made her more interested. The spell on the paper must have detected her uniqueness. It would make sense with the old soul part of the text. She looked up at Kayd. "Think I'll be setting off at dawn. The sooner I get there to see what this is all about, the better."

Kayd smiled. "That's me girl."

Lara leant back, studying the note while Kayd finished his stew. Her eyes focused on the men again, some looking ready to pass out. In the morning, most would be still here waking up at the table, with very thick heads.

She looked at the parchment and tried to imagine what type of character Malaki would be; if he would be stuffy and old like most sorcerers she had met. Lara found it all intriguing. She was interested in knowing more about the dragon he faced, but expected, like most things, it had been exaggerated over the years. He would still have some interesting stories to tell her, as well as finding out what exactly he needed her skills for.

CHAPTER 2

K AYD AND LARA had gone to their rooms late that night. The group of Swords broke into song, to the amusement and dismay of the other customers. From what Lara could hear from her room, they had continued drinking and singing into the early hours. When she walked down to the mostly deserted inn at dawn carrying her saddlebags and sword, she found the remaining Swords had passed out at the table which was covered in discarded tankards and spilt ale. She stopped at the table next to the one she had known well among them. She pulled his face out of the pool of stale ale as he snored merrily and gave him a little pat on the back. She regarded him and the others. Whoever Kayd needed to see, he would not get much from them when they finally came around.

Her mind turned to Malaki as she left the inn and headed towards the stable. He seemed fascinating, and the hidden message had sparked her interest. She saddled her mare wondering what did a sorcerer need a Sword for exactly that he could not have solved himself. Her instincts were telling her it would be no ordinary contract, especially after how the rest of the message had magically appeared. It had to have been from her own magical energy which was another reason she wanted to get to Great Moor as soon as possible. Yet she questioned if Kayd had been compelled to want her to have it, and not just for the money.

The only issue getting there was the outpost. She would have to pass through Bighdarum. There could be some complications after last time, but it should not be too much of a problem. She pursed her lips. There was a longer route where she could avoid it, but then again, she was not that type of girl. She mounted the mare, and tapped her heels into the horse's sides. "Come on, girl."

The horse started walking towards the gates. Lara glanced back at Eagle Heart, the large town slowly coming to life, and wondered when she would be this way again. With the lack of details on the contract, it was hard to say, but it should keep her busy for a while. She mused over what the contract would entail. From the hidden message, it seemed to be an issue with demons which would be more in line with her area of expertise. The sorcerer had written the contract in a way to deter the time wasters. The part about 'young heart, old soul' made her curious. She was older than she looked and could be considered an old soul these days. She still wondered what triggered the rest of the message to appear. *Did it sense what I am? Or was it when it knew Kayd had given the message to his best Sword?* If she rode hard, Lara would get her questions answered within a few days. She just hoped there would not be any trouble at the outpost. Hopefully, if she kept her head down and to a brief night's stay, everything would be alright. It was only one person who could make it a problem.

It took four long days for Lara to reach the outpost. The rough-looking makeshift, yet now, permanent town of Bighdarum had high wooden walls surrounding it. Watchtowers stood on each corner and above the large wooden gates into the settlement which were there to discourage anyone from trying to rob the town of its profits. The northern and southern gates were always open and welcoming during the day, but locked tight at night. That, of course, did not help any traveller who wanted to continue without rest. The dwarves had built the town between the primary route and the mountains, but over the centuries it had expanded from the mountains in the west, to the coastal cliffs in the east. To head north or south on the main road, every traveller was forced to ride through the town. Of course, the dwarves, and humans alike, made sure that there were several opportunities to purchase anything from food to weapons, along with many rooms to stay the night, or for any other pleasures they may wish to partake in. Hence why Lara partly wanted to avoid it. But taking the longer, more unpredictable route through the mountains themselves or going across the desert was too much of a risk. It was still better to head through the town itself.

The once small settlement had always been dwarven, as with most of the mining outposts, but this one, still had a large dwarven population. It seemed, with other outposts that were mostly occupied by humans, that over the years the dwarves had abandoned them. They either went to cities for more profitable businesses away from mining or, for those more devoted to the mining cause, had built settlements in the mountains away from the other races and kept to themselves.

Lara glanced up at the watchtowers and pulled her hood further over her head. The security in Bighdarum was tight, yet not for entering the town, just leaving. Bamur was so paranoid that someone may steal from him, that on leaving the town, everyone was searched. She hoped that Bamur's men would be too focused on anyone leaving to notice her, but at this time of the day, there would not be many. Lara looked around carefully. She did not want to have to deal with that deceiving dwarf while she was in town. She pursed her lips. If she could just get to the inn near the south gate without being spotted, she could lie low till dawn. Then hopefully slip out with as few problems as possible. The innkeeper at the inn where she was going to stay did not trust Bamur, and he could be relied on. It was just getting there that was the issue and having no choice but to ride through the town's main street, Lara would have to keep alert. Taking a deep breath, she rode into the town, keeping her head down and riding as fast as she could without drawing attention.

The principal route was busy, even late in the day. Lining each side of the road were shops, several of which offered coin for any crystals. It was the major source of income for the mining town. It had once been silver and gold, but many magic users sought after the rare crystals found only in the caves of Bighdarum. The price for crystals had overtaken any other precious metal or stone. The bigger the crystal, the more versatile it would be and a sorcerer or sorceress, witch or warlock would pay. All magic users carried a small one on their person so they could teleport. But larger crystals gave them even more opportunities, from communication to travelling between continents.

As she rode, she kept a close eye on the two inns owned by Bamur. She turned when she heard a shout. It seemed the dwarven owner of the whorehouse was offering services from elves, dwarves, and humans. They looked up at her, offering a reasonable rate. She shook her head and kept riding. Her eyes wandered to the busy market stalls selling everything one could just about think of. The street in front of the stalls was teeming with customers, all haggling for a fair price.

Lara kept riding south, her eyes constantly moving, making sure none of Bamur's men were in sight. She looked ahead, seeing the sign for the Rock and Axe Inn near the south gate. It seemed she would avoid Bamur on this occasion, much to her relief. Reaching the inn's stables, she dismounted and ensured the stable lad settled her horse. As she collected her saddlebags, a voice boomed, just a moment after she picked up the familiar metallic scent.

"LARA!"

She paused, knowing the accent far too well, and cursed. Lara put down her bags and slowly turned, facing the slightly overweight dwarf. Bamur had a very impressive full auburn beard, and his jerkin was finely made, as were his trousers and boots. He stopped in front of the stall her horse was in, and Lara noticed several of his stubby fingers were adorned with gold rings when he folded his arms across his chest. He was ensuring she could not leave without talking to him.

She grinned. "Bamur! *What* a surprise."

He looked up at her, his blue eyes narrowed with suspicion. His bushy eyebrows were as impressive as his beard. "So ya were gonna pass through without saying a quick greetin'?"

Her smile wavered, wondering how he had got to her so quickly. Someone must have spotted her shortly after she entered through the gates. Even though he was a dwarf, who was a little on the heavy side, he was still quick on his feet.

She regarded him. "Of course I was. I just needed to get settled first."

The dwarf studied her, scowling slightly. "I ain't some daft, half-wit, Lara. I know ya were hopin' to get through 'ere without me men seeing ya."

She sighed, folding her arms across her chest. "Well, aye. I was hoping not to cross paths with you after last time."

Bamur laughed without emotion and slapped his thigh. "*I knew it!*"

Lara looked sheepish. "It seems your men are just too good, and they spotted me."

The dwarf looked up at her, his clenched fists resting on his hips. "Ya didn't finish ya job from last time."

Lara studied him sternly, remembering the contract all too well. She had dealt with the low-level demon that was hiding in the mine, but in the process, it had killed his men. It had not been her fault, as she had specifically told him to keep his men out, but unknown to her, when she had headed in, Bamur had sent in some of his men to keep an eye on her. With three of his men ending up dead, he refused to pay the full payment after the demon had been dealt with. When Lara told Kayd, he took Bamur off the books. It was not good business to have someone who would not pay up.

Lara stated, "Bamur, Kayd has blacklisted you. You'll have to look elsewhere regarding any current problems that you have."

The dwarf's features grew red from anger. "*BLACKLISTED!!*"

Lara smirked. It seemed no one had had the courage to tell him. "Sorry, Bamur, but you refused to pay after I had fulfilled the contract. Kayd had little choice. It isn't good for business."

Bamur paced back and forth and muttered under his breath, several very coarse sounding dwarven words among them. Lara could tell from the tone they were not polite. He looked back up at her and gave her a toothy grin. "Lara, me girl. Can't we come to some *agreement*?"

She looked at him suspiciously, knowing, like anyone in a mining town, to be wary when someone wanted an agreement. Dwarves especially thought they could resolve anything with the right amount of coin. She looked down at him, her arms still folded. "What are you asking, Bamur?"

The dwarf looked her straight in the eyes as well as he could from his smaller stature. "How about twenty gold pieces? If ya could just deal with our *little* problem?"

Lara regarded him. Bamur had to be desperate if he was offering her that much. She took a breath and thought it through. The last one took her a day and would have been less if Bamur had kept his men back. A day extra here would not make too much difference to the contract at Great Moor, and Bamur would make it hard for her to leave if she refused.

She sighed. "What do you need?"

The dwarf slapped his hands together and rubbed them with satisfaction. "Well, we 'ave an issue in the mine. Seems we 'ave one of those Kanfors again."

Lara sighed, remembering how she had warned him more would come unless he ensured talismans were put up. It seems her advice had fallen on deaf ears. Lara looked down at him like a scolded child. "I can help you, but you *must* do what I told you about the talismans."

Bamur snorted. "They don't do anything."

"Really? So, did you put some up?"

Bamur peered down at his feet as he shuffled them. "Er, well, I was busy and me lads are *useless* at independent thinking."

Lara sighed. "Then how do you know they don't work? And remember, Bamur, I'm the expert here when it comes to issues like this. You know mining. I *know* demons."

The dwarf nodded impatiently. "Aye, ya right. But if I do what ya ask, will ya deal with it?"

"I will." She stepped closer to him and leant down, looking him directly in the eyes. "This time. When I say to keep everyone out. I mean. Keep everyone *out*!"

Bamur looked sheepish. "Understood."

It went against her better judgement, but also knew how savage Kanfors could be, so she could not just walk away. She glared at him. "I want that mine cleared by dawn. Nay exceptions. Now I'm going to have a drink."

Lara strapped her sword to her back and grabbed her saddlebags. Then left the stable, not waiting for a response from Bamur. She had been wanting a drink for the last hour, and after this conversation, she needed it even more.

Once in the inn, Lara went up to the counter and waited for the man to finish with his customer. She looked around, unable to see the innkeeper who had been there the last time she had stayed. Then again, mining towns usually have a high turnover, for miners and non-miners alike. Usually, with the non-miners, it was the lifestyle; they just could not stick with it for too long. For miners, it was prosperity; they had made their fortune, but they usually returned after a year or two when they had spent it all.

The middle-aged, bald, stocky man turned to her. "Aye?"

Lara smiled at him. "I was hoping for a room. Where's Von?"

The innkeeper rummaged under the counter and placed a brass key in front of her. "It's the room at the back, first floor, name on the door is Emerald. As for Von, his daughter gave birth to her first child in Great Moor. So, he put me in charge for now. Do ya know him?"

"Not well, but he was a friendly fellow. I stayed here two winters past. Thank you for the room. Can I order a groc?"

The innkeeper eyed her. "That's potent stuff, girl. It ain't for a lightweight like ya self."

Lara smiled, forgetting how she still only looked twenty-one, and apart from her muscle from training and being a lycan, she did not look like someone who could handle her liquor. She responded, "Don't worry, I can take it."

The innkeeper shrugged. "Well, I've warned ya."

He went to the back of the counter and pulled out a small demijohn full of a purple-coloured liquid. He poured some into a small beaker and passed it to her, then placed the demijohn out of sight again. Lara grabbed the beaker and took a big swig. She smiled at him as the strong alcohol burned its way down into her stomach, where it felt like an explosion of warmth.

She smiled at the man. "Thanks."

He looked at her, slightly astonished, and shook his head in disbelief. "Well, seems looks can be deceivin'."

Lara nodded, grabbed her saddlebags and drink, and went to find a quiet table at the back. Removing her sword, Lara sat down, placing it beside her, then leant back, and studied the room. Non-miners and travellers, and miners who just wanted a quiet night, always favoured the inn as it was never overly busy. The inns further in town were not for the faint-hearted, always packed, and had at least three or four fights a night. She took a sip of her drink, savouring the strong flavour in her mouth, and thought about the conversation with Bamur. She sighed. He had drawn her in again, but then, there were good people in town, and she could not just stand by and do nothing. Getting killed by a Kanfor was not something she would wish even on her worst enemy.

Although she was tempted to go there now and take care of it, Lara knew that even a hybrid needed a rest and she wanted to make sure that they cleared the mine before she ventured in. Lara did not want any casualties like there were last time. Savouring her drink, she thought about Malaki again. She would be delayed by a day, but there was not any time frame on the contract. A day in Bighdarum to deal with a demon would not be an issue.

She turned back to the inn, listening to the buzz of conversation as she nursed her drink. After an hour, she went to her room and settled down for the night. She would be up by dawn and get the mine cleared of the Kanfors for Bamur. Again.

CHAPTER 3

THE ENTRANCE TO the mine had been carved into the side of the mountain several hundreds of years before. The wide pathway snaked down deep into its depth and darkness. Mining carts had created well-used ruts in the ground from leaving filled with the treasured minerals, then going back empty. Those very mining carts and other equipment were strewn about outside with everyone being told to leave quickly at the crack of dawn. A crowd had formed near the inns that were closest to the mine. All had ale in hand, watching Lara with a mix of hope and suspicion. As she peered into the darkness of the tunnel, she kicked some small rocks out of the way. She could see the gradient heading downwards into the depths, her keen nose picking up the powerful scent of upturned earth and rock.

She looked back at Bamur. "Is it empty?"

The dwarf nodded from where he stood facing the mine, close to one of his inns, with his arms folded across his chest. "Aye, all clear."

"Good. Now don't send *anyone* in after I go down there."

"Nay, we'll all stay clear and keep out."

Lara eyed him with suspicion before she said, warning him, "This may take a while."

Bamur nodded. "What about the talismans? I've sent one of me men to get some from Eida. She's a witch close to 'ere."

Lara kept her eyes on the tunnel as she responded, "When I come back out, send your men to me." She looked over her shoulder at the dwarf. "I'll show them where to put them."

Bamur nodded, and Lara could tell he was taking her advice seriously this time. As Lara entered the mine, Bamur bellowed, "There be lanterns just to the side so ya can see down there!"

Lara looked back at him and nodded. But she would not need one. She could see perfectly fine with her wolf vision. She would need to keep her hands free if facing a Kanfor, and the light would alert them, which she did not want. She strolled into the mine, taking the main tunnel down the centre. From what Bamur had told her, they had seen the creature down in the deepest section. It would take her a while to reach the heart of the mine. Using her vampire speed, would be quicker, but she wanted to ensure the creature had not headed further up with the mine being empty. Yet, from what she could smell once she was deeper into the tunnel, the Kanfor's scent was faint and as she walked further down, it was clear that it was still in the depths. After walking a little further, and certain it had not ventured up, she ran down the main tunnel, following the scent, which grew stronger the deeper she went. Lara reached the deepest part of the mine in half the time that it would have taken anyone else. Lara glanced back in the direction she had come from, determined to retrace her steps at a slower speed to avoid arousing suspicion among the townspeople.

Leaving the main tunnel, she stopped in a large open cavern which was storage for lanterns and carts that could be used in case of any mishaps without having to go back up to the top. She looked around the area which was almost as clear as day with her lycan vision. She could smell the Kanfor strongly, it was close. Several tunnels led off from the area, she just had to pick the right one. She took in the Kanfor scent and narrowed it down to the tunnel ahead of her. Lara pulled her sword free, and as she walked towards it; she saw movement in the tunnel mouth and stopped.

She peered into the opening and watched. Just a little ways in was the Kanfor, its limbs almost folded back on themselves as it held on to the wooden framework on the wall and ceiling. Its short, black fur acted as camouflage, hiding it against the darkness and the rocks. It had the build of a small child with oversized ears, enormous eyes, and a roundish face. Even though the creatures looked harmless, they were dangerous, with quick reflexes. She regarded it. From its size, it was only a young one, and it seemed timid. Yet its timidness was not the reason it was hesitant. Like most other demons she had faced over the years, her scent always confused them, unsure of what kind of threat she would be. That was always an advantage, as they would venture with caution, but it was unclear if this Kanfor would be. They were not known to be cautious, especially when cornered as the last one had been. But she was wary about this one. With it being what looked like an adolescent, she knew that they were more unpredictable.

Lara's eyes focused on her sword for a second as she gripped the leather wrapped hilt more firmly. The expertly made silver sword was well balanced in her hand. It had been her trusted weapon since she found it amongst her mother's possessions when she and her brother had to leave their childhood home. She had added runes to the blade years later, using them whenever she had to deal with demons.

Staying in the centre of the cavern, Lara's eyes never left the Kanfor, knowing it could pounce at any moment. She clenched her sword as the creature jump down and slowly stood up straight. She visualised the rune of fire in her head and murmured the word softly. The rune associated with it on her sword glowed red for a moment and the whole blade shimmered.

The Kanfor stepped forward, its body short and thick, its long, double-jointed limbs made it move oddly. With their flexibility, and the three claws that were on its feet and hands, it could tear at its victim's flesh rapidly. Its mouth was filled with small teeth and its saliva was a deadly neurotoxin, meaning that its bite would be fatal. It was not a creature to cross unless one was well prepared.

The Kanfor slowly emerged from the tunnel, sniffing the air, still unsure what Lara was. Its large ears moved individually, listening to see if any others were about. She stood her ground. Her sword at the ready. Waiting. It was wise not to make any movements and wait for the creature to make the first move. It looked around the cave, then back at her and growled, showing its razor-sharp teeth, the neurotoxin giving them a green tinge. Lara just stared back, looking as neutral as possible. Kanfors attacked aggressively if the victim made any sudden moves. That had been the mistake Bamur's men made. If they had stayed still when Lara told them to, most of them would have been alive today.

Lara watched it, knowing she could at least match the Kanfor, maybe even be faster than the adolescent demon. But she needed it to come closer. The creature would not know what to do with a victim that did not run, and she hoped its curiosity would get the better of it. That would give Lara the advantage. It could even work for humans too, if they could keep their nerve. If the Kanfor got close enough, she could inflict a mortal wound. It had one major weakness, its midsection. If it was in close proximity and the aim true, then it could be brought down in two blows. The bonus of a silver sword, powered with a fire rune, would ensure her strikes were even more effective. Yet nerves of iron were needed to wait and let it get within a lethal range of its claws.

The Kanfor slowly moved towards her sniffing the air, sizing her up with its large, cold, black eyes. It was unsure why she was not running or even getting scared. Lara kept her focus, smelling its foul breath. The Kanfor flexed its fingers, which looked longer with the razor-sharp claws. The creature then stopped, just over an arm's length away from her. Its round features cocked to one side as it scrutinised her with its enormous eyes. Lara firmed her grip on the sword and attacked so fast that the demon almost did not see it. But the Kanfor was still able to dodge the sword, and her blow only nicked its midsection. Lara cursed, unable to make the fatal strike, the Kanfor was more aware and quicker than she had expected. Lara moved towards the Kanfor again.

The demon was swift, but had not expected her to be as fast. She cut it across the chest. It hissed in pain; the silver burning its flesh, the fire rune aggravating the wound. It went to slash her with its claws, but Lara jumped back, and it missed. It then hissed again, from frustration. Lara smirked. It was cursing as she had earlier. It slashed at her again. Lara jumped to the side, parrying with her sword. The claws clashed with the blade, creating sparks. She spun around, cutting deeply into the Kanfor's arm. It screamed out in pain. The eerie sound echoed around the cave.

It took all of Lara's strength not to cover her ears from the piercing sound to her lycan ears. She shook her head, the sound so deafening it frazzled her senses for a moment. Lara took a deep breath, focusing again and moved, clipping the Kanfor. This creature was a lot faster than the last one and she needed to make the killing blow before it made a run for it. If it ran, it would have the advantage, and that was the last thing Lara wanted. It lunged at her again, slashing with its claws. A couple sliced across Lara's shoulder as she spun around to counterattack with a fatal strike. The Kanfor stopped in its tracks, then stumbled backwards falling to the floor. Its body cut in half. Dead.

Lara stood over the two sections of the creature, her shoulder already healing. She kicked it just to make sure it was dead but could already tell from her vampire senses. She wiped her sword clean and sheathed it. Lara grabbed one of the creature's arms and dragged the top half up the tunnel and headed out of the mine. Its weight surprised her, considering how it was built, but she wanted to make sure she could show Bamur proof of death.

The Kanfor's upper body lay on the ground outside the mine. The late morning summer sun baking the dead flesh, the smell of the innards getting stronger. Bamur looked at the corpse with disgust, trying not to smell the stench. His men all stood back looking on with fear.

The dwarf turned to Lara. "So that's what a Kanfor looks like? The feckers move so fast, I never got a clear look."

Lara nodded. "You just have to have the nerve to stay still, so they get close enough to kill them."

Bamur looked up at her. "Aye, ya a tough 'en Lara." He eyed her. "And not a scratch on ya, well, apart from that one." He pointed with his stubby finger.

Lara sighed, glancing at the torn shirt sleeve, a little blood staining the material. She had healed completely, but no one could tell. She shrugged. "All part of the job."

The dwarf chuckled. "I bet ya want ya money?"

"Aye, and nay swindling me like the last time."

Bamur held up his hands in defence. "I wouldn't do that."

Lara just raised an eyebrow. The dwarf looked a little sheepish and unattached a small purse from his belt, then passed it to her. "Twenty gold pieces, as agreed."

Lara took the purse and could tell it was correct by the weight. She looked back at the dwarf. "Do you have the talismans?"

"Aye, me men will go in with ya."

Lara led the way back into the mine with Bamur's men, who were all a little skittish. They would not have lasted long against the Kanfor if they had gone in, but it seemed the dwarf had had a firm word with them as they all did exactly as she ordered. After a couple of hours, the talismans were in place, and they all understood to check on them every few days and replace any that were damaged. All soon relaxed, knowing it would hopefully stop any Kanfors or other nocturnal demons from using the mine as their home.

Once back out on the surface, Bamur insisted on a drink at his best inn, aptly named Bamurs, which was in the centre of town. It was a typical miners' inn, rough and extremely popular. His other inn, named Pa's Axe, was just as rowdy and only a few doors down. Bamur bellowed to everyone in the inn when he entered. "The Kanfor is dead!"

All the miners in the inn cheered, and the dwarf added, "Ale all around!" He turned to Lara. "And groc for our demon killer!"

Everyone cheered again, Lara feeling uncomfortable with everyone staring at her. But that was Bamur, always making a spectacle of everything. She glanced around. "Can we just sit down?"

The dwarf looked up at her, realising how uncomfortable she seemed. "Oh. Aye, sorry me girl. There's a table over 'ere."

Lara followed him through the inn to a table near the enormous fireplace. It was slow going as everyone wanted to shake Lara's hand as she passed. Reaching the table, Lara made sure she was facing the main part of the inn.

Bamur sat beside her, grinning. He turned to her. "Thank ya, Lara. We can now get back to full operation."

She glanced at him sternly, taking a sip of her drink. "Just remember this was a favour. I won't be able to work for you again."

The dwarf nodded. "I know." He pursed his lips. "I'm still in shock that Kayd has blacklisted me. Think I need to go have a word with 'im."

Lara studied the dwarf. "Don't do anything foolish, Bamur. Kayd has connections, so you're best to just leave it be." She paused, focusing on the dwarf's blue eyes. "I like you Bamur, don't let me find out some misfortune came to you."

"Me? Nah, I'm an iron ox." Lara raised an eyebrow, and the dwarf added a little more under his breath. "But get ya point."

She nodded and turned back to her drink and watched the inn, which was getting a little more raucous with all the free ale. It would not be too long before a fight broke out and Lara would be wise to make her excuses as soon as she could. The last thing she needed was to be in a bar fight. It never ended well for the ones who started them. She wanted to make sure she left here in high spirits, not with a cloud over her head from having to knock everyone out. She savoured her drink and listened to Bamur as he told her one of his many stories. It was about how he was once stuck down a mine shaft with a couple of humans and some other dwarves. Lara had not the heart to tell him he had told her the same story several times over the years, and every time, it would get more elaborate. Lara wondered what extra horror he would add this time.

The evening rolled on and the inn was very loud. To Lara's surprise, not one fight had broken out. She needed an early start and wanted to find a good hunting spot before she reached Great Moor. When the opportunity arose, she made her excuses and left them to celebrate.

CHAPTER 4

LARA LEFT JUST before dawn, a little sore headed, but the ride would soon clear it. Bamur's men did not stop or search her when she left. The dwarf had given orders the night before that she had free passage. The men at the gate nodded in gratitude, and Lara realised that even without the dwarf's orders, they would have let her pass. Her thoughts turned to Bamur and the others at the inn. A lot of ale was drunk, and by the time Lara left, most had passed out. When Bamur started telling her how much he was attracted to the human female, especially one who could wield a sword with skill, Lara called it a night. She chuckled as she rode. The dwarf would have a very sore head when he finally woke, and would instantly regret everything he had said to her the night before. She hoped that by the time she returned, the memory of the night's festivities would have faded.

It would take at least three days to get to Great Moor, with an inn a day's ride from the mining town. The Traveller's Rest was only half full compared to the ones in Bighdarum. With that, it was easy to get a room and have a quiet drink while the other customers chatted amongst themselves.

Leaving the inn behind at dawn, Lara continued. She would have to camp out overnight, and it would be the perfect opportunity for a hunt. There was a large forest to the north of Great Moor, called The Forest of the Sea, because of the colour of the evergreen trees, which grew to the coast. It would be a good place to find something to eat and vast enough for her to have a good run. Her wolf had been itching to stretch its legs. After the last contract and waiting for Kayd, she had to hunt more sparingly. At least in the vast forest, she could clear her head and make her wolf happy with a good hunt and run.

As the light faded, she made camp on the outskirts of the forest. With everything secure, Lara turned into her wolf form and ran into its depths. As she raced through the woods, she wondered what the sorcerer would be like. If anything like the others she heard about or had met, he would be a man of authority. She just hoped he was not like the one she had crossed paths with a few years back. He had been too cocky for his own good.

She soon found a good hunting area and, having made a kill, ate her fill. Lara lay where she was for a while after she had eaten, just listening to the trees, and focusing on the feeling of her other self. The wolf felt content and glad of the run and good hunt.

Lara paused as the forest suddenly fell silent. She tensed, sniffing. Something was not right. She felt a coldness in the air for a moment and then it passed. Lara stood and investigated the depths of the trees, sniffing her surroundings. Woods never usually fell silent unless there was a demon around. She listened carefully to the night air, but could not pick up anything. Then, as suddenly as the silence had fallen, the sounds of the woods came back to life. Lara stood for a moment, wondering why she had a feeling of dread. Yet it had been short-lived and the forest seemed normal again. She shrugged it off. Whatever it was, had headed away. It could have just been a demon looking for prey. Taking one final sniff of the air, Lara turned and trotted off back to her camp. The kill she had just had would sustain her for several days, and by then, she would probably leave Great Moor behind.

By mid-afternoon on the third day, Lara reached Great Moor. It was a large, affluent town, with trees and filled flower pots everywhere. Yet it had no large, fortified walls like others with such a prosperous population. Centuries ago, there was a major conflict between the north and south kingdoms affecting the settlements that had been closer to the border. However, unlike the neighbouring villages and towns further north, this town had never experienced the same level of suffering. Even though the war had been won by the south to bring peace throughout the land, some towns had still constructed walls for additional security.

There were guards all dressed in dark green uniforms with a royal crest on the shoulder. Although the lands had been peaceful for centuries, the royal family of the southern kingdom had made a decree to ensure all the southern towns had a presence of authority, with or without walls. They were there to keep the peace, but mainly they were to make the residents feel safe. Most of the guards would see no action, apart from the odd drunken fight or skirmish. The guards helped lost travellers, helped citizens with their everyday tasks, or chatted with the local girls who were fascinated by them. Lara smirked. The number one reason most young men joined was to impress a girl.

They had posted guards on all the major routes into town, but as they never really dealt with any trouble, the ones she passed looked relaxed. Several were not even armed. One was too busy chatting to a flirtatious local girl than watching the travellers going in and out of the town.

The main street was busy, with shops on either side and the sounds of a market ahead in the large square, which was in the centre of town. Lara let her horse walk at a slow pace as she took in the hectic atmosphere. It had been several years since she had last passed through, and the town had changed little. As she rode past the side streets, she looked down at them to see nothing untoward. Most large towns had some sort of darker side to them, but this one was the exception. It had surprised her that there was no non-human quarter. Then again, it was mostly the larger cities that had those. The pack she and Derwyn had met years before had their farms to the south and that was another reason the town had few issues. Unknown to the locals, the lycan pack was keeping them safe, more so than the visible guards on the streets. If she had not been here for the contract, she would have ventured down to see the pack and catch up on old times.

As she carried on, she saw a dwarf blacksmith up one of the side streets and made a note to have her horse's hooves checked before she left. She doubted there would be any trouble, and whatever Malaki wanted, it was not about an issue here in town. She had a few hours till dusk and wanted to have a good look around and find Malaki's residence. But first, she needed an inn for the night.

There were a couple of inns at the edge of the main square. Both looked reputable. Lara rode to the one that Kayd had used before. He had recommended it several times, as the innkeeper had good prices and made a fine stew. Dismounting outside the inn, she fastened her horse to the hitching post and ventured inside. It was quiet because of the time of day, but there were still some customers. Lara went over to the main counter and nodded to the innkeeper.

The large man gave her a broad, friendly smile. "Can I 'elp ya?"

"Can I get a room for a few eves and stabling for my horse?"

He nodded. "Aye, take the horse around back. Me lad will take care of it for ya. And I 'ave a few rooms spare, I'll give ya one upstairs at the back, it's one of me best."

Lara nodded, took the key, and walked back out to take her horse to the stable. With her horse settled and her things secured in her room. Lara had a walk around the town. The last time she had been in Great Moor, all those years before, she had stayed with the pack on their farm. She just passed through on the occasional visit to the pack, or whenever she returned from a contract. Having never had the opportunity to really explore the town, it was nice to finally be able to do so.

After wandering for a while, she asked one local where Malaki could be located. It seemed he had a tower to the north, and was well-liked by the locals. Lara walked that way and soon found the tower. It was hard to miss. A lush garden surrounded it with a straight, tree-lined path leading up to the door. Lara decided not to introduce herself as she wanted to find out more about him from the locals, and from his message, he wanted to meet at dawn. Lara would respect his wishes, as sorcerers were wont to be set in their ways.

She turned on her heel, heading back towards the main square. At the inn, Lara ordered a drink and asked the innkeeper about the sorcerer.

The large man smiled. "He's a fine man. He has 'elped the town on several occasions over the years. Think he's 'elped the lasses round here give birth on more occasions than I can remember. He 'elped me wife with two of ours."

Lara took a sip of her drink. "So, a man who keeps his word?"

"Aye, miss, he will." The innkeeper eyed her. "Why do ya ask?"

"I have business with him and just want to ensure it wouldn't be a misadventure."

The innkeeper chuckled. "Ya will be fine with him, miss. Ya can have a word with him, ya self. He always comes in 'ere, of an eve, for a drink."

Lara raised an eyebrow. "I may just do that, thank you."

The innkeeper nodded and turned back to his chores, Lara took a table at the back to relax. His contract stated to meet him at his tower. But if he was going to be here at the inn tonight, then Lara was not about to miss an opportunity to at least watch and see what he was like. The pack never mentioned the sorcerer during any of her visits. But then again, they would have wanted to keep their distance, as he would have been aware of what they were. But he must have known they were nearby. She surmised that he left them alone because they helped protect the town.

That also made her wonder, depending on his powers, if he might sense what she was and venture over. Yet, if he were as good as the innkeeper stated, then he would not try anything, especially once he realised she was here for his contract.

By early evening, the inn got busy with late-arriving travellers, and a few locals who would greet the innkeeper and pass on any local gossip. A local bard also started playing and singing songs in the far corner. He seemed very popular with the locals who would sing along with him and barmaids smiling at him warmly. Lara raised her eyebrow as she watched some exchanges. It seemed he had been very close to two barmaids from their interactions. She smirked. The bard was most definitely a ladies' man, probably promising all his lovers that he would write a song after them.

It was not long after the bard had begun to play another tune that a tall, handsome man entered. He wore a full-length purple cloak, black polished boots, black trousers, and a white shirt. His immaculate, well-trimmed beard, along with his dark skin, made quite an impression. It had to be Malaki. She took a deep breath, taking in his scent, which seemed floral and calming. She studied him without making it obvious; he was younger than she had expected from what Kayd had said, but then again sorcerers had ways of always looking youthful if they wished. He looked around the room. Everyone nodded a friendly greeting to him. The bard also acknowledged him as he continued to play his ballad. As the sorcerer continued to survey the occupants, his eyes lingered on Lara for a moment before he walked with confidence to the innkeeper. She leaned back, trying to watch him without being obvious, but could hear him effortlessly, even with all the singing.

He stated, with a smooth, deep voice, "Good eve, Jacob. Some of your fine wine."

The innkeeper nodded. "Good eve, Malaki."

The innkeeper placed the goblet of wine down and Malaki asked quietly, "The young woman over there? A traveller that I don't believe has passed this way before."

Lara stayed relaxed, taking a sip of her drink. She wanted to turn towards them when he mentioned her but did not want to give away that she could hear them.

The innkeeper smiled. "She's 'ere on business. I think with ya self, as she was askin' about ya."

Malaki glanced over at her, Lara just making out the movement from the corner of her eye. "Then I should introduce myself."

Lara casually looked around the room, noticing the sorcerer picking up his drink and walking in her direction. She now looked at him more obviously as he came over to her.

He nodded a greeting and asked, "May I join you?

Lara made a quick nod and watched him as he sat opposite her. She smiled and stated, "I'm Lara and you?"

His blue eyes gazed at her. "Malaki, but then again, you probably already know that with your lycan hearing?" Lara raised an eyebrow. He was good. In just a few moments, he had already figured out who she was. He studied her, a furrow of confusion on his brow. "But your mystical aura seems tainted." He paused and added, "Well, in all my years." Then chuckled. He focused on her eyes. "I thought it wasn't possible."

Lara took a sip of her drink, not taking her eyes from his. "It isn't. But it seems for me, it was."

Malaki leant back, chuckling deeply again and took a sip of his wine. "So, am I to expect you at my tower at dawn?"

"Aye, clever with the message on the contract."

The sorcerer leant forward. "I wanted to ensure I had someone with wit and brawn." He paused for a moment, studying her. "You're a little young for a Sword."

"I'm older than I look."

"Oh!"

Lara leant forward. "So do we wish to talk business now, or is this to be a more relaxed meeting?"

Malaki smiled, studying her intently. "I think we leave business till the morn. I want to get to know you first."

Lara nodded, taking in his floral scent again, feeling tranquil in his presence. "The same here. Few sorcerers that I've met are so well-liked."

He raised a perfect eyebrow. "Indeed. It seems we are intriguing each other."

Lara studied Malaki's blue eyes. It seemed all sorcerers had the same eye colour. *Was it because of the magic?* She felt his hand gently lay against her lower back, their naked limbs still intertwined, and her body relaxed. "Well, is this your way of getting to know someone?"

He smiled softly, looking very content. "Only for those who truly intrigue me, and you are a very rare find, Lara."

She smiled, her fingers tracing over the lean muscles on his smooth chest. "I hadn't expected such an attractive sorcerer."

He sat up slightly but ensured they stayed intertwined. "Were you expecting some old, grouchy man?"

Lara looked up at him, wincing slightly. "Sorry, but, aye. I was."

He chuckled, making his chest vibrate with the deep sound. "Then again, I have to say, I wasn't expecting such an attractive Sword."

Lara sat up, studying him. "Just understand I'm not the type of girl who beds just anyone."

Malaki brushed a strand of hair from her face. "Don't worry, I wasn't thinking that. We're just two souls sharing a connection for one eve. Nothing more. But I could not pass on this opportunity." He paused and regarded her. "With what you are, have you connected intimately with anyone?"

Lara glanced down for a second, remembering Carn; she had not thought about him in months. "Once. But we both knew that it wouldn't last."

Malaki nodded. "A curse we both share. I will not live as long as you will, but we sorcerers live for several lifetimes."

"So, you understand. When there's a connection . . ."

He smiled, his full lips parting. "It's worth those moments."

Lara detangled their limbs. "They are."

Malaki sat up, glancing out the window. "It's almost dawn. Could you meet me at my tower, say mid-morn? The contract I have for you isn't a topic to discuss in the bed of a lover."

Lara nodded. "Understood." She regarded him for a few moments. "I hope we agree that this was just one eve, nothing more."

He nodded. "I believe that is to both our satisfaction."

CHAPTER 5

LARA WALKED ALONG the immaculate white gravel path towards Malaki's tower. It was wider than she had first thought the day before. Windows were scattered all the way to the top. The light sandstone of the tower shone in the sun like a beacon. It was impressive. From the grandeur of the gardens, Lara suspected the inside of the tower would be just as ornate and immaculate. After meeting Malaki, he seemed to be a man who was proud of his appearance and his possessions. She doubted it would be a cluttered mess like some other sorcerers' places. Her mind wandered to the night before. She had not expected to end up having sex with him, but there had been something about him; and a mutual attraction. She smirked, looking up at the tower, but, it was back to business. He had refused to talk about the contract last night, and Lara was still curious about what it would entail.

Reaching the main entrance, the large oak door opened on its own accord as soon as Lara reached the threshold. She tentatively entered the tower. The entranceway opened to a small, lush, enclosed garden. She looked up to see it was a large atrium. In the centre was a small fountain which reflected a tranquil escape. Malaki looked up from where he sat on a bench near a small tree, off to the side of the fountain. He snapped shut the book he was reading, and as he stood, he said, "Good morn."

Lara nodded, looking around at the garden. "Nice place."

The sorcerer smiled. "It helps me think." He walked towards her, wearing a full-length dark blue robe, which seemed more befitting of a sorcerer. "Come, we have much to discuss."

Lara followed Malaki from the garden to an archway at the side where he headed up a winding staircase which was situated around the edge of the tower. There were windows looking out at the grounds, but on the other side, open arches offered a view into the atrium to see all the plants below and the vines trailing on the walls. The stairway then became enclosed, and continued upwards to more rooms. They stopped half way and entered an extensive study. There were shelves covering almost half of the walls, all crammed full of books of all kinds. The only empty space was to the right of her, where a window was located. On the opposite side of the entrance, there was a large map hanging on the wall behind a grand desk that was covered in books and scattered paperwork. Lara raised an eyebrow. She had not expected a room to look so cluttered after such an immaculate garden and atrium. The tall sorcerer leant against his desk, studying Lara, who stood opposite him.

She asked, "So the contract?"

He nodded, twisting round to grab a large parchment from his desk. Turning back, he unrolled it and studied the content before looking up at her. "What I am asking you to do won't be a straightforward task, but think, with your skill set, you will be the best Sword to deal with my issue."

"And your issue is?"

Malaki moved some books on his desk and rolled out the parchment, then used the books to keep it from rolling back up. Lara came to stand next to him and looked at the unrolled document. An herbal scent that he wore invaded her nose, different from the more floral one he had the night they met. This one seemed less relaxing. Lara wondered if that had been a factor in the events of the night before, but shook the idea from her mind and returned to the task at hand.

The writing on the parchment was in a language she did not recognise. She asked, "So, what am I looking at?"

"This is an ancient text. The language is old and lost, but I still know it well. It's about a crystal, one that was recovered deep in a mine hundreds of years ago. This crystal was dangerous and held powers that, if held in the wrong hands, would destroy life."

Lara whispered, remembering the books she had read as a child, "A necromancy crystal."

Malaki glanced at her. "How have you heard of it?"

"My papa had a lot of old books, mainly on demons and mystical creatures. I read them all as part of my education so that I would be well versed. I remember one book that covered myths spoke of that crystal, even in my homeland of Moonstar."

Malaki gazed at her. "The crystal is nay myth, but I know it is widely known across our world as one. Many do not realise that, as well as the crystals we use to teleport, there are more rare ones that contain other forms of magic. Light and, in this case, dark."

Lara studied him, thinking back on the night before again, no longer seeing the attraction that had drawn her. His face seemed a little older, and cold. "So, what is it you're asking me to do?"

Malaki looked down at the parchment and sighed. "The crystal had been in my safekeeping for many years, but recently a colleague wished to study it, to see if we could harness the power within for good." He turned to her, his eyes focusing on hers. "Unfortunately, the crystal was . . . stolen."

"So, you want me to find it?"

"Aye. I have spoken to my colleague, Alistari, at great length, but feel he is hiding something from me. I believe, you may get more information."

"I see. Then am I to follow the trail and destroy it?"

Malaki shook his head. "Nay, to return it here where I can keep it in safekeeping once more."

Lara regarded him. "But shouldn't something as evil as that be destroyed?"

"True, but to destroy such a crystal would take such immense power that whatever is within, we may not contain."

"Do you think there's something in it?"

Malaki nodded. "When studying it, I could sense this evil, and knew something was within. Even Alistari said he sensed something. I then wondered if we could ever use the power within it for good."

"So, I am to return it to you?"

"Aye. I have a containment for it, below this very tower. It has been safe there for centuries, so know, once it is returned, it will be locked in there forever."

Lara looked up at him. "And remain a story of myth and legend?"

He nodded. Lara looked back at the parchment. She thought of what the risks would be. She remembered the stories in her father's book; it was something not to be played with. It was not her normal remit, and would be an unusual challenge. But also, with what she was, she was probably the only Sword who could get it back.

She took a breath and turned to Malaki. "I'll take the contract. Where do you suggest I start?"

"Thank you. I suggest you go to Alistari first. He's a bit of a recluse and has his tower in the mountains of Dragon Nest." He pointed to a map on the wall behind his desk and added, "It's north of here, about a four-day ride."

Lara raised an eyebrow, studying the area on the map of a crescent shaped range of mountains. "I hope it isn't an actual dragon nest."

Malaki chuckled. "Nay, not for a few hundred years."

Lara studied him. "So, are the rumours true you faced one?"

He smiled. "I did, many, many years ago in my youth. He was a formidable beast, and I had nay choice but to kill it."

Lara sighed. "A pity it had to die. I had always thought they were just myths. But had still always wondered what they would have been like, if real."

He gazed at her, focusing on her green eyes. "Alas, few now remain, most flying to the far north." He paused and then added. "Everything in our myths and legends were derived from something real. Even the ones that are far-fetched are based on some fact." He studied her intensely. "To some, lycans and vampires are just stories."

Lara smiled and nodded. "Very true." She looked at the parchment. "Is there anything in there that may help me or warn me to be careful of?"

The sorcerer gazed at her. "All that I can say is to be wary when you find the crystal. It can prey on the weak-minded. But I feel with what you are, you cannot be turned."

"Turned?"

He nodded. "It mentions it taints the holder. This is the other reason I believe something is within it, and feel if it could find the right person who is weak in mind, it will escape."

"But you said it would need immense power."

"Aye, but first it would need to influence."

Lara asked, "Could it have tainted your friend?"

He sighed. "Aye, unfortunately, I believe so."

Lara regarded him. "Do you think I could be walking into a trap?" He looked down with a glint of guilt in his eye. Lara sighed. "I see. Any tips?"

"Be on your guard. I don't believe that he still has the crystal, but think he may know more than he's saying. Hence, why I think it may have tainted him, even if only to turn a blind eye when it was taken."

Lara nodded. "I best return to the inn and prepare to leave."

Malaki studied her intently and took her hand in his. "Be careful. I don't know where the crystal could have been taken to. You must be on your guard."

"Don't worry, I can take care of myself."

He added, "Aye, but I do not wish any harm to befall you."

She studied his blue eyes, wondering if Malaki had been more invested in their night of passion than she realised, or if there was some other motive behind his concern.

"Thought last eve was a nay strings attached kind of thing."

"Aye, it was. But you're one of a kind."

She smiled coldly, realising he was more fascinated by what she was. She pulled her hand free of his and said, "Aye, I am. My knowledge and experience as well."

Malaki nodded, seeming to get a hold of himself, his features becoming neutral once more. "Once you have been to Dragon's Nest, go wherever the information takes you."

"What if there isn't any?"

He sighed. "Then you will have to follow the trail of death and destruction."

She nodded, knowing, from what she had read as a child, what the crystal could do. She looked at him. "Hopefully, I won't have to."

Malaki added, "I will contact my acquaintances and see if they have any information that will help. If I have, you will be informed."

Lara frowned. "How?"

Malaki smiled. "We sorcerers have our ways."

CHAPTER 6

L ARA STROLLED BACK to the inn, lost in thought. She would need to get her horse's shoes inspected by the blacksmith. She did not want her horse throwing a shoe if she would have to travel for some time. Lara would use the rest of the day to prepare, and then have a good rest before leaving at dawn.

She would fulfil the contract, but felt a little leery of Malaki. Her wolf self was warning her that something seemed off. The Malaki she met the night before had been different to the one present at the tower. When she thought about it, it seemed her feelings around him had changed and was suspicious that it was down to the scent. *Did I succumb to a type of spell?* His scent last night had made her feel relaxed and trusting. But the one she had picked up today seemed neutral, yet cold.

Lara pursed her lips as she reached the stall in the stable where her horse was. She felt a little foolish that a spell had tricked her, and wondered why he would feel the need to do it in the first place. Then again, from experience, it was wise to never fully trust a sorcerer, or his intentions. At the tower, he was more interested in her being a hybrid, just like all the others had been. Once the first part of the contract was complete, she would have to be cautious. She sighed as she bridled her horse. *Then again, was this all overthinking?* She had other nights with men that, afterwards, she had wished she had not. Last night was no exception. Taking her horse from the stable, she walked it across town to the dwarf blacksmith. She focused on the business at hand once more, putting the past behind her, and determined not to be fooled again.

The dwarf tipped his head in greeting Lara and patted the horse's flank while Lara explained about having the shoes checked. He nodded and put her horse at ease as he checked the shoes, indicating that it would be wise to get three replaced. As he got to work, he chatted away, telling her of all the gossip in the town. Yet, as all she could see of him was his backside as he worked, he had no clue if anyone was even there. Lara smiled politely, wondering if she should leave and if he would even notice. Then his conversation sparked her interest.

". . . And well, it seems Malaki still has a way with the ladies. He bedded a traveller last eve, at The Ox and Bull. Lanthrel, the innkeeper there, was tellin' me this morn, that she was a fine-looking lass too." He grunted, grabbing a new shoe, then stroked the horse's leg and nailed it in place. "Anyway, Malaki left at dawn, so think they had a good eve."

He chuckled and stood up straight, patting his hands together to get rid of the dust and dirt from working on the hooves. Looking up at Lara for the first time since she had arrived with her horse. His features paled slightly, realising he had gossiped a little too much. "Oh. Sorry lass, I . . ."

Lara responded, "It's interesting to know that I'm the gossip of the town."

He glanced down, a little guilty. "Nay, lass, honest ya not. It's just between me and Lanthrel."

Her eyes hardened as she added, "Then shall we keep it that way?"

The dwarf nodded and turned back to the horse, patting its flank. "This is a fine animal. Ya look after her well."

Lara smiled softly, seeing how embarrassed the dwarf was. "Aye, she is. She's seen me through a few scrapes over the years."

The dwarf looked up at her. "Well, if ya ever want to put her out to pasture, I'd be interested."

Lara nodded and asked, "How much for the shoes?"

"Just two."

"Two for three shoes?"

The dwarf nodded. "Aye, I think ya deserve a discount after all me chatting."

Lara chuckled and passed over three coins. "Let's just keep what happened between myself and Malaki quiet."

The dwarf nodded and bid her a good day. Lara took the reins of her horse and walked back across town. The last thing she needed was to be the gossip of the town. From what Lara could tell, it was more than likely the gossip would spread from the dwarf more than the innkeeper.

When she returned to the stable, she paused, seeing a wolf dozing next to a black horse. Lara smiled softly. The wolf was old, but that scent was all too familiar. She put her horse back in its stall and strolled over; the wolf woke as she approached.

The stable lad, who was clearing out some stalls, said, "Be careful. It don't like strangers."

Lara glanced at him. "It's alright, she'll remember me."

The wolf looked up at her and sniffed her outstretched hand. The animal recognised her instantly and nuzzled against her. Lara combed her fingers into the wolf's soft fur and whispered, "So, is your master inside, girl?"

The wolf looked up at her and grunted. Lara took a breath, her stomach twisting. It had been over fifteen years since she had seen Carn, and she wondered how he would react. She slowly stood, letting the wolf doze again. She left the stable, a little apprehensive, and walked inside the inn. It was busy for the time of day, but there were still empty tables dotted around.

Lara picked up Carn's scent as soon as she entered. But her stomach was full of butterflies. She walked over to the counter first. Ordering a drink, she took a big gulp to steady her nerves. Lara turned from the counter and surveyed the large room. She paused, seeing Carn in the corner, at a table by himself, drinking ale. Lara's heart skipped a beat, her throat tightened. It was good to see him, but as she gazed at him; she was a little shocked to see he had aged. She knew he would have, and calculated he would have to be in his mid-forties. A sprinkle of grey coloured the temples of his dark hair, which was a little longer than he used to wear it, and a new scar marred his cheek. He had also grown a beard, which was well-trimmed, and it suited him. She guessed it was to hide the scar, but there was still a faint line visible where the hair did not grow. Lara was curious about when he had got the scar and wondered if he would tell her. That is, if he was as welcoming to see her as his wolf was. She hoped so. They had left on good terms, but being over fifteen years, life moves on.

Lara had never felt nervous before. She downed the rest of her drink and ordered another. She glanced back towards him as she waited for her second drink, her fingers strumming on the countertop. From the way his black jerkin fitted him, he still held the same physique, and her body instantly reacted. She took a breath, trying to keep focused. Grabbing her drink, she took another big gulp and walked over.

His eyes were looking about the room and then locked on hers when she was only halfway across. Lara's heart skipped a beat, pausing mid-step, her chest tight in apprehension. As she focused on those strikingly blue eyes, her skin flushed, remembering his touch all those years before. He gazed at her, and for a moment he appeared almost in a daze, as if he wondered if she was real. Then he beamed. Lara's apprehension vanished when his features lit up in warm recognition. Her legs moved her forward, seemingly of their own accord, until she arrived at his table. She put down her drink and said, "Is this seat taken?"

Carn stood and grinned, his eyes never wavering. His familiar, smooth, deep dulcet tones said, "By Rosh, aren't you a joy to behold."

Lara returned his smile and her body zinged at the memory of the last time they had been intimate together. He moved around the table and embraced her in a bear hug, his body as muscular and broad as she remembered. She felt the familiar sense of safety of his embrace; it was so good to feel him once more. As they parted, gazing into each other's eyes, their lips hovering close together. Lara breathed, "Good to see you."

They stood like that for what seemed like an eternity, both lost in each other's gaze. Carn slowly leant forward and kissed her gently and passionately. Lara's whole body shuddered at his touch. They parted when someone behind them coughed awkwardly. Both turned to see the barmaid holding a tray with food. "Ya order, sir."

Carn nodded reluctantly, letting Lara go. They parted and instantly noticed the attention they were getting. Carn quickly sat; Lara doing the same opposite him. Once the barmaid had placed the order and left, Carn took Lara's hand from across the table and said, "You haven't aged a day."

Lara smiled. "The years have been kind to you." She nodded towards the scar. "That's new."

Carn sighed, his hand going to it absentmindedly. "I forget it's there now. Happened about ten winters ago." He studied her intently. "Let's say the other fella was worse off."

Lara smiled gently, touching the scar, his beard soft against her fingertips. "I have missed you."

"Aye, the same. Kept wondering what became of you and Derwyn. I cleared the contract on you over a hundred days after you had gone. I was half tempted to get on a ship and try to find you."

Lara studied him. "Why didn't you?"

"I couldn't find where you disembarked. The captain of The Black Raven wouldn't give me any information. He ensured he didn't tell a soul, good at protecting you, but frustrating for me. The fact he stopped at so many ports it would have been the will of Rosh if I chose the right one. So, unable to find where you had gone, I thought it was best to let you go." He paused, looking a little forlorn, then glanced around. "So, where's Derwyn?"

Lara sighed, leaning back in her chair. She gazed at Carn for a few moments, just taking in the sight of him. "He has a family and lives in Warrior Sword."

"Impressive." Lara noted a glint of sadness in his eyes as he added, "And you?"

Lara gave him a sideways glance. "I became a Sword. With an excellent reputation, too."

Carn laughed. "Bet Derwyn wasn't too happy about that."

Lara chuckled. "He was a Sword for a while, too. Meeting you changed his views on them."

Carn nodded, taking a sip of his ale, forgetting about the food in front of him. His eyes focused on hers and he smiled. "It is *so* good to see you."

Lara leant forward, raising an eyebrow. "So, did any good woman tie you down?"

Carn leant back and replied, almost coldly, "None."

Lara smiled softly. It seemed she had touched a nerve. She looked back up at him and their eyes locked. She changed the subject. "So how long have you been in Barberium?"

Carn took a deep breath. "Came in on a ship over ten days past."

"Business?"

Carn studied her, shaking his head. "Nay."

Lara glanced down at her drink, noting the coolness in his voice again. "Oh."

Carn's hand slowly took hers into his again. He smiled softly, probably noting the sharpness of his reply. "To be honest, I needed a new start, and I heard this was a good place for Swords to get work."

"That's true, and a good place to start fresh."

Carn gazed at her and sighed, his hand never letting go of hers. He glanced down, then stated, "I had met someone. Thought I wouldn't after you, but she was a fine woman . . ." he trailed off.

Lara could see the sadness in his eyes. "You don't have to tell me."

Carn's lips turned upward slightly as he regarded her. "I know. But you're about the only one I would want to tell."

Lara tilted her head to one side. "So, what was she like?"

Carn smiled, with a mischievous glint in his eyes, so similar to how he would look, from when they were together on Moonstar. "She was loving and caring." He looked at Lara. "She reminded me of you." He paused, his eyes distant, his face long, remembering the past. "She was stunning."

Lara regarded him, seeing the hurt in his eyes. Whatever had happened, it had scarred him. The Carn she knew had changed, was broken. Lara squeezed his hand. "You don't have to continue."

Carn looked up at her, raising the corners of his lips slightly, and nodded. He took a big gulp of his ale and took a breath. "So, what have you been up to?"

Lara leant back. "Where to begin. Killed a few demons. Saved a few towns."

Carn chuckled, glad of the change of subject. "Nothing much then."

Lara shook her head and smiled. "You'll like it here. I know I do."

"Aye, it's a fine place. Just finished a contract."

"So, still a Sword."

Carn smiled, studying her. "Aye, it's in my blood. I'm working for this man called Kayd. Just come back here to wait on a new contract."

Lara stared at him. "You work with Kayd?"

"Aye, do you know something I don't?"

Lara leant back and laughed. "So, you're Larn!" Carn frowned, wondering what she meant. Lara gazed at him. "I work for Kayd too. He mentioned he had a new Sword, but said his name was Larn."

Carn laughed and studied her. "He keeps moaning. Seems he can't understand my accent."

Lara sighed and lost herself in his eyes again. "He told me I may cross paths with you, and when I did, I'm supposed to convince you to take some of the more lucrative contracts."

Carn smiled, his fingers interlacing with hers again, his thumb gently stroking hers, almost absentmindedly. "You mean the ones that line his pockets more? I don't take those." He paused, seeing Lara's guilty glance. "Do you?"

She shrugged. "A few. I'm the best on his books for dealing with demons." She paused and regarded him intently. "But if they aren't causing a threat, I deal with it amicably."

Carn nodded, studying her, lost in her eyes. "I can't believe you are here in front of me. I half wondered if we would cross paths, but never dreamed . . ."

She smiled, lost in his gaze. Carn took a deep breath and said, "So, why are you here?"

"In Great Moor?" he nodded. Lara could tell he was not sure if they were friends, or still more, and was treading carefully. He had not let her hand go, so he had to be leaning towards more, yet she could understand his hesitation. Fifteen years was a long time. She smiled and added, "Just picked up a new contract, a very interesting one, too."

"So, you're leaving in the morn?"

"Aye."

Carn nodded. He glanced down at his hand holding hers, like he had not realised he was holding it. He looked back up at her and cocked his head to the back of the inn. "Sooo, could I help you find your room?"

Lara regarded his features, getting lost in his gaze. Then she grinned, she had been hoping he would ask. She raised an eyebrow. "I may need help with my things, too."

Carn beamed, quickly finishing his ale, his food, cold and forgotten. He pulled her to her feet and let Lara lead the way.

As soon as they entered Lara's room, they kissed passionately. Carn pulled her towards the bed, not wanting their embrace to end. Lara broke the embrace, gazing at him. After all these years, it felt like they had only made love a few days before. Carn focused on her eyes and smiled, his lips brushing hers again. His hands roamed down the front of her shirt, unfastening the buttons, slowly. Once her shirt was open enough, his hand slipped beneath the material and cupped one of her breasts. Lara gasped, feeling his familiar touch, her skin buzzing in delight. She hooked her fingers into his thick hair, deepening their kiss. His hand roamed down her body, reaching for her belt. He unbuckled it and his fingers went to her waistband. Lara's loins shuddered in delight and pushed him back onto the bed. Carn grasped her trousers, pulling her with him. Lara landed on top, straddling him, and gazed at his features. Her hands slid down to his trousers and began undoing them. Carn closed his eyes for a moment, the bulge in his trousers portraying how his body was reacting to their closeness. Lara gazed at him and smiled. She leaned forward, capturing his lips with hers.

Carn pulled up her shirt, his hands sliding up and down her back. His fingertips slipped beneath her trousers, brushing her buttocks. Lara gasped. She stopped kissing him and pulled off her shirt, discarding it. Carn gazed at her firm breasts. Leaning forward, he sucked one of her nipples, making Lara moan in delight. He then grabbed her around the waist, flipping her over on the bed so he was on top. He stood up, gazing at her, then quickly undressed. Lara doing the same from where she lay.

Once they were both naked, Carn leant forward, sucking her nipples again, his lips roaming across her breasts and down her chest. He placed kisses across her abdomen and ventured further. His lips brushed her pubic hair before he went lower. His tongue was warm and welcoming against her flesh. Lara closed her eyes as he continued to lick, making her thighs shudder in delight. He glanced up at her, savouring her familiar taste and then crept back up her body. Lara opened her legs further when his groin laid against hers, feeling his phallus against her thigh. As Carn captured her lips with his, he entered her. Lara raised her hips slightly, letting him slide further in, making her body tingle. Their hips moved in unison as he went deeper. He grabbed her arms, moving them above her head. While he continued to rotate his hips, he leaned down and sucked her nipples again.

Lara lost almost all control of her body; it was no longer her own. Carn's magical touch made her buzz with delight. She had had a few lovers since Carn, but none could make her body react as he did. Her surroundings disappeared as time seemed to stand still, frozen in the moment. Fully focused on the feelings inside her, her body wanted more, even as it neared its peak. She shuddered, feeling Carn doing the same as they orgasmed together.

Lara gazed at the sleeping Carn; their naked limbs intertwined. As soon as they reached her room, their apprehension vanished. It felt so good to be with him again. She was not about to push to know what had happened on Moonstar that hurt him so much, but if a night together could help distract him, she would not refuse. Lara studied his lined features; it was hard to see him aged when she was still as she has always been. Times like these made her remember all those years ago when she spoke with Fashor, the first vampire she had met after she had been turned who was kind enough to give her some pointers about having ties. She felt it with Derwyn, but seeing Carn, it somehow hurt even more. Her eyes focused on the scar across his cheek, her fingertips slowly traced across it, into the salt and pepper beard. She sensed his heartbeat change as he woke. Lara turned her attention to his eyes as they flickered open, and she smiled. "Good morn."

Carn focused sleepily on Lara and took a deep breath. It had felt like the night before had been a dream. He had never expected to cross paths with Lara again. Yet it felt good to have her in his arms. His whole body zinged remembering how they spent the night. He returned her smile. "Good morn."

He kissed her passionately and pulled himself up on his elbow to study her, still taking in the fact she was here after fifteen years. He stretched his neck and sighed. "Why is it, as you get older, you ache more?"

Lara laughed. "Wait till you're my age."

He raised an eyebrow; he had not expected Lara to have any aching joints as he had. The life of a Sword was hard on the body, and it felt as if it was finally catching up with him. "You ache?"

Lara nodded. "I may be immortal, but that doesn't mean I don't get some aches and pains. I know my body heals, and not fully sure it is more like a memory, but I ache a little from time to time."

Carn chuckled and gazed at her lovingly. *Is she just saying that to make me feel better?* He did not care. He had her in his arms after all these years, and it felt good. "Well, there you go." He glanced towards the window, the morning summer sun seeping in through the thin curtains. He turned back to her. "It's odd that you haven't aged a day." He brushed her cheek. "I knew you wouldn't, but it is still odd to see."

Lara smiled softly. "I know, with being immortal, that I could live for several hundreds of years." She studied his features. "So, that was another reason it was time to part ways all those years ago, because of this."

Carn sighed and kissed her, placing his rough hand gently on her cheek. Losing himself in her beauty. "I don't care. Seeing you again was just so unexpected."

Lara smiled. "It's good to see you, too. I missed you." She paused and studied him, her hand on his chest, and he wondered if she could feel how much his heart was pounding. She added, "It's odd seeing you with a beard."

Carn smiled, rubbing it with his knuckles. He had been so conscious of the scar that he had grown the beard. The scar was still visible, but it seemed to help. "Thought it made me look wiser."

Lara laughed, raising an eyebrow. "Really?"

Carn frowned, seeing the mischievousness in her green eyes. "Hey!"

Lara kissed his lips gently and regarded him. "Aye, I do have to agree. You look *wiser*."

Carn smiled and sat up more to study her. He glanced across at the books on the side. "Still have your head in books."

She looked over at them. "Aye, always will."

He gazed at her, remembering their last few days together. Whenever they were not making love or riding, she would be reading. He sighed, still finding it hard to believe they had found each other again, and thanked Rosh, as the god must have had a hand in it. His hand cupped her cheek, feeling her soft skin against his. Now that he had found her, Carn felt he did not want them to part again and wondered. "This may seem a crazy idea, but what if I went with you?"

"With me?"

He nodded, the glint in his eyes almost gleaming. "Look, I came here to start afresh, but seeing you . . . I feel alive again, and that's what I need. But I will only join you if you will have me."

Lara stopped herself from instantly saying yes. She missed having someone with her and, like Carn had said, she felt the same. Seeing him again, she felt alive. She pursed her lips, not giving him the satisfaction of an instant answer. "Well, I'm not sure." Carn looked at her forlornly, and then Lara chuckled. "Of course, I'd want you with me."

Carn smiled, beaming from ear to ear. "Excellent decision."

Lara regarded him, wondering if he would ever tell her everything about what happened on Moonstar. In her heart, she did not care. To have Carn with her again was enough for her. The time would come when age would catch up with him, but for now, it was good to just enjoy the company.

Carn kissed her passionately. "So, I know I should have asked this first, but what's the contract?"

Lara smiled and placed her hands on his chest, studying him intently. "It's not for the faint-hearted. I need someone good with a sword, won't back out of danger, and will give me one-on-one attention in the evenings."

Carn chuckled, kissing her again. "Hmmm, not so sure, now." He gave her a side glance and pursed his lips. "Think that's more than I'm willing take on."

Lara went to hit him, and Carn grabbed her fist in his hand. "Alright, I will."

She smiled and kissed him, looking towards the window. "I could stay here all day, but . . ."

"Aye, I know, come on."

They both reluctantly climbed out of the bed, but being together again meant they would have many nights like this one.

CHAPTER 7

LARA PULLED BACK on the reins and looked up at the dark mountains ahead. They were a formidable sight; like razor-sharp teeth tearing into the late afternoon clouds. They were dangerous, not just from rumours of dragons, but from the conditions making them impossible to cross, much less climb. The mountains were as black as night and made from a strange, almost crystallised rock. It had been said they had become that way from thousands of years of dragon fire.

It had taken the two about three days to get to Dragon's Nest, which seemed less with having each other for company. Lara had not realised how lonely her life had become, especially in the evenings, till she had Carn at her side. She glanced at the Sword as he rode up beside her, his wolf running ahead, sniffing the ground and surroundings. Lara smiled. Saying they had been apart for fifteen years, certainly did not feel like it. After one night together, it seemed like it had only been days. He was still holding back about what happened on Moonstar, but she knew when Carn was ready, he would tell her.

He smiled, looking up at the mountains. "So that's the edge of Dragon's Nest?"

Lara replied, "Can't see any tower."

Carn pursed his lips. "You said that Malaki mentioned he was a bit of a recluse, maybe further in?"

"Aye, didn't think it would be that easy."

Carn looked ahead; his features puzzled. "Is there a way in?"

Lara glanced at him and smiled. "From what was on Malaki's map, they are in the shape of a crescent. So, there should be a point of entry."

They continued and soon could see a more open section. It was very uneven ground, but would give them access to the centre of the mountains. As the horses struggled across the rugged terrain, they eventually reached an expansive clearing, with the mountains forming a flawless crescent around them. The two looked up at the rocky landscape which seemed even more foreboding up close. Around the sizeable area, they both noticed a few trees, but still no tower. It seemed they would have to venture even further in to find it. As they rode on, Lara understood why it had the name and why it had once been used by dragons. It was well-protected, and a good place to hide. She looked at the mountains surrounding them, wondering if there were still any dragons there. Most said they had left a long time ago, but with the vastness of the mountains, who was to know. They could hide in these mountains for centuries, and no one would find them.

They both stopped when they were about two-thirds into the extensive area. The terrain was getting a lot rougher and more rocky, with a few more trees and shrubs scattered about, but otherwise open. As they looked around, Carn's wolf made a bark-howl to get their attention. They turned in that direction and Lara finally saw the tower. It was off to the side, up in the mountains themselves, and not a straightforward route, especially by horse. After riding as far as they could go, they both dismounted. The rest of the way would have to be on foot. They secured their horses by a tree. Carn looked up at the tower, whistling to his wolf to heel. As he strapped his sword to his back, he said, "So, that's it?"

Lara nodded. "Just need to get to it."

She scrutinised the mountains and the tower as she strapped her sword to her back. There had to be some sort of pathway. They made their way up the steep rocky ground with no access in sight. Lara glanced back at Carn and shrugged. He came up beside her, looking at the rocks. "Looks like we are going to have to climb."

She turned back, looking at the large boulders in front of them when Carn's wolf growled, then barked, to get their attention. The wolf went up to the large boulder blocking the way, sniffing the floor, then vanished. The two looked at each other. Carn whistled to his wolf, and she came back into view. Lara stepped closer to see a hidden pathway. It was cut into the rock with such precision that it could not be seen unless standing right next to it. Lara glanced back at Carn. He smiled and strolled up to his wolf, giving her a fuss.

They walked up the winding, narrow trail, wondering what reception they would receive once they reached the tower. It took some time, as the route wound backwards and forwards, up the side of the mountain to it. They had not gone far when ahead of them, long brambles suddenly grew across their path. Within moments, a wall of thick, thorn-covered branches blocked the pathway in front of them. As Lara approached them, they seemed to have a life of their own, and flicked out towards her, snatching on her jerkin sleeve and cutting across her hand. She stepped back and glanced at her skin as it slowly healed.

Carn cursed. "This fecking sorcerer is making sure it's hard to get to his tower."

Lara nodded and looked back at the branches. She pulled her sword free and tried to hack at the bramble. Carn came up beside her, pulling his sword free and did the same. But as quickly as they cut a branch, another appeared, flicking out at them and cutting their hands. It seemed hopeless.

They stepped back, looking at the plant. Carn glanced at Lara's blade, seeing the runes, and raised an eyebrow as he sucked on a cut on the back of his hand.

Lara smiled. "They come in handy."

He responded, "I may have to consider some if I'm going to be working with you."

She gazed at him. "There's a witch in Warrior Sword who can add them."

Carn looked back at the brambles and then at her sword. "Could a rune help?"

She looked at the branches and then at the runes. She smiled and then envisioned the fire rune and whispered its name. The fire rune glowed for a moment on her sword. She then looked at the brambles and hacked at them again. This time she cut through with ease and none grew back. As she hacked her way in further, the brambles shrunk back, slithering under the rocks as quickly as they had appeared.

The path in front of them cleared once more, Lara sheathed her sword and smiled at Carn. "Told you they come in handy."

Carn chuckled, sheathing his sword, and continued up the pathway.

As they approached, Lara glanced up at the tower. It was narrow and not as impressive as Malaki's. She walked up to the large oak door, Carn at her side. She shrugged and knocked. As they waited for a response, Lara glanced up at the tower again and noticed it had been partly built into the mountain. She wondered if most of the living space was hidden and if the tower was just for show. After a few moments of nothing. Lara knocked on the door harder, thinking that the occupant had not heard her. She sighed, looking around. After waiting for a while more, Lara stated, "Nay one's home."

"Let me try." Carn banged his fist on the door, making a louder sound than Lara. Still nothing. He shrugged, grabbing the door handle and turned it. The door swung open. He looked at her and gave her a cheeky grin.

Lara cursed under her breath for not thinking of the obvious. She pursed her lips, pulling one of her daggers free. She looked at the empty entryway. With no response, the sorcerer was either: deaf, not there, or unable to answer because of potential danger. Lara needed to know that the sorcerer was unharmed. They would have to continue with caution.

The door opened into a small hallway, leading to a staircase that winded around the edge of the tower heading upwards and downwards. Lara entered first. As she glanced back to see if Carn was following, the door slammed shut. Lara turned to grab the door handle, but it was stuck fast. She slammed her fists on the door and snapped, "Feck!"

She beat her fist on the door again and again, then tried the handle, but it would not budge. It seemed the sorcerer wanted her alone. Lara could hear Carn banging on the other side, his shouts muffled. Yet there was nothing either of them could do. Carn would wait or try to find a way in. Until then, Lara decided she might as well continue. Turning, she listened carefully, her keen lycan hearing picking up something faint below her. She looked up, knowing that there were probably some rooms above, but it seemed the activity was below. Lara sheathed her dagger and slowly headed down the stone staircase.

It got cooler the further she ventured down and assumed she must have been in the interior of the mountains. The stairs ended and there was a corridor ahead. The sound was louder, from what she could make out, someone was mumbling spells. There was a clinking of glass and lids being lifted off containers and a scraping sound from something getting mixed together. Lara walked carefully down the hallway, noticing the smooth stone. She traced her hand along it; it had been carved out with magic as it was too smooth to have been made by handheld tools. She looked around as she entered a cavern, impressed by its size. Cluttered bookshelves lined the walls. In one section was a small bed and a desk, and in the centre was a large table. An old man in a grey robe stood at the table mumbling and mixing potions. His attention was fully on the task at hand, yet he suddenly stated, "It is rude to stare, young lady."

Lara turned to the man. "Sorry, I didn't want to disturb you."

He glanced up at her, his grey hair short, his beard well-kept, but long to his chest. "You did by banging on my door. It seems your companion still is." He stopped what he was doing and studied her with wise blue eyes. "So, why are you here?"

Lara walked toward him and stated, "Malaki sent me and my companion."

"Ahh, I see. Well, your companion can stay outside for the moment, as it was only you who talked to Malaki." He paused, regarding her. "Well. Haven't come across a lycan in some time. But not just any lycan either. You are a rarity."

Lara smiled coldly, wondering how he knew only she had seen Malaki. *Had he talked to the other sorcerer or did he know by other means?* That was one reason she was always wary of sorcerers. They always seemed to hold secrets and used magic to ensure they were one step ahead. She had read as a child that sorcerers were selfless and it was warlocks that were the ones to be careful of. But in her experience, the lines were often blurred.

"So, if you know I was the only one to talk to Malaki, then you know why I am here."

The old man nodded, walking towards the corridor where Lara had come from. "Aye. We best talk, haven't we?"

She fell in step beside him. His scent was heavy with herbs, but with an earthy undertone to it. "What can you tell me?"

He looked at her, taking the lead up the narrow stone steps. "I think some tea first."

Lara gazed at his slightly arched back as he ascended the steps. It seemed the sorcerer was not in any rush, or as concerned as Malaki was about the crystal going missing, especially when it was in his care. Lara's instincts told her to be on her guard. Something felt off with this sorcerer, and he was hiding something. She also did not like how he was making sure she was alone and hoped Carn was alright outside. The Sword would pace with frustration, hoping she was alright too.

As they passed the main entrance they heard a large thud. Carn must have run at the door with his body weight, yet the door hardly moved. The sorcerer tutted under his breath. "He won't be patient, will he?"

Lara responded. "Then let him in."

The sorcerer chuckled, shaking his head. "I don't think so, dear." He studied her for a moment before continuing up the steps.

Lara glared at his back as she followed. She disliked this sorcerer and was going to remain on guard. They entered a small, cluttered study. The old man smiled at her and checked a teapot on the small stove in the corner and muttered to himself as he prepared tea. Lara looked around the room. Every surface was covered with books or rolled parchments, all of which were covered with a fine layer of powder. Most sorcerers' studies seemed to be the same whenever she had come across them, yet few would make tea. But what drew her attention was the fine layer of dust. It would not be there if he regularly used the room, unless there was a source that made lots of it. Lara eyed the back of the sorcerer. Something was off. Lara took another deep breath, taking in the man's scent. Up here, away from the cave, it was musky and earthy. She tried to look at him with her vampire vision, but a spell blocked it. She turned her attention to the surfaces again and trailed her finger over a book, feeling the dust between her fingertips. It was a fine powder, like clay. Lara turned her attention to the man again and remarked, "So Malaki said he enjoyed your visit a few weeks ago."

The sorcerer nodded. "Aye, aye. It was good to see him too."

"And the crystal. Is it safe?"

He turned to her and smiled. "Oh, very."

Lara nodded, wondering where the real sorcerer, Alistari, was being held. Probably back down in the main cavern. It had a more herbal smell down there, like for masking a spell. She mentally remembered the books she had read as a child and more recently, there had been a few entries on doppelgangers, and only one about golems. It was a powerful spell, and the victim had to remain alive. She just had to remember how to disable it. She recalled that if she stunned it and looked under its hairline on its forehead, she could remove the first letter from the word, *Emet*, which would be written there. But she needed to get it to be still long enough for her to do that. *But where is the real sorcerer?* She had not picked up his scent, so a spell shielded him. But then she wondered if the herbs down in the cave were meant to mask the golem, the real sorcerer, or both. Lara questioned whether the golem was clever or just a ruse for anyone who happened to get in. She took a gamble and smiled at the creature. "So, are you going to tell me where the real Alistari is?"

The old man paused and studied her. After a few moments, he sighed, looking around the room. "It's all the dust, isn't it?" Lara nodded. The golem sighed. "Should have been tidier, but the dust keeps coming back."

Lara shrugged. "The natural effect of drying clay."

He gazed at her. "So now what?"

"Well, I need to talk to the actual sorcerer of this tower. Are you his work or someone else's?"

The golem sat down and sighed. "His. He doesn't enjoy talking to strangers and has locked himself away in his study."

"Shielded by a spell?" It nodded. Lara pursed her lips. That was why she had not picked up his scent and with all the herbs down there, it had shielded the golem too. "Will you take me to him, or do I have to deal with you first?"

The golem sighed. "I'll take you."

Lara regarded it, wondering how much power it had. "Did you stop my companion from entering?" It shook its head, and she added. "But did he give you some powers?"

"Just a few basic ones and made my senses keen. I'm kind of like a guard dog, really. Keep out the riff raff."

Lara raised an eyebrow. "So, I, and my companion are riff raff?"

It shrugged. "Just doing my job."

"And the tea?"

The golem looked back at the teapot, almost forgetting what it had been doing. "Oh that. Well, I was hoping to, you know, slip you a sleeping draft. So, he could study you."

Lara glared at him. "I am not an object you can experiment on!"

It looked down guiltily. "Sorry, but you intrigue him."

Lara drew her sword. "Then I want to meet him. *Now!*" She added, "And let my companion in!"

The golem sighed. "Sorry, that is something only Alistari can do."

"Then let's get down there, shall we?"

They made their way back down the stairs, Lara pausing at the main door. She was going to make sure Carn could get in somehow.

The golem sheepishly led Lara back down to the sizeable area belowground. They passed by the large table where she had found him working, and continued to the back of the room. There was a solid rock wall, which was also closer than it had seemed. She quickly realised the large room was a lot smaller than she had first thought. A good way to hide a second room.

When the golem placed his hand on the wall, the rock shimmered and revealed a wooden door. Lara took a deep breath as the golem went to open the door and she picked up the real sorcerer's scent. Herbs masked it well, but there was no mistaking it. It impressed Lara that the spell masked him, even from her powerful sense of smell. Years before, back on Moonstar, she had been able to find a covenant of vampires, even with a cloaking spell. Whatever this sorcerer used was far stronger, and wondered what was in it to stop her from picking up his scent.

The door opened to reveal a large room, filled with even more books, a second small bed in the corner and a large table in the centre with various bottles of potions. It was almost a mirror of the room they had just come from. Lara wondered if the first room was just an illusion, like the rock wall. The old man looked up from where he was bent over the table, writing. He was the spitting image of the golem. He studied his double for a moment, looking disappointed, before turning his attention to Lara. "You are a clever girl. Few get past my golem. Did Malaki tell you about it?"

So, Malaki knew of this. *Why didn't he tell me? Or was it a trick question?* Lara smiled. "He didn't, so I think this is a more recent addition. I am more curious about how I could not pick up your scent."

He chuckled. "Wolfsbane in the potion, helps hide scents from vampire's and lycan's keen senses."

"I see."

Alistari put down the quill he was holding, and stood up straight, arching his stiff back. "So, with you having spoken to Malaki, you will be here about the crystal."

"I am. I want to know exactly what happened and how it was taken." She paused, glaring at him. "But first I want you to let my companion in."

CHAPTER 8

ARN WENT TO follow Lara into the tower, pulling his sword free, when the door slammed in his face. Cutting him off.

He shouted, "LARA!" Then slammed his fist against the door.

Besides him, his wolf growled at the closed door. Carn grabbed the handle, yanking at it, but it would not budge. As he sheathed his sword, he could hear Lara hitting the door on the other side. He sneered at it and hit the wood hard in anger. He cursed in frustration that the woman he loved was trapped on the other side.

He shouted again. "LARA!"

Carn looked around frantically, hoping there was another way in, even though he knew there was none. He hit his fist against the door again, then he paced as his wolf sniffed around the area. Lara could take care of herself, but that was not the point. He just wanted to make sure she had some sort of backup. There was nothing he could do. Being powerless was something he hated. He stopped pacing, staring at the door, wishing it to open and hit it again for good measure. He looked up, wondering if he could climb, but the surface of the tower was too smooth and the surrounding rocks were too steep. It was in the perfect location, no other way in except through that door.

"*Feck!*"

His wolf stopped and looked up at him. He studied her. "Can't get in there, girl."

He paced again, clenching his fist and glaring at the tower. Carn just hoped Lara was alright. He cursed again. Now and then giving the door a good kick.

Carn sat on the ground, throwing small rocks at the boulder in front of him, bored out of his mind. His wolf dozed at his feet. It felt like he had been sitting here for hours, but looking up at the sky, it had been a fraction of that time. He had been randomly hitting the door, hoping the next one would force it open, but it never happened. He had even run at it, full force with all his body weight. It felt like he had hit a brick wall, the door never giving way. His shoulder still ached as he wondered what to do next. He would stay for days if he had to, and get whoever came out, force them to take him to Lara. He leaned back and took a deep breath, letting the air out in frustration.

Suddenly, the door creaked open. Carn slowly looked towards it, wondering if it was a figment of his imagination. His wolf stirred and sniffed the air but did not seem concerned. Carn grabbed his sword slowly off the ground next to him, wondering if someone would emerge. Yet with the fact that his wolf was relaxed, he did not think there would be anyone. Then he heard a voice. "Sorry, old chap, but would you like to join us?"

Carn got to his feet, brushing the dust off his black trousers and strapping his sword to his back. With a brief hesitation, he walked up to the doorway in case it slammed into his face again. He turned to his wolf, signalling to her to stay. He tentatively stepped over the threshold; the door, then slowly closed behind him. The disembodied voice stated, "Head down, we are at the back."

Carn walked down the stone steps. He looked around; the tower had been built into the mountain itself and it was getting cooler the further he descended. He walked along the corridor, entering a large room. Seeing the door ahead, he picked up the pace, striding towards it, hearing Lara asking someone. "So, have you let my companion in?"

When Carn entered the room, he saw two identical sorcerers and Lara. He walked over to her, placing his hand on her shoulder. "You alright?"

Lara turned to him and smiled. "Aye. Seems Alistari doesn't like visitors."

He turned to the two sorcerers. "Which one?"

The real one smiled. "That would be me. Sorry I locked you out, but I thought it wise to have only one of you in here."

Carn glared at him. "Well, you know Lara is far more dangerous than I am."

The sorcerer chuckled. "So, it would seem."

Carn glanced at the golem and frowned. It smiled at him, looking a little sheepish. Carn could tell something had happened, but knew Lara would tell him when they were alone. He turned back to Lara. "So, have you found anything out?"

Lara glanced at him. "Just about to," she turned to Alistari. "So, what happened and how was the crystal taken?"

Alistari looked a little guilty. "Did Malaki tell you he spoke to me at length about it?"

"He did, but feels you may talk to me more freely."

The old man smiled. "Aye, he is right. I feel that with your abilities, it would be wise to talk to you freely and to be honest. You see, I did something foolish and well . . ." He looked at her and then at Carn. "You won't tell him, will you?"

Lara shook her head. "Whatever you tell us will remain between us, except information on the location of the crystal, if known."

He sighed, looking at Carn with a knowing smile. "Well, it's foolish really, but she was a fine-looking woman. Hard to resist."

"Woman?" frowned Lara.

Alistari replied, "Aye, the one who took it. It was foolish of me, but that crystal has a power about it, and will prey on your weaknesses, and it did so with mine." He looked down, a shadow of guilt crossed his features.

Lara sighed. "Don't any of you men ever not think with your dick?"

Carn could not help but smirk, knowing that a fine woman would always be a man's weakness. He glanced at Alistari, and it seemed sorcerers were just as bad.

Alistari nodded. "Aye, even us sorcerers can be weakened by it. Of course, I felt too foolish to let Malaki know. They, indeed, tricked me out of it, but it was a more vulnerable position that I was in when it was taken from me."

Carn made a short laugh, imagining the position the sorcerer may have been in. Lara gave him a stern look and turned back to the old man. "So, what can you tell me?" she paused. "And save me all the seduction details."

"Well, as I told Malaki, they entered the tower and took the crystal. I just failed to tell him I had sex with the woman and that I was in a naked slumber when she took it. My hands a little tied."

Carn snorted with amusement again, and Lara gave him a sharp look. She stated, "So, she knew where to go and that you had it? How do you suppose she knew this?"

Alistari shrugged. "As far as I was aware, only I and Malaki knew of its exact location."

Carn asked, "Are you sure nay one else knew?"

"Well, nay." He paused. "But if the girl did her research and knew who to ask, she would know that the guild stored it in a safe place."

"Guild?"

"Aye, the guild. Ah, of course, Malaki may have thought it was of nay value to tell you."

Lara pursed her lips. Carn was all too aware of that look which showed how annoyed she was.

Alistari responded, "You are wondering why Malaki didn't tell you, aren't you?"

Lara looked up at him. "I think it may have helped to have known that."

Alistari smiled. "To Malaki, it is just a trivial piece of information, one that wouldn't be needed in his eyes."

Lara responded, "Well, he was wrong. Can you tell me more?"

Alistari nodded. "Of course. Well, I, Malaki and another four sorcerers took an oath many years ago, when we joined the guild. The guild has always had six members, for many hundreds of years, and has been protectors of the crystal. Of the six, only two would know the exact location, but all would guard the secret to ensure it never fell into the hands of man. In Dalimor, there are texts about the guild, and if she knew where to look, she could find who to ask."

"Do you think she has spoken to the other sorcerers, or someone who knows them?"

The old man nodded. "Probably all."

Carn stated, "But you all took an oath to remain silent."

Lara asked, "So how would she know you had it?"

"That I do not know unless it was just luck."

Carn added, "Or someone who wasn't as honourable told her."

Alistari raised an eyebrow, partly not looking surprised at Carn's statement. Carn regarded the sorcerer. The woman could have just been in the right place at the right time, but it was more than likely someone told her where to look. According to Lara, Malaki would not have been easily seduced, but Alistari seemed to be the person who could have been. Yet something still did not feel right. There was something that Lara said about Malaki that made him wonder if there was more to this than met the eye.

Lara sighed. "So, where did she go and when did she leave here with it?"

Alistari shrugged. "I have lost track of time. I think it was about fourteen days ago, maybe more. As for where she went; now that she has the crystal, I believe she may head east towards Dark Cloud. That is the place where the crystal originated from, in the mountains to the south."

Lara studied him, frowning. It had been missing for fourteen days. That meant the woman took the crystal the day Kayd received the note to give to Lara, which felt odd. Carn eyed the sorcerer something still was not right. Quite a few things did not add up, and he could tell by the look in her eyes that she was not sure if it was wise to trust either sorcerer. Lara asked, "Are you sure that's where she's heading?"

Alistari nodded. "I saw it when studying the crystal. It has always been drawn there, and I think it will guide the woman there too."

"Do you think someone clever enough to find the crystal would be that weak-minded?"

Alistari chuckled. "She was not weak-minded, but was driven by greed for power."

"And the crystal could use that?" asked Carn.

"Aye."

Lara sighed and glared at Alistari. "Is there anything else you can tell us that may be of use?"

He thought for a moment, then walked over to one of his bookshelves. Looking carefully, he pulled out a large dark-coloured book and placed it on the table. He beckoned them over as he flicked through the yellowing pages and then stopped. "Here. This is what it looks like. Be always on your guard as you do not even have to touch it for it to know your darkest secrets and weaknesses." He looked up at Lara. "And I know that would be your vampire side?" He then glanced at Carn. "And for you, it would be Lara?"

Carn and Lara studied the image of a three-sectioned dark red crystal, set in a black onyx-like rock. Lara looked at Alistari. "But my wolf side keeps the vampire one at bay."

Alistari studied her and Carn. "You will need to keep clear-headed when it's near," he focused on Lara. "I hope that wolf side is strong."

"It is."

He studied her intently. "I hope it is, for your sake." He turned to Carn. "As for you, it will try to trick you. Keep your mind focused, always. Then you won't lose another loved one."

Carn's breath caught in his throat, memories flooding back instantly. He quickly nodded, trying to look unphased that the sorcerer seemed to know about what had happened in his past. He wondered if his memories were that easy for a sorcerer to sense. Then again, with what happened, he was no longer the man he once was. Carn glanced at Lara, seeing a puzzled look in her eyes. It seemed it was time to let her know the full reason he left Moonstar. He glanced back at the old man, but not with him present. He needed to tell her when they were alone.

CHAPTER 9

WHEN THEY LEFT the tower, Carn's wolf was dutifully waiting near the door. She sniffed the back of Carn's hand as he strolled up to her, and then the wolf trotted ahead as they walked back down to the horses. Carn looked across at Lara as she mounted her horse. He felt like he was in a daze, still shocked that the sorcerer seemed to know his past. The Sword sighed, gazing across at the woman he loved. He had to talk to her. He just was not sure when. What Alistari said about losing a loved one troubled him deeply. Carn was sure he could not take it if he lost Lara as well. He mounted his horse, chewing his lip nervously. He had been gathering the courage to tell Lara everything that had happened after she had left since they had been reunited. But whenever they camped, he felt too much pain in his heart to pull those memories back to the surface. But how Lara looked at him after the sorcerer's comment, Carn would have to find his mettle and do it sooner than later. He turned his horse around to follow her. It was strange how he could rush to face a demon but was reluctant to tell Lara about what happened. He glanced at her as they rode back the way they had come. It was going to be painful to talk about what happened on Moonstar. If they were about to venture towards something that would latch onto their fears and weaknesses, then it was the time to get everything out in the open.

They rode their horses towards the opening to the mountains and then followed the primary route once more. Carn was feeling tense, not just from having to tell Lara everything, but from knowing they would have to be on their guard at all times. He thought about how Alistari had warned them so forcefully. The sorcerer knew how powerful that crystal was, so it was not wise to take his warning lightly. Carn went over the events Alistari had told them and was convinced someone had given the woman the information. It was not down to luck. The Sword wondered who the source had been, and his suspicions leaned towards Malaki. He had not met the sorcerer, but in what Lara had told him, and from Alistari's comments, Carn's instincts told him Malaki was behind it. His mind immediately questioned what the man would do once he had all that power. Carn looked ahead. He did not want to know what Malaki would do, but the thought filled him with dread if an already powerful sorcerer was behind it all. Carn took a slow breath. He had to stop overthinking, his eyes moved to Lara as she looked ahead.

He turned to Lara and asked as they rode, "So, how do we get to Dark Cloud?"

Lara glanced back at him as her horse pulled at its reins. "It's across the River Slangor from here. The inlet was named Great Channel before travellers realised it was just an inlet to the river. So if we could cross here, we would need a ship."

"Is there a dock near here?" He paused. "You said, 'if'."

"Aye, there is nay access this far south. Mountains cover the southern tip of that area, so it's too dangerous. There's a section a little further north, but it's all swamp land and also very treacherous."

Carn raised an eyebrow. "Sounds like such a lovely place."

Lara smirked. "Aye. Past the Black Mountains, it is more dangerous. The land to the north has Gor, which is a prosperous city. Gor seems to be a part of Barberium, but from what I have heard, the southern section is different. Saying that, it's only separated from here by a river."

"So, how do we get across?"

"We must travel through Bighdarum, then head further north. It's a few days' travel but the Great Channel narrows becoming the River Slangor. At that point, we take the road to the riverbank where the two sections of land are closer together. We can cross from there on a ferry." Lara paused then added, "Thinking we should stop at the Travellers' Rest and then ride through Bighdarum. I'm not keen on stopping at the mining town, as it could delay us."

Carn nodded, having heard mixed messages about Bighdarum. He knew it was rough-and-tumble type of town. Also, that Kayd had mentioned something about a dwarf not paying up and being blacklisted due to it.

He looked ahead, his mind returning to the sorcerers' troubles. As he pondered which way the woman would have gone with the crystal, Carn became more inclined to believe it would be a similar route. He just hoped they did not come across any devastation that Alistari and Malaki had mentioned.

Leaving the mountains of Dragon's Nest behind, the two travelled a good way before the light faded. Leaving the principal route, they stopped in the open brushland and made camp. It would take them about three days to reach an inn, so it was camping out under the stars till then. While Lara made a fire, Carn took care of the horses. With what would lie ahead, his mind thought of how he would tell Lara everything. He brushed down the horses, trying to keep a firm hold of his emotions. Carn had tried, since reuniting with Lara, to be the man she had met back in Moonstar, but the pain was still there in his heart. It seemed less since being with her, but he knew, deep in his soul, that he was no longer that carefree Sword Lara had known all those years ago. He focused on the open land around him. *Could I ever be that man again?* Carn sighed, knowing that part of him had died that dreaded night. He took a deep breath and patted the horse's neck, regarding its eyes. It would be hard, but he could do it. He had to tell her what had happened. Maybe tonight, if his courage held.

Once the horses were secure and settled, Carn came and sat beside Lara. He warmed his hands against the fire and smiled, trying to stop his stomach from twisting with nerves. "I was worried when you were locked inside the tower."

Lara smirked. "I was alright." She paused, looking at him. She took a deep breath. "I must ask you something. Since the tower, you've seemed distant and I think it's to do with what Alistari said. And well . . . do you know what he meant about the loss of a loved one?"

Carn's throat tightened, and his stomach dropped like a rock. He gazed at her. He felt the pain deep down, trying to bubble to the surface, yet, somehow glad she had brought the subject up. Even though he wanted to tell her tonight, he did not know how he would have broached it, and may not have done so. He took a deep breath. "As we left the tower, I knew I needed to tell you everything." He glanced away from her eyes. "It's just . . ."

Lara gazed at him, taking his hand in hers. "If it's too painful . . ."

Carn smiled sadly. His heart ached, but if he could not tell the woman he loved, then he would never say it out loud. He looked back at her features. "Nay, you need to know."

Lara gazed at him and waited. Carn focused on the flames of the fire for a few moments, lost in thought, struggling with his inner demons. Trying to place all the events in order in his head. The light from the flames put Lara's features in shadow as he took a breath and gazed at her. He could do it.

He bit his lip then said, "As I told you, I had met someone. Her name was Isabel. She was a wonderful woman, and I loved her dearly." He paused; Lara squeezed his hand but remained silent, letting him collect himself. He looked into her eyes, lost in their depths. They had always anchored him. "She was like you. Very independent, loving and caring, and that was what drew me to her." He smiled softly, remembering how they had met. "I first met her at The Black Ox Inn in Palasses. It was about seven years after you had left, and I still missed you greatly."

Lara smiled softly, brushing his cheek. "I missed you too."

Carn took a moment, all the memories of Isabel resurfacing. Lara studied him softly as he slowly told her how he had met Isabel. He told her that when between contracts, he would dwell on Lara and drown his sorrows in ale. Isabel had been a barmaid. Whenever he was at that inn in Palasses, she would always come over and talk to him, making him feel less alone. He smiled, still remembering her grey eyes; they were as clear as Lara's. Isabel was part elf with their slender figure and almond-shaped eyes. She would always wear her jet-black hair up, accentuating her elven features. Over time, they would talk more and more. Carn found he enjoyed her company, and what had been at first a friendship, developed into something more. Carn glanced at the fire; his features shadowed by sadness. "We settled in Palasses, and after a year, we found out she was with child. We had never been so happy."

Lara regarded him. Carn, able to see his pain mirrored in her eyes, looked up at the clear night sky, trying to keep control of the emotions he had locked away for so long. He smiled sadly. "I put up my sword that year. I was done. If we were to have a family, I wanted to make sure we had a happy life. We had a house and a farm that I could work on." He paused, remembering the night like it was yesterday. "Then it was time. The babe was on the way . . ."

He took a shaky breath. His heart ached, the pain like a dagger, ripping it apart. "But . . . but there were complications with the birth."

Lara gently placed her hand on his cheek, making him face her. "You don't need to go on."

He stroked her cheek and kissed her gently. Tears welled in his eyes. "Nay, I need to tell you."

Lara nodded, studying him softly. Carn took a deep, shaky breath. "There were complications, and the babe . . . she was stillborn, but something else wasn't right. Isabel wouldn't stop bleeding . . ." Tears rolled freely down his face, a sharp sob escaping before he could stop it. "That eve I lost Isabel, and Iesha, within hours of each other."

"Iesha?"

Carn turned to Lara; his vision blurry from his tears. "Our daughter. We named her before Isabel took her last breath."

Lara pulled Carn close to her, giving him a loving hug. As soon as her arms enveloped him, Carn could not stop the tears from falling, and he sobbed as he had that night all those years ago. He pulled Lara closer to him, having missed her embrace for so long. His body shook as more sobs bubbled to the surface, all the pain he had held for so long breaking through. Opening to Lara and telling her all that he had lost made him feel raw, but strangely relieved. When he could not cry anymore, he slowly pulled away, gazing at Lara, and seeing her features also tear ridden. He kissed her gently and sighed. "I'm sorry."

Lara brushed his cheek, studying him with her loving gaze. "Nay, don't be. I'm honoured that you have told me. I felt there was something. You seemed so broken, and I didn't know what to do. I did wonder where the Carn I knew had gone, but now I understand, and will be here for you whenever you need me."

Carn smiled, lost in her gaze; he cupped her cheek in his hand. "I wonder what Iesha would have been like if she had survived. She would have had her fifth winter now."

Lara smiled and kissed him gently on his cheek. "She would have been wonderful, and I would have been honoured to meet her."

Carn smiled sadly and sighed, studying Lara. "I only knew one thing after all of my grieving. That if I ever found you again, I would never let you go. I lost Isabel and Iesha, I just couldn't lose you, too."

Lara kissed him gently and gazed into his blue eyes. They embraced again and were soon fast asleep in each other's arms.

CHAPTER 10

LARA WOKE EARLY, morning dew covered their sleeping blankets. She felt the heavy arm of Carn draped over her body, still relaxed in sleep. Lara turned slowly and studied his sleeping features. Everything he had told her the night before weighed heavily on her heart. She had hoped that when she had left Moonstar, Carn would have had a happy life. Instead, he had felt such deep pain and loss. She gazed at his handsome features; she could never give him a child, but she would ensure his life was full of happiness. Lara was glad he had told her everything, knowing that he must have felt some relief in doing so. She slid from under his arm and sat up. Hoping that the loss would not be the weakness the crystal would use against him, not wanting the man she loved to have to relive such a horrible event. She focused on the wolf sleeping at Carn's feet, not surprised he had brought her with him. He could have found another wolf pup, but he had trained her so well and had a bond he would not have found easily with a new pup. Lara gazed at the animal. She was old and probably only had a couple of winters left in her, but it seemed Carn just could not part with her yet.

She turned back to Carn, waking him gently with a kiss on his full lips. She smiled when he took a deep breath and opened his eyes. His features warmed seeing her and he sat up slowly. "Good morn."

Lara smiled, pulling the blanket from her legs. "Thank you for telling me about Isabel and Iesha last eve."

Carn nodded, still looking a little forlorn. His wolf woke and focused on them both as Carn said, "I have been wanting to tell you for days, but just didn't know how."

Lara kissed him and stroked his cheek. She looked up at the cloudy sky and sighed. "Are you alright to continue?"

Carn nodded, stretching his arms. "Aye. To be with you is all I need."

Lara nodded and kissed him on the cheek, then got to her feet. She packed up camp as Carn ate breakfast. It was not long after that they were riding along the river's edge, continuing north, Carn's wolf trotting ahead. Lara looked up at the impressive mountains as they rode. Beneath them were hundreds of mineshafts. She wondered how many of the crystals found in those mountains could be as dangerous as the one they were tracking. That crystal could not have been the only one and others would have to be out there, or maybe not been found yet. Lara hoped that any that were mined were quickly hidden away as the other had been.

She thought about Malaki and wondered if there was anything else he decided not to tell her. She glanced at Carn and thought over what he had stated about it not being just luck. He had mentioned it was odd how the woman had found the crystal and Lara had to agree. Something did not feel right. She was still suspicious over the night they spent together. She was convinced even more that it had been some sort of spell by the way it made her feel secure and trusting of him. She bit her lip. It had worked. Yet now, with her ruminating over it all, she would not trust the sorcerer again. She would fulfil his contract, but that would be it. Take her money and go. Yet she knew she would have to stay on her guard. The way he remarked about what she was, she could only hope he did not have plans for her. She glanced at Carn riding beside her. She was not on her own anymore. If Malaki tried anything, she had an extra sword.

They had ridden for a couple of days when Lara decided she would need to hunt. After making camp in some shrub land, Lara left

Carn tending the horses. She ran off to find a fresh kill, knowing it was her last opportunity before they reached Bighdarum. The simple pleasure of just running through the brush gave Lara a brief respite, lifting some of the sadness in her heart for Carn's painful past. Not to mention the doubts that were growing from having taken Malaki's contract.

She stopped near some bushes and took in the night air. It was always good to be in her wolf form and when she was, she could connect with her other self more easily. Taking a few moments, Lara could sense that darkness and nature seemed out of balance. Her wolf was concerned, being more sensitive to the magical side of the world. She wondered if it was because of the crystal. From what her wolf could sense, the woman with the crystal had been through the area. Lara worried of what may lie ahead, and could only hope no one had suffered harm.

Having found and hunted her prey, Lara laid down and devoured it, her mind switching between what Carn had told her and the crystal. She needed to focus on the task at hand. But her mind wandered to Carn and what his life would have been like if tragedy had not struck. She glanced at the night sky. Lara was heartbroken that he had not had a happy life as she had wished. But she was also glad he came back into her life. She had missed him, but she had not realised just how much. Once her meal had been eaten, she stood, taking a deep breath of the night air. She turned back towards the camp and ran, longing to be in his arms once more.

Back at the camp, Carn looked up from fussing his wolf as Lara came trotting towards the fire. After changing back into a human form, she dressed and sat down next to Carn. She snuggled up to him and he curled his arm around her. They just seemed to value each other's company even more after the night Carn shared his painful past with her. They did not broach the subject again as he seemed to have returned to his old self, if still a little distant.

Lara gazed at the fire as he asked, "Good hunt?"

"Aye. I should be alright now for several days."

Her eyes focused on Carn's wolf as it curled up near the fire. She had been studying the animal the past few days and was concerned for her. The wolf seemed healthy enough, but with Lara's senses, she was aware of something developing because of her age. She turned her attention to Carn and said, "I have to talk to you about your wolf."

Carn gazed across at the sleeping animal and then at Lara. "I should have left her on Moonstar, but I just couldn't. She had been with me for so long; I knew she wouldn't survive without human contact."

Lara smiled softly. "I know wolves can have a long life, and she has done exceptionally well."

Carn regarded her features, seeing her apprehension. "But . . ."

Lara sighed. "Well, with my senses I can see things others can't, and . . ."

He gazed towards the animal. "How long has she got?"

"Maybe one or two winters. But with the fluctuations of her heart . . ."

Carn's eyes held sadness. "With all the travelling, it could be less."

Lara nodded. "Aye. I can ask Derwyn to take her once this contract is over."

"Do you think he will?"

Lara responded, "Aye. I haven't been to Warrior Sword in a while, so we could pay a visit and ask."

Carn pulled her closer to him and said, "I want her to have a suitable home. And if Derwyn will have her, I know she'll be happy."

Lara responded, "She will have fields to hunt in whenever she wants."

Carn smiled softly, keeping his arms firmly around her. He stifled a yawn. "If she can have a loving home, and a place to run, then that's all she needs."

Lara leant her head against him, savouring their embrace. "She will, and also have twins doting on her."

Carn gave a lop-sided grin. "That would make her happy."

Lara glanced up at him and kissed his cheek. He yawned again and laid back, pulling her with him. Lara snuggled up against him, his hand gently squeezing her shoulder, keeping her close. He closed his eyes and savoured their embrace. Lara laid her head on his chest, feeling him relax. Once he was asleep, she listened to his heartbeat. The rhythm relaxed her and it soon pulled her to the depths, too. Both were fast asleep in each other's arms.

They finally reached the Travellers Rest inn after a day's ride, Carn's wolf looked tense and growled when she looked towards the route to the north. They secured their horses outside and Carn calmed his wolf down before they went inside with caution. The atmosphere was not right, and the inn seemed too quiet. There were very few customers compared to when Lara had been there several days earlier. Lara could also sense fear in the air.

When they walked up to the nervous-looking innkeeper, the large man studied them with fear in his eyes. "This is not a safe route to be on."

Lara regarded him and glanced around the half-empty inn, then at Carn, who raised an eyebrow with concern. This was always a popular inn, and she had never seen it so quiet. Turning back to the innkeeper, she asked, "What happened?"

"Some days past we had a group pass through. They were not the type ya would want to meet on the road. There was something about the leader, a woman. She had something evil about her. One of the young lads from a nearby village got a little mouthy with 'em. Then, moments later, he was on the floor. Dead!"

"Did one of the group fight him?"

The innkeeper shook his head, looking pale. "Nay. The woman just looked at 'im and he clutched his throat, and then started coughing blood. Then dead." The innkeeper shook his head, whispering a prayer to any god that was listening. "It ain't right. That was dark magic she used. Then that eve there be somethin' out there, somethin' evil. In the morn, half the customer's horses were dead," he paused and leant forward. "In an *unnatural* way." He looked around, cleaning a pewter mug more from nerves than from necessity. "Since then, this place has been almost empty. I'm thinking of shutting up and heading for Dalimor, where me cousin is."

Lara looked around, sensing the tension and fear in the air. "Do you know which way the group went?"

"North, but stay clear of 'em, lass," he looked at Carn. "Both of ya."

Lara responded, "Don't worry."

He shook his head, fear in his eyes. "Even the best Sword would avoid 'em. The woman ain't right, and those that follow her has somethin' wrong in the head."

Carn nodded. "We'll try to avoid them."

The innkeeper responded, looking a little less concerned. "So, do ya want rooms for the eve?"

"Aye, we were hoping to. Our horses are outside," responded Lara.

He nodded, passing her two keys. "Have me best two rooms. I ain't busy and nay extra cost. Me lad will deal with ya horses for ya."

Lara nodded, feeling sorry for the innkeeper and had not the heart to tell him one room would do. She ordered drinks, while Carn went to find a table that looked out on the inn. As the innkeeper prepared the drinks, she added. "If I were you, I'd pack up in the morn, and head to your family in Dalimor for a while."

The innkeeper studied her. "I'm tempted."

She gazed at him with concern. "With what has happened, I doubt there will be many on the roads for a while. You're concerned enough to warn two strangers, and I believe you should heed your own warning."

The middle-aged man smiled at her and nodded. "Aye. I can't rest here with what has happened."

Lara took the drinks. "Then see your family. Return when you feel it'll be safe to do so."

He nodded and returned to serving drinks to a small group of customers but heard him telling them he would close the inn for a while. Lara walked over to join Carn, looking around, but it was not worth watching anyone as the few that were there kept to themselves and looked concerned. One traveller nodded a greeting to them both but kept to himself. Lara took in the scents in the room and could still make out what had to be the woman and her men. There was something odd about the scent, an aroma of death. Lara could use that to her advantage to track them. The group would also pass through Bighdarum, and that concerned her. Lara hoped nothing bad had happened to the town. Maybe a night's rest here was even more worth their while.

While Carn ate, they spoke quietly, Lara stating, "Something doesn't add up."

Carn looked at her, his features full of concern. "I know. Something about all of this feels strange."

Lara nodded, taking a sip of her drink. "There's something about what Alistari said regarding *when* the woman took the crystal. If his timing is correct, it was the same day that Kayd received the note."

Carn raised an eyebrow. "That's interesting. Do you think what Alistari said was correct? I don't trust him, but Malaki even less."

Lara sighed. "I don't know what it is, but my instinct is telling me not to trust either of them. Now, with what has happened here, in only a few days, something's off. The woman should have been further ahead of us than this."

"What do you think?"

Lara leant forward. "I think she went somewhere else first, after getting the crystal."

"You mean to meet someone?"

"Aye . . . I don't know. But I think there's more to this than meets the eye. I think Malaki, and even Alistari, know more than they are letting on."

Carn leant back, glancing around the inn. "Do you want to go back to Malaki and say nay to the contract?"

Lara shook her head. "Nay. When I find that woman, I'm going to be asking a lot of questions."

"I agree. We need answers, and I think she can give them to us."

Lara studied him. "I'm glad you're with me on this. At least I know it isn't just me being paranoid."

He smiled softly, taking her hand in his. "We work well together, and don't worry; we'll find out what's going on with all of this."

After Carn had eaten and they had had drinks, they went up to the rooms, taking the closest one. They lay in each other's arms while Lara told Carn about Bighdarum. "It's a rough mining town and Bamur is . . . well, it takes a bit of time to warm up and get used to him."

Carn studied her, tracing his fingers along the base of her back. "Seems to be a character."

Lara chuckled. "Aye, that he is. His heart's in the right place, but just watch him. He'll try anything to make a good amount of coin."

Carn asked, "He doesn't happen to be the dwarf who Kayd blacklisted?"

Lara smiled, studying his handsome features. "Aye, it is, and it didn't go down well with Bamur when I told him. So best not to mention it." She paused and added. "Bamur is like any dwarf, and rather annoying, but I do like him."

Carn smiled. "You have a soft spot for him, don't you?"

Lara nodded slowly. "I do."

Carn focused on her eyes and gave her a lingering kiss. His hand slowly slid down her torso and raised his eyebrow, a mischievous glint in his eyes. Lara shifted her body slightly as his hands slid further into her pubic hair. His fingers played with her gently, making her moan softly. His lips captured hers as he moved a little, to ensure his fingers could continue to play with her as he kissed her. Lara's legs widened as he played with her more, her thighs beginning to tingle in delight. Removing his hand, he repositioned his body and entered her. He moaned softly, feeling her warmth surround him. He kissed her deeply, Lara arching her back, forcing him to enter her deeper. They moaned in unison as their passion grew, both lost to the moment. Carn lifted himself up, pulling Lara into his arms, yet not breaking their connection. In this position, he continued to move, his length going deeper, making Lara tremble in delight. His callused hands cradled her bare back, and they continued to move rhythmically. Lara lost all control, her body shuddering at Carn's gentle, but powerful, touch. He sucked on her nipples as Lara closed her eyes in delight. Then their movements became faster. Both climax at the same time. They shuddered and fell into each other's arms. Carn gasping gazing at her with raw, loving affection.

Lara kissed Carn softly, gazing at his flushed features. He smiled and said softly, "Why does it seem more amazing every time?"

Lara regarded his features and kissed him on the lips. "We love each other too much to hold back."

He laid back, pulling her into his arms. "With all the darkness around this land now, the light we have keeps me grounded."

She stroked his beard, lost in his eyes. "Aye. Same."

He took a deep breath, savouring her, like he did not want to forget anything. He closed his eyes and smiled softly. "Just stay in my arms forever."

Lara rested her head on his chest and whispered, "Always."

W HEN THEY REACHED the outskirts of Bighdarum, they slowed their horses once they saw the large open gates ahead were deserted. Lara tensed and turned to Carn, stating, "Something's wrong. They don't leave these gates unguarded. Bamur's just too paranoid."

Reaching the entrance to the town, Lara stopped, her horse unsettled. She took a deep breath through her nose, picking up the acrid stench of death. She considered the empty main street before them. Not a sound. She turned to Carn, seeing his features mirrored her concern. Carn's wolf was skittish; growling, and reluctant to go any further. Lara slowly dismounted, fastening her horse on the gatepost and stroking its neck to keep it calm. She turned to Carn as she slowly drew her sword. Carn did the same, calling his wolf to heel.

They then walked, hesitantly, into the silent town. With no people about, the once lively town felt eerie. Keeping a firm hold of her sword, Lara continued further in. Walking with caution, glancing around at her surroundings, and taking in the scents. Carn was a little behind her as he looked down the side alleys and streets, ordering his wolf to investigate. Lara stopped mid-stride, picking up something that she had not expected and turned to Carn, signalling for him to be on his guard. She could pick up at least three Kanfor scents. She knew from experience they would never come out to the surface, unless . . . She swallowed. It had to be the crystal that had forced them out. That would be why the town was so quiet. All the people were dead or hiding. She hoped most were hiding.

Carn came up beside her and asked, "What have you picked up?"

"Kanfors and the stench of death."

Carn's features paled slightly. "Those things are brutal. But they won't be here now, in the daylight." He glanced down at his wolf. "She hasn't picked up any signs of life yet, but that doesn't mean they aren't hiding somewhere."

Lara responded, "I know there must be someone here. They could be down in the cellars. As for the Kanfors, nay, they are nocturnal. But they wouldn't normally venture from the mines either. I think it has to do with the crystal."

Carn nodded in agreement. He looked around and added, "Think if any of the townspeople have survived, they're lucky."

She agreed, and they continued walking slowly down the main street, surveying the buildings. Smoke invaded their nostrils, a shop up ahead was on fire. Lara turned, hearing a door creaking as it swung in the light breeze. It was the inn where she had stayed only days before. Its main door hung on what remained of its hinges and the windows were shattered. The Kanfors had ventured that way, the stench of death radiating from inside. As she focused through the open doorway, she could see the white of bone from body parts. She grimaced; it seemed the Kanfors had had a feast. The rotting flesh festered in the warm summer air. From the broken windows and splintered furniture, the attack had been sudden. Lara doubted if anyone survived. She regarded the row of buildings as they passed. Others were damaged, like the inn, but some had their shutters securely closed against what was lurking in the shadows. Lara felt sorry for everyone once night fell. The Kanfors would emerge, and no one remaining would stand a chance. If they made any sound, the creatures would find them in an instant.

Keeping a firm hold of her sword, Lara looked towards the mine entrance. The Kanfors scent was stronger that way. Carn also looked on with concern, knowing that was where they were hiding until sundown. They suddenly heard a low whistle and turned towards it. Further down the road, Bamur had poked his head out from the doorway of his inn. He shouted, in a hushed tone, "Lara! It's not safe, lass!"

They both sheathed their swords and hastened towards the dwarf. Carn's wolf at his heels. The dwarf ushered them in and locked the door again when they were all inside. The animal sniffed the dwarf for a moment, who gave it no mind, then went and curled up nearby. Bamur's body language showed a man who had not slept in days.

He eyed Carn with suspicion before turning to Lara when she asked, "What happened?"

He responded, keeping his voice low. "Some lass and her henchmen passed through a few days' ago. There was somethin' strange about her, and then it was like a cloud of death came over us all. When eve fell, they came out of the mine."

"The Kanfors?"

"Aye and *other* things." He looked towards the door in fear. "We didn't stand a chance. They just ran through the town into shops and inns, killing anything that moved. All that could, boarded up and locked up tight as soon as we heard the screams. Others weren't so lucky. Me men tried to fight the things out there, but few lasted the eve." He shook his head, looking frightened. "The screams."

Lara sighed, studying the dwarf. She had never seen him look so afraid. She needed to know what they were up against. "You mentioned other things?"

"Aye."

"Can you describe them?" She smiled softly, knowing the dwarf did not want to remember the horrific past events, and added, "It will help us know what we must fight."

"Fight?" Bamur shook his head, glancing from Carn to Lara. "Lass, don't do it. Ya won't stand a chance."

Lara sighed, focusing on his eyes. "It's my job, and Carn's, Bamur. You know, we're about the only ones here that could deal with this."

"Aye. Even so, I wouldn't wish my worst enemy out there."

Lara smiled. "Wasn't I, several days ago?"

Bamur chuckled and looked up at her with affection. "Not as much as Kayd."

"I don't think anyone likes him." She turned serious again. "Now I need to know, Bamur. I know how to deal with the Kanfors but need to know what else we may face out there."

He nodded slowly. "Well, I didn't see much, but the sound wasn't anythin' I had heard before."

"So, something that's not as well known. Can you describe anything?"

"It had a large wingspan, and black as a moonless sky, as me men that got back said. It would fly over them, the beating of the wings enough to knock them over. Erm, one of them said somethin' about a body like a snake."

Lara nodded, going over all the creatures she had memorised over the years. She needed her demonology book from her saddlebag to be sure, but, from what he was telling her, she could think of only one.

She looked at Carn as he whispered, a questioning look in his eyes. "A Quetzal?"

She was inclined to agree. They were more of a legend than anything, but with the crystal, it would not surprise her that something so vile had been summoned or awakened. If one was roaming around, it would sleep in the depths of the mines during the day. Too deep to find, they would have to wait until dark to deal with the Quetzal and any Kanfors still round. She knew that if one of the flying beasts had come out, even the Kanfors would not linger. Anything in the Quetzal's path would not last long, demon or not. She sighed. There was no guarantee she could defeat it, even with Carn's help. But they were the town's only hope. Lara turned to Bamur. "Do you know how many people are safe?"

The dwarf shrugged. "I ain't too sure. It was such chaos that I don't rightly know."

"Are any of the stables secure?"

The dwarf thought for a moment. "There's mine. And, I think the one behind Jake's shop is, why?"

"We need to get our horses, and stable them somewhere before eve."

Bamur folded his arms and pursed his lips. "Then head for the one behind Jake's. Mine is full with a couple of cattle as well as me men's horses. His has a couple of cattle too, but think some stalls are free."

Lara responded, "Then we need to check on as many places as possible before the light fades." She paused and studied the dwarf. "Are any of your men still fit to fight?"

He shrugged. "I think a few, but they won't stand a chance."

"I'm not asking them to risk their lives. We need traps set up in the square where there's some space. I know your men will have the skills to help."

He pointed at her. "And May, at the smithy. She's a good trapper, and think she's still alive."

Lara nodded. "Good. Can one of your men check? I need every abled body here to help set up before eve, and for everyone else to keep secure."

Bamur touched her arm as Lara went to leave with Carn. "What ya plannin'?"

Lara looked at him. "To free the town."

Lara regarded the men and women who stood or sat on the chairs Bamur had brought down from the inn into his cellar. It was about the only place they could discuss plans without drawing attention as the sun lowered in the sky. Carn stood at her side, along with Bamur.

One of Bamur's men asked, his bald head covered in old scars, "So ya can beat these things?"

Lara regarded the group of fifteen. They were all that remained who could help or fight. "The Kanfors are easy, but I'm going to need help with the Quetzal."

"How?" asked one of the tough-looking dwarf women standing at the side.

"We need to trap it. Once it's on the ground, I will have more of a chance of killing it."

"That's why Bamur asked for me, isn't it?" asked a dark-haired woman at the front.

Lara nodded, studying May. "Bamur said you're a good trapper."

"Aye, I am. So how big is this Quetzal thing?"

"About the size of a small dragon. Unless it's an old one from the depths, then it could be bigger." Everyone gasped and there was some muttering at the back. Lara added. "But from what

Bamur said, it is going to be big; but not a size we couldn't manage if we have the right equipment."

May regarded Lara intently. "To trap something that big, I need a lot of netting. I have a number in me barn, but will take a couple of days to stitch it together and make it strong enough to hold. From what ya said of its wingspan, it will be hard to trap and keep it down."

"Aye, it will be strong. But could you do it?"

May paused for a few moments, calculating in her head, scratching her chin. "Aye, but I would have to set up a trigger rope high enough for it to snag. And to get the net over it, we'll need people out there to help pull it and release the anchor points."

Again, more murmurings and more fear in the voices this time. Lara sighed; she did not want anyone out there apart from herself and Carn. "Is there another way?"

May shook her head. "Not with a net that size. It would be too heavy with pulleys alone. Ya would need manpower."

Lara sighed and pursed her lips, glancing at Carn. "I was hoping to keep you all out of harm's way. If you need people out there, then volunteers only, but with those demons about, you'll need protection." Lara turned to Bamur. "How close is your nearest witch?"

"That be Eida, who did the talismans for the mine. What do ya need her to do?"

"Protection spells and to be honest, I want her here, in case."

"In case?"

Lara studied everyone in the cellar. "A protection spell should make whoever goes out there shielded from the demons, but the spells can weaken. So, unless I know the full habits of these creatures, we could have to wait for a few hours. If you are going to be out there with that Quetzal, I want you all well protected."

All muttered in agreement, one young lad shouted, "I can go get Eida in the morn at first light. Me horse is fast."

Lara nodded thanks and added, "Make sure you tell her exactly what we are facing, as she will need the right potions."

Bamur slapped his hands together and studied the members of his town. "Well, ya heard the lass. I need to know who's gonna be out there and am giving the rest of ya jobs to help where ya can. Understood?"

All responded, "Aye."

Bamur smiled. "Good! We be gettin' our town back from these beasties."

Lara regarded them all. "Thank you for helping, but don't put yourselves in danger. Let Carn and I deal with the creatures, as we have the skills to face them. The main thing is getting the trap to bring the Quetzal down. Remember, once it's grounded, I *should* be able to kill it."

Carn started organising everyone by finding out what skills they had as it helped to know where they would be best suited. Meanwhile, Bamur pulled Lara to one side, his eyes darting behind her as he asked, "So, who's the new fella?"

Lara glanced back to study Carn as he spoke with everyone in the cellar. Turning back, she smiled. "An old friend."

The dwarf pursed his lips, eyeing Carn from a distance. "Not from around 'ere, is he? He talks funny."

Lara nudged his shoulder with her hand. "Hey now. He's from the same land as I am."

Bamur looked at her and glanced back at Carn. "Well, I understand ya, but he has a stronger accent." He paused, pursing his lips, and squinting as he peered at the Sword. "And he's too tall for my likein'."

Lara chuckled. "You're not jealous, are you?"

Bamur gazed up at her, his features looking astonished. "Me? Nay!" He raised an eyebrow, studying Lara. "Methinks he's more than a friend, the way he looks at ya. When he thinks nay one's lookin'."

Lara smiled softly. "True."

The dwarf looked up at her intently. "Just be careful, lass. Those older Swords aren't always after the same thing."

She gazed at Bamur and then looked across at Carn, realising that to anyone looking at them both, there was an age difference, but unknown to all concerned, she was the older one. She squeezed Bamur's shoulder. "Don't worry, we both know what we're doing."

He added, placing his hand over hers and patting it, "I'm just sayin', as I don't want to see ya hurt, lass."

Lara smiled, glancing back at Carn, thinking about what the dwarf had said. Contemplating the situation, she would have to remember that at some point Carn would bear a greater resemblance to her father rather than a lover. She shook the thought from her mind; she needed to think clearly about the task at hand.

They strolled back over to the group. Eight had volunteered to help with the trap, which May stated would make it even quicker to pull the net over the Quetzal. Carn's and Lara's plan was simple. As soon as night fell, they would go out and face whatever emerged. The Kanfors would be easy, but the Quetzal was the tricky one, and they hoped the trap may even up the odds. If they could ground it, they had a chance of tackling it, although it would be more Lara than Carn, but he would do his bit. Lara had the advantage of her speed and senses, nevertheless, facing such a creature would not be a simple task. By the time they arranged everything, it was past midnight. Lara and Carn left them all sleeping safely in the cellar and ventured up into the boarded-up inn. Lara looked at Carn and whispered, "I need to go out there and see what we're up against."

Carn studied her. "You sure?"

"Aye, a lycan out there won't cause too much suspicion. Demons usually give us a wide berth."

Carn responded, "I can keep a lookout and with everyone asleep, you should be safe to turn."

Lara nodded and stripped off her clothes. Carn studied her naked figure for a moment, his eyes lingering. She gave him a sly smile and quickly changed into wolf form. Carn quietly let her outside, he stated softly as she left, before closing the door. "Be careful."

She growled quietly and sniffed the air. If she kept to the shadows, she could scout the town with ease and see what they were going to have to fight.

Venturing around the town, it seemed the Kanfors were wandering around looking for anything moving and fighting each other for scraps. Lara made sure she kept upwind. If they were this desperate for food, they may decide to try their luck with a lycan. She had not been out for long when the Kanfors suddenly became frantic and ran off towards the mine. Lara then heard the beating of large wings. She looked up towards the west and the mountains to see a large dark shadow heading for the town. As the Quetzal got closer, she moved further out of sight. She noted that it seemed to be drawn only to Bighdarum, and wondered why it had not ventured north or south to other towns. She guessed that the crystal had left something that was drawing it. Since the inn, she could feel something cold and evil in her gut. When she focused on it, she could sense a pull, but it did not feel that strong to her. Lara was certain the creatures felt it too, but stronger. Lara wondered if, once there was nothing left alive in the town, it would follow the crystal's trail. That was something she was not willing to find out, and had to deal with before it devastated any other towns and villages in the path of the crystal.

It flew overhead, Lara watching it as it circled above the town, the sound of its beating wings unsettling in the night air. The creature appeared to be searching, then it dived, seizing something, then soared back upwards. The Quetzal swooped round, and landed with a thud on a building opposite where she was hiding, damaging the roof with its claws and weight. It held a writhing Kanfor in one of its powerful front limbs and tore off the demon's head with its razor-sharp teeth. Lara backed slowly into the shadows, not letting her gaze leave the creature. Once at a safe distance, she trotted back to the inn, having seen enough. Reaching Bamurs, she turned into human form in the shadows of the building. Quietly, she re-entered and locked the door.

Carn looked up from where he was sitting near the entrance, glad to see her. "So?"

Lara pulled on her clothes. "It seems to be Kanfors and the Quetzal, nothing else. I also got a good look at the Quetzal. It's feeding off the Kanfors for now, and it's big, so food may soon become an issue. It's not too big that we can't manage it, but we'll definitely need the trap."

"Let's hope our plan works."

She sat down, pulling on her boots. She gazed at him. "Try to get some sleep. I'm going to read up on it and see if the book I have has anything useful."

Carn nodded, watching her as she rummaged in her saddlebag that was placed near the fireplace along with their other belongings. He made himself comfortable in a chair, gazing at her. But sleep soon drew him to its depths. Leaving Lara alone, reading in the candlelight.

CHAPTER 12

A T THE CRACK of dawn, the town was busy. The young lad left at first light to get Eida. Bamur gave him a note for the witch, so she understood how imperative her assistance was. While the rest helped May with the nettings and ropes for the trap, the others that were not busy made sure the ones unable to help were safe.

From what May had calculated, it would be a couple of days before the trap would be ready to capture the demon. Checking the town with May, Carn and Lara, found the perfect spot in the main square to position the trap. The buildings were spaced evenly apart to support the net and with structures on each side, it would corral the Quetzal and they could spring the trap, dropping the net over it. If Lara and Carn could lure it there.

Leaving May to sort out the netting, the two Swords investigated the area to plan out how they could get the Quetzal to be where they needed it to be. The problem was the Kanfors; they did not need them getting in on the act when trying to bring down such a big demon. It was decided that their best option was for the two to go out that night and try to thin the herd while making sure they did not spook the Quetzal. With fewer of the smaller demons, they could focus on the bigger one the following night, if May was ready by then. Lara did not want to worry the townspeople, but they had just one shot, and if it failed, it would get very messy.

By midday, the young lad had returned with Eida. She was a tall, elegant woman with long, black hair and piercing grey eyes. Lara could sense Eida's powers and because of that, she would know her secret. The woman studied her intently. "You are a rarity."

Lara smiled, whispering. "Not many know."

Bamur smiled and stated, misinterpreting the comment, "Aye, Lara is. She's one of the best at dealing with demons I've ever met."

Eida raised an eyebrow. "I would be surprised if she wasn't."

Lara chuckled when Bamur coughed uncomfortably, sensing the tension between the two, and again misinterpreting it. He looked at Lara and glanced at Carn, who was smirking at the dwarf's mistake. "I thought ya liked men?"

Lara smiled, the comment easing the tension. Eida laughed and studied the dwarf. "It was just admiration to see a good swordswoman, Bamur." She glanced at Lara. "And nothing more."

Lara made a quick nod toward her, knowing that her secret was safe. Yet Lara knew that once these folks saw her fighting the Quetzal, that may no longer be the case, and wondered if she should tell Bamur. It was the least she could do. But in telling him what she was, it might jeopardise the entire plan. That was something she could not risk. She wanted to ensure the town was safe. She decided it would be best to talk to Carn first, to find out what his thoughts were.

She turned her attention to Eida and said, "So, do you think you can make at least eight protection spells against a demon? I need the townsfolk to be undetected."

Her vivid eyes focused on hers. "Aye. I have the right ingredients to do that. What about one for you and your companion?" Her eyes lingered on Carn for a few moments.

Lara shook her head. "Nay, I need the demons to see me and Carn. We are quick on our feet. We just need to be sure we won't have to worry about the ones dealing with the trap and can focus on our objective."

Eida nodded. "I understand, and I will ensure they are safe. I may be able to help you lure the Quetzal."

Carn responded, "That would be useful. We want to trap it in the square. If we can get it grounded, we have a good chance of killing it." He paused. "Well, Lara will know more where to make the killing blow, but I will make it bleed."

Eida studied them both. "Understood. When it is in the nets, I may be able to daze it, if the need arises."

Lara smiled. "Thank you. That would be helpful. I know it's rough size, and from what I could see last eve, it's big. About four horses in length, its wingspan twice that."

The witch pursed her lips. "Sounds like it is an old one from the depths. How did it emerge? I have noticed a change recently, something evil was near."

Lara studied her. "Aye, a crystal of dark magic was stolen. Carn and I are tracking it. Seems that when it passed through here, it awoke the Quetzal as well as the Kanfors. But we can't continue until we have freed this town."

Eida nodded. "I understand. Will you be able to get the crystal and destroy it?"

"My contract is to take it back to the man who has been guarding it."

The witch studied her intently. "That much evil can *never* be contained. It needs to be destroyed."

Lara nodded. "I have to agree, but Malaki has a place where it has been safe for centuries."

"Malaki?" Eida said with a bitter taste in her mouth.

"Aye. Do you know him?"

"I know him, aye. Not a man to cross with. Be careful Lara, his intentions may not always be what you believe."

Lara pursed her lips, glancing at Carn, remembering the conversation with Alistari and the one at the inn. "Do you know how it could be destroyed?"

"Aye, but it will not be a straightforward task. But if you are in need of my help, I could get what will be needed."

Lara replied, "Aye. Can we discuss that after we have taken care of the demon issue?"

The witch nodded in agreement. Then she followed Bamur into his inn and found a place where she could develop the protection spells that were needed.

Lara turned her attention back to the task at hand, satisfied that everyone knew what they had to do. She went over to speak to Bamur about thinning the herd of Kanfors. If they attacked before the Quetzal came out to hunt that night, then there would be less to deal with when they laid the trap the following night.

Bamur agreed but was also concerned. "Ya fella and ya self are our only hope. Don't do anythin' stupid that will make ya unable to deal with that beastie."

Lara studied him. "Don't worry. We just need to reduce their numbers. We can't be having to deal with all of them, and the Quetzal when we've grounded it."

"Just be careful, lass."

Lara nodded. "We will."

"And not just with 'ere. Getting that crystal doesn't seem a simple task."

"It isn't. That's why I was hired, it's part of my skill set. And just know; I'm always careful. I also have Carn to help me."

The dwarf gazed up at her. "We may 'ave had our differences, but I do care for ya." He paused. "And wouldn't like anythin' to happen to that fella, either."

Lara smiled at him. Bending down, she gave him a big hug. "I knew you had a soft side, Bamur."

The dwarf reluctantly pulled free and studied her intently. "Don't ya go around tellin' anyone though, I have a reputation to keep."

Lara chuckled. "My lips are sealed and rest assured; we'll get this town free of all those things."

CHAPTER 13

L ARA SURVEYED THE street, Carn at her side wiping his sword clean. They had killed seven of the Kanfors, but it was time to get back inside. The beating of the Quetzal's wings could be heard in the distance and they did not want to be seen by the larger demon when they were so close to being ready to bring it down. All the nets were ready, and as soon as it was light, they were going to get them into position. They had gone over the plan several times, but tomorrow they would put it to the test. Once the Quetzal was killed, any remaining Kanfors could be dealt with swiftly. Eida would make more talismans to put in the mines and around the town to ensure none came back.

Carn locked the inn door behind them, his wolf trotting over, having been curled up at Bamur's feet. Carn had left her inside as they did not need her when they had been fighting the Kanfors. He gave her a fuss, and she went to curl up near Bamur once more, having become friendly with the dwarf. Even though the dwarf would not admit it, Carn could tell he had a soft spot for the animal and was probably giving her treats.

Bamur glanced at the two as he drank some ale. "Did ya get 'em?"

Lara replied, "Aye, a few."

"Better than nothing, lass."

She nodded, but would have preferred, and Carn agreed, that they had killed more. Yet once the Quetzal arrived, most of the Kanfors usually rushed back into the mines, and that was pure self-preservation on their part. It was just the waiting before it arrived; fewer Kanfors would make it easier for the volunteers to move about. Lara would just have to accept that things do not always go according to plan. The primary aim was the Quetzal. But Eida's skills to shield the townspeople from being detected by any of the creatures gave Lara hope that the trap would work.

The dwarf beckoned them to sit with him, and they noticed two pewter mugs, one filled with groc, the other with ale, waiting as well. Lara raised her eyebrow and glanced at Carn as they sat down. She nodded to Bamur. "Thanks for the drinks. I'm guessing this is a serious talk?"

The dwarf responded, studying her with affection. "Aye. It's gonna be a big eve on the morrow, and think it's time we had a wee chat."

Lara took a sip of the strong liquor. "I hope you aren't going to get soppy like last eve."

Bamur sniffed, looked around nervously and glanced at Carn. "Well, as we said, let's tell nay one of that."

Lara chuckled and raised her mug to his. "So, what is it?"

The dwarf leant over the table; his blue eyes focused on hers. "So, there's been somethin' I've been wanting to talk about for a while now." He glanced at Carn. "I'm hopin' with 'im being an old friend, I can talk freely?"

Lara eyed Carn. "There are nay secrets."

Bamur nodded and continued. "So, I thought with what's gonna happen on the morrow, it may be best to get things out in the open."

Lara studied him, wondering what Bamur was about to tell her. She had known him for years, but he still surprised her. She took a sip of her drink. "Go on."

Carn sipped at his ale and quietly waited.

Bamur coughed, and shifted in his seat. "Well." He paused, scratching his thick red beard. "Well, ya see . . . I think I know what Eida was talking about when ya met."

"I see, and what's that?" Lara studied him, wondering if he knew, or that, like earlier, he mistook the conversation for her liking the same sex.

Bamur studied her and Carn, then said, tapping his temple with one of his stubby fingers. "Well, ya see, I ain't that dumb and a lot sharper than most folks think for a dwarf." Lara nodded. Carn remained silent and just listened a slight smirk touching his lips. Bamur continued, "So, I've been thinkin' and, well, ya very good with that sword and have abilities I haven't seen before." He held up his hand and curled down each fat finger in turn. "Ya, fast. Ya have nay issues in the dark. Ya seem to know people are coming well before anyone else. Ya seem to need little sleep and . . . well . . . on me pa's axe, lass, ya don't eat!"

Carn chuckled at the last statement. Lara realised some people would be able to figure out what she was with a lot of interaction, but stayed quiet in case Bamur was still way off the mark. She regarded him and waited as he nervously scratched his beard again. He studied her, belatedly realising she was waiting for him to continue. "So, what I'm saying, lass, is . . . well, ya know, I think ya maybe more than just a lass."

Carn raised an eyebrow and glanced at her. "He's pretty much nailed it."

Lara smiled; Bamur had realised she was different, but he had not figured out in what way. She sighed. She had wanted to tell him earlier and with his prompting, it was the perfect time. She leant back. "Alright Bamur. What I'm going to tell you, only Carn knows. So, this stays between us."

"Eida knows, doesn't she?" Bamur studied her.

"Aye, she could sense it."

Bamur looked around and leaned forward. "So, lass, what are ya? Part elf?"

Carn chuckled. "Nay, she's not an elf."

Bamur paused, looking at Carn, then studying Lara. "But the speed? I watched ya deal with some of those Kanfors, and I don't know any Sword with that speed or reflexes. Are ya a witch?"

Carn chuckled again. Lara kicked him under the table and glared at him. Bamur was about to guess again when she shook her head. "Let's not have a million guesses, Bamur. To be honest, I want to tell you."

He leant even further forward, his beard dipping into his ale, but being so eager, he had not noticed. "Well?"

Lara took a breath and then a big swig of the groc. "I'm not a witch. I'm something unique." Bamur raised an eyebrow, his entire body tense, waiting. Lara looked him right in the eyes. "I'm a lycan –"

He interrupted as he sat back. "That explains the speed."

Lara eyed him. "But I'm also a vampire."

Bamur choked on the ale that he had just taken a sip of. "What? But that ain't possible."

Lara smiled. "I told you; I'm unique. I'm possibly the only one, well nay. I *am* the only one."

"How?"

"Long story, but I have the skills and speed of a lycan *and* vampire."

He gazed at her. "I wondered how some young lass had such an old soul." He raised an eyebrow. "If ya don't mind me askin', how old are ya?"

"Well." She paused for a second, working it out in her head. "I have seen about forty-five winters."

Bamur leant back, his features astonished. "But ya look like ya only seen twenty." He looked at Carn. "So ya are about the same age?"

Carn nodded. "Well, she's a little older than me."

Lara smiled at Carn, then added. "They sired me when I was twenty-one."

The dwarf leant forward again and took her hand in his. "But ya warm to the touch. Thought vampires were cold?"

"Have you met any?" Bamur shook his head. Pulling his hand away, Lara continued. "I don't know why. All I can think is it's my wolf side, which is the most dominant, and I hunt every few days or so."

"Do ya?" Bamur pointed to his neck. "Ya knows."

Lara shook her head. "Nay, never. I won't let that side take control. If it did, I fear I'd lose myself."

The dwarf nodded, downing the last of his ale, and he looked back at her. "So ya, more dangerous than I had thought." He looked at Carn. "I admire ya being able to keep up."

Carn smiled, studying Lara with affection. "Well, I try."

Lara gazed at Bamur, taking his hand in hers. "I'm still me, Bamur. I just don't tell people due to them seeing me differently or because fear drives them away. But with what I am, I know I'm the only one, well with Carn's help, who can deal with this situation and deal with that crystal." She studied him intently. "Do I have your word you won't tell anyone?"

Bamur looked up at her and placed his other hand on hers, that was still holding his. "On me pa's mining axe, ya have me word."

Lara smiled. "Thank you."

The dwarf responded, "I knew ya were different, but hadn't expected that." He picked up his mug, noticing it was empty. "I need another drink."

"Same here."

Carn lifted his. "Me too."

The men got up and went to get more ale and Lara followed for more groc. They stood at the counter waiting for their drinks, the dwarf passed Carn his ale, and he strolled back to the table, fussing with his wolf.

Lara said, "With what I am, Bamur, I like to move on after a few years. So, if you don't see me again, you'll know why."

He looked up at her. "Aye, understood." He glanced across at Carn. "What about the fella? Will he go with ya?"

Lara gazed over at the Sword where he sat at the table, giving them some time to chat. She smiled. "Aye, I think he will. We have known each other for a long time."

Bamur nodded and chuckled softly. "Ya love each other deeply, don't ya?"

Lara turned her attention back to the dwarf. "Is it that obvious?"

The dwarf smiled. "Aye, lass." He paused, studying her. "Ya a fine lass, Lara, and thank ya again for helpin' save the town."

"It's the least I could do for a friend." She looked around at the inn. "I have some fond memories here, Bamur. Even when we had that disagreement for a while."

Bamur chuckled. "Well, if I had known who ya were, I wouldn't have argued with ya in the first place."

Lara smiled and said, "A toast to Bighdarum."

Bamur tapped her mug with his. "Aye, to Bighdarum." He regarded her for a moment. "And friendship."

Lara nodded. "And friendship."

Bamur chuckled and gazed at her. "Still find it hard to believe what ya are, Lara. But I can see why ya have the reputation ya have as a Sword."

She smiled. "Well, I have had a lot of experience."

He took a sip of his ale and said, "I have had one of me men secure a room upstairs for ya both. Thought ya may like a bit of privacy."

"Thank you, Bamur."

He looked across at Carn. "Least I could do for ya. Saves ya fella and ya self sleeping on the chairs down 'ere. And with fighting those beasties, I thought ya both want a decent bed to sleep in."

Lara smiled at him. "Thank you."

CHAPTER 14

IN THE CHILLY night air, the main street in Bighdarum was silent. Kanfor bodies were scattered all around. Lara and Carn stood in the centre, making sure they were visible. The town had gone eerily still only moments before. The remaining demons that were in other parts of the town looking for food, were scurrying off towards the mine. That meant the Quetzal had to be approaching. Lara looked to the west to see its silhouette in the clear night sky. She took a firm hold of her sword, still stained from the Kanfor's blood that she had just killed. To one side, and out of sight, was Eida casting a spell to lure the Quetzal towards the trap. Lara held her breath, hearing the creature's wings beating in the distance. She glanced at Carn, who gripped his sword, looking tense. He had held his ground well with the Kanfors, but this creature would be more of a challenge for both of them.

Lara heard the creature getting closer. It was time to see if the trap would work. They had gone over every plausible scenario that day. When the Quetzal was in position, they had to act fast. Lara looked towards the square, seeing the volunteers above on the rooftops, in the moonlight, ready to move. She focused ahead to see the Quetzal flying towards them and it looked like its path was true. It dived low and glided along between the buildings towards Lara and Carn. They both held their nerve as it swooped closer, ready to attack with its long, curved talons. Right then, Eida cast the spell to daze the Quetzal. Then the villagers pulled their ropes, and the nets dropped over the creature as it lost momentum, which forced it down. The Quetzal roared and tumbled to the ground. Lara looked up to see May and the others using powerful crossbows to fire large, thick bolts; some shooting more ropes over the creature, and others securing the net into the surrounding ground.

Lara took a breath; the Quetzal was larger than she had expected and hoped that the nets and ropes would hold. Its wings struggled to unfurl under the netting, as it tried to break free, straining against the ropes. Lara just needed it to hold long enough for her to get in and make a fatal blow, but with its size, that would not be a simple task. She glanced at Carn, who nodded. He was ready. They ran at it. Carn dealt with keeping the Quetzal distracted with blows from the ground. Lara, with her skill, jumped up high and landed on the creature's large neck. Its muscles instantly tensed when it felt her. The Quetzal struggled even more. Carn had to jump back, and Lara was nearly thrown, when the creature tried to slash at him with its claws. She focused on its neck, her vampire vision enabling her to see its blood vessels. She soon found the major artery. Lara thought of the ice rune, whispering the words to activate it, and sunk her sword deep into the skin. The flesh smouldered from the reaction of the silver and the rune. The Quetzal strained under the nets, some ropes snapped. Luckily, the whiplash from them breaking was clear of herself and Carn. Then she heard Carn cry out but she dared not look as she needed to keep focused. Yet, from the corner of her eye, she saw him stab his sword into the creature's front leg, and knew he was not badly injured. Lara had to move fast, the trap would not hold it for long, and withdrew her sword. Another rope snapped, and Lara had to dodge as it lashed across her vision.

She focused on the demon and plunged her sword into its neck again. With all her strength, she sliced across, making the opening large enough for its blood to flow, and cutting the net in the process. The blood spurted out in a torrent, pulsating with the creature's heartbeat. The black liquid surged freely with such speed that it splashed all over Lara and Carn, who was below. She spat some out of her mouth and continued attacking the creature while she tried to keep her balance as it struggled. With the net cut, it would soon be free if she could not kill it quickly. But as the blood continued to pour from its wounds, the movements of the Quetzal slowed. Lara jumped from its neck, landing near its head. Lara turned to see its gigantic eye focused on her. Slowly, the lizard-like pupil dilated, and the beast stopped moving, its breathing shallow. Lara wiped the viscous, black fluid from her face and sheathed her sword as the Quetzal took one last, rattling breath. Carn walked over to her, panting lightly, covered in the thick, black liquid. He had sheathed his sword and was examining a gash on his upper arm.

He wiped his face and smiled at her. "We did it."

For what seemed like an eternity, the town fell silent, everyone watching the Quetzal, in case it started moving again. Then Lara heard something, but it was not human or Quetzal, it was the Kanfor. Lara turned to Eida. "Get everyone inside, now."

"Why?"

"Kanfors."

The witch nodded and with her magic spoke to everyone telepathically, telling them to get inside quickly. Eida glanced at Lara. "Can you deal with them?"

Lara nodded, turning towards the mine where the Kanfors had been hiding. She glanced at Carn. He nodded, rotated his shoulder where the Quetzal had caught his arm, and pulled his sword free. Lara could hear them coming out from the depths with the threat of the larger demon gone. Compared to the Quetzal, the remaining Kanfors would be easier, yet, would still take all their skills to deal with. From what she could sense, there were only six of them. The creatures ran from the mine entrance on all fours, at speed. They could not sense the townspeople, but they would sense her and Carn. Yet, when the Kanfors emerged, they ran past them both, straight for the Quetzal. Lara realised it was a feeding frenzy. The perfect opportunity to deal with them. One Kanfor did slow and looked at her. Lara realised that the Quetzal's blood would mask their normal scents. It sniffed the air, focused on Carn for a moment, then ran to the carcass. Even though the two were covered in Quetzal blood the Kanfors were only interested in the Quetzal.

They turned to the carcass to see the six Kanfors climbing all over it, pulling its flesh free with their teeth. Seemed they were ravenous. Lara took a firm hold of her sword and ran at them, Carn close behind. She jumped onto the carcass and killed three before they realised they were in danger. The remaining Kanfors turned to her, ready to attack. These were not as hesitant as the one she dealt with in the mine. But they also had not realised how fast she was. One was dead moments later, another had jumped down and was attacking Carn. But the last one on the Quetzal's carcass was larger, and that meant older, and not such an easy target. She needed solid ground to fight this one, not on the back of a dead Quetzal. The Kanfor, with its double joints, used its odd angled limbs to stay atop the Quetzal, which was not to her advantage. She jumped down and faced the creature. It stood on the back of the carcass, all four limbs holding on to it, studying her, baring its teeth. It was not sure what she was, and would not attack blindly. Lara slowly stepped further back, her eyes never leaving the Kanfor. Slowly, the creature crouched, preparing to jump, its black eyes never leaving hers. It bared its teeth again and flexed its claws. Lara took a firm hold of her sword and moments later the Kanfor pounced. Not at Lara, but at Carn. He yelled out in pain as the Kanfor's claws slashed across his back, his attention on the other Kanfor he had been fighting. Lara cursed and ran at the creature, needing to get it focused on her, knowing Carn would not stand a chance fighting two, let alone an elder. Lara swung her sword at the larger Kanfor, and it turned to face her snarling. When it lunged at her, she dodged it with ease. She swung her sword, slicing at its midsection. It squealed in pain as the silver burned its skin, yet the injury was not deep enough to be a fatal blow. She envisioned the fire rune and whispered its name, activating it on her sword. The Kanfor slowly moved around her, sizing her up. She took a quick look to see Carn had dealt with the other Kanfor, but he did not look good. His face was etched in pain.

She snapped, "Get to the inn, now."

He hesitated, wincing in pain, his sword firmly in his hand. "I can help."

She shouted, "Nay! Go!"

Lara turned back to the other Kanfor, yelling at it when it looked towards Carn again. She stood her ground, keeping her eyes focused on it. It was better to let the Kanfor make the first move, as she could match its speed. Yet, it was not moving. She yelled at it again when it watched Carn as he ran towards the inn. Still, it stayed where it was. There was only one thing to do. She slowly lowered her sword enough for it to think it had an opening to attack. For a moment, the Kanfor still did not move and Lara wondered if her trick would work. Then it pounced with lightning speed. It froze a hairbreadth from her face. Her silver sword protruded out its back. Lara studied its features, seeing surprise there. It grimaced, shuddered, and then went limp. Lara pushed the corpse off her sword with her leg, and it slumped to the ground, lifeless. She slowly looked around at her surroundings, unable to pick up any life except the townspeople huddled within the buildings.

Lara looked down at her sword, then her arms and pulled a face in disgust. Her body was smeared with the foul-smelling Quetzal and Kanfor blood. It amazed her she could pick up any other scent, as the smell was so strong. Sheathing her sword, she slowly walked towards Bamur's Inn. Shaking her arms to get as much of the gooey mess off her as possible. She needed a bath, but first, she had to check on Carn.

When Lara entered the inn, Bamur pulled a face. "Not another one covered in that stinky stuff!"

Lara glared at the dwarf and removed her sword from her back, then shook the foul fluid from her hands. "It's a mix of Quetzal and Kanfor blood."

Bamur retched. "It'll take weeks to get rid of that stench!"

She sighed. "Thanks, Bamur."

She looked around to see Carn sitting off to one side, Eida tending to his wounded back. He had removed his shirt and jerkin, but he was still covered, though slightly less, in the sticky goo and looked exhausted. Lara strolled over, concern etched fully on her features. "Carn?"

He looked up and winced. "I'll be alright, it's just a scratch."

Eida raised an eyebrow. "More than that, you're lucky it wasn't any deeper."

Lara came round to see his back and winced, seeing the three gashes. Eida was wiping them clean and applying ointment on them.

Eida looked up and said, "But you both need a bath and then I can deal with any wounds with ease."

The dwarf agreed. "I want this stink gone!"

Lara glared at him. He looked abashed, adding, "Well, let's get ya a bath and get those clothes washed." Then muttered under his breath, "A good hundred times." He studied Lara. "And thank ya for savin' the town."

Lara smiled, wiping a glop of black goo from her nose. She could feel the blood running down her back, beneath her shirt, and just wanted to get out of her clothes as quickly as possible. "I could do with some groc."

Carn looked up. "Ale for me."

Bamur nodded. "Aye." Then he shouted to no one in particular, "*Where're the fecking baths? Get some drinks!*"

Lara slumped down in the chair next to Carn as he leaned forward, letting Eida deal with his wounds. He smiled at her and said, "I think I am going to be smelling this stuff for weeks."

She gazed at him and smirked. "At least we'll both smell the same."

Carn went to laugh, then winced in pain. Eida tutted that he should not have moved while she was dealing with his wounds. He glanced back at her and apologised, then Lara thanked Eida for her help. A barmaid came over with their drinks. Both Swords took the beakers and gulped down the respective liquids. They glanced at each other, both realising how much the drinks were welcoming after the long night of fighting.

Lara leant back in the warm water and closed her eyes; it was the third bath since she had defeated the Kanfors and Quetzal and there was still a lingering smell of their blood. It had taken four washes to get the stuff out of her hair, and her skin felt raw from all the scrubbing. Carn had been in at least five baths, Eida wanting to make sure it cleansed the slashes on his back and the wound on his arm from the Quetzal. He was laying on his front with a green paste over his wounds, dozing on the bed in their room. She could hear everyone downstairs in the inn rejoicing, but in the morn, they would need to face reality and assess the damage.

She felt triumphant in freeing Bighdarum, but also exhausted. Once she rested, she would need to hunt, but for now, she was going to enjoy her bath and the third beaker of groc. Lara's mind wandered to the crystal; she would need to follow its trail as her contract was not completed yet. She looked across at the sleeping Carn and hoped he would be alright. Eida had informed her he just needed rest and to take it easy for a few days, but would be fine. He was as stubborn as her and would not do anything to jeopardise the contract. But staying here to help Bamur had left them far behind. She just hoped they had no more towns or villages to rescue enroute. Lara took a deep breath, needing to think less of what she still had to do. For the next few hours she needed rest.

When she had been in the bath long enough, Lara climbed out and dried herself off. Slowly, she climbed onto the bed, laying down next to Carn. She kissed him gently on the cheek. He murmured for a moment, but did not to stir. She laid back, her joints aching. *Why were they aching?* Too exhausted to care, Lara ignored it. She just wanted to close her eyes and have some peace. As she closed her eyes, Carn's arm curled around her. She glanced at him. He was still asleep but had sensed her close and taken her into his arms. She hooked her fingers over his and smiled softly. She would just savour the moment for a little while, then think about hunting.

CHAPTER 15

LARA SIGHED, HER hands on her hips, studying the horse's mutilated bodies. From the smell, they had been dead for a couple of days. It seemed the stable was not as secure as she had thought. The Kanfors had had a feast on the horses and the cattle. Annoyed, she headed back to the inn. They were down two horses, and they could not continue the contract without any. She hoped that even with the town's folks trying to rebuild, and the fact they would be down horses too, some may part with a couple for the right price. If not, they would have to walk to the nearest town or farm. From what Lara remembered, none were that close by, and more time would be lost, which they did not need.

When she entered the inn, Carn was slowly coming down from their room, wincing slightly. Lara waited for him and asked, "How are you feeling?"

He gazed at her, smiling. "Sore, and probably wise not to lean on my back for a few days, but I'll be alright." He frowned, regarding her concerned features. "What's wrong?"

Lara sighed. "The horses. Both are dead. It seems the stable wasn't as secure as I thought it would be."

Carn cursed as he perched on the edge of a table. Rotating a stiff shoulder. "It will take us even longer on foot, and we are already behind."

Lara agreed and looked towards Bamur, who was at the bar checking on the stocks. "I'm going to ask if the town has any to spare. I know Bamur had a stable, but there wasn't room for our horses."

"Worth asking, otherwise it will be a long trek."

Bamur sighed, studying the two. "Well, I think I may have a spare couple. One belonged to one of me men, but he didn't make it. But to be honest, it's the least we could do for ya both for helping the town."

Lara nodded. "Thank you."

The dwarf sighed, eyeing them both. "Don't thank me yet. They ain't young'uns but will get ya to a place where they will have somethin' decent."

They followed Bamur to his stable, behind the inn. This one had fared better than the others. It was evident it had been full from the amount of cleaning up the stable boy was doing. Bamur led them to the middle stalls, where there were a couple of older mares, one eating oats. He was not wrong. The sandy-coloured one and the black one had both seen some years, but were still healthy enough to do the mileage, just not as spritely as their horses had been. Carn turned to Bamur as he patted one mare's neck. "Thank you."

Lara studied the dwarf. "Thank you, Bamur." She paused and added, looking at the view of the town from the stable. "There will be a lot of work getting this town up and running again."

Bamur grinned. "Ahhh, don't worry, lass, it'll be back to its old self in nay time."

Carn's wolf trotted up to them and the dwarf absentmindedly stroked the animal's fur. Carn stated, "She's not friendly with many people."

Lara agreed. "That's true."

The dwarf looked down at the wolf, giving her a fuss around an ear. "Well, she has good taste."

Carn glanced at Lara, who smiled, remembering their conversation before they reached Bighdarum. The plan had been to ask Derwyn, but the way his wolf was with Bamur, there was no doubt where she would be happy. And with the tasks ahead, Carn was concerned it would be too much for her. When he saw how friendly she had become with the dwarf, Carn suggested his idea to Lara, and she had to agree. It was the perfect home for her.

The Sword regarded Bamur and said, "I was wondering if you could do me a favour." Carn looked down at his wolf and crouched, giving her a fuss, looking a little forlorn. He looked back at Bamur. "As you get on so well, could you look after her?"

The dwarf looked a little shocked and studied the wolf. "But she's yas?"

"Aye, but she's old now, and she needs a loving home, and I think she would fare better here in her remaining years."

The dwarf looked a little choked at the offer. "Well, I . . . I," he paused, gazing at them both, then smiled. "I'd be honoured."

Carn gave the wolf a big fuss, whispering in her ear. He stood and smiled, taking Bamur's hand in a firm shake. "Thank you."

Bamur nodded and looked from the wolf to Carn and back again. "I'll look after her well, I can promise ya that. She knows a good place when she sees one."

Carn chuckled and patted the dwarf on his back. "Thank you. It's been good getting to know you, Bamur."

The dwarf looked up at him and grinned. "Aye, and ya, even though ya talk funny."

Carn laughed. He turned to Lara and said, "I'll sort out supplies and equipment." Then walked out of the stable.

Lara watched him leave. He probably wanted some time alone. He had a close bond with the wolf, and had trained it from a pup. It would be hard to part, even though it was the right thing to do.

The dwarf turned to Lara. "I can see why ya like 'im."

Lara's lips curled up slightly, placing her hand on his shoulder. "I know a good man when I find them."

The dwarf blushed a little and looked down at the wolf. "And for him to ask me to look after her."

"It was a hard decision for him to make, but he knows she'll be happy here."

Bamur smiled. "Aye, I'll treat her well." He took a deep breath. "Well, this town won't sort itself out. I better get to it."

Lara smiled and watched him go, knowing the dwarf hated to show his soft side. She glanced back at the horses, pursing her lips. The mares would not help them catch up too much on the time they had lost, but it was still better than being on foot. Leaving the stable, she walked towards the main gates. Lara needed to hunt before they went anywhere, and to clear her head. After talking to Bamur about what she was, it made her wonder if it was time to move on from the continent of Barberium. In her heart, she knew Carn would go with her, and it seemed the right time to start again. Also, the contract was giving her more attention than she wanted. After last night, a number had seen how she fought, and some may wonder what she was. Lara would fulfil the contract, but then she needed to start fresh somewhere else. At least this time she would have Carn for company.

After her hunt, Lara found Carn in the stables preparing the horses and equipment. She strolled over to him and smiled. Carn kissed her gently and gazed at her. "Did the hunt help?"

"Aye." She focused on his eyes. "I also decided that after this contract, it may be time to move on."

He laced his fingers into hers, pulling her closer to him. "I wondered. You seemed a little distant after that conversation with Bamur."

Lara looked up at him, raising an eyebrow. "Was it that obvious?"

"It was to me, but I know you."

Lara smiled softly. "I know you only just got here, but would you come with me?"

Carn kissed her passionately, then said, "Of course I will. I told you a few days ago, I am not losing you again."

Lara melted against his lean chest, feeling him wince when she curled her arms around him. She looked up. "Sorry."

Carn pulled her close, enveloping her in his muscular arms. "It's fine. I'm not about to lose the opportunity for a hug."

Lara smiled softly, savouring their closeness, realising how much she had missed it. Carn kissed her on the top of her head, taking a deep breath. Lara closed her eyes, listening to Carn's heartbeat. All the events over the last few days melted away.

One horse snorted, breaking their tranquillity. Carn sighed. "Well, we should say our farewells."

Lara kept her body close to his. "Just a little longer."

Carn leaned his head against hers and smirked. "Not going to refuse."

After a few moments, they parted and Lara gazed up at Carn. Already looking forward to other adventures with him.

Returning to the inn, they found Bamur snapping orders to his remaining men. They had a lot of work ahead to get the town up and running again, and the dwarf was a hard taskmaster. Once his men had left, Lara sat next to him at his table while Carn went to their room to get the rest of their belongings. Lara studied the dwarf's old features. "It has been good knowing you, Bamur."

The dwarf focused on her eyes. "Ya leaving for good?"

Lara glanced down for a second. "Aye, I think I am. I was thinking about it all while hunting. Once this contract is done, it may be time for me to move on. Even though I know you'll keep my secret, the story of me saving this town will get out, and will spread. What I don't want is getting more attention than I need."

"But ya a hero."

Lara smirked. "But there are some out there who do not want something like me existing, even if I am a hero."

Bamur sighed. "Is ya fella goin' with ya?" Lara nodded. Bamur smiled and said, "So, a drink for the road?"

"Of course, then we must be on our way. I want to stay and help more, but the woman who has the crystal is way ahead of us. So, I need to make up some time."

"Understood. Those mares ain't young, but they will get ya far."

Lara gave him a sly look. "Better than on foot."

The dwarf chuckled. "It's been nice knowing ya, Lara."

"And you Bamur. Once this is all over, I may pass this way again, but if not, I just wanted to make sure we had a farewell drink."

The dwarf looked up at her with affection. "Any idea where ya will head?"

She shrugged. "Not sure. Carn and I will discuss it once we have fulfilled this contract."

"There are some fine lands to the southwest. Or there are the northern ones, but they can be a little harsh."

"You seem to know a few places."

Bamur chuckled. "Aye, lass. I did a bit of travelling in me youth. Then I took this place on and haven't left since."

"Do you miss the travelling?"

He shook his head. "Nay." He looked around at the inn, stretching out his arms. "This is my world now, and I 'ave too much responsibility to go gallivanting off."

Lara smiled warmly. "Well, this is a fine town."

"On my pa's axe, it is, and one that I will run for many years to come."

Lara regarded him, knowing it was hard to figure out the age of a dwarf. They had a pretty long life span. It seemed in Bamur's youth he did not want the responsibilities and had travelled for several years. Yet now, Bighdarum was in his heart after his family had built this town up from almost nothing. From not wanting to take his father's place, he would now always put the people of Bighdarum first. Lara knew, even though this town had taken a good beating from the demons, it would soon thrive once more.

After a farewell drink with Bamur. Lara found Eida, as the witch had stated she could help them if she was needed, and Lara wanted to see if the offer still stood. Eida was packing up her things, ready to leave in the morning. She studied Lara intently. "So, you are heading off to find the crystal?"

"Aye. Carn is sorting everything else while I said my farewells to Bamur. You mentioned you may be able to help."

"I did, but need to find some information, and cross-reference it with my books."

"Understood, but we can't wait any longer. The crystal is already to far ahead of us."

Eida touched Lara's arm. "Don't worry. I have a teleportation crystal. I use it sparingly, but I will find you both when you're ready."

"What do you need from us?"

Eida pulled a hairpin from her hair. "Just a little blood from one of you, and you will need a location stone."

Lara nodded, holding out her finger. Eida pricked it and placed a few drops of blood into a small glass vial. Rummaging in her saddlebag, the witch passed Lara a small, polished, black stone. "Keep this on your person at all times. Then, when I'm needed, think of me clearly, and I will teleport to you within the day."

Lara smiled. "Thank you. Do you think you'll be able to help us destroy the crystal?"

"I'm hopeful, but need to read my books to be sure of what spell will be required. Yet you must understand, to destroy something that evil, there will be a cost."

"Cost? To you?"

Eida nodded. "And to you. It will take a lot of magic and I may need to channel some of your own to help me."

"I understand. Do you know what it will do to us?"

Eida shrugged. "I'm unsure, but with you being vampire and lycan, it may weaken you, so the vampire side may take over for a time."

"Oh." Lara looked pensive. "That side's unpredictable if not kept in check."

"Understood, and I'll ensure I have precautions in place."

Lara studied the woman. "And what about you?"

Eida sighed. "I'm not immortal as you are. So I may age a little, but it's a small price to pay."

Lara said sternly. "If it means the loss of your life, we'll look for an alternative."

Eida smiled softly. "The crystal has to be destroyed. Whatever the cost."

Lara nodded, but did not want Eida to lose her life in the process. "Let's hope we don't have to find out."

Eida slowly nodded, yet Lara felt there was something the witch was not telling her. Her instincts made her feel that it would not be wise to take the crystal back to Malaki. *Would I be able to make that sacrifice?* She sighed and hoped it did not come to that.

After she had spoken to Eida, Lara met Carn outside the stables and they were soon on their way, leaving Bighdarum behind. They had a lot of ground to cover, but even though slow, the horses seemed up to the task. The plan was to head for the inn near the River Lan before heading across the country to the riverbank, where there was a small ferry across the narrow section at the River Slangor. They were not sure what to expect, but if the woman took a similar route, then no other town or village should have been affected, except for the inn and maybe at the ferry crossing. Lara looked ahead. It would not be an effortless task, but with Eida's and Carn's help, she hoped it would be successful.

125

CHAPTER 16

LARA AND CARN slowed their horses when they could see the inn ahead in the fading sunlight. Yet as they got closer, the summer breeze changed direction and Lara picked up the scent of decay. Focusing ahead, Lara could see someone outside the inn vomiting. As the two reached the building, the traveller looked up at them, his plump features pale. "Don't go in, it ain't pleasant."

Lara regarded the older man. "I've seen worse. Are you heading south?"

"Aye." He glanced back at the inn. "Whatever happened to them, it wasn't a human that did it."

Lara dismounted and took a deep breath, picking up another scent beneath that of the decay. She drew her sword. Whatever she had picked up was still close by. When Carn dismounted, she turned to him and whispered, "There's a demon in there. I should do this on my own." She turned to the traveller. "Do you have a sword?" The stocky man nodded. "I suggest you stay here with Carn and keep alert."

The man swallowed. "Am I in danger?"

Lara glanced around. "Aye, if you don't stay alert. But Carn is an excellent Sword, so you'll be safe."

Carn nodded to the man before drawing his sword and stated, "Stay focused and do what I say if anything happens."

Lara turned her attention to the inn. and slowly pushed open the door that was barely on its hinges. The smell of decay hit her, and the buzz of flies filled the silence within. The bodies were scattered inside, all torn apart and bloated. Limbs were tossed across the blood-covered floor, maggots already feasting on the rotting flesh. From the greenish colour of the torn flesh, and the dark brown of the dried, flaking blood, it had happened several days before. Lara tried to focus. The smell of blood and rotting flesh was rancid, making her body want to retch. She understood why the traveller had been sick. Lara tried to focus on the scent of the creature that was still in there. She carefully avoided stepping in the blood where it was still tacky from pooling in large amounts. Keeping a firm hold of her sword, she slowly surveyed the room. Tables had been knocked over, alcohol had spilt all over the floor and had mixed and dried with the blood. She looked at the mutilated bodies; it was hard to tell if anyone defended themselves, it seemed to have happened fast. Her foot touched a sword tip. Lara crouched down and examined it. The blade was coated with a dried black substance. Demon blood. Someone had managed to at least wound the thing that did this.

Lara paused. She could pick up the other scent more clearly. She turned to the door leading to the cellar. A draft coming in from the open door propelled the scent her way, it seemed it was down there. That made sense; cold and dark, the perfect hiding place. Taking a firm grip on her sword, Lara pushed the cellar door open slowly and headed carefully down into the dark depths. She stopped on the stone steps and took a deep breath. She could smell the demon, something she had not encountered in a long while; a Vacnor. All the carnage upstairs had masked its scent of decay and its blood from the wound that it had received from whoever wielded the sword upstairs.

Vacnors were nocturnal from what she could remember, but they were vicious, known to rip its victims apart with its claws and eat the livers. It was hard to tell from the bodies, but was certain that on closer inspection, she would find the livers would be missing from all of them.

She continued carefully down the steps, then stopped, hearing movement. In the corner was a small bipedal creature. Lara paused. It was smaller than she thought it would be, but still as deadly.

It turned towards her, sniffing the air, and paused, its large, bat-like eyes focused on her. Lara stopped at the bottom of the stone steps, sword firmly in hand. But it just turned away, not interested in her at all. Lara paused; she had expected it to at least defend its territory. Yet the last one she had come across seemed disinterested, too. Maybe her liver was not tasty enough. But the other had still been territorial. Whatever the reason, Lara could not leave the demon alive in the cellar to kill more innocents. But Lara wondered why it was not attacking. She sheathed her sword and slowly walked towards it. As she got closer, she could see the reason. It was severely injured across its midsection and sat in a pool of its blood. Whoever had been wielding that sword had, even inadvertently, aimed true. The Vacnor could not attack because it was dying. Lara stopped only a few steps away, and the creature looked up at her forlornly. Then Lara understood. It wanted her to end its misery. Lara pulled out her sword and made the fatal blow, the Vacnor not even resisting.

Lara walked out into the early evening sun. The traveller's demeanour was anxious. Carn, standing to one side, looked more relaxed. The Sword asked, "Well?"

She looked at the two men. "I'm going to have to burn this place down." She focused on the traveller. "I suggest you keep travelling south and camp out tonight."

"Is it safe?" the man asked, his voice a little nervous.

"As safe as it normally is. But this place needs to be destroyed."

The traveller nodded. "Let me help ya both."

Lara thanked him, and they soon torched the inn. The building and its contents were soon in full flame. Lara looked at the inn, a little saddened. She had never come across a demon wanting her to kill it before. It made her realise even more that not all of the creatures were heartless. She sighed. Then again, humans thought lycans and vampires were heartless, too. Lara mounted her horse, and with Carn at her side, they watched the traveller heading south.

Carn turned to her once they were alone and asked, "What happened?"

Lara told him about the demon, and he pursed his lips. "Makes you understand not all demons are evil. You did the right thing."

Taking a breath, she said, as they turned their horses away, "Let's travel a suitable distance away before we make camp."

Carn agreed, and they headed east across the country to the river, wary of what they would come across next.

They reached the ferry crossing in the late afternoon, after a couple of days. For most of that day, it had rained, and both would have valued a night at an inn, but there were none on their side of the riverbank. They could see the small hut for the ferryman to shelter, and the dock, but both looked deserted. Carn pursed his lips, looking at the fast-flowing water and then back at the dock. The ferry was nowhere in sight. They dismounted, keeping their cloaks firmly around them against the rain, and went to take a closer look. It seemed the ferry had taken the woman across, but whatever happened to it, and the man who looked after it, happened on the other side.

Carn peered through the rain, across the far side, to see the large, raft-like ferry, slightly further downstream, caught on some low-lying trees. There was no sign of anyone. "Feck!"

He turned to Lara, hearing her curse as well. Their access across was gone. Someone had broke the chain that pulled the ferry back and forth and stopped it from being pulled along by the current. They looked at the horses and hoped they would be willing to enter the water. It was fast, but if the mares kept calm, they could make it. That was why the ferry was so popular; it made passage safe for the horses, and carriages could also cross.

Carn glanced at Lara, her features in shadow from her hood. "So, what now?"

She shrugged. "The only other place to cross is at Slangor Pass, but that will take several days, and we are already too far behind."

Carn cursed again and looked across at the fast-flowing river. The ferry had been their best option. Carn glanced at the horses, then the river again, and said, "Are you a strong swimmer?"

Lara eyed him. "Why?"

He tilted his head toward the horses, the notion barely seen from under his large hood. "If they panic, we may have to think of an alternative."

"That may be our only option, if it comes to pass. But then we'll have to walk to the nearest town once across."

Carn shrugged. "Aye, but still save us more time than riding to Slangor Pass."

Lara nodded in agreement. She pulled her hood back slightly to look at the late evening sky; the rain beginning to slow. "We should set up camp and then deal with this in the morn." She paused, studying the horses. "Let's hope they like swimming."

They guided the mares to the small hut near the ferry dock. If the mares were reluctant, they would have to leave them here and hoped they fared well. Yet Carn was feeling confident that they could cross. By the time they had unsaddled the horses, the rain was turning to a drizzle. Looking inside the hut, they found a bed, a small fireplace, and cooking supplies. On one wall was a shelf with a couple of well-worn books and a trunk in the corner with spare clothes. It seemed the ferryman had little but it sufficed for him. Even though small, it was nice to get out of the rain they had been riding in all day. Lara set up the fire while Carn got out food for himself and passed her water. He looked across at the bed. It was just big enough to take them both, so at least a little more comfortable than the floor. Once the fire was burning well, they removed their cloaks, sat down, and rested.

Carn studied Lara in the firelight, wondering what was ahead for them. As he ate, he asked, "Do you think we'll need Eida when we find the crystal?"

Lara regarded him with affection. "From what she knows of it, we will. I'm just reluctant, as it may be costly."

Carn nodded, having not been with Lara when she had spoken to the witch, but understood that magic always had some sort of cost. "Until we find that woman, we won't know for sure. I think it would be advisable to have Eida in case."

"Aye, which is my feeling as well." She gazed at Carn and asked, "How's your back?"

Carn shrugged; he could feel where the Kanfor had slashed through his skin, but with Eida's herb paste they were healing. "A little stiff, but it seems alright."

Lara responded, "Let me see. Eida told me to check on the wounds every few days for you."

Carn gave her a sideways glance. "Are you sure it's just not an excuse to get me to take my clothes off?"

Lara thumped him playfully on his shoulder, raising an eyebrow. Carn chuckled and removed his jerkin and shirt. Lara moved round to look at his back. The green paste had dried over the long slashes, and they were healing well. Carn could feel

Lara's gentle touch making his skin tingle, then he felt her lips on his shoulder and said, "So, is that inspecting my wounds?"

Lara kissed his ear gently and whispered, "I'm making a very detailed examination."

Carn smiled and twisted round to face Lara, kissing her passionately. "I can think of something else that will make it better." He glanced over at the bed. "It can take the strain."

Lara smiled, lost in his gaze. "But you can't lay on your back."

Carn grabbed her, spinning her around onto the bed, and covered her body with his. "There are other ways."

Lara kissed him passionately, her hands sliding across his firm chest. She gazed at him for a moment before he began undoing her jerkin. Within moments they were both naked, Carn on top of Lara kissing her breasts, entering her. The bed creaked under their movements as they made love, but neither noticed, both lost in each other's embrace. Lara's hand slid across Carn's back, making him wince. She paused, gazing at him. He leant forward and breathed, "Don't stop."

Lara continued to move her hips with his, her body shuddering with delight. Carn thrust deeper, making her gasp as she slowly lost control. She leant up to him, keeping her hips moving, and kissed him passionately. Her fingers combed into his hair and pulled him towards her. Her loins tingled uncontrollably as they moved faster, both coming at the same moment. Lara grabbed his shoulders as Carn leaned against her, gasping, his body covered in sweat. She kissed him gently, lost in his eyes. Carn smiled and kissed her again. "I love you."

She brushed his cheek and whispered, "I will love you always."

He regarded her with affection, his love clear to see. He leaned his head on her chest and they both held each other tenderly, never wanting the embrace to end.

CHAPTER 17

A T DAWN, THEY packed up their things and went over the plan to get across the river. Carn was hoping they could ride across if the horses did not panic. But if the horses were unsettled, then they would have to strap what they could to their backs and swim. Whichever way they crossed the river, by horse or swimming, the contents of their saddle bags would still get wet. Because of this, the food would spoil. Carn ensured he had a hearty breakfast, but the remaining food, except the water bottles, would have to be left behind. Lara, in the meantime, could not leave her books, and wrapped them in as many of her clothes and then with her cloak, hoping to give them some protection.

Carn teased her. "You can't go anywhere, can you, without a book?"

She looked at him and stated, "Yet these books helped at Bighdarum."

He gazed at her. "Aye. You win."

Lara looked at him, knowing Carn was right. She went everywhere with a book in hand. Even her brother said she always had her head in a book. She looked at the saddlebags, hoping the books would not get too wet. She then said, "When we get to the other side, I can go hunting for food. Then when we reach the first inn or village, we can resupply."

He nodded in agreement. Once Carn had eaten, he packed everything up. Then they stripped to the bare minimum of clothing, in case they had to dismount from the horses and swim. They packed up all their clothes into the saddlebags or strapped them to the saddles when the bags were full. Most of their clothes would still get wet, but if needed, they could swim with ease, taking off anything that would get heavier when they were in the water. They could then dry out their clothes on the other side. With it being in the warmer months, the sun would help, and Carn would not end up getting chilled to the bone.

With the bags secured to the saddles and their swords strapped to their backs, the two then turned their attention to the flowing water. It would be a hard swim, but both, them and the horses, would make it. Mounting the mares, they rode them a little way from the dock to where the riverbank was shallow. The horses snorted and neighed nervously upon seeing the fast water. But the two rode the mares to the water's edge, stroking their necks and trying to keep them calm. Carn's horse patted its front hooves at the water and, with a little encouragement, ventured in. Lara's was a little more reluctant, but when it saw Carn's swim, it calmed a little and ventured in too. The horses snorted, Lara and Carn tensing as the freezing water hit their bodies.

They had not swum far on the horse's backs when Lara glanced over her shoulder to see they were already downstream. It seemed the currents were stronger than they had expected. Lara focused on her goal on the other side and held to the horse's neck, letting it swim. Carn was only a little behind on his, patting its neck, keeping it calm. The horses fought against the currents, swimming at an angle to reach the riverbank.

It felt like forever until they finally made it to the shallows and stopped being carried away by the current. The horses trotted quickly onto the sloping riverbank. Lara and Carn pulled them to a stop and dismounted. Both slumped down on the grass, soaked through. The horses were calm and chewing on the grass near their feet. Lara looked back across the river for a moment to survey where they had come from. She could not see the ferry dock and realised it was further upstream than she had expected. Lara was not too worried. At least they had made it. She laid back in the sun for a few moments as it warmed her chilled body and let everything dry off. She glanced at Carn to see he was already welcoming the warmth of the summer sun after the cold water.

After a few moments, Carn sat up, looking at her. "I could stay here all day, but I know we need to get moving."

Lara nodded and was reluctant to stand, but they had too much time to catch up on. They checked on the horses. Taking some clothes from the saddlebags. They both left their boots fastened to the saddles, letting them dry in the sun, along with the wet clothes they had changed out of. Lara checked her books. They had fared well in the materials that were wrapped around them, soaking most of the water.

Mounting their horses, they left the river behind and headed southeast, hoping to find a village or town. Carn glanced at Lara as they rode. Crossing the river had been tougher than he thought it would be. The horses had been a little reluctant, and his panicked slightly when the current pulled it downstream. He had to keep a firm hold of the reins and calm it down. His soothing words worked, and the mare regained control. His back ached from the strain and he rotated his shoulder as that ached, too. He sighed. These last couple of years he had noticed he was aching more, and it was just age slowly catching up with him. He looked across at Lara; she seemed just as strong, and of course still never ageing. Yet she had changed. Seeing her fight at Bighdarum, he could see she had become a fine swordswoman, a lot better than even himself. She had also become more brutal. That was down to fighting demons; if you hesitated, you were dead. She no longer did and made the killing blow more aggressively. She was still the Lara he knew, but there was a harder edge to her. Carn sighed. They had both changed over the last fifteen years, but the one thing that was steadfast had been their feelings.

He looked ahead. The land was more barren compared to the mainland. There were trees scattered about, but the ground was dry and dying. It seemed the entire land was no longer thriving, almost like life was being drained from it. Carn glanced across at the imposing mountains to the south of them and beyond, wondering if everything mined from them was evil. The wind picked up and swirled around them, pulling up debris and dust, making them both cover their eyes as they rode. Carn tried to see ahead, but the wind was obscuring everything. The wind died down for a moment and Carn could see a small hamlet. But his eyes focused further ahead on the dark storm clouds. He turned to Lara and pointed; she nodded. He asked, "Do you want to keep going, or take shelter there if that storm is heading our way?"

Lara surveyed the hamlet ahead as the wind picked up again, blowing dust in their faces. She responded, "Let's see when we get there. I can't see any movement."

Carn looked ahead, wondering how, then remembered her eyesight was far superior to his own. Neither of them knew how far Dark Cloud was, but both had expected at least one village or town before then so they, and the horses, could have a rest. He focused on the hamlet ahead, already thinking of a bed at an inn and some welcomed ale.

When they reached the small hamlet, both sighed. It had been deserted for some time. The buildings were still standing, but just barely. A couple had been destroyed, the remains in a heap of burnt beams and rubble. Carn sighed, patting his horse's neck when it snorted nervously. He had hoped for an inn and a nice pint. Carn turned to Lara. "What should we do? We could make camp here, but there's still several hours of daylight."

Lara sighed, looking around at the buildings, her mare pulling on the reins. "I think we keep going." She took a deep breath and added. "There have been ghouls here. The scents are still fresh. Think that's one reason the horses are restless."

"Are we heading towards them?"

She shook her head. "Nay. They went towards the mountains, southwest of here, and as far as I can calculate, Dark Cloud is south. But . . ." She paused, glancing at the dark sky ahead. "Towards that storm."

Carn sighed. "Sooner face that storm, than ghouls."

Lara studied him and smiled. "Have to agree."

Carn scanned the barren land. "Aye, so would the horses. I was really looking forward to a good pint of ale, too."

Lara chuckled. "Aye, I agree there, too. When we get to Dark Cloud, we'll make sure we have some." She looked around and sighed. "Hopefully, there will be something for the horses if we find a decent area to camp. And you'll need food soon. When I go hunt, I'll bring you back a rabbit."

Carn leant over in his saddle towards her and gave her a quick kiss. "Come on, let's get moving."

They had made good progress seeing the town of Dark Cloud in the distance. They had camped out the first night, the storm never reaching them. The horses had munched on local plant life while

Lara hunted, bringing back a meal for Carn, who cooked it on the fire he had made. They then rode all day, reaching a quiet inn for their second night where the horses could have a good brush down in the stables and a meal of grain. Checking with the innkeeper, they found they were heading on the primary route, and they would reach the town in less than a day.

By late afternoon they reached Dark Cloud, riding up to the imposing gates. It seemed the land was not as desolate as stories had made it out to be. The town was thriving. Most of the rumours must have been from traders trying to keep the competition out. Whatever the reason, it still seemed to be the only town for miles. At least they could have a rest and get information. From the activity here, it did not seem that the woman had ventured this way, yet Lara's instinct was telling her they were heading in the right direction.

Riding through the busy streets, they headed into the heart of Dark Cloud, looking for an inn. It seemed to be as rough as any mining town, and it would also be their principal source of income. They came to an inn that did not seem too busy, left the horses with the stable lad, and went in. They ordered food and drink. Finding a quiet table near the back, they sat facing into the inn and watched all the customers. Carn took a large gulp of his ale, and then sat back, soaking up the atmosphere. He smiled at the barmaid when she brought the food; the girl looked questioningly at Lara as she had not ordered anything. She just smiled back at the girl and continued to drink her strong drink.

Carn glanced at her and whispered, "You could always go back to ordering for two. I'd be happy to eat it all."

Lara glanced at him and smiled. "I'm surprised you didn't. You eat like a lycan."

He chuckled and gave her a big grin. She leant back and took in the scents and conversations as Carn ate the sausages and potatoes. There were no rumblings of the crystal or the woman and her men. That confirmed to them that the woman must have taken a different route. Maybe she wanted to get to her destination quicker, or they had made an error in the direction they were heading. But Lara could sense the crystal. It was pulling at her vampire side, so she was confident they were heading the right way. It seemed the woman was just avoiding any more trouble.

Lara suddenly tensed, picking up a faint smell of lavender. She looked towards the entrance to see a couple of hooded men had entered moments before. Lara focused on them and took another sniff, the circulation of air in her favour. Lara turned to Carn and whispered, "We have vampires here."

Carn raised an eyebrow questioningly, Lara nodded towards the two without making it too obvious. Carn looked in the general direction and responded, "Look like seasoned Swords to me. Just look at their stances."

Lara glanced over casually and had to agree. Then she remembered something the old vampire, Fashor, had said all those years ago and wondered if these were the cleansers he had mentioned. The ones she came across in Kerlish had seemed new, but it was enough for her to understand they were not vampires to cross. The situation was not good. If they picked up her scent, it would cause issues. She observed them as they ventured further into the inn, away from them. She was glad they were moving away, but curious as to why they would come into an inn, even if quiet. Then she saw a young man across the room, looking nervous, his attention fully on the two. It seemed he was their target. A good time to go. Lara turned to Carn. "We need to leave now."

Carn paused, two-thirds the way through his potatoes and sausages. "But I haven't finished."

Lara slowly stood. "Sorry, but I think they're cleansers, and we best leave before they pick up my scent."

Carn slowly stood, taking a few quick mouthfuls, then grabbed his belongings. "Won't they, anyway?"

Lara gave him a sideways glance. "Aye. But I want to be away while they're busy."

He looked over to see one of them sitting in front of the lone young man, the other standing to the side, blocking his escape, and Carn nodded. "Oh, aye, we best get moving."

She watched the two, who were too focused on their victim, and quickly left the inn. No one in the inn seemed to mind that a lone customer was in distress. But Lara had the impression that no one would step into other people's business in this town. As soon as they left the inn, Lara picked up the pace, making sure they kept upwind of the inn. Carn glanced at her as they walked, the light fading fast. "What about the horses?"

Lara looked back, pleased to see no one following. "Nay, time to saddle them. I want to be a good way from the inn before they come out. I think we need to stay out of sight till morn. Then come back for the horses."

"Maybe a stable would help. The horses would mask our scent."

She nodded. It was not ideal but might work, just not one so close to the inn. She hoped that by moving around a bit, the cleansers, if they picked up her scent, would lose it quickly. Carn asked as they kept to the side streets and alleys. "Have you come across them before?"

Lara looked at him. "Briefly, at the vampire's coven in Kerlish. But not since then. I was told about them by a vampire many years ago. He warned me to stay clear of them."

"At Kerlish? But you said nothing."

Lara eyed him. "Nay, I thought it best to say nothing, and then it was nay longer an issue when we left."

"I see. What do they do? From the name I am gathering, they deal with rogue vampires?"

Lara replied, "Aye, but not just vampires, any rogue demon, and anyone like me. They would want anything like me dealt with as soon as possible. Lycans like to keep the pack pure, but from what I have been told, vampires are even more strict."

Carn nodded, seeing what looked like a stable ahead down a side alley. "Then we better keep a low profile."

As they entered the side alley, someone ahead stepped out. Lara heard the whoosh of a crossbow bolt and deflected it with her sword. Carn only realised what was happening when the bolt fell to the floor harmlessly. He turned to the person ahead, one more stepping out behind them. The light had faded more, making it hard for Carn to see who they were, but he slowly drew his sword when he heard Lara curse.

The one with the crossbow walked toward them. From under his hood, his pale features became visible in the moonlight, which was just peeking through the clouds. The man had slender features and purple-coloured eyes that seemed centuries old. He focused on Carn when he was a few feet away and stated in an ancient accent. "We do not quarrel with you human. Stand aside so we can deal with this abomination."

Carn glanced at Lara, seeing her features full of disgust. Carn slowly stood in front of her and said, focusing on the two men. "Sorry, I can't do that."

Lara stepped forward. "Carn these are vampires. You won't stand a chance."

The vampire leader glared at the two and smiled without emotion. "Very true, human. You would be dead in moments. And why would you protect this *thing*?"

Carn snarled at him, standing his ground. "Well, that's my concern, not yours."

Lara stood beside Carn and sneered at the vampire. Her eyes lingered for a moment on the one waiting behind him. He was standing perfectly still, like he was awaiting orders. She focused on the leader once more. "We have caused nay issues. Why don't you let us be on our way?"

The vampire smiled and cocked his head to one side, studying Lara, his eyes looking her up and down. "I am surprised you survived the process. All have died."

Lara's lips curled in disgust. "Well, I'm unique."

The vampire pursed his lips, seeming not to even acknowledge she was talking. He looked at her and smiled. "So will you submit?"

Lara took a firm hold of her sword, slowly moving ahead of Carn. "Would you even listen to my response?"

The vampire sighed. "It seems not." He signalled with a wave of his hand and the other one behind him drew his sword.

Lara pushed Carn behind her and snapped, *"Run."*

Carn stepped back a little, giving Lara room, knowing he would not be able to match their speed or hers. Yet refused to leave her. The vampires advanced down the alleyway, but the one behind the leader jumped high, landing behind Carn, blocking his way out. Carn would have to fight this one, but with him having fought vampires before, he knew what to do. Yet this vampire was faster and a far better Sword. But the vampire was not fully fighting him, just making sure Carn did not escape or interfere.

Lara focused on the leader as he drew his sword. She quickly glanced back to see the other one was making sure Carn was busy. Lara turned back to the leader, remembering what Fashor had told her. These were not normal vampires and had centuries of training. Lara was faster, but it would not be an easy fight. Lara stood her ground, making the leader come to her. She wanted him to make the first move so she could get an idea of his fighting style.

The leader walked casually toward her as he passed his longsword from hand to hand in a cocky way, thinking he was superior to her. Lara pursed her lips. It may be his undoing; he thought she was like dirt under his foot, and not a skilled Sword. Once close enough, the vampire regarded her and took a firm grip on his hilt. Lara held hers, ready for anything. He made a move at lightning speed, his sword aimed at her neck. Lara counteracted by deflecting his sword and bending backwards to avoid his blade when he swung again. He raised an eyebrow, impressed with Lara's moves. But she was not going to wait, and attacked. He jumped back, but Lara was faster than he had anticipated. He hissed when the tip of her sword sliced across his lower chest. Lara gave him a sly smile, knowing he had not expected her to be that fast, or skilled. She kept a close eye on him as the vampire slowly circled her.

Lara envisioned the ash rune and murmured it under her breath. As she turned to keep facing the vampire, she glanced towards Carn to see him dealing with the other. It seemed both vampires, thinking they were superior, had not had to fight skilled Swords before. They would have only been dealing with vampires and other rogue demons who would turn and run, not ready to stand up and fight.

Lara parried another attack from the vampire leader and counterattacked. He deflected her moves, not letting her strike him again. Lara needed to act, as this would just continue till dawn. She went for him again, and then suddenly spun and jumped over him, landing with ease behind him. Before he could turn, Lara lunged, her sword digging deep into his midsection. The vampire cried out, drawing his companion's attention. Yet, Lara was already onto her next move. She went to strike his chest. The ash rune and silver blade would make a killing blow, but her blade ricocheted off metal. The vampire laughed. It seemed he was prepared for such a blow. He lunged at her. Lara spun out of the way, and then partly changed, making her features wolf-like. If she could not strike him in the chest, there were other ways. He went for her again, but Lara sidestepped and bit down on the vampire's neck. He cried out.

Lara snarled as she stepped back, turning back to human form. "That was a lycan bite. You will be dead in hours."

The leader cursed and swung at her with his sword, but his emotions clouded his judgement, and he missed. Suddenly his companion ran at Lara, but she was already prepared, her sword slicing the vampire's head clean off. As it fell to the ground, the head, and then the body turned to dust. Lara spun back to the leader, who was already feeling the effects of her bite. She glared at him and, in one swift move, sliced his head off. As he disintegrated to dust, Lara turned to Carn. He had a few cuts, but otherwise was unharmed.

He stated, as he sheathed his sword, "Think we best head out of here in case there are more."

They hurried back to the stables behind the inn and saddled their horses. Moments later, they were leaving Dark Cloud behind and heading south. It was better to camp out than stay in the town any longer, in case any other cleansers were around and came looking for their companions.

As they rode away from Dark Cloud, Lara focused on the contract. From the lack of evidence of anything untoward, the woman and her men had not ventured to the town, and had, more than likely, gone directly to the mountains to the south. That was where Alistari had stated the crystal had originated from. Lara wondered what the woman would do when there. *Would the crystal be stronger with it being close to its origin?* Maybe it was time to call on Eida, as they were going to need her help to destroy the thing.

Setting up camp near a small coppice of trees, while Carn made a fire, Lara found the stone to call on Eida. Lara sat cross-legged by the small campfire and clearly thought of the witch and what was needed. After a few moments, Lara could sense Eida. She had received the message. Placing the stone back in her saddlebag, Lara turned her attention to Carn and sighed.

He studied her and smiled. "How long for Eida to get here?"

"A few hours, then we can continue to the mountains."

Carn nodded and looked up at the sky. "Once this is done, where should we head?"

Lara shrugged. "Not sure. But I think we go to Dalimor, see what ships are there, and where they are heading." She studied him and added, "I know you haven't been here for long, but for me, it's time to move on."

"Aye, and as I have said, I'm not losing you again." He paused. "What about Derwyn?"

Lara smiled softly. "I haven't been that way in a while and would like to see him and his family before we leave."

"It would be good to see him, too."

"Then, as soon as this is all over, we'll travel to Warrior Sword. I think he'll be pleased to see you, too." She focused on the flames, thinking of her brother. It would be hard leaving the land where Derwyn had made his home, but that day would have come eventually. The attention she was getting from this contract was just moving things forward.

CHAPTER 18

LARA WAS GAZING at the predawn, red sky from where she sat near the smouldering fire. There was a sudden flash of light and a portal opened near the camp as a light breeze carried Eida's scent her way. Lara leaned over to Carn, where he slept beside her, waking him up gently. Then turned her attention to the witch as she walked over.

Eida smiled warmly. "Good morn."

Carn nodded a greeting as he stretched his stiff limbs, yawning.

Lara stated, "Glad you could find us."

The witch sat down opposite them both; she glanced around at the open plain. "This is very deserted." She studied them. "It surprised me you weren't staying in the town."

Lara shook her head, looking north. "Not the most welcoming of places."

Eida sighed. "Aye, this entire island isn't the most welcoming. Gor to the north is the most civilised here. But once you get south of the Black Mountains, it's even more challenging."

Carn asked, thinking about his theory when they arrived. "Do you think it's anything to do with where the crystal originated from?"

"Aye," Eida said, looking south towards the mountains. "I can sense the evil from here."

Looking to the south, Lara had to agree. She had sensed it for the past few days, the draw of it becoming stronger the closer they came to the mountains. With her heightened senses from being a hybrid, Lara wondered if she was just more attuned to it. It seemed to even seep down into her bones. She would be more than glad once she destroyed the crystal.

Lara turned to Eida when she asked, "So, what's the plan?"

Lara glanced across at Carn as he took his packed things across to the horses. She rolled to her knees and rolled up her sleeping blanket. "Not sure yet. I want to see what we're going to be facing. The primary plan is, with your help, to destroy that crystal for good."

Eida responded, "I have what I need, but will have to borrow some of your magical properties, Lara, to fulfil it."

Lara raised an eyebrow. "How will you take them?"

"Just from my touch." She gazed across at the mountains. "But that isn't what's concerning me. My instincts feel that whatever we face will be a challenge. We all need to be on our guard."

Carn regarded the two women as he saddled Lara's horse. "Well, my sword is ready."

The two nodded and Eida said, "And it will be needed. I do not know how much control the woman will have over the crystal. She may conjure creatures or only be able to use the power of illusion. But she has been exposed to it for some time, and am fearing the worst."

Lara took a deep breath and placed her packed things on her horse. "Then we will be ready."

Leaving the camp behind, they rode slowly south towards the mountains. Carn let Eida ride his horse while he walked alongside. Lara asked as they all looked ahead. "Eida, what will you need once we have the crystal?"

The witch glanced at them both and said, "I must recite a couple of spells. I found, in one of my books, what I need. One spell should destroy the crystal and that will release the power within. Once it's free, I need to contain it and then destroy that too, with the second spell." She glanced at Lara. "That will be when I need those magical properties that you possess."

"Will it be enough to help?"

"Aye, I think it will be. You are a mystical creature, and even though you can't create spells, you still hold a lot of magic within you. It should be enough to boost my powers."

"So, what Carn and I need to do is ensure we have dealt with all other obstacles before we focus on the spells?"

"Aye. We'll both be exhausted once I have cast the spell." She looked down at Carn as he walked beside Lara's horse. "We'll need you to protect us and be ready in case there are any unforeseen issues."

Carn nodded. "I'll protect you both, if needs be."

Lara stated, "Hopefully, most will have been dealt with before then."

Eida asked, "What will you tell Malaki?

Lara sighed. "I haven't thought that far ahead yet. I know he won't be happy, but this crystal can't be in anyone's possession."

Carn agreed and Eida said, "I agree as well. It's too powerful. What we saw at Bighdarum was horrible, but in the hands of someone who could control it, the devastation would be unimaginable. And like I told you before, I just don't trust Malaki."

"Then we will ensure it doesn't fall into his hands," stated Lara with determination in her voice.

They reached the base of the mountains after about three days. Lara pointed towards some shrubs, where they would get some shelter from the cool night air when they camped. She glanced around at the dry rocky plains, realising she would need to ensure she was at full strength with what lay ahead. In the dusk light, Lara could sense wildlife to the west and could find a good couple of small animals to eat, as well as bring back a couple for Eida and Carn.

Lara turned to the two. "I need to hunt."

Carn smiled, and studied her with a loving gaze as Lara stripped.

Eida responded, "Hard to believe you are a lycan and vampire."

Lara placed her clothes on one side. "I won't be gone long, but need to make sure I have hunted before we venture any further." She paused. "I will bring something back for both of you to cook, too."

"Understood." Eida smiled.

Lara kissed Carn and then turned into her wolf form, trotting off into the night. Venturing off into the shrubland, Lara found a rabbit and a couple of other vermin to keep her vampire side at bay.

As Lara trotted back, with a fresh kill for Carn and Eida, she surveyed the mountains ahead and ventured closer to see what they would be facing. Keeping to the shadows and moving further into the mountains, she found the main path. It was not passable by horse, so they would have to be left where they were camping, but otherwise, it looked like a good, clear route. Setting down the rabbit, she took a few deep breaths, taking in the scents. She picked up the group; they had come this way, only a few days earlier. Trotting carefully down the uneven path, and keeping out of sight, she soon made out a cave entrance in the distance. That was where the group had gone. She looked around, yet could not see anyone on watch, but she could sense a lot of magic. That was something for Eida to deal with. Picking up the rabbit, Lara ran back to camp to tell Carn and the witch what she had found.

In the dawn light, Eida regarded the cave ahead of them and glanced at Lara and Carn as they all kept out of sight. "Aye, there's a trap. A magical tripwire, near the entrance. As soon as we pass through, they will be alerted, and something may attack us."

Lara asked, "So, how do we get past it?"

Eida smiled. "Now that I know they are there, it's a simple spell to deactivate them."

They moved as quickly and as quietly as they could to the cave entrance. Lara and Carn kept watch while Eida deactivated the trap. Once done, they continued inside. The cave was dark and damp, but Lara could see with ease and saw some lanterns ahead. She could also make out distant voices, which sounded like they were reciting a spell. Lara turned to the two and whispered, "They are chanting something, deep in the cave."

Eida nodded, straining to hear. "I keep forgetting you have those wolf ears. We best hurry as they may be trying to access the full power of the crystal."

The three picked up their pace. Eida stopped them whenever she sensed a trap as they ventured further into the cave. As they got closer, the chanting became more evident. Eida looked at Lara, concern in her eyes. "We need to stop them."

Lara pulled her sword free. "Best find a vantage point before we deal with them."

The witch gave a quick nod and went to find a safe position. Lara and Carn turned their attention to the sound of the group ahead and walked carefully towards the cavern where the group was located. When they reached the entrance, they could see five men standing in a circle, the woman in the centre holding the crystal in the air, which was glowing from the spell.

Lara inspected the enormous cavern. There was mining equipment scattered around. They were where the crystal must have been found. Looking closely, she could also make out the mummified remains of the miners who had probably discovered it. Something dreadful had happened, and they did not survive. *How did the crystal even get out of the mountain. Had someone survived? Well, at least long enough to get it out of here, or had it remained here for some time before it was discovered?* Looking around the cavern, it seemed like it had not been touched since the initial discovery. From the magic Lara was sensing, the crystal was getting stronger by being at its source.

Lara turned her attention back to the circle. From experience, they needed to break it, as at least then it would slow the spell down. The group were all focused on the task at hand, giving Lara and Carn the element of surprise.

After assessing the situation, she sheathed her sword and then pulled her dagger free. It would be better to kill at least two without being detected. They had to act now before it was too late. She glanced at Carn, who nodded; he was ready to go, pulling his own dagger from its sheath. Lara focused on one of the larger men. Creeping up behind, she slit his throat. Carn doing the same with the one next to him. When they fell to the floor dead, the spell instantly broke.

The woman who was standing in the centre turned when the crystal stopped glowing. Her lips curled in distaste when she focused on Lara and Carn. The woman's features were gaunt, her eyes as black as night. It had to be from the extended exposure to the crystal. Then the remaining men turned towards them, all with similar features, almost looking like the dead were walking. They all lunged toward Lara and Carn, the woman moving back, letting her men protect her, as she muttered a spell. Lara threw her dagger at the men, hitting one in the leg. As soon as she threw the dagger, she pulled her sword free, ready for the counterattack. Carn was ready beside her, having done a similar action, with his dagger finding the shoulder of another.

The men were powerful, seemingly undeterred by the daggers finding their marks. Yet none could have anticipated the skills of the two Swords. Lara parried with one man, then rolled out of the way of the second. Meanwhile, Carn matched blow for blow of the third. The man was fast and skilled, but still no match against Carn. He glanced at the one Lara had dodged, Lara in a full fight with the other. All three men were seasoned warriors and fast on their feet. His attention turned back to the one he was fighting, just in time to dodge a dirty blow from the side, and swung his sword round to make a fatal blow. But a sword swung down on his. Carn looked up to see the man Lara had dodged had turned his attention to him. The Sword sneered and kicked the enchanted man away. The man recovered quickly and soon they were fighting, the blades of their swords clashing.

Lara landed a kick to the man she was fighting as he tried to strike. She looked over to the woman who was keeping to the back of the cavern, letting her men do all the work. Lara took a breath and stood her ground, waiting for the one to come at her again. She glanced to see Carn dealing with the other, both matching the other's moves. Lara parried and dodged her attacker's strikes with ease. Spinning around, she sliced his head clean off. She turned to see if Carn needed help, but he had just delivered the fatal blow to his attacker. The third man rushed to attack Carn, Lara grabbed her dagger out of the dead man's leg and threw it. Her aim was true and the blade sunk into the man's skull, right between the eyes.

When Lara heard a roar, she turned her attention to the back of the cavern. A portal had opened behind the cadaverous-looking woman and a large demonic creature stepped out. It was huge. It had two large, curled horns on the side of its head, and the humanoid demon's arms and legs had long, vicious claws. Its skin was black with red cracks, like that of hot lava. Its black, lifeless eyes focused on her. Lara's widened in fear.

She turned back to Carn; they would both need to deal with the creature. Then Lara frowned, seeing Carn suddenly stop dead in his tracks. His eyes focused on something, but not the creature behind her. He whispered, "Iesha?"

Carn made the fatal blow on the possessed man attacking him. He could tell he had been a seasoned warrior, but under the influence of the crystal spell, the man seemed twice as strong. Carn rotated his aching shoulder, turning to Lara, ready to deal with the woman and the crystal. But then he saw a portal opening behind her with a roar. Lara turned to look. Carn swallowed. Something was about to step out. Yet, as he focused on Lara, his vision blurred. Carn shook his head, feeling fuzzy, and then Lara vanished. In her place stood Isabel. She was covered in blood, her arms outstretched, holding the tiny dead body of Iesha, the umbilical cord still attached to her. She was crying out his name. Carn felt his throat tighten, his stomach dropped in reaction. He whispered his daughter's name in shock. Then, like a wave, all his memories, and the misery of that night came flooding back. Carn dropped his sword and clamped his hands to his head, trying to stop the pain. In the back of his mind, he could sense it was just an illusion from the crystal, but he could not focus. His mind flooded with emotions that he could not control. The fresh smell of blood invaded Carn's nostrils. It mixed with the smoke from the fireplace, and the melting wax of the candles in the room of the farmhouse on that fateful night. He could even smell Isabel's fragrance. Lilies. She always wore that scent when he saw her at the inn. All he could hear was Isabel crying out to him. Carn clawed at his head, trying to stop her screaming voice, telling him it was all his fault.

Before Lara could acknowledge Carn was being tricked by a vision, pain suddenly shot through her head, like someone had stabbed her through her temple with a dagger, making Lara cry out. Confused, she turned and focused on the woman who was mumbling a spell, her cold eyes focused on her. Lara felt dazed as the sensation shot through her head again, her ears buzzing. Then she focused on the creature as it moved slowly toward her. Lara had to stop it from killing her and the others. She took a few breaths, taking a firm hold of her sword. She dodged the creature, but the lancing pain tore through her. Lara cried out, staggering to the side. Then the creature lunged again. Lara was not quick enough, yet the creature's claws passed right through her, like mist. It was an illusion, just something to try to make them run. Yet before she could say anything, more agony burned through her. She could faintly hear Eida shouting to run. Lara turned towards the witch to tell her it was a trick, but her head throbbed even more. Lara cried out again, dropping her sword as the torment increased. She clamped her hands over her head, then fell to her knees, the pain resonating through her body. Lara bit her lip. She had to get control, but it was just too much. Lara tried to focus on Carn as he fell to his knees crying out, his face contorted with emotions. His hands clamped over his ears like he was trying to stop some excruciating sound.

Eida ran into the cavern from where she was waiting and froze when she saw the creature emerge from behind the woman. She turned to Carn, and wondered why was he was not moving, he needed to fight. Eida turned to Lara when she cried out as she tried to fight a creature. She backed away from the large, horned demon, fear in her eyes. She shouted at Lara to run, but she was in no condition to hear her. Eida turned her attention back to the creature. She needed to figure out how to deal with that, as well as free Carn and Lara. The magic in the air from the crystal was suffocating. She turned to the creature; she would have to daze it long enough to help the others. Then the creature walked straight through Lara like it was mist. Eida focused on it, looking at the creature more closely, and saw a shimmer. It was an illusion! The witch looked at Carn, who had his hands on his head, his features full of suffering and distress. She then quickly looked at Lara when she cried out again. Then her eyes focused on the woman. The crystal was channelling through her, allowing her to create the apparitions. But Eida could not face her alone. She needed help. The witch had to act fast; she turned to Carn as he was the closest.

Lara watched Eida as she mumbled something, focusing on Carn. Lara crumpled on her side as pain burned through her and looked up, seeing the creature walking slowly towards Eida. But the witch ignored it, she must have realised it was just an illusion. Lara knew Eida needed to break the spell on her and Carn. She turned towards the woman at the back of the cave. Ignoring the pain, she struggled to her feet. Lara had to stop the woman and the crystal so Eida could help Carn. Yet, when Lara went to move, she was stuck on the spot, her feet locked in place. Then pure agony hit her again, this time in her gut. As Lara folded over, she saw a look of satisfaction on the woman's gaunt face. Lara frowned, then gasped in pain, wondering what was happening to her, and how the woman was doing it.

Suddenly, Carn snapped out of the vision, and the torture stopped. His wife and child, and the creature had gone. He could see Lara again, but she was crying out in pain, doubled over in agony. He picked up his sword and ran to her, grabbing her arm. "Lara! The spell is trying to take over . . ." He did not finish as Lara cried out again. When he focused on her features, he saw the edges of her eyes turning red as the vampire side tried to take hold.

Then, as suddenly as it had stopped, the suffering and anguish of that night came flooding back to Carn. He dropped his sword again, clamping his head as it pounded with pain. His vision blurred and Isabel was there once more, her body torn open with blood everywhere. He dropped to his knees, the torment more intense this second time, as his grief from that night overpowered him.

Lara cried out as an intense stabbing sensation burned through her body. She could not make out what Carn was saying, but she saw fear in his eyes. Eida was chanting something, fully focused on the woman once more. Lara fell to her knees, and could feel her body fighting. She realised the woman was trying to control the vampire side of her, but Lara's lycan side was fighting back, hence the pure agony ripping through her body. She could not take much more, it had to stop before it was too late. Lara forced herself to move, almost crawling towards the woman, who continued to mumble something. Lara stopped her body from convulsing as the pain increased.

Then Lara felt a warm hand on her back. She turned slightly and saw Eida kneeling next to her, quietly chanting; the throes easing, and Lara was getting control over her body. Eida had broken the spell keeping Lara frozen in place. Then the woman moved towards the centre of the cave, she was going to attack Eida to stop her. Lara turned towards Carn to see him on his knees, holding his head. His eyes were closed as he cried, trying to not let the visions take over again. Eida could not help him as she concentrated on helping Lara. There was only one thing she could do. Change.

There was no time to strip. Lara needed to be in her lycan form as quickly as possible. Then she could protect Eida and Carn, and hopefully stop the spell in its tracks. She quickly unbuckled her scabbard and her belt, as the leather would not give. As they dropped to the floor, she changed. The material of her clothes ripped apart as Lara turned. She pulled as much off as she could in the transition, but she had to be fast. Over the years, she realised her body could change quicker than any lycan or werewolf. Moments later, torn clothes at her feet, Lara was in her wolf form. She glanced at Eida, who nodded. She looked across at Carn, who was holding his head, crying out in pain. Lara knew what she had to do.

She ran at the woman and jumped. The woman tried to deflect Lara with a spell. Eida already was counteracting, and a beam of light shot from her hand, pushing the woman back. As Lara crashed into the woman, the crystal dropped from her hand. The two fell to the ground with Lara on top.

Lara was about to make a fatal bite when she paused, seeing the woman's features. They were drawn and pale, but with the crystal out of her grasp, her eyes had returned to normal and were full of tears and fear. The woman whispered with emotion, "Kill . . . me."

Lara stared at her and grunted. The woman was fighting to resist the control of the crystal. "Malaki . . . he . . . tricked us. Please . . . end it."

Lara turned to Eida when she shouted, still trying to help Carn. "Quick, before it takes back control!"

Lara looked back at the woman, seeing her features begging her to end her torture. Lara nodded her head and bit deep into her neck, snapping it. The woman's features mirrored relief as she took her final breath. Lara stepped back and looked at the body, then turned to Eida and Carn. The Sword's misery instantly stopped with the spell broken, but still looked dazed. The witch, gasping, walked up to her. "If this is your strongest form, stay as you are."

Lara growled softly. Eida turned her attention to the crystal laying on the ground nearby. She took a firm hold of Lara's strong wolf's neck, and began chanting.

Lara could feel the magic flowing through her. At first, it was ecstatic, but then she felt it being forcefully pulled from her, taking her vitality. She looked at Eida who also seemed to be in pain. Then a bright light burst from her hand again and shot at the crystal. As her energy waned, Lara watched the crystal slowly begin to crack, and then it snapped in two like an old, dry twig. Eida stopped chanting, and the sensation of her wolf magic being drained stopped.

Then a grey mist slowly swirled from the crystal. As it moved upwards, the crystal turned clear and the air in the cavern became cold. From the mist emanated a faint, but chilling, laughter, and whispering voices. All three were unnerved by the evil presence that had escaped from the crystal.

Eida turned to Lara. "Now the hard bit."

The witch took a breath and began chanting again. She directed the ray of light on the mist. The fog tried to flee, like it had a mind of its own, the voices coming from it cried out, and cursed in pain. But the light from Eida's hand engulfed it, stopping it from escaping. Lara felt her energy diminishing, this time faster. The light grew brighter, almost filling the entire cavern. Lara suddenly felt weak, unable to stand. As Eida continued to chant, her voice sounded strained and grew hoarse. Lara felt herself changing back to human form. She was too weak to stop it. She convulsed as the light became a big burst of brightness and then vanished. Moments later, Lara and Eida lost consciousness.

CHAPTER 19

WHEN LARA REGAINED consciousness, pain was radiating from all her limbs. She tried to focus on the cave ceiling, her naked body shivering. Her head throbbed and her mouth was dry. She struggled to sit up, her body burning in pain at the movement. She murmured, "Carn?"

A faint voice said, "He's gone to check there are nay others in the mine. He'll be back soon." Lara cradled her head, feeling dizzy, as she tried to push herself up with her elbow. The person added. "It will take you time to regain your strength."

Lara turned towards the voice to see an old lady sitting next to her. Then, as she looked closely, she realised who it was. "Eida?"

She slowly nodded, then looked down, showing her black hair streaked with grey. "Aye."

Lara turned her attention to her as she struggled to sit. "What happened to you?"

She smiled softly. "The spell needed more than I had anticipated."

Lara gently touched Eida's withered face. "This was too much."

"But it was a sacrifice worth taking. The evil power has gone."

"Why didn't you take more from me? I would have been alright."

She shook her head. "You would have died, and I couldn't have that. I knew the risks, and I had to take them. I couldn't ask you to."

Lara sighed. "Aye, I could've."

Eida's withered hand gently stroked Lara's cheek. "To let such beauty die? I simply couldn't do that."

Lara studied her and kissed her gently on the cheek. "This land will shine less without you, Eida."

The witch chuckled. "I knew there was a spark there between us."

Lara smiled, then started shivering again. Eida pulled off her jerkin, struggling slightly from her now arthritic limbs. "Here."

Lara placed it over her naked shoulders and looked back at the shattered crystal on the cavern floor, then at the body of the woman. "She said something just before she died."

Eida asked softly. "What?"

"Malaki tricked us." Lara turned to Eida. "She begged me to kill her."

Eida sighed and glanced over at the woman's body. "The crystal had taken control of her. Her will, nay longer her own." She paused. "I think Malaki knew that."

Lara responded. "Hence the trick."

"I knew he couldn't be trusted. I think he arranged for her to come here so she could get the full power of the crystal. Then he planned to somehow take it back. Either by pulling the power from her, once he knew how it worked, or taking control of her."

"But how? The crystal's power would be too strong. Look what it's done to you for destroying it."

"Aye." nodded Eida, looking down at her withered hands. "But to control it would be far easier than destroying it, as it wanted to live. Knowing Malaki, he would have wanted to harness the power, but without him losing his control. I think he would have used the woman as a vessel, and kept her secured in his tower."

Lara sighed, pulling her knees up to her chest when she shivered once more from the dampness of the cavern. She gazed across at the body. "A fate worse than death. I know now why she wanted me to kill her."

"Malaki sees only power, not suffering, or freedom."

Lara glanced at the witch and crinkled her nose. "And I slept with him."

Eida raised an eyebrow and chuckled. "So did I. And I don't like men!"

Lara sighed and studied the witch. "It seems this isn't over until I deal with Malaki." She regarded Eida with concern. "This is something you will have to remain out of. I need to get you home, and then I will face him."

"Aye. I think my travelling days are behind me now." She paused for a moment. "Can you help an old woman up?"

Lara nodded, feeling her energy beginning to return. She slowly got to her feet and helped Eida to hers just as Carn re-entered the cavern.

He ran over to Lara, taking her in his arms and kissing her. "I was so worried about you."

Eida nodded and smirked. "Aye, he was. That's why I told him to check the mine. He was getting annoying. He wouldn't stop pacing."

Carn glanced at her. "Even when I was concerned about you?"

The witch squeezed his arm. "Nay, I welcomed your concern." She gave him a sly smile. "But you were impatient, and giving me a headache."

Carn sighed and kept his arms around Lara, not wanting to let her go.

Lara kissed him gently, savouring his warmth from the chill she still felt. She said to Carn. "We were discussing Malaki and how he tricked the woman. She wanted me to kill her."

He looked across at the body. "She was a pawn in his big plan? Poor woman."

Both nodded, and the witch stated, "I have something in my pack that will help you against any spells when you face Malaki."

"You had it with you?" asked Lara.

"Aye, just in case."

Lara studied the witch. Eida had known from the start that this had been a one-way trip for her. Lara sighed; that was something she had not wanted to happen. If she had known, she would have done it without Eida, and even Carn. But without the witch's power, they would not have defeated the evil trapped inside the crystal. Lara just wished Eida had told her all the risks.

Eida hobbled over near the entrance to the cavern. She sat down heavily and rummaged in her pack. She pulled out a simple pewter ring and turned to Lara. "Here. I placed a protection spell on it."

Lara looked at her. "Wouldn't this have been useful earlier?"

Eida looked a little guilty. "Aye, maybe so. But I would have been unable to pull from your magic when doing the spell to destroy the crystal."

Lara nodded and placed the ring on her left index finger. "Understood."

Eida glanced at Carn. "Sorry, but I only had enough to make the one. I suggest when Lara faces Malaki, you stay out of sight till needed."

Carn nodded, looking at the witch with concern.

Lara gazed back at the bodies and then at the two. "We should head back," she studied the witch. "Do you need to rest?"

The old witch regarded her. "I should be alright for now, but we will need to take it slow."

"Once back at the camp, you'll ride one of the horses."

Eida nodded. Lara turned to the bodies of the men nearby and pulled a shirt off one of them. As she put on the shirt that was like a tunic on her, she realised she would need boots. Lara turned back to the bodies. The men would be too big, so she went over to the body of the woman and pulled her boots off. She checked them against her feet, seeing it would not be a perfect fit, but would do for now. Lara pulled them on, then walked back over to Eida and Carn, picking up her belt, scabbard, and sword on the way. Once back at the camp, she could change into some of her spare clothes.

Leaving the cave behind, they made the slow walk back to camp, where the horses were still secured and waiting. As the group rested for the night, Lara meditated, focusing on her wolf self. Her strength was returning, and from what she felt, her alter ego would soon be back to her old self in a day or two. But she innately knew that it would not be wise to transform for a few days, not until she was back to full strength.

They rode to Dark Cloud in the morning, after a good night's sleep. Even with Carn and Lara sharing a horse, it took longer with Eida needing to rest more often. They reached the town after a few days, but Lara was reluctant to stay the night at an inn after what had happened with the cleansers. But Carn insisted, as Eida needed to rest, and a night inside, with a bed would do them all some good. Lara's energy was nearly restored by the time they reached Dark Cloud, but Eida's would never recover. She put on a brave face, but Lara could sense she was struggling. The spell had been at too high a cost.

The three sat at the back of a quiet inn while Eida and Carn ate a hearty meal and Lara nursed a strong drink. She watched the inn closely, her senses on alert.

Carn looked up at her from his stew and said, "Relax."

Lara glanced at him. "I would, but with the knowledge of cleansers being around here, I won't be able to."

The witch asked, "Have you come across them before?"

"I crossed paths with them once, then here. And hope never to again."

"But you dealt with them, as you are an excellent swordswoman," stated Eida.

Lara smiled. "Thank you, but they are known for being exceptional. The vampires make them train hard before they become part of the elite group where they remain a cleanser for centuries, honing their skills. They are ruthless and will kill anything in their way. We were both lucky then. I'm not sure what the case would be if we met any again, especially now."

Carn agreed. "They were hard to fight, and the gods Laycain and Rosh were in our favour. But agree with Lara; we don't want to cross them again so soon."

Eida smiled. "So, you are concerned about my welfare? Don't worry about me. I may be old, but I can still feel the power within me." She looked around. "How certain are you that there will be more here? They may be just in small groups."

"True, but I still don't want to hang around to find out." She studied Eida. "You're still weak. We'll stay tonight, and we can get going at dawn. I'll need to hunt as soon as we leave here."

"Alright."

Lara added. "But when we reach the ferry crossing, we may have to swim."

Carn added. "Nay. Eida, you can ride the horse, and I will guide you across. Although it pains to admit, Lara is more than capable to cross on her own."

Eida sighed. "I forgot about that." She looked at Carn and smiled. "Thank you."

Lara took a sip of her drink. "The ferry will eventually get repaired as it's a well-used route, but I don't think it will be by the time we get there."

The witch finished her stew. "We'll just have to wait and see." She smiled at Lara and Carn. "Knowing these lands, it's probably being worked on as we speak."

Lara shrugged and finished her drink. It would be good if it were, as it would make the journey easier. Yet Lara was just taking it one day at a time. Once Eida was back home, Lara would sort out a plan to deal with Malaki with Carn's help.

CHAPTER 20

THEY REACHED THE ferry crossing after a few days' ride. They had taken it slowly, as Eida's joints had been aching since they arrived at Dark Cloud. Carn and Lara had again shared the other horse, but with it carrying two, they could not go as fast as they wanted to. But then, with the crystal destroyed, they did not have to worry about time as much as before.

As they got closer to the area of the ferry dock, they noticed a lot of activity. It seemed Eida had been right. Travellers had come to the ferry crossing and, with the help of local farmers, were trying to fix it. Lara nodded to the men and looked across at the far side to see some horses eating the grass gleefully and others harnessed up to help the men in pulling the ferry back upstream. Lara helped Eida down so she could rest. Then Lara and Carn volunteered their services and their horses to finish getting the ferry up and running again. They needed strong swimmers to recover the chain. Lara and Carn were strong enough, and knew they could get the job done. Lara had the big advantage of being able to stay underwater for an extraordinary length of time. In truth, she could stay under indefinitely, but to the people she was helping, and with Carn's convincing acting, they just thought she was an excellent diver and nothing more. By sunset, they had the chain reconnected to the ferry, and the crossing was up and running once more.

Lara, Carn, and Eida were the first to cross and made plans to camp on the other side. With some explanation and coin, Carn was able to acquire an extra horse and then settled down at the camp with Eida and Lara. The others set camps up on the far side of the river, as most were heading towards Dark Cloud, not away.

Lara glanced at the distant fires and turned back to Eida. "Will you be able to manage the rest of the journey?"

The witch studied Lara and Carn, who sat on the opposite side of the fire from her. "Aye, don't worry about me. I'm stronger than I look. I have recovered most of my strength now." She sighed. "Alas, not my youthful appearance."

Carn smiled softly, studying Eida's aged features. "Sorry this quest was at a cost."

"Don't be. And this." Eida pointed at her face. "Is still preferable to having that dark magic free in the world."

Lara smiled. "That is true."

Carn looked up at the clear sky. "You both should get some rest. I'll take the first watch."

Eida nodded and settled down for the night. Lara turned to Carn as they sat by the fire and snuggled up to him. He curled his arm around her and said, "So you won't fall asleep on me this time?"

Lara glanced up at him. "Sorry, nay. With Eida taking that magic from me, it drained me more than I had thought."

He kissed her softly on her head. "I was worried when you were unconscious in the cavern. I just wished I hadn't succumbed to the visions."

Lara smiled, looking up at him. She was curious to know the full story since visiting the cavern. "What happened to you? I heard you whisper your daughter's name."

Carn sighed. "When we had dealt with the men, I suddenly had a pain in my head. Then, instead of seeing you, all I could see was Isabel holding Iesha. I couldn't believe it. I felt all the grief and misery again after their deaths. She stood there with Iesha, their bodies covered in blood. She was screaming at me, saying horrible things, things I had thought myself. Eida broke the spell for a moment, and everything just vanished. But then when you went down, she had to help you. The visions, and the agony, came back and had to force myself to concentrate. But if you hadn't broken free of that spell and dealt with the crystal, I don't know what would have happened. I was so overcome with grief, I couldn't focus."

Lara kissed him gently. "They warned us that that could happen. But even prepared, it was something we hadn't truly anticipated."

Carn studied her and gently brushed a stray hair from her face. "We made it. That's what counts."

Lara nodded and looked across the grassland towards the mountains in the distance. She took a deep breath and wondered where they would head next once the contract was complete. She poked the fire with a stick and pursed her lips. "We still have to deal with Malaki."

Carn agreed. "Do you want to have a visit with Alistari first, see if he will stand with us?"

Lara looked up at him. "I don't even know if he can be trusted."

"Aye, I understand. The whole golem thing, and what you told me about him wanting to study you . . . it's a little unsettling."

"Aye, it was. I think we go directly to Malaki and face him. Since Eida only made the one talisman, I'll go in. But having someone on the lookout will be helpful, just in case."

Carn smiled and kissed her. "I know you can manage yourself against Malaki, but will be there if you need me. Do you think he knows what has happened?"

Lara shrugged. "I don't know. It's a risk we'll have to take."

Carn kissed her again. His arms curled further around her. "Well, we'll face it together."

Lara smiled, looking up at him, seeing how tired his features were. She suddenly realised with her being so exhausted on the ride to Dark Cloud, he had stayed awake to be on watch longer than he should have been. "Do you want to rest?"

Carn smiled softly. "Let's just stay like this a little longer."

They sat in silence for a while, savouring each other's embrace. Lara looked up at him, seeing his eyes becoming droopy. He was tired, and now he was older, he would feel it more, but just did not want to admit it. She rested her head on his chest, listening to his heartbeat and breathing as it slowed, sleep pulling at him. Carn was resting for the first time in days after she felt his weight on her. She smiled softly, savouring this moment of peace and Carn's embrace. They had fought well together, and they would be there for each other for many years to come.

They reached Eida's small cottage, which was just north of Bighdarum, after a few days. The witch looked relieved to finally be home. Lara ensured all was well with her, while Carn stabled one horse. Then Lara and Carn continued to the mining town, where they would get a good night's sleep at an inn before continuing to Great Moor.

The townspeople had accomplished a lot of rebuilding in such a short time, surprising them as they rode into Bighdarum. It did not look at all like the town had been on the brink of being wiped from existence. The only evidence there had been any demon activity was the stalls selling Quetzal and Kanfor souvenirs. Lara shook her head, not too surprised at the way the town was making a profit from their misadventure. They rode to Bamur's Inn, fastening the horses up outside, and the two wandered in to find the dwarf. Once inside, they spotted him giving orders at the bar.

They walked up to him, Lara patting him on the back, while Carn ordered drinks and food. "Good to see you again."

The dwarf turned to look up at her. "Lara!" He smiled broadly, hugging her. When he realised they were getting too much attention, he quickly pulled back. He coughed, looking a little awkward. "I hadn't expected to see ya both again this way. So did ya succeed?"

Lara smiled, knowing how the dwarf hated anyone to know he had a softer side. "Aye. We're heading to Great Moor to complete the contract."

"Hope he pays up."

Lara chuckled. Bamur did not need to know the full story and, for his safety, it was probably for the best. "We will see." She turned to Carn when he passed her a drink and indicated he was going to find a table. She nodded and said to Bamur, "Anyway, I see you have rebuilt most of the town already."

"Aye, that we have. It'll take a while to get up to full mining capacity, with the loss of men, but we'll get there, or me name isn't Bamur!"

Lara smiled and nodded. "If anyone can get a town back up and running again, it would be you."

The dwarf chuckled. He looked up when his name was called by someone entering the inn. "Well, duty calls, lass. Ya can have one of me best rooms."

Lara watched the dwarf walk out of the inn, barking orders as he went. She strolled over and found Carn at a table near the back. He was fussing over his wolf. When the animal saw Bamur leave, she trotted off to follow him. Carn watched the wolf go, looking a little sad but also happy, and then took a sip of his ale. Lara sat by him and decided not to say anything. She relaxed, taking a sip of her drink, then closed her eyes and focused on her wolf.

When she was done, she glanced at Carn just as he sat back, having devoured his meal, and took a sip of his ale.

He said, looking around the inn before focusing on her, "It seems we're the talk of the inn."

Lara looked around the room for the first time, without making it too obvious. Everyone was talking amongst themselves, and looking across at them both every now and then. Lara sighed. "This isn't what I need." She looked at Carn and added, "Think it may be time to go to our room."

Carn raised an eyebrow and gulped down his ale. He then gave her a sly smile and winked. Lara grabbed his hand as he stood. Collecting their belongings, they ventured up to their room.

They lay in each other's arms, having made love, their naked limbs entwined. Lara's head rested on Carn's chest, listening to his heartbeat.

"Where do you want to go once the contract is done?" Carn asked softly.

Lara replied, her fingers caressing his firm chest. "Warrior Sword. I want to see Derwyn before we leave."

"So, we are leaving?"

Lara pushed herself up on her elbow to focus on his blue eyes. "Aye. I think it is time."

"I agree. Just from the attention here, I can sense you're uncomfortable with it."

Lara smirked. "I also think with that run-in with the cleansers, I don't want to push my luck. I think we stay at Warrior Sword for a few days and then travel to Dalimor. They have a large port with ships sailing out far and wide. We are both excellent Swords and could easily get work elsewhere."

Carn smiled, lost in the depths of her green eyes. "Aye, that's where I landed." He paused, studying her features, and added, "I'll follow you to the end of this world. So, wherever you go, I will follow."

Lara kissed him gently and said, "The same. Together, we can face anything."

He pulled her close and took a deep breath, burying his head in her hair, and kissed her. After a few moments, he pulled back and said, "There's so much out there to explore. We'll never see it all in my lifetime, but I know in yours, you will."

Lara gazed at him lovingly. "Let's not think about that. I want to live my life with you."

He nodded, focusing on her eyes. He could sense Lara did not want to talk about it, but she was immortal. He was not. She would be on Zentos for hundreds of years, maybe even more. Yet, after the events in the cavern, and seeing Isabel's and Iesha's deaths again, he realised he wanted Lara to always be happy. After he was gone, he wanted her to live. Maybe it was not the time to talk about it, but Carn could not help thinking about it. Knowing, in the grand scheme of it all, that his life would be far shorter than Lara's would ever be. They would live together to the fullest. But he wanted to make sure Lara did not stop once he was gone. He pulled her into his arms again and savoured the embrace. He would, and had, always loved her. Isabel, he had loved deeply, but with Lara, it was more. He could sense that their connection was deeper, and their paths were always meant to cross. Since finding Lara again, all he could think about was being with her. He closed his eyes, feeling Lara, savouring their embrace, and soon they were fast asleep in each other's arms.

CHAPTER 21

WITHIN A FEW days, they reached Great Moor and rode to the inn where they had reunited all those weeks before. As they rode, both agreed on what to do. The plan was for Lara to face Malaki as soon as possible, as they were uncertain if he would know what had happened, and it was not worth the risk of waiting to find out. They would leave their horses and belongings at the inn and head straight over to the sorcerer's tower. If he was aware of what had happened to the crystal, it was best to face him head-on; before he realised they were in town. As otherwise, he would be able to either escape, or take them by surprise. They were also counting on the fact that Carn had not joined Lara till after she had met with Malaki, he would be her secret backup, if needed. Once their horses were secure in the stable, and their bags stored in a room, they walked across town towards Malaki's residence.

Lara looked up at the tower. She pursed her lips; it seemed too quiet, and her instincts were telling her to be on alert in case there were magical traps. She looked towards the far side and noticed an old brown mare chomping on the lush grass. Somehow, she knew it did not belong to Malaki. She turned to Carn indicating to the horse and said, "Think he may have company."

Carn responded, looking up at the tower. "Do you still want to go with our plan?"

Lara nodded. "Aye, but be alert."

He watched as she walked up to the door, and when she was about to knock, it opened of its own accord. Lara took a bracing breath. The sorcerer was expecting her. She looked back at Carn, his body tense, but stayed where he was, watching. Entering the tower cautiously, Lara inhaled deeply, picking up Malaki's scent and that of Alistari. Then she heard an argument upstairs, and briefly wondered if Alistari could be counted as being on her side.

Lara took the steps up to the study carefully. Her hand itched to take a grip of her sword as she heard the voices getting louder. But it was wise to remain unarmed until needed.

Alistari snapped. "This is *not* what the guild is for, Malaki!"

Lara entered the main area that was Malaki's study to see the two men. Alistari stood in the centre of the room, Malaki, pacing near his desk, looking annoyed. Lara remained quiet as Alistari stated, "The crystal is too dangerous. Attempting to harness the power is not the way, and you know it!"

Malaki turned and focused on Lara; his voice was bitter. "Well, well, the one who *breached* the contract."

Lara moved into the room as Alistari turned towards her. Muscles tense and not taking her eyes off the two sorcerers, she coldly stated, "Happy to disappoint." She glanced at Alistari before focusing on Malaki. "Does Alistari know you tricked the woman and were going to make her a prisoner here?"

The older sorcerer turned toward Malaki. "Is that true?"

The younger one looked at them both and laughed. "She was a *whore!* I was giving her something nay human had ever had the honour to harness."

Lara snarled, "At the cost of her free will!"

Alistari shook his head, studying his old friend. "To want to harness that power is one thing, but *that* is not right, Malaki. That is everything our guild stands against."

Malaki sneered. "To live a meagre existence when we could harness unlimited *power?*"

Alistari turned to Lara, then back at Malaki. "This woman did what had to be done. That crystal couldn't be possessed by any one person, which is why we had the Order!"

Malaki shook his head, looking at them both with disgust. "Pss, how would you know *anything?*" He pointed at Lara and declared, "This hybrid monstrosity should have been destroyed!" He glared at her and then at Alistari. He regarded his fellow sorcerer for a few moments, then asked, "Have you been tempted to study her?"

Alistari glanced at Lara, who glared at him. The old sorcerer turned back to Malaki as he added, "We could keep her here. In the vault. Use her uniqueness to our advantage! Nay one would know."

Lara stiffened, feeling the tension in the room build. Her hand tingled, wanting so much to draw her sword, but that would make things escalate too quickly. She needed to see how Alistari reacted to Malaki's last comment, she needed to wait and see how it played out. But if something happened, she would have to move fast.

Alistari stepped towards Malaki. "My friend. You seem unable to see that it is wrong to imprison someone that way. Aye, Lara is unique, and she certainly fascinates me. But you know this isn't the way, and if you continue thinking like this, there will be consequences."

Malaki laughed. "More for you both than me!"

Lara glanced at Alistari, seeing him tense. With her senses heightened, she could feel the static in the air. A small ball of energy grew in Alistari's hand that was behind his back. Lara slowly moved backwards, knowing it was wise to keep out of it and let the two battle it out with magic until she needed to step in, or defend herself. Alistari brought up his free hand as a calming gesture. "Malaki, please reconsider before it's too late. The crystal has corrupted you. It has made your judgement clouded."

Carn tensed when he saw several armoured men on horseback galloping towards the tower. He glanced back, looking up at it, wondering if Lara was alright and then turned back to the men when they all stopped and dismounted. Carn did not draw his sword, but kept alert. The men did not look aggressive. They wore helmets, but none had visors, so he could see they looked disciplined. His instincts were telling him they were on his side. The leader of the men walked up to Carn asking, "Do you work with Malaki?"

Carn shook his head. "Nay. Also, my companion is inside."

The man stated, his grey eyes stern. "And your companion, do they work with Malaki?"

Carn looked up at the tower. "Nay, we took a contract from him. But he tricked us."

The man studied him. "Ahhh, you're the ones who destroyed the crystal," Carn nodded, and the man added. "Then you're our allies."

The man turned to the tower, signalling to his men to follow. Carn added. "I'm going with you."

The man regarded him for a few moments and nodded. He and his men then ran in, Carn close behind. He followed them up the staircase and was surprised by how silently the soldiers could move while wearing heavy armour. Something not known to be a good choice for stealth. He looked ahead to see Lara tense as the leader reached her, but the man went straight past her into the room. When Carn reached the top, the armoured men had circled Malaki. Lara stepped back to let them fill the room. Carn came up beside her.

Alistari stated, "These guards of the guild are here to arrest you. Please come willingly, Malaki."

The younger-looking sorcerer snarled, and went to move, but Alistari was ready, and propelled the ball of blue static at him. The orb connected with Malaki which caused him to have a seizure and fall to the floor, unconscious. Lara and Carn quietly studied the scene as the guards shackled the unconscious sorcerer and carried him out of the tower.

Alistari turned to Lara, as she said, "Well, I had expected I would've had to confront him."

He smiled. "Nay. After you both left my tower, I did some investigating, and found things that didn't add up. I have had my suspicions about Malaki for some time. But when I found out that the woman had inside help, I soon found that it appeared to trail back to Malaki."

Lara looked at him. "Why didn't you tell us?"

He shrugged. "I wasn't sure if you were working more with Malaki than just taking a contract. I couldn't take that risk. All I could do was make you understand he wasn't trustworthy, without stating it to you bluntly."

"Ahh, the bit about him not giving me all the information."

Alistari nodded. "If you weren't with him, it would have planted a seed of doubt that he really wasn't giving you all the facts. I didn't know if you would seek out more about his plan or not, but I couldn't risk saying anymore. Just in case."

Lara responded, "A witch gave us more information and, to be honest, we both had our doubts. When I confronted the woman, I knew Malaki had to pay." She looked down the stairs to where the guards had taken the sorcerer. "What will happen to him now?"

"The guild will put him on trial."

"And then?" Asked Carn.

"Imprisoned. They have enchanted cells, where he will live out his mortal life."

"Mortal?"

"Aye. They will strip him of his powers in the cells. This will, of course, shorten his lifespan considerably."

"I see. That's a fitting punishment, saying what he was going to do to that poor woman. And what he had suggested doing to me."

Carn glanced at her with concern.

Alistari nodded. "When he suggested taking you, I realised how corrupted he had become." He sighed, glancing at Carn's concerned features. "I assure you; I would not have let that happen."

Carn replied, "Neither would I."

The sorcerer smirked and then looked around the room. "I have some work to do here, as the guild will need all of Malaki's books and spells confiscated."

"Do you need help?"

He shook his head. "This will not be a quick task, but it's one I must do." He paused, studying them both for a moment. "What of yourselves?"

Lara sighed. "Time for us to move on, I think. For me, being immortal, it's best not to stay in one place too long."

Alistari looked at Carn. "And you?"

Carn smiled, glancing at Lara. "I go where she goes."

Alistari chuckled. "A wise man." He turned to Lara and took her hand in his and squeezed it, looking between them both. "As nay one else will say this, I thank you for destroying that crystal." He focused on Lara. "And for freeing that poor woman from her imprisonment."

He let go of Lara and pulled a small purse of money from his belt. "Here's the payment that's owed to you."

Lara shook her head. "Nay we . . ."

The sorcerer pushed it firmly into her hand. "Take it. Pleasant journey to both of you."

Lara nodded, taking the heavy purse and placing it on her belt. She then turned to Carn, and they left the tower, heading back to the inn for a well-earned drink.

CHAPTER 22

A S THEY RODE slowly into Warrior Sword, the large, popular, market town still had travellers coming and going, even in the late afternoon. Like Great Moor, the town had no walls for protection. The war in the north centuries before had never threatened their safety nor encroached their borders. Yet there were still guards, all dressed in dark green uniforms, some with swords strapped to their backs. They were stationed near the major routes to the town, chatting with each other. They would casually look up as people passed by and nod a greeting, looking relaxed and bored.

The main street that weaved through the town was busy with locals and travellers alike, buying and selling goods. A few of the guards strolled along, helping anyone who asked, but did not behave like they were necessary to keep the peace. The busy street was lined with shops, a couple of inns, popular taverns and blacksmiths, as well as the occasional house scattered amongst them. As the two rode along, they glanced toward the side streets and alleys to see even more inns and shops.

Lara gazed ahead, feeling apprehensive about seeing Derwyn. It had been some time since she had been this way. It flooded her with memories as she soaked in the atmosphere. They made her think about the first day they had arrived in Great Moor, and when Derwyn's thoughts on his future had changed, finally deciding to make his home in the affluent town. Thinking of the past made her focus on what she planned to do next. It would be her first time to journey to another land without her brother. Lara smiled softly. At least Derwyn had found someone, and had a loving family; he would be alright. He no longer needed his older sister to protect him. He was a formidable lycan all on his own.

They rode straight through the town as Derwyn's house and grounds were just outside, to the southwest. Every time Lara saw it, it reminded her of their family home. Even though he had been young, the memory was enough that it was the reason Derwyn built the house where he had. There was a lycan family in the town itself, but Derwyn had wanted to live on the outskirts, giving his family more room to hunt. Lara smiled when she saw the house ahead and wondered what reception they would get.

When they rode into the main courtyard, they could see a boy and a girl playing. The boy and girl looked towards them, and Lara saw her parents reflected back at her in their similar features. The girl's dark locks had come loose from her plait while playing, her colouring and eyes matching Derwyn's. The boy's light brown hair was cut short, but it was his similar green eyes, mirroring her own, that made Lara realise that even though she would never bare her own child, part of her lived on in her nephew. Within moments of them entering, both ran to her, shouting. "Auntie!"

Lara smiled broadly, pulling her horse to a stop. "Let me at least dismount."

The children stepped back, letting Lara climb from her horse. Yet as soon as her feet touched the ground, they were on her, giving her as tight a hug as they could. Lara could not help but chuckle, never used to such a welcome. She looked up at Carn as he dismounted, a broad smile on his face.

With all the commotion, a petite blonde woman in a blue dress came out to see what was going on and beamed. "Lara!"

Lara struggled to turn towards her with both children hugging her so tightly. She smiled at her sister-in-law and said, "Good to see you, Skylar. I wish I had such a fond welcome elsewhere."

Skylar laughed and glanced at Carn, raising an eyebrow. He smiled, stepping forward. "I'm Carn, an old friend of Lara's."

Skylar glanced at Lara, who nodded. The woman added sternly. "Children, let Lara go, so she can at least get inside to see your papa."

Lara smiled as the children did as their mother said and then asked, studying the younger woman. "Where is he?"

"In the study. He has alpha Caleb with him. They're going over some pack business."

"We can wait."

Skylar shook her head. "Nay, please go in. They won't mind, and it may make them remember to have a break."

Lara nodded, remembering how her father would be in his study for hours. They left the children in the courtyard and went inside the house. Lara remembered where the study was on the ground floor. It was not the same layout as her family home, but every time she visited Derwyn's house, it still reminded her of it. Her brother was seated in an armchair, a large muscular man sitting opposite, when she entered the study. Lara paused for a moment. Whenever she saw Derwyn, it always took her aback by how much he looked like their father, even more now that he was older. "I hope we aren't disturbing you."

Derwyn turned and jumped to his feet. "Lara!" He paused, seeing who was behind her, a broad smile of recognition spreading across his face. "Carn!"

Derwyn rushed over and gave his sister a big bear hug. Lara melted in his grasp, so happy to feel her brother's embrace and his scent invading her nostrils. She never realised how much she missed him until they saw each other again. When they parted, he looked at her. "How long has it been?"

Lara gazed up at her brother; his shoulders were broad and had the air of an alpha about him. If the time arose, as Caleb had no children of his own, she felt her brother would be the pack's successor. "I've lost track, maybe over a year?"

He smiled and studied her. "It feels longer."

She shrugged, seeing faint lines around her brother's eyes. "It's so good to see you."

Derwyn turned to Carn, giving him a big hug. "I've missed you, big guy."

Carn chuckled, studying Derwyn when they parted. "I knew you would settle down. You have a fine family."

Derwyn nodded, smiling with affection at the Sword he had once hated. The pack leader stated, interrupting the three's moment, "It's good to see you, Lara." And made a quick nod of acknowledgement of Carn.

All turned to the larger, muscular man with dark, salt and pepper hair. Lara nodded. "And you, Caleb."

He turned to Derwyn. "Let's leave pack business for later. You should spend some time with your sister, and her friend."

Derwyn nodded thanks, and Caleb left the study, the children giving the large man some hassle of wanting him to play with them. Lara heard Skylar having to chastise them a little so Caleb could leave. Lara turned to her brother and smiled. "I see family life agrees with you."

He nodded, studying his sister. "It does. You should both stay for a while."

Lara glanced at Carn. "Aye, we would like that."

He gave her a suspicious look. "But I feel there's something else."

Her eyes gazed downward, a little sullen. "Aye."

"So?"

Lara sighed, gazing at her brother with affection. "I think it may be time to move on."

"Oh." Derwyn regarded the two. "Is it because of the talk going round of a couple of Swords saving the land from imminent doom?"

She eyed him, raising an eyebrow. "I wouldn't say imminent doom."

Derwyn chuckled. "It's all people talk about, and how you were the saviour of Bighdarum. I even heard the local bard singing something about it, too."

Lara sighed. "Damn, I'd've hoped those stories wouldn't have reached this far."

Carn responded, "But knowing Bamur." The Sword raised an eyebrow. "Always wanted to be part of a song."

Derwyn chuckled. "It's very catchy."

Lara glanced at the two men. "Catchy or not. I don't like it." She sighed. "I should've told Bamur to keep quiet. Then again, he could never keep anything to himself."

Derwyn chuckled. "We are talking about Bamur, after all."

"Aye, he's got a big mouth, for his size."

Derwyn smirked. "Very true. I wondered if the rumour was true when I heard you might be moving on. But at least here, you can have some peace."

"Thank you. Rest would do us both some good. But then, I think it would be wise to move on."

Derwyn replied, "Understood. But till then, spend some time here. Samuel and Miriel have missed you."

Lara nodded. "I've missed them too."

He looked across at Carn. "It's good to see you. We have so much to talk about."

Carn responded, "Aye. Lara tells me you became a Sword for a while, too."

Derwyn chuckled. "Aye, I did. You were a bad influence." Carn laughed and Derwyn added, "Come. I think Skylar has made dinner for the children, and we can have a good drink and catch up."

Lara nodded, squeezing her brother's arm. "I have missed you."

Derwyn smiled. "Aye. I'm happy here, but miss our days of travelling."

She gazed up at him, hooking her arm through his as he left the study.

They filled the evening with laughter and alcohol. The three told Skylar about adventures they had been on together or separately. Skylar regarded Carn as he drank his ale, glancing at her husband. "So, Derwyn didn't like you?"

Carn nodded, eyeing the younger man. "It was bad enough that I was a Sword, but I was also sleeping with his sister."

Lara took a sip of wine. "It's true. Derwyn kept trying to get me to leave Carn behind."

Carn looked at her, a little shocked. "He did?" Then looked over at Derwyn, who became a little sheepish.

Skylar frowned, glaring at her husband. "But when we met, you were a Sword."

Derwyn held up his hands in defeat. "Aye, Carn's ways rubbed off on me." He glanced at Carn and added, "But it's true. I disliked Carn, and kept telling Lara she could do better." He placed a hand on Carn's broad shoulder and continued, "But as I got to know you, Carn, I realised what my sister saw in you. A good man. And I respected you a lot."

Carn smiled, patted Derwyn on his back, and nodded. "Thank you. You're a good man too, Derwyn. Lara brought you up well."

Derwyn studied his sister with affection. "Aye, she did." He glanced back at Carn and added, "Didn't realise how much of an effect you had on us, Carn, until we had left Moonstar. It felt odd not having you around, and took Lara a long time to stop thinking of you."

Lara gazed at Carn's features. "I never really stopped."

Carn focused on her eyes, lost in their depths. Derwyn suddenly cleared his throat and turned to his wife. "It's late. We should get some sleep."

Skylar nodded, smiling at the two, lost in their thoughts. "Aye, good eve."

Carn and Lara nodded, not listening, everything around them had vanished. They did not even see Derwyn and Skylar leave. Carn combed his fingers into Lara's hair and kissed her passionately. Lara melted at his touch. Slowly Lara stood, trying not to break the kiss, pulling Carn to his feet. Fumbling their way up the stairs, they found their room and, as soon as the door closed, they stripped. Carn paused, studying Lara. "I never stopped loving you. Even when I loved Isabel, you were always in my heart."

Lara cupped his face in her hands and kissed him gently. "I'm so glad you're here now."

He pulled her towards the bed, kissing her again. "Me too, and I'm never letting you go."

Lara smiled, pushing him onto the bed. "Less talk."

Carn chuckled, curling his arms around her waist, and making love to her all night.

CHAPTER 23

L ARA AND CARN spent over a month with Derwyn and his family. The two lovers had a lot of quality time together. When they did venture into Warrior Sword, Lara took Carn to see a witch she knew well and recommended runes for Carn to add to his sword. He ended up with similar ones that Lara had, which were ash, fire, and ice. Once back at the house, Lara taught him how to activate and use them. Not all demons they hunted would need the addition of a rune, but Lara had found, over time, that the ones she had were the most effective.

When Lara had the opportunity, she would run with Derwyn in their wolf forms in the nearby forest, and it felt like old times hunting together again. Carn noticed Derwyn's wolf was black whereas Lara was grey, however they both had a patch of silver fur. Lara's had a spot just above her right eye and Derwyn had one on his left ear. When Carn had remarked upon it, Lara explained that they got it from their father who had a tuft of silver on his back left foot.

The siblings also hunted with Skylar, leaving Carn with the children. The arrangement amused them, as on one occasion, they returned to find the renowned Sword tied up and begging for help. Carn stated the twins were far more dangerous than any demon he had ever faced, and asked not to be left alone with them again. Yet once free, he then smiled at the boy and girl, telling them he would teach them other tactics on how to bring down an enemy larger than themselves.

For Lara and Carn, always being on the move, it felt good to not have to travel or have a contract to fulfill. During their time with Lara's brother, they planned their next move. Derwyn found information on ships known to dock regularly in the large city of Dalimor. Yet the two were still unsure of their destination. They had gathered all the details regarding the ships and would decide once they arrived at the port. The docks in the city were large, and most ships that moored there would head out to sea to other islands or continents. Wanting to start afresh would be good for them both, and at least this time, they would be together.

Even though they had had a fond time at Derwyn's home, it was soon time for them to move on. They said their farewells, both reluctant to leave, but knowing they had to. They travelled west for Dalimor, where they could have a choice of ships. There were a few possibilities; Derwyn mentioned Lost Island, which was beautiful, but was rumoured to be lawless. Many went there to be lost, so no one would ask about their pasts. It was a good place to start over, and a place for Swords to get work. Lara was not sure when they would return, and she would miss her brother greatly, but he had a good life and family. She did not have to worry. Maybe the next place would be where she and Carn could live for many years, or maybe they would soon move on. All they knew was they would not be going their separate ways again.

Dalimor was as impressive as they remembered. It had been over a year since Lara had last visited the city, but every time, it took her breath away. The city was on the coast at the end of a natural point of a curved section of land that lined a large crescent-shaped cove. Dominating the skyline, away from the coast, was the majestic Castle Dalm, where the southern royal family resided. They had constructed Dalimor's walls out of a sandy-coloured stone, with watchtowers placed around it and at every gate. Each watchtower had a banner fluttering in the sea breeze in deep blue and silver. The city walls gleamed in the sunlight, even though they were incredibly old, they were well-maintained and impressive. They had withstood the battle from the north centuries before and, hopefully, would never see war again. Where the walls reached the large docks, the sandstone tapered off at the edge of the cliffs. Watchtowers were also scattered around the docks, all built on natural rock formations in the seawater or on clifftops. All had beacons to help guide ships in bad weather when entering the cove and the docks.

The two came into the city via the major route from the north. Lara looked up at the ornate carvings on the massive oak gates, which were tall enough to allow a ship in full sail through if it were on land. Lara never understood why they had to be so tall, but it was an imposing sight. The city itself was busy and affluent, which was not a surprise with it having a royal family in residence.

Their horses trotted through the busy cobbled streets. People rushed back and forth and merchants shouted about their excellent merchandise to everyone who passed by. The scents of flowers, spices, alcohol, and the crowds of people going about their business invaded Lara's senses. She looked ahead to the main square and indicated to Carn the inn she used whenever she visited the city. Lara knew the innkeeper well, and he gave a good deal for his rooms, but, more importantly, never asked questions. Stopping outside the inn, Lara dismounted.

Carn stated, as he did the same, "I'll take the horses to the stables while you sort the room."

Lara nodded and took the saddlebags, then headed inside as Carn walked the horses round the back. Lara went up to the innkeeper, and he gave her a big, beaming smile when he recognised her. "Good to see ya again."

Lara smiled and stated, "Can I have one of your best rooms, my usual drink, ale, and your daily special?"

The innkeeper smiled and passed her a key. "Alicia will bring ya order over to ya." He paused, looking around, ensuring no one was listening. "I got in a batch of groc. Would ya like some of that?"

Lara smiled and nodded. The last time she had been here, she had asked if they had it. Grabbing the key, Lara weaved her way through the busy inn and found a table near the window. Putting the bags down, Lara sat facing the inn, her sword placed at her side. She focused on taking in all the scents, seeing if there were any that would need her attention. A vampire odour that was several days old, the stench of multiple humans and a metallic smell from a dwarf. She knew there was a dwarf blacksmith close by and had seen him in the inn before, enjoying a well-deserved drink. She smiled softly to herself when she picked up Carn's unique fragrance of cloves and leather. She focused on the Sword as he entered. He scanned the inn carefully, looking for her, and smiled when he did. He came over and sat opposite her. "Horses are being looked after by the stable lad."

Lara nodded and waited to talk as the barmaid, Alicia, arrived with their order. Carn took a deep breath, taking in the food's aroma. He thanked the young woman who gave him her best smile before leaving them be. Carn was completely oblivious of the barmaid flirting with him.

He turned to Lara as she said, "In the morn, we'll go down to the docks to see what ships are in or arriving."

Carn nodded, trying the food. "I think Lost Island seems a good choice."

Lara replied, "I agree. I'll also need to go into the east quarter once we have been to the docks."

Carn looked at her questioningly. "What's there?"

"Witches. I need something to help me with the voyage."

He stopped eating and asked, "Why?"

Lara explained what had happened before and how the amulet had helped her. He nodded. "Aye, that seems a good idea. Do you need me with you?"

Lara shook her head. "Nay. Can you look at selling the horses and get a good price for them?"

He said, before returning to his food, "Aye, I can."

"We'll keep the saddles and all that, but we can purchase new horses when we get to our destination."

Carn nodded, taking a sip of his ale. "Aye, that's what I did when I came here." He looked around the inn. "I wonder what Lost Island will be like. I found here to be very similar to Moonstar."

Lara had to agree. There were differences, but still had traits that reminded her of home. She leant back and took a sip of her drink and then turned to Carn. It felt good to know he was going to be with her and wondered what adventures lay ahead.

Carn looked up at her as he finished his food. "So. We have a few years yet, but seeing Derwyn in his home, with his family, made me wonder; would you ever want to settle down somewhere?"

Lara focused on Carn, knowing he had made a home, and hoped for a family, till tragedy struck. She studied his blue eyes, realising he was hoping she would be with him till his last day on

Zentos. "Aye." She glanced down. "But we could never have a family."

Carn's hand slid across the table, taking hers. "And I'm not expecting one. To be with you, is all I need."

Lara squeezed his hand, lost in his gaze. "Build a cabin in the woods?"

Carn smiled, nodding. "Aye. Our swords above the mantle, gathering dust."

She grinned, loving the idea, remembering the simple cabin she had built with Derwyn all those years ago. One built with the man she loved would be perfect. She breathed. "I like that idea."

He smiled softly. "Then that's the plan. When we have had our fill of adventure, we'll build that cabin. Maybe on Lost Island or somewhere else undiscovered yet."

Lara agreed, and when they came to the right place, they would know. But first, they needed to find a ship to leave Barberium behind to start their new adventure.

CHAPTER 24

LOST ISLAND
TEN YEARS LATER

THEY HAD BOARDED up the inn, everyone inside remaining as quiet as they could, sitting at the back of the building, huddled together. The barmaid whimpered when they heard the claws scraping across the door. She placed her hand firmly over her mouth to keep silent. The scratching stopped, and then they heard a loud howl. The glow of the full moon seeped through the wooden shutters. The innkeeper, Roclus, looked towards the barred door hoping the Swords he had promised to pay good money to could deal with the werewolf. He would know if they had succeeded by dawn, but hoped with two working together, they would have the odds in their favour. If they did not return, then yet more had fallen. He would then have little choice but to leave for good.

Carn anxiously glanced around the dark forest, standing alone in the small clearing, large trees packed close together, surrounding him. He strained to see through the branches; the light of the full moon dimmed by the clouds in the sky. He clenched and unclenched his fists, trying to stay relaxed. He whispered, "Seriously, is this your best plan?"

He knew Lara could hear him muttering from somewhere further out in the dense forest as she waited upwind for their target. He looked around, wanting to draw his sword, but Lara had instructed him to look unarmed, so he had hidden it off to the side, under some bushes. They had gone over the plan that day while at the inn. At the time, it seemed the most logical, but now with him standing alone in the dark forest as bait, Carn was beginning to wonder why he agreed. He took a deep breath and slowly searched the trees, scanning for any movement. He muttered, "I don't have night vision like you. How am I supposed to see it?" Carn knew not to expect a reply, but he felt better telling her how he felt.

He paused when he heard movement to the northeast. *Could this be it?* It sounded big. He clenched his fists and stood his ground in a fighting stance. Then the trees seemed to explode as a large werewolf jumped out at him, growling. It was over seven feet tall, and ran on two powerful hind legs. It stood like a man, but twice the size. Its whole body was covered in thick black fur, and the head was that of a wolf. Its enormous jaw was menacing, with huge, sharp teeth. It swung its powerful arms at the Sword, its razor-sharp claws glinting in the moonlight. Carn ducked and rolled out of the way. It jumped towards him, its large, claw tipped hand landed with a menacing thud a hairbreadth from Carn's face. He cursed, rolling out of the way, grabbing the scabbard sword that hid in the nearby undergrowth and drawing his sword. *Time to fight this thing.*

Jumping to his feet, Carn faced the werewolf. It was not the first he had fought, but it was the largest. That meant an alpha. For werewolf packs, they were the strongest, and the most aggressive. That was not good, it would be stronger than him. A lot stronger. He wondered if Lara knew they were fighting an alpha. The werewolf turned to face him, growling and flexing its hand. Carn looked up at it, getting a firm grip on his sword. All he had to do was keep it distracted long enough. He visualised the thorn rune he recently added to his silver sword, and whispered the word.

Carn focused on the enormous creature before him. It was a typical werewolf, but being an alpha, everything about it was huge and vicious. Carn looked up at the full moon, now breaking through the clouds. The only time a werewolf had no choice but to change, it was also when they were the most aggressive, and their bite was contagious. What he absolutely could not let happen was to be bitten by that thing. Carn cursed under his breath. "Where are you, Lara?"

The werewolf sniffed the air and growled, almost smiling in glee at the thought of Carn being its next victim. It snarled, showing off its menacing teeth. Carn kept a firm stance and a firm grip on his sword. The werewolf will well and truly be fecking pissed when its skin got burnt by the silver blade. The thorn rune ensured it delivered its damage with an extra painful twist.

The creature attacked. Carn was able to fend it off with his sword, the claws sparking off his blade. It lunged again, and Carn swung his sword, cutting across the werewolf's upper arm. It hissed in pain as the skin smoked and blistered from the silver. It stepped back, sizing Carn up. The Sword was ready for it to make its move. He took a steadying breath, his joints already aching, his body feeling the fight more, now that he was older. But it was not the time to show any weakness. The werewolf pounced again. Carn parried the claws with his sword, dodging out of the way. Yet it swiped again, a claw nicking his shoulder. Carn cursed, and the werewolf prowled around him, sizing him up. Carn had to show strength, and prepared for its next attack. It ran at him, ready to strike with its long arm. Carn held his breath, but suddenly, the creature was flung sideways as a large, grey dire wolf attacked from the west, clamping its jaw around the werewolf's throat.

Lara started running through the forest once she heard the werewolf reaching Carn, she had to get there fast. Carn did not want to admit it, but he was not as fast as he used to be. She saw the werewolf ahead and cursed. It was an alpha. It was also about to make its move on Carn. She pounced, her powerful jaw clamping down on its large neck. It forced the werewolf to the side with the momentum of her jump. The two landed on the ground, and the beast rolled free. Lara spun around, facing the werewolf, making her body as big as she could, and growled menacingly. It checked its neck, seeing the blood on its claws. It then focused on Lara and growled, baring its teeth. Lara glanced at Carn to see him getting ready to defend himself, his breathing slightly laboured. She could smell the blood from his wound, he needed to rest. She turned back to the werewolf, her turn to deal with the alpha.

The werewolf growled and paced in front of her. It was sizing her up, trying to figure out what she was from her scent. Her wolf body was as long as it was tall and almost level with his stomach. She pounded her paws into the ground extracting her claws. It watched her as it paced and flexed its claws, making them gleam in the moonlight. Lara glared back. It had a cockiness about it, a typical alpha. She saw it move slightly, knowing it would lunge at her. Yet it would not have been expecting her speed for her size. It landed on the empty ground, spinning around in frustration that it had missed her. Lara did not give it a chance to recover, her jaw clamping down over its upper arm, tearing the flesh. The werewolf howled and swung wide with its other arm, but Lara leapt clear. In frustration, the werewolf ran at her, and Lara jumped, landing on its back. Her jaw clamped down on its neck, then she forced her body round to its front, and knocked it down to the forest floor. Lara kept it pinned down as Carn ran over, plunging his silver sword deep into its side. The werewolf tried to fend them off, hitting Carn and sent him flying into a tree with a dull thud. Lara kept her jaw clamped, not daring to look, but then heard Carn groaning and cursing. With that foul language, she knew he was alright, just his pride taking a beating. The werewolf struggled to break free and, with sudden force, flung her from him. She landed a few feet away, gracefully on her paws, ready to pounce again. The werewolf checked its side and growled at all the blood. It struggled to its feet and was ready to attack again. Lara stood her ground, baring her teeth. It should be over soon. The alpha was weakening from blood loss, but would not give up easily. She ran straight towards it, then feinted a jump, but darted right, and bit down on its wounded side and tore at the flesh. Blood spurted out aggressively from the fatal wound as the werewolf fell to its knees. They had to act quickly. She looked towards Carn who was getting back to his feet, and she growled, getting his attention. They needed the silver sword with the activated rune to strike it again, otherwise the werewolf would keep going till its dying breath. Lara ran at it again, mauling it, keeping it distracted long enough. Then Carn made the final blow. His sword plunged into the werewolf's heart from behind, killing it.

Carn staggered back, exhausted. Lara jumped free of the werewolf as it changed back to human form. She studied the man; he was not that old, but even in human form, he was big. Lara turned when she heard Carn cursing. He was studying his wounded arm and checking his ribs, where he sat on the ground nearby. Lara trotted over, studying his lined features with affection.

Carn looked up at her wolf's features and smiled. "I'll be alright."

Lara changed back into her human form and inspected his wounds. "They need to be looked at."

Carn nodded, rotating his aching shoulder. "I keep forgetting I ain't as flexible as I used to be."

Lara sat beside him, studying his features. Carn was in his mid-fifties and still as handsome as ever. She kissed him passionately. He winced, and she smiled softly. "Let's get back to the inn. Think we both deserve a good drink."

Carn smiled, studying her naked body. "Think you better get some clothes on first."

Lara chuckled, cupping his face with her hand with affection. In the privacy of the forest they could be lovers, but once back at the inn, they would have to put on the father-and-daughter act once more. She took a breath. It was for the best that they had to lie. She glanced through the trees. "I left them in that direction."

Carn slowly got to his feet. "I'll catch up." He looked at the naked body of the man. "What about him?"

"His pack will find him."

Carn glanced at her. "Is that a good idea?"

Lara smirked. "We killed their alpha, and from what I found out, the pack is small. The others will just scatter. If they come back, we can deal with them. Roclus knows how to get hold of us. Most werewolf packs usually move on when their alpha has been defeated."

Carn nodded, sheathing his sword, wincing at the movement. Lara studied him with concern. Carn waved his hand at her, gesturing for her to go. "I'm alright," he reminded her.

She nodded, knowing it was best not to fuss over him, even though he would suffer from stiffness and pain for days. She ran to where she had left her clothes and was fully dressed and waiting for Carn when he finally caught up to her. They then walked back to the inn. Roclus would be pleased that the route with his inn and the nearby town would not be bothered again by the werewolves.

The two sat at a table near the fire, having returned to the inn just before dawn. Roclus, the innkeeper, brought over food and drink for them both. The barmaid and patrons thanked the Swords for saving them from certain death. Roclus herded them away, telling his customers that the two needed some rest. Carn and Lara nodded thanks and were glad to have some peace finally. The barmaid had brought over supplies so Lara could tend to Carn's wounds. He leaned back and sighed. "I think I'll sleep for days after that."

Lara gazed at him and smiled. "I'm sorry. If I had known it was an alpha . . . "

Carn looked at her. "Don't. The plan worked, and that's all that matters."

She nodded and gave him a sideways glance as she finished cleaning his wound. "You do know I could hear you moaning."

"Good," he smiled mischievously.

They sat in silence, Carn finishing his food, Lara savouring her drink. She closed her eyes and relaxed. But she was soon tense when she picked up a scent. It was lycans. There was a pack at Shadefall, but there was no good reason for them to be at the inn at this early hour. She sat up and saw two men at the bar talking to the innkeeper. He, in his joy, was informing them about the werewolf kill and, of course, her and Carn. Lara nodded to them when they looked over. Lara slowly squeezed Carn's thigh under the table and whispered, "We may have trouble. Lycans."

He looked up, seeing the two men. "Oh."

The two walked up to the table and the dark-haired one stated, "So, you killed a werewolf."

Carn responded coolly. "Aye, we did."

The men turned to Lara, the dark-haired one taking a deep breath and sneering. "*What* are you?"

Carn stated, "None of your business, lad."

The dark-haired man turned to him. "Not your concern, *old man.*"

Carn snapped, "Hey, less of the *old!*"

But the man's attention was fully on Lara. She glared at him firmly and stated, "Do you want to cause a scene here?"

He glanced around and whispered, "Don't meddle in our business."

Lara raised an eyebrow. "Really? It seemed you weren't doing anything when these kind folks were living in fear."

The man smirked, keeping his voice low. "You have nay clue what you've stepped into here, and what you may have caused."

Lara responded, her gaze fixed steadily on his, "Enlighten me."

He shook his head and looked around. "We don't want to cause any trouble for these kind folks, now do we?"

Lara smirked. "True."

Carn glared at the two, the silent one having been staring at him the whole time. "Listen, we were just helping them out, nay harm."

The two men smirked. The dark-haired one stated, "Best leave here by this eve."

Lara was about to protest when Carn placed a hand on her arm. The two men studied them both. The one who had remained silent leant forward, his eyes on Lara. "We don't like things like you around here."

She glared back at him, but it was wise not to make a scene. The two men then turned and left the inn. Lara cursed under her breath.

Carn stated, "Why are they always so superior?"

Lara sighed. "Not all lycans are."

Carn looked at her and smiled softly. Roclus came over and said, "Do you know those folks?"

They both shook their heads. Lara added. "Nay, they just wanted to say a thank you."

Roclus nodded and headed back over to the bar when a customer shouted for another drink. Carn turned to Lara. "So, what do you think we stumbled on?"

She shrugged. "With them not helping here or the local townspeople, I think they had made some deal with the werewolves. Odd, as they usually can't stand each other. But if it were to keep the peace, say in Shadefall, then that may be why."

He pursed his lips. "Would make sense. So, are we heading north or east?"

Lara glanced at him. "I think you know me too well. East. I want to know why lycans would make such a deal."

He grinned. "That's me girl." He grabbed his tankard and took a couple of large gulps. He then glanced at her and added. "But not for a few hours."

She gazed at him and smirked. "Don't worry, we'll have a few more drinks before we go anywhere."

CHAPTER 25

THEY REACHED SHADEFALL after a couple of days. The city was large and prosperous, with several inns popular with new arrivals or travellers leaving Lost Island behind. While the taverns in the city were always full and busy, the main customers were dock hands and, because of this, considerably louder. With such a busy port with ships big and small docking, the city never seemed to sleep. When the dockhands were not resting or drinking, they would move crates and barrels all day and night. With so many supplies arriving, the shops were always well stocked. The market square was open most days where locals from the nearby towns and villages came to buy and sell. Like any city of its size, it also had a bustling non-human quarter where more specialised shops lined the streets. Those catered to spells or talismans needed for long voyagers, or helped to change one's appearance to vanish into a new life. Like any other major city, an impressive, grey stone wall surrounded it with enormous iron gates at the two main roads heading north and south. There were unused watchtowers on either side, as they needed most guards within the walls. Mainly to ensure the peace was kept when the occasional dockhand had a little too much ale. With all the access roads, which included three smaller ones, the gates were always open. They had been left in position for so long that they had rusted and would not be able to close even if they tried. The only section where there was no wall was at the large port. There were tall lookout towers surrounding the dock to help guide ships in bad weather.

It was at those very docks where Lara and Carn had landed all those years ago. Lost Island being almost lawless, had only been rumours. The land was prosperous and peaceful. As anyone who came here to be lost did not want trouble. Those who would think of causing issues never did, as it was a haven that they could need one day. The island had become a place where no one ever asked about people's pasts. It was also lucrative for Swords for hire. If there was any trouble, most wanted it dealt with quietly. But few had Lara's and Carn's skills. As, overall, it may have been a peaceful island, but it had issues with demons daily. After only a few days of arriving, they had more contracts than they could deal with.

The two rode through the busy streets, heading for an inn they had used before that was off the main square. From the crowds coming and going, a ship must have recently docked, and both hoped they would not have any issues with finding a room. Lara gazed ahead. She roughly remembered that the lycans had their residences to the north of the city. If she could get to see the alpha, they may get some answers.

Reaching the inn they dismounted, Carn headed in while Lara took the horses to the stables at the back. Once the horses were settled, Lara walked in with their saddlebags and supplies. Carn was sitting at a table near the back, but with a good view of the inn. She walked over and sat down next to him just as the barmaid came over with the food and drinks Carn had ordered. She asked if Lara wanted anything to eat and she declined. The barmaid nodded and left them in peace. Lara took a sip of her drink, looking around the not-so-busy inn.

Carn stated, "I have two rooms upstairs for us."

Lara nodded, eyeing him. Only one room would be required, but with them looking more like father and daughter, it was always wise to get two. She took another sip of her drink and scanned the room, letting the scents invade her nostrils. She picked up a lycan one, but it was a few days old, so the inn was not one of its regular haunts. She turned to Carn. "I'll patrol the city tonight. See if I can spot or find out anything that may be useful."

He nodded, studying her. "Just be careful."

She smiled. "Always."

Carn turned his attention to the food before him while Lara leant back and relaxed, taking in the inn's atmosphere. She eavesdropped on a few conversations, most were on the topics of taxes and trade with cities overseas. As usual, not much trouble except the odd drunken dockhand and bar brawl. It seemed the lycan pack in Shadefall kept the locals safe, unknown to them all. Lara wondered why the lycans they had encountered had such a strange reaction to the werewolf being killed. Maybe it was down to the peace held here. She wondered again if the werewolves had caused issues in the past forcing the lycan pack to make a deal with them. She sighed. She would go out tonight, and hopefully, talk to the lycan alpha in the morning. They had never crossed paths with that pack before, but Lara did not like the two who had threatened them at Roclus's inn, and she wanted answers.

Carn opened the window to their room, letting in the cool night air, and looked down. The side alley was empty, and a sloping roof that covered the building on the other side broke the drop. Lara would have no issues with jumping from the window, even if the wooden overhang had not been there. He turned back to see her naked; she smiled, giving him a passionate kiss. "See you soon."

She then went down on all fours and changed into her wolf alter ego. Carn always marvelled at her wolf form and ran his fingers through her soft grey fur, cautioning her, "Be careful."

She grunted and jumped out of the window, landing silently on the roof and then to the ground. Carn left the window open for her return. Lara trotted through the city, keeping to the side alleys and streets. As she headed north, she picked up scents from vampires and a couple of other night demons. Lara would have been more surprised if she had not picked up anything. It was the norm in a city like this to have a good mix of demons. If there were none, then something would be amiss. What did surprise Lara was how few people believed that those demons even existed. She snorted as she continued in the shadows. People would soon have a shock if they ventured out at night down these quiet side streets.

Lara continued heading north and soon neared a house used by the lycans. It was impressive even from a distance, and she hoped that was where the alpha's family was. As she got closer, she picked up several lycan scents and wondered if they were having a meeting. But she paused when she picked up another scent. Werewolf. She looked up at the full moon. There was still another night to go before the werewolves would have control again. That meant if one was there, it probably was not for a friendly chat. She trotted a little closer, picking up the sounds of a fight. It seemed it had not been invited. Lara focused on the house. The werewolf would not stand a chance with that many lycans and their alpha. But werewolves were never a race who thought rationally, especially on a full moon. Lara listened for a while. The fight had quieted down. Lara looked at the house and considered whether she would be welcomed if she visited in the morning. She returned to the inn, but questioned if they would even welcome her. She sighed, remembering the pack on Barberium that had welcomed her there. Yet from the lycans at the inn, she did not think she would get the same benefit here. The few times they had been in Shadefall, they had not stayed long, and had not come across the pack. With the town being a place to lose oneself, few ventured into other people's business. Even the pack seemed to keep a low-key presence in the city. Yet they would probably know of her and if not, they would soon.

"So, a werewolf?"

Lara nodded as she lay next to Carn on the bed. "Aye."

He gazed at her features. "Are you sure it's wise to visit in the morn?"

Lara shrugged. "Maybe not, but I want to get answers."

"As do I. So, we will see. Carefully . . ." He gave her a mischievous glance. "Unless none are left. The werewolf may have outsmarted them all."

She arched her eyebrow. "One werewolf on a full moon, against a pack of lycans and their alpha? I think all will be well, except for the werewolf."

Carn chuckled. "I know. I was just teasing."

She jumped on top of him, pinning him down. "Best watch that mouth of yours. It will get you into trouble."

Carn laughed, grabbing Lara around the waist, and pulling her close. "Already has."

They kissed passionately as their limbs intertwined. Lara gazed at him as his hands stroked her back, feeling his groin growing as she straddled him. She leant forward and kissed him softly. Carn slid his hands up to her breasts, cupping them in his large hands. Lara changed her position slightly, letting him enter her. She moaned softly, feeling him inside her, moving their hips, slowly at first. Carn pinched her nipples as he played with her breasts. Lara's skin shivered in delight as his hips moved faster. She leant forward, kissing him again. Carn suddenly grabbed her firmly and adjusted his body weight, rolling himself on top while holding her tightly so their connection did not break. In the new position, Carn thrusted deeper, making Lara gasp. He grabbed her arms, moving them above her head, and he kept his hips moving to gaze at her as they reached orgasm. Lara closed her eyes, her body buzzing in delight. Carn gripped her hands tightly as he lost control of his body and climaxed along with Lara.

Carn slumped on to her gasping, both covered in sweat. Lara curled her arms around him. Feeling him still throbbing inside of her. She kissed him gently, savouring his embrace, feeling his heart pounding. His testosterone overwhelmed her senses. She had lost count of how often they made love and every time it felt like the first. Carn sighed, his head resting on her chest. They laid like that for a while, just savouring the moment. Lara smiled softly when she felt Carn's breathing change as he drifted off to sleep. She closed her eyes and was soon asleep, too.

CHAPTER 26

LARA WOKE TO find the other side of the bed cold and empty. She rolled over, wondering where Carn had gone. Then she picked up his scent outside, mingled with food. It seemed he had gone to get breakfast. The room door opened, and Carn entered carrying a tray of fruit and juice for himself and water for her. His shirt was loose and untucked from his black trousers. He smiled and said, "Good morn."

Lara pulled herself up as Carn came and sat back on the bed, placing the tray down between them. As Carn ate the fruit, Lara sipped at her drink. Lara stated, "Once ready, let's walk across town and see the lycans. I want it out of the way as soon as possible."

Carn nodded, glancing at her as he ate. "Then when they tell us to leave town, we have a good day to ride south."

Lara smirked. "That isn't what always happens."

He studied her. "True, but we both know they don't really like you, and me for being with you."

She sighed. "You don't have to rub it in."

He gave her a loving side glance. Lara had resigned to her fate with other packs years ago. "You say that every time."

Lara smiled softly. "Aye, I do. But I'm always hopeful that another pack will go against the norm."

Carn squeezed her hand. "As am I. It happened before and I know it will again."

She took a sip of her drink and smiled at him. "I like your optimism."

"Always good to have."

Lara kissed him on his cheek and leaned back while he ate. She wondered what the lycan family would be like, and hoped the alpha would at least talk to them.

Once dressed, they walked across the city to the house Lara had seen the night before. They strolled up to it, Lara picking up several scents within. The werewolf one had faded since last night, but she could also pick up the smell of decay. It had not survived. Lara glanced at Carn. "Remember, follow my lead."

"Aye, you know lycan politics better than I do."

She smiled and turned her attention to the house. As they reached the main door, it opened. It was one of the men from the inn, the one who had remained silent for most of the time. "What do you want? We told you to keep out of lycan business."

Lara glared at him. They must have picked up their scents as they had walked to the house, being downwind of it. She responded, not looking submissive. "I have to talk to your alpha."

The young lad smirked. "Why would I let you?"

Lara responded. "Maybe because of the werewolf corpse in your house."

The dark-haired man, the other one from the inn, came up behind the lad. He sneered as he took the lad's place at the door. "I told you to move on."

Lara smiled coldly. "Not a member of your pack, so don't have to abide by your orders. Now I want to see your alpha."

The dark-haired man glared at them both. "Nay."

Lara pursed her lips. "Humm, I wonder what the werewolf pack will say when I tell them you have one of theirs rotting in your cellar."

The man glared at her, not backing down. Lara stood her ground, staring right back at him, hoping the alpha could hear their conversation. If so, she just had to wait. The man went to say something when a voice boomed as a larger man walked up from the corridor behind him. "Let them in. Tomlin."

Tomlin paused for a moment, longer than a pack member should when given an order by the alpha. Then, slowly, with reluctance, opened the door. Lara glanced at Tomlin, the lad who was silently standing to the side and then at the alpha, who was walking towards them. The alpha and Tomlin had similar features, so were probably brothers. That would make sense with lycan packs usually being family oriented. She glared back at Tomlin for a moment before fully turning to the older man. With him being the alpha, that meant he was the eldest in the family. Yet by the way Tomlin reluctantly obeyed the order, Lara wondered if he was just biding his time to find his moment to challenge his brother. Lara looked the alpha directly in the eyes. The large, muscular man studied her. His features were hard and broad. "So, why are you here? Are you to tell me you're with Tomlin's child?"

Lara glared at the alpha, not becoming submissive. She glanced at Tomlin with disgust. It seemed he had a reputation, as from the alpha's response, he had to deal with matters like this before. "I'm here to talk."

He nodded, his nostrils flaring as he took in her scent. "So, you're the hybrid." He turned to Carn. "Travelling with a human, an odd match." He took in a deep breath and raised an eyebrow and studied the two. "And not papa and daughter."

Lara smirked and stated, "Not here to talk about personal lives. I'm here to find out what is going on with you and the werewolves."

The alpha smiled coldly and nodded. "To the point I see." He turned to his brother. "Take some of your men and deal with the situation from last eve and then the matter is closed. As for our guests, I will talk to these two alone."

Tomlin nodded reluctantly and left them, the young lad dutifully following. The alpha smiled. "I'm Dray. Come, we can talk in my study."

They followed Dray back to the room at the end of the corridor where he had come from. Lara said as they entered the large room full of books. "You know Tomlin is going to challenge you?"

Dray chuckled. "Aye. And as before, he will fail." He sat down behind his large desk and regarded them as they took the seats opposite. "So, you want to talk about werewolves?"

Lara replied, "Aye, from the disagreement you had last eve with one, and your brother not being so happy that we dealt with one in Old Wood, I'm thinking you have some agreement with them?"

Dray chuckled. "Nay, not an agreement. An understanding, which with what you did the other eve, has now ended."

Carn snapped, "I thought lycans were protectors?"

Dray looked at Carn with disdain and turned back to Lara. "We protect Shadefall. Those werewolves wanted to start their own pack. They tried their luck here, and we informed them to leave. Tomlin let them know that if they kept away from Shadefall, we would leave them be."

Lara studied him. "So, the werewolves were threatening to cause issues here?"

"Aye. For the greater good, Roclus and his fine establishment were a sacrifice that had to be made."

Lara snarled. "But it wasn't just Roclus. The village of Diran was being affected, too."

Dray raised his eyebrow. "Really? Well, that place is full of scum, anyway."

"Aye, but still has innocents." Lara leant forward. "I think there's more to this. If those werewolves were that rogue, you would have culled them."

Dray studied Lara. "You seem to know lycan law, well."

"Aye I do. My family is pure blood and goes back generations."

Dray snarled. "Unfortunately, not you."

Lara clenched her fists, seeing Carn tense. This alpha was trying to rile her, and Lara would not let him. "Enough about the past. What's the real reason you made a deal with them?" She studied his features, seeing a slight twitch near his eye at her last question. She took a punt. "They have something on you, don't they?"

Dray remained calm, but Lara sensed his heartbeat quickening. She had hit a nerve. Lara leant forward. "We may be able to help you." Carn went to say something, but Lara gave him a stern look, and he backed down.

Dray looked at them both and stated, "Work with a *thing* like you?"

Lara just smiled, not giving him the satisfaction of a further reaction. She had found a weakness that the werewolves were taking advantage of. She just had to figure out what it was. "Well, our skills may be to your advantage."

The alpha studied them both and thought for a moment. Then scoffed. "You have nay idea. You are just clutching at daggers."

Lara kept her features calm. "Is it a risk you're willing to take?"

She was calling his bluff. She could sense his heart rate and how his muscles tensed. She just needed to push a little more and hoped he would open up. She regarded him; he did not have a ring claiming he was promised to another, so it was not an issue with a lover. She took in the scents in the room and picked up a new one. It was several days old, and not from any of the pack she had encountered. It was female. Yet when she carefully took another deep breath, the woman had not been intimate with Dray. She thought fast. An alpha would be very protective when it came to family. There was no love lost between him and his brother, so it was not that. Then Lara took a guess. "They have your child."

Dray's face paled, and he glared at her. "You're just guessing."

Lara studied him. "We're not here to threaten. We can help."

The alpha glared at them. "How can you help? You're just some hybrid."

"A hybrid with the strength of an alpha and vampire."

Carn added. "True. She could leave you standing."

Dray regarded them both. Lara added. "So, they have your child or know who does. You and Tomlin have told them to stay out of Shadefall, but otherwise, they can do what they want. With that, you're hoping they may give you the information you're after?"

Dray slowly nodded. "But you killing their alpha has caused a problem and now they won't give us the information we need."

Lara stated, "They sent one here last eve with a deal, didn't they?"

Dray answered, "Aye. But Tomlin and he argued. It didn't turn out well for the werewolf."

"What of your child?"

Dray looked at them. "My daughter? We got something from the werewolf last eve before he died. It seems she's north of here with another pack of werewolves."

"Another pack?"

"Aye. Not sure where, though."

Lara asked, "How did they get your daughter?"

He glanced down. "If you must know, she was travelling west, and a pack attacked her and my men. They killed all my men but one. He came back badly injured and gave Tomlin a message before he died. He had said a pack of werewolves had taken her."

Lara leant forward; she had never heard of werewolves kidnaping before. "Why would they do that?"

Dray shrugged, "That's what I want to find out."

"So, the pack here knows where?"

Dray focused on her. "Aye, I believe so. But none seem willing to say exactly where." He took a deep breath. "Tomlin had been talking to them. He had been hoping to get more information. Till you two fecked it up."

Lara studied him. Something felt off. Werewolves keep to their own. *Why would they take a lycan girl? And why was Tomlin talking to the werewolves?* From what she had seen of him, she did not think he would do anything to help his brother. Unless the girl was a tool for him. She focused on the alpha; he was not telling them everything. He seemed to trust Tomlin, but Lara did not. It was not surprising, from what she could tell of Tomlin, that the alpha's brother was also hiding something. For the time being, she would keep her theories to herself and go along with what Dray was telling her. "We could track your daughter. Find where she has gone."

Dray snarled. "Don't you think I have done that with my men?"

Carn stated, "Aye, but we are incredibly excellent trackers. Nothing we can't find."

Dray regarded them both and pursed his lips. Lara was aware that if he was not interested, he would have called his men in. That meant not all his pack knew everything, or he felt they were not all loyal. It also would not surprise Lara if Tomlin had men that would do anything; even betray their alpha. She silently waited while Dray studied them both. He then said, "So you could track them?"

Lara nodded. "Aye, we could."

Dray leant forward. "But you want something in return."

Carn and Lara nodded. She stated, "You tell your pack to leave us be."

The alpha looked at Carn and then Lara and slowly nodded. "Agreed."

Lara stood, turning to Carn. "Time to go."

He stood, and they walked to the study door. When Lara opened it, Dray's men were waiting outside, blocking their way. Lara turned to Dray, who nodded to his men to let them pass. The men moved away from the doorway, making a path to the main entrance. Except for Tomlin, who still blocked Lara's way, as he snapped at Dray, "You made some deal with *this*?"

Dray glared at his brother. "Aye, and you will obey my order!"

The lycans looked at Dray and then his brother and waited. Lara glared at Tomlin. The last thing they needed was to be in the middle of a power struggle. She looked Tomlin directly in the eyes. "Out of my way."

He stood his ground, glaring back. Carn tensed, his hand creeping towards his dagger on his belt. Dray snapped, having come up behind them. "Enough! Move aside, Tomlin. *Now!*"

Slowly Tomlin looked around at the other lycans. He put his face inches from Lara's as he said, "Don't cross my path, as I'll put you down."

Lara smiled, not looking intimidated. "You have nay idea what I am capable of."

Tomlin slowly moved to the side but never took his eyes off Lara. If she crossed paths with him again, she would have to act fast, as otherwise, she could see there being repercussions.

As they walked back to the inn, Carn stated, "You know Tomlin may follow us."

"Aye, I know. He's looking for any excuse to overthrow his brother. Like it or not, I think we're in the middle of it."

Carn glanced at her. "Do you think Dray was telling us everything?"

She eyed him. "Nay. There's more to what has happened to his daughter than he was saying. I think the werewolves will have more information."

"And Tomlin?"

"He seems to have his own agenda, and I think he may be behind Dray's daughter disappearing."

Carn studied her. "You do?"

Lara nodded. "It seemed convenient that the survivor told him the information, not Dray. I don't know what yet, but my instinct is telling me he's behind it somehow."

"Well, that's never wrong. So, do we deal with him?"

Lara glanced at him. "If he interferes then, aye. Otherwise, we just need to be on our guard, and not trust any of Dray's men, either."

Carn studied her as they reached the inn. "What do you think is going on?"

Lara shrugged. "I'm not sure, yet. But something's brewing, and I think because of Dray's ego, it won't be good."

Carn sighed, opening the inn door. "So, we're hunting werewolves."

Lara smiled at him as they went inside. "You know how much you love it."

Carn chuckled. "Aye. But can I not be bait next time?"

Lara smirked. "But that plan worked."

Carn eyed her, not saying a word, his disapproving features telling her clearly; he did not fully agree.

Wanting to head south as soon as they could, they packed up their things and left Shadefall behind. They reached Roclus's inn within a couple of days, veering slightly from the primary route. It was good to have somewhere to stay for a decent night's sleep. Carn took the horses into the stable while Lara went inside the inn to get rooms and find out how the inn and town was fairing after they had killed the alpha. It surprised Roclus to see them so soon, but he told Lara that they had been werewolf free since they had left. Lara was pleased, but also disappointed, as she had hoped to track a werewolf down to get some information. The small village of Diran was to the south, and being in the same vicinity, may still have the odd werewolf hanging around. For them, it was worth a look.

After procuring keys to a couple of rooms and drinks, Lara found a table and waited for Carn. He entered a little while later with their saddlebags. He sat opposite her and smiled. "Horses are settled. Anything from Roclus?"

"They have been werewolf free, but that also means none for us to track. So, I think Diran may be the best place to look."

Carn nodded, taking a sip of his drink. "We'll be backtracking on ourselves, but you're right. There may be one or two still lingering around."

"Aye. I just need one. Hopefully, they'll talk."

"If not?"

Lara raised her eyebrow. "I have means."

Carn chuckled and glanced around the quiet inn. "It's good to see nay one terrified of staying here, but it's just not as busy as it once was."

Lara nodded. "They'll come back in time. Once word has spread that the route is safe." She paused. "Well, as safe as it once was."

Carn nodded, studying her. "Do you remember when we came here soon after we had arrived?"

Lara smiled. They had been on Lost Island for ten years now, and it only felt like five. "Aye, and we've had some fine adventures while we've been here."

He nodded, his gaze lost in her eyes. "And we'll have many more."

She smiled and leaned forward a little. "I want to kiss you right now."

Carn smirked. "Best not, I'm supposed to be your papa."

Lara chuckled and responded, "Think I better help you to your room, *papa*."

He raised an eyebrow and quickly drained the rest of his ale. Standing, he gestured towards the back stairs. Lara got to her feet and smiled, leading the way to a room.

CHAPTER 27

THEY CONTINUED TO the small village of Diran the following morning and reached it by dusk. Lara and Carn rode slowly up the main street. The village was quiet, only a few were out going about their business. As they looked around, they could see evidence of werewolf attacks. Windows were boarded up and the townsfolk that were out, looked nervous. The centre of town had been where the major event occurred. Both felt guilty that they had been unaware, and could not have helped them. Lara took a deep breath and picked up old and new werewolf scents. Some had not gone too far when the alpha was killed.

She glanced at Carn. "There's still at least one werewolf here."

He looked around. "You sure?"

"Aye, they must still have some connection to this place. Let's find an inn. Then we can investigate."

He nodded, and then pointed to an inn sign further up the road which was too worn to read. "Looks as good a one as any."

They rode up the dirt road to the inn. Fastening the horses outside, they took their belongings and ventured in. Lara took a deep breath as they entered, picking up all the scents. But none belonged to a werewolf. Glancing around, she saw a couple of dwarfs talking and getting drunk quietly, but the others scattered about the inn were human. Carn nodded to the innkeeper and asked about rooms while Lara went to claim a table. While she waited, Lara leant back and took in the inn's scene, glad to be out of the saddle. She focused on Carn as he spoke to the innkeeper, ordering food and drink. The innkeeper was very talkative and asked where they had travelled from. Carn had always been good at directing idle chit-chat and changed the subject without the large man even realising.

She sighed, remembering what Carn had said the night before at Roclus's inn. She gazed at him, she had almost forgotten that he was in his mid-fifties. It seemed odd to her, the reality was that she was the elder. Yet, to everyone in the inn and all who they passed by; he looked like her father. Lara recalled what her vampire mentor, Fashor, had said to her all those years ago about being immortal. She had noticed the difference between Derwyn's and Carn's ageing. Derwyn's lycan blood slowed down the process slightly, but that would not happen with Carn. She regarded his ageing features and realised how time had frozen her. Some years from now, there would be that moment when life would deal a crushing blow to them both. Lara bit her lip. She would not change a thing, though. They seemed fated to always be together, so she would not end it just because he looked older than her. To Lara, she saw only his heart and soul, and she would love him for eternity.

Carn walked over and frowned, studying her faraway look. "Everything alright?"

She smiled softly, knowing it was not a good idea to burden him with her thoughts. "Aye. I'm just wondering where the werewolf or wolves would be."

He sat opposite her and passed her a drink, eyeing her, but did not push. "Let's investigate in the morn. I'm aching all over." He smiled. "And only one room is available, so we're sharing."

Lara raised an eyebrow. "So, nothing different there then."

Carn responded. "Aye, but the innkeeper is getting a bedroll, so I can sleep on the floor." He leaned forward saying, "The Innkeeper said, 'As you are a fine fellow and will give your daughter the bed, I will get you something so that sleeping on the floor isn't too uncomfortable.'."

Lara chuckled and gazed at him. It was frustrating with the father and daughter act, but it could also be very amusing.

Early the next morning, they left the inn after Carn had had his breakfast. The Sword gave the impression he had rested in the bedroll, although it had not been used. Lara did not care what people thought, but Carn wanted to keep up the act in public, so she went along. As they walked to the main town square. Carn asked, "So, where do we start? I'm guessing the werewolf or wolves will have either family or work here."

Lara responded, "Aye. I just need to pick up a scent. I picked it up faintly when we entered the town, so the main square may be a good place to start."

Carn agreed, looking ahead at where the market traders were setting up for the day's business. Lara slowed as she picked up a scent. "I have one. It's north of here."

Carn followed Lara as she walked through the market to the north of the town. As they left the square, Lara picked up the scent again. It was stronger, and she followed it up a side street. Ahead of them was a blacksmith, both could hear him working on something in his forge. Lara focused on the large, bearded man as he worked. The hammer rang down the street as it beat the metal into shape. The scent had to be coming from him. She glanced at Carn. "I think we've found our werewolf."

Carn looked ahead, nodding towards the blacksmith. "Him?"

"Aye." She looked at Carn and smiled.

He sighed. "I know that smile all too well. So, am I needing my sword repaired?"

Lara nodded. "I want to see his reaction with the silver blade. I'm downwind, so he won't pick up my scent, but he may on you. So, keep downwind and in the smoke from his forge, as it will mask it."

Carn nodded and walked up the narrow street. Lara stayed back and hid from sight, but could still see and hear what was happening. When Carn reached the blacksmith, he called out, "Good morn."

The blacksmith emerged from the forge. The large man wiped his hands on a cloth and eyed Carn with suspicion. Lara saw Carn was keeping downwind and in the direction the smoke was heading, so the blacksmith would not be able to pick up his scent easily. The blacksmith asked, "How can I 'elp ya?"

Carn smiled and pulled his silver sword free. "I was hoping you could look at this for me."

The blacksmith moved forward to take the sword, then froze, flexing his fist. "That will need a more specialised craftsman. Ya will need to head for Shadefall."

Carn stepped forward, pointing the sword towards the man. "Can't you take a quick look?"

The man eyed him and shook his head. His eyes apprehensively glancing at the blade. "Nay, not for me."

Carn reluctantly sheathed the sword. "Alright." Carn paused, then smirked. "Not sure why you won't take a look unless you are a werewolf or somethin'."

The blacksmith laughed awkwardly and stated, "Not me thing."

Carn nodded, not realising he had stepped out of the direction of the smoke. The blacksmith took a deep breath and glared at Carn. "Then again, you mingle with somethin' off."

Carn cursed, realising his mistake, but before he could react, Lara was next to the blacksmith. When the large man turned to her with suspicion, she stated quickly, "We just want to talk."

He glared at her, ready to run. He took a big sniff and snarled, "What are ya? Ya smell off."

Lara kept calm, blocking his path to stop him from running. Yet also making sure they were not seen as a threat. "Like I said, I just want to talk."

"'Bout what?"

Lara could see him tense. She stepped back, raising her hands. "We aren't here to fight you."

She kept her eyes on him. It was a full moon when werewolves were forced to change, yet, they still could, at will. The downside of that meant they just were not as strong compared to when there was a full moon. She was not about to show her true nature, unless she had to, and he probably did not realise she would know a werewolf's limitations. But even in a weaker state, they could still be quicker than a human, so Lara ensured she was close enough to Carn to get between them, if needed.

She stated, "We want to know about the lycans at Shadefall and the deal they made with your pack."

The blacksmith smirked. "Not me pack. I know there wasn't nay deal, just a truce."

Carn asked, "Not your pack?"

The blacksmith replied, "Nay. I've lived here for years. The pack who caused the trouble came from the north. Well, some of them did. I had to be careful as locals don't know what I am, and have a business to run. So, I made a deal with 'em; they leave me be and I do the same."

Lara nodded. "I can understand that. What do you know?"

He sucked through his teeth, scratching his bearded chin, and regarded them. He stretched out his hand, eyeing the two of them. Carn nodded and pulled some coins from his pocket. He placed them in the man's grubby hand. The blacksmith glanced at the coins, then smiled and pocketed them. He said, "Well, seems some of them had left a pack up north to start their own. Think the new alpha didn't get along with the other one. Most of them were young'uns, and they wanted to make their mark. Seemed they tried their luck further east but the lycan pack at Shadefall weren't too happy. So, they headed 'ere."

Lara asked, "Know anything more about the pack to the north? And why did this one seem able to have a full run here without being stopped?"

The blacksmith studied her for a moment. He then held out his hand again, beckoning with his fingers. Carn dropped more coins into his dirty palm. The black smith pocketed them. Then leaned towards Lara and said, "Well, I 'ave known for years that the lycans at Shadefall don't give a feck about us small towns and villages. And sayin' they're supposed to be watchin' over 'em. Which, to be honest, suits me fine. Yet it seems somethin' happened. The alpha was boastin' that he could do what he liked here and the lycans wouldn't stop 'im. Then one night, after they'd had a few, I heard one of them say they 'ave some lycan wantin' shelter with, um, up north. Seems they're protectin' one from her pack. So, wonderin' if that had anythin' to do with a deal or somethin', I dunno."

Lara raised an eyebrow. This differed from what Dray had told them. "I see. Did you hear anything more? Maybe as to why she's with them?"

He shrugged. "Nay, they didn't say much 'bout that. Only that Shadefall was off-limits, but they were free to set up 'ere and 'ave nay interference from the lycans. Saw the cocky alpha of the pack having dealin's with a dark-haired lad, the younger brother of the lycan alpha. Thing is, most of the time they kept pretty quiet, till all that talking with the young lycan. He seemed to almost encourage 'em to cause trouble. A few times, I'd see 'im drinking with the young alpha and egging 'im on with the local girls. Most of the trouble came after too much drinkin'."

Lara nodded, wondering if the lycan was Tomlin and why was he stirring trouble. She asked, "Do you know where up north the female lycan is?"

"Think one mentioned Silver Wood once. But their alpha didn't seem to like many to know. Sayin' he'd boast 'bout it if he could, and I knew he didn't, as I heard the lycan ask, and the alpha just said north. Think the lycan was getting annoyed that he wasn't tellin' him more. The werewolf alpha was all cocky, like he knew more, but from what I've gathered from the other pack members, he didn't know much. They said he was simple in the head. Seems they were getting a little disgruntled with 'im and if he hadn't been killed, they would've left anyway. Which I don't think would've gone down well with the lycan. He was still askin' about the lycan girl up to the day before the alpha was killed. To be honest, I think the lycan was gonna kill 'im if he hadn't died already."

Lara nodded. "Thank you. We'll let you get back to work."

She turned to leave when the blacksmith added, "Just to warn ya, those lycans at Shadefall? Best keep out of their business, they don't like anything that ain't them. This confused me with 'im being chatty with the werewolves, but think he was after where the girl was. Be real careful of that younger brother. He killed Sara, from up the road, for sayin' nay to 'im." He glanced round and quietly added, "I think the lycan lass said nay to 'im too, and she ran."

"Again, thank you. And we'll be careful."

He nodded and returned to his forge. Lara glanced at Carn and they headed back towards the square.

Carn broke the silence, "Knew that Tomlin was trouble."

"Aye. Think if our paths cross again, we may have to deal with him."

Carn agreed. "Think it would be wise."

When they returned to the square, they wandered around the meagre market. Carn wanted to pick up food supplies before they headed north. Lara stayed as it was nice just to wander and it reminded her of her time on Moonstar before her change. The market was not as busy, due to what they had recently gone through, but it was still interesting. Both also knew they would welcome their coin. She paused at a toy stall and remembered how she would pick something for her brother whenever she was at the market back home. She sighed and turned from it, feeling a little sad; she had not seen Derwyn for over ten years and wondered how his family was doing.

Carn placed a hand on her shoulder and whispered, "Thinking of Derwyn?"

She looked up at him, frowning. "How?"

Carn gazed at her lovingly. "I saw you looking at the toy stall."

Lara smiled softly, seeing sadness mirrored in his eyes. "Aye, I was wondering how he and his family are. It has been so long."

"They'll all be well."

Lara nodded. Carn would have similar feelings when seeing a toy stall. It had hit Carn hard when he lost Iesha and Isabel. Now and then, she would catch him lost in thought, obviously still thinking about them. But even though they both had dark moments, they would help each other through them.

Lara smiled at Carn and said, "Let's get a drink."

He nodded. "Sounds good to me."

Lara squeezed his hand and pulled him towards the inn.

They sat at the back of the inn, Lara savouring her drink while Carn was on his third ale. He belched and apologised, then looked across the nearly empty room. "So why didn't Dray tell us the truth?"

Lara looked at him. "I knew he was hiding something. I think it would affect his status if they knew his daughter had help in escaping from the pack. Yet, I'm more inclined to think he doesn't know who aided her." She paused and then added, "I think Tomlin may have been the cause for why she left."

"You think so?"

Lara shrugged. "Not sure. But my instinct is telling me he could have been the reason. If he had his sight on taking control of the pack, then the girl could have been a threat to him. If he had her killed, then it would unsettle Dray, and make him irrational. With her dead, Tomlin would gain full rights to the pack if he challenged his brother and won. I'm wondering if things didn't go according to plan, and if that's why he kept asking the werewolf the same question. Maybe he was trying to fix a mistake. So, another reason to be on our guard."

Carn agreed. "So, this northern pack, do you think they'll be welcoming or like all the others?"

She took a sip of her drink. "I don't know, but we'll find out. Think they'll take a dislike to me, but if we manage it right, we'll still get something out of it."

Carn sighed and finished his ale. He leaned back and raised an eyebrow. "Time for bed, I think."

Lara gave him a mischievous grin. "Aye, I agree."

As soon as the door closed, the two started pulling each other's clothes off, and stumbled to the bed, kissing as they went. Lara climbed on top of Carn, straddling him. Lara traced her fingers over Carn's lean muscles. For his age, he was still in fine form. She paused, gazing into his blue eyes, and breathed, "I love you, Carn."

He looked up at her, focusing on her green. "You know, I never tire of hearing that."

They kissed passionately, and Lara gasped as he entered her. She lost all sense of time and focused only on Carn's caresses and connection. The sadness from hours before melted away for them both.

Lara lay entangled in Carn's limbs, tracing her fingertips over the scar on his chest. He had received it from a demon fight five years before. "Does it still hurt?"

Carn glanced down at her and kissed her on the forehead. "A little, but just one of many."

Lara smiled softly; most wounds would heal, but a demon one would always leave its mark. She thought of the ones on his back from Bighdarum. They had taken weeks to fully heal, and they still plagued him. With her lycan and vampire healing properties, she never got any scars, but with Carn being a human, his body took the toll. She hated it when he was in danger and got wounded. But being a Sword was his life, even before they had met all those years ago.

She leaned on her elbows and studied his features. "I was thinking about that cabin. Once this is over, do you want to have a go, and build it?"

Carn grinned. "In that clearing we saw?"

"Aye. Think we need somewhere, and with all the years here, I think we should have something."

He kissed her gently. "Thank you. I know you would feel restless to move on after so many years here. But I think for us, this will be good."

She nodded, and it was true, she had always felt the need to move on. Yet in finding Carn again, the urge to move had lessened, and this time she wanted to stay. Her stomach twisted with dread at the eventual outcome, but Lara did not care. She had many years ahead of her, how many, she did not rightly know, but she wanted to spend the rest of Carn's with him.

CHAPTER 28

BY SUNUP, THEY were leaving Diran behind and heading to Silver Wood, a small village to the far north of the island. With little success from the market, they decided when they reached Roclus's inn, they would get supplies and ask after any news. There was also a chance they could bump into Tomlin if he had followed them. If so, they had decided to deal with him, then and there.

They reached Roclus's inn after a day's ride. Roclus was as chatty as ever, but there was no significant news of werewolves or any sign of Tomlin. After a good night's rest, they picked up supplies and continued their journey the following morning.

While at Roclus's inn, they made their travel plans to save time and avoid issues. The major towns and cities were all to the east or west, and very few needed to travel north, but, if they had to, they took the long way and stuck with the major routes. They would take the direct route north, then ride through Old Wood, a large, ancient forest. There were rumours of demons and wild cats within, and most would avoid it at all costs. Yet, if one wanted to get to the smaller villages and hamlets to the north quickly, Old Wood was a shortcut. It was a route used by excellent trackers to save time. All the safe paths that went through the forest were hard to find. Lara had an advantage and could spot anything that would cause them issues in advance. Along with Carn's tracking skills, they could take the risk.

As they ventured further in, they entered the oldest part of the forest. The density of the trees became tighter, and the darker it became. It was difficult for them to tell the time of the day with no reference to the sun. Both agreed to continue until they felt the need to rest. After a decent ride, with Lara able to see clearly in the forest's darkness, they finally set up camp. Carn made a small fire to keep any demons or creatures away, and to take away the slight nip in the air. Lara studied Carn over the flames of the fire, feeling the need to hunt. It would also help, as she could track ahead and see if it was safe. Lara gave Carn a quick kiss, then stripped and changed into her wolf form. While Lara trotted off into the trees, Carn sat at the campfire, cooked food, and kept watch.

Lara ventured between the large trees, taking in the surrounding scents. This section of the forest was old. Lara glanced around, surprised she had not picked up any demon scents yet. They could be further in. She slowed when she picked up the scent of a few rabbits and a deer, but no wild cats. It seemed this part of the forest was safe. She focused on the rabbit, as that would be easier prey and enough for what she needed. Yet as she hunted it, Lara picked up another scent. Demon. She paused and took a deep breath, trying to pinpoint it. It was not familiar, something she had not encountered before. Since she was unsure as to what it was, the last thing she wanted was for them to cross paths with it. But it was also on their potential route north. If they had to, they would need to be prepared. Leaving the rabbit to live another day, Lara crept towards the scent, wanting to know what type of demon it was.

The trees were even more compact, and a small stream towards the east flowed between the trunks. Then she noticed something moving over the forest floor. It was the demon. It was huge, resembling a large centipede, but only had twenty thick legs. Lara crept closer, keeping herself low to the ground and making sure she stayed upwind. Her wolf eyes regarded the creature from where it stood in a small clearing. As she watched, it spun around in a circle, digging itself into the ground. It was soon covered in a thick layer of newly upturned dirt. Lara then picked up the scent of the deer she had detected earlier. It seemed that it was going to be its next prey.

Lara watched, fascinated; but realised it would be valuable information for when they headed this way later. She did not have to wait long before she could make out its trap. Lara noticed what looked like young plants on the ground where the creature was hidden. Lara focused on them, inspecting them as well as she could from a safe distance. When the demon buried itself, those were not there before. At a quick glance, they looked like plants, but there was something strange about them. Lara sniffed as a soft breeze came her way, and could smell fresh vegetation. But when she focused on the greenery using her vampire vision, she realised they were some sort of tendrils. Very clever. If the breeze changed direction, the deer's senses would pick up the smell of vegetation. But Lara could see exactly what it truly was.

Keeping still and low, she waited. The deer moved slowly into the clearing, lured by the green tendrils. It tentatively sniffed the air, as the breeze changed direction for a moment, but still lured in. Once the deer was close enough, the tendrils shot upwards, wrapping around the animal at a phenomenal speed. Then the ground exploded with the creature emerging. Within moments, it secreted a green gel, cocooning the deer. Then, with its front legs, the creature threw the deer up into the air and Lara heard a splat. She slowly looked up to see the horror of the creature's nest. Entombed in the green gel, were several animals: wild cats, deer, and other creatures, all in various stages of decay. The bodies seemed to be more like husks. The demon then slowly stretched upwards, standing on its back legs, the insect-like head reaching up to the deer that could not even struggle in the solidified gel. Lara turned away as it punctured the body of the deer with a spike on its tongue. It slowly sucked out the animal's innards, leaving another husk in its collection. Lara felt sick. They needed to avoid that demon at all costs. She noticed the wind changing direction again, and she ran from the nest area before it could pick up her scent.

Lara returned to the camp but had still ensured, even after seeing the demon's nest, that she hunted. When she reached the campfire, she changed back into human form. As she dressed, Lara stated, "We may need to change our route."

Carn looked up from the fire. "What did you see?"

"I'm not sure," said Lara with disgust in her voice. "Some insect-like creature, it traps its prey and then devours the innards."

Carn wrinkled his nose. "Sounds pleasant."

"Even more so when you see it in action."

"Oh," responded Carn as Lara sat beside him. "That's bad."

She nodded. "Nay clue what it is, though. I have never encountered one before, and I hope we never have to again."

Carn replied, "Well, it's deep in the forest, so not sure anyone would have encountered one till they head this way. Was there only one?"

"Only picked up the one scent."

"It's not ideal, but shall we go around?"

Lara pursed her lips, wondering if they should deal with it, but it was so off the beaten track, it really did not seem worth it. "Aye, we'll avoid it. I saw how it got its prey, but with not knowing its weaknesses, I think it would be wise to avoid." She eyed him. "Also, we won't need to worry about wild cats, as that thing has eaten them all. If not, they'll stay clear."

Carn responded as he yawned. "I'm glad this route isn't well used."

Lara smiled. "Think the rumours keep most out." She gazed at him lovingly. "Get some sleep. I'll take watch."

He nodded, knowing how little sleep Lara needed.

Once Carn had settled down. Lara rummaged in her saddlebag, pulling out her leather-bound notebook. Using the firelight, she quickly sketched the creature and made a few notes about the trap it used. It was not much, but at least she had something written.

After a few hours, Lara woke Carn. From a rough calculation, it had to be nearly dawn, and it was best to continue. Lara took the lead so that they could avoid the area with the demon of unknown origin. After making the note, Lara also decided that when they ventured back to Ra, she would go to the extensive library there. It had an intensive section on the demons of Lost Island and another one that covered other lands as well. She hoped there would be something on the forest demon, and if not, she knew the librarian well enough to know that they would want her account added to their records.

The detour through the forest added a few more hours to their trip, but it was better than risking an encounter. By dusk, they reached the edge of the woods. It was good to see the sky once more. Making camp, Lara let Carn rest while she took the first watch. She looked up at the sky and then back at the forest. The demon was the apex predator and over years had taken out the wild cats and other demons that had been rumoured to be living there. She did not get a detailed look at its nest, but suspected that there would be several layers of corpses. The ones she had seen seemed to be old, and they went high into the trees. If she could find out more about it, then it may be worth coming back to Old Wood and dealing with it. There will be a point when its food ran out, and then it would need to find an alternative source.

She glanced north toward Silver Wood and wondered what they would find. If what the werewolf at Diran had said was true, Lara would want to talk to Dray's daughter to make sure she had all the information. Yet once she had, she was unsure of what her next move would be. Lara strongly suspected that somehow Tomlin had some involvement in the situation, and if he was, then it was no longer her concern. It was a battle for leadership. Yet Lara wanted no more innocent people getting stuck in the middle. Maybe if she told Dray's daughter what was happening, then something could be resolved. But she would not get further involved unless Roclus's inn or Diran were stuck in the middle again. Then Lara would not just stand back and do nothing. What surprised her was they had not come across Tomlin yet. She looked back at the forest; he was probably tracking them and making sure he kept upwind. As that would be what Lara would do. Whatever the case, if they crossed paths, it was wise to deal with him.

By dawn, they were riding north again, towards Silver Wood. They had not gone far when it started raining, and as time passed, the rain got heavier, to the dismay of the two. Their cloaks kept them dry to a point, but with the rain becoming heavy, it slowly seeped through. The north did not have the harsh winters like they did in Barberium and Moonstar, and the rain was still preferable to bitter snowstorms. Yet, even though rain was better than snow, by the time they reached the small village and inn, they were soaked to the bone. Lara looked north, to the woods in the distance similarly called Silver Woods. She could see why it had the name with the grey-green leaves of the trees. The wind whipped up and swirled around them, making the leaves move, looking like a wave of silver. She surveyed the trees; the wood was dense and looked substantial. A good place for werewolves to hunt unseen.

Stopping outside the inn, both wanted to get into the dry as soon as possible. Lara gave Carn the saddlebags, and he headed inside to get rooms and food and drink. Lara had spotted a stable to the back and took the horses there so they could rest. Entering the stable, Lara wondered how busy the inn would be, as the stable was less than half full. She found a couple of stalls and brushed down the horses, ensuring they had a supply of oats before she ventured out into the rain again and then to the inn.

When she entered, it surprised her at how busy it was but realised most of the patrons were probably locals. She took in the scents, and all were human, but there was a faint trace of an older scent that was a werewolf. Just none were there that evening. She removed her rain-soaked cloak as she searched for Carn, glad of the warmth of the inn's fires. Even though small, the inn had two fireplaces in the main seating area for patrons, one at each end. Being further north, the winters were probably cold to the townspeople, yet for Lara and Carn, Lost Island was almost tropical compared to the lands they had been to before.

She soon spotted Carn seated at the fireplace near the far end, where it seemed a little quieter. He had taken off his cloak, which he had draped over the back of his chair, letting the fire's heat dry it out. Lara walked over to Carn and draped her cloak over her chair, like he had, and sat down next to him.

He gazed at her as he took a sip of his ale, then said, "I will be glad to have a decent night's sleep and get out of these wet clothes."

Lara agreed. "I'm wet to the bone. I would welcome a bath."

Carn replied, "Already thought of that. I asked the innkeeper to set one up in your room."

Lara smiled. "My room?"

He nodded. "Thought it best I booked two." He leant back and winced. "This rain is making my joints ache."

"What about your back?" asked Lara, knowing the wound always gave him more trouble in the cold or damp.

Carn sighed. "It aches."

Lara took a large gulp of her drink, letting the alcohol burn its way down to her stomach. She did not actually feel the cold, but she still remembered the feeling from when she was just a lycan. It was silly she could recall the feeling, but for Carn, it made her seem more human if she moaned about the cold and dampness, even though it was not an issue for her. Yet she did like, and longed for, a bath. It was more likely a subconscious habit that seemed to make her feel relaxed. The barmaid came over with food, a selection of sausages and potatoes, and bread. Lara could see why Carn had ordered it, so it would look like they were both going to eat instead of just Carn. Lara had tried a few times over the years to consume food, but it was always the same. Tasteless as sawdust in her mouth, and she found it impossible to swallow. She even tried to think about when she hunted, but that did not help. Only raw meat was palatable, and asking for that at an inn was not the wisest thing to do. She would just sit back and enjoy her drink while Carn devoured the lot. He did not have the appetite of a lycan like Derwyn, but he still ate more than the average man. It was his warrior build which gave him the energy to fight as he did. Whatever, it worked, and even in his fifties, he was still as lean. She gave him a sly look and knew when they got to 'her' room, they would enjoy the bath together.

It did not take Carn long to devour his food. He then nodded to the innkeeper that they wanted the bath prepared, and by the time they had finished their drinks, it was set up, and readied in Lara's room. She thanked the barmaid when she came over to inform her. The two then headed up to their rooms, yet Carn never made it to his. Lara opened hers, seeing the hot steaming bath waiting for her. Carn sighed. He was probably wanting it more than her. She took his hand in hers and pulled him into her room, locking the door behind them. She gazed at his blue eyes and whispered into his ear, "Let's get you into that bath."

He raised an eyebrow, looking over at the medium-sized circular bathtub. "Looks big enough for two."

She smiled, kissing him. "Well, I need someone to give my back a scrub."

He pulled her into his arms and kissed her passionately. He said, his lips just a hairbreadth from hers, "I can think of something else to do than that."

She smiled, her hands fumbling with the buttons on his shirt. "We should get in before that water gets cold."

It did not take them long to strip and soon they were in the bathtub, enjoying the water's warmth and their closeness. Carn sighed with delight as the hot, herb-filled water helped his aching joints and muscles. Lara positioned herself behind him and massaged his back, her fingers tracing the claw marks across it from the battle at Bighdarum. She tried not to focus too much on the scars that ravaged his body. So many were from battles they had had together against demons. Her scars were a faded memory, but for Carn, they were a reminder every day. She felt guilty knowing how humans suffered from scars dealt by demons.

Yet whenever Lara asked him about them, he never complained and saw them more like trophies.

Carn glanced back at her and said, "They don't bother me that much anymore."

Lara studied him, her hand resting on his firm, muscular shoulder. "But you will still feel them. I feel guilty that I don't have scars like this."

He turned in the tub facing her, making some of the water splash out onto the floor, and cupped her face in his wet hands. "Don't. I've told you before; they remind me that I survived fights that few humans would. And all I feel is honoured as they also remind me I fought by your side."

She smiled sadly, and pulled him close to her, kissing him. When they parted, she said, "But I will always feel like I should be the one who feels all the pain of those battles."

He studied her and smiled. "Don't Lara. Without you, I'd've been dead years ago. So I get scars, yet, we fight well together. I'd sooner have these to fight by your side, than a scar-free body and never to be with you." He paused and chuckled. "Even if sometimes you use me as bait."

She smiled and kissed him passionately and then said, "Well, you're good as bait."

He glared at her and grabbed her, pulling her close. "So, I'm just bait, am I?"

Lara giggled as he nibbled on her neck. "Oh nay, you are more than that."

He looked at her, lost in her green eyes. "I'm yours till my dying breath, and if that means being bait, so be it."

She studied him and kissed his full lips. She would live for hundreds of years, but these years with Carn would always remain her fondest.

CHAPTER 29

AFTER DAWN, THE two left the inn and walked along the main road that wound through the small village, both wondering how they could go about finding the werewolves. The village was more like a hamlet, with a blacksmith, a couple of shops, and the inn. The rest were houses, scattered along the road and nearby, with farmland to the north. As they walked along, Lara could not pick up any definitive scents. Most were a few days old. The werewolves had been in the village, and to the inn; they had to live in the nearby area. But not being in the village on a daily basis meant only one other place.

Lara looked north towards the wood and wondered. It was a good place to hide. When the werewolf at Diran said they were at Silver Wood; that did not mean just the village. She grabbed Carn's arm. "I think we need to explore in there."

He nodded towards it. "You think they're in the woods?"

"Aye. The scents are days old and, to be honest, it looks like a good place to hide."

"Then let's go."

Turning from the village, they walked north towards the woods. Lara felt it in her gut, they had to be in there, and her instincts were never wrong. When they reached the edge, Lara picked up a werewolf's scent, and it was recent. She glanced at Carn. "They're here."

Carn pursed his lips. "Then we better be on alert." He studied her. "Are we going in as we are, or did you want to change?"

Lara surveyed the woods. "Nay, as we are. Don't want to spook them more than necessary." She glanced at him. "Be alert. They won't be at their strongest, but they'll still be fast."

Carn nodded. "Always am."

They slowly made their way into the woods. The trees were large, old, and remarkably close together. There was a natural pathway off the primary route from the village, but Lara kept away from it, Carn close behind. They were on full alert, and Lara kept her senses sharp, not knowing when they would come across a werewolf. If she was correct, the pack would be in the centre, to the north. They were upwind, and she would pick up their scents first. They soon fell into the darkness of the dense wood and Lara, with her keen vision, could see a respectful distance. Carn kept close, relying on Lara.

She stopped, hearing something ahead. She wondered if it had detected their scent. They were not visible, but as a gentle breeze headed in their direction, she could smell the werewolf. She gently took hold of Carn's arm and placed her fingers to her lips, then pointed in the werewolf's direction. He nodded, understanding. They moved slowly ahead, toward their objective. As they moved around some trees, Lara could see it ahead. It was in werewolf form, but seemed oblivious to them.

They have keen senses, similar to mine. Seems strange it hadn't picked up our movement; unless it was . . .

There was a low growl behind them. Lara cursed. It was a common ruse, and she fell for it. Lara slowly put up her hands and whispered, "We're here to talk, nothing more."

The werewolf ahead of them walked over and snarled. It sniffed them both then growled, picking up Lara's scent.

Lara stated, "Aye, I am different, but I am not your enemy." She looked the werewolf directly in the eyes. "I want to talk to your alpha."

The werewolf looked at the one behind them and then nodded slowly. Lara and Carn followed when gestured for them to go with it. Lara glanced at Carn. He looked tense, but knew not to do anything foolish, and to let her take the lead.

They walked through the woods, taking longer than Lara had thought. It seemed the werewolf was trying to hide the exact location of where they were living. After several more minutes, the werewolf entered a clearing. In the centre was a large house with vines covering the walls. The clearing had once had an ornate garden but had become overgrown. Though the house was old, it looked well-maintained. Lara looked around. At one point, there would have been a clear path to the house for carriages and horses. It seemed whoever lived there years ago had wanted the house to be hard to find. She wondered how many generations of werewolves had lived there, as that would explain why it was so well hidden.

Once in the clearing, Lara could pick up several more werewolf scents and one lycan. It seemed Dray's daughter was here. As they reached the house, the door opened and a tall, blond, plain looking man with broad shoulders stood on the threshold. He stated, "Few venture into these woods, and never voluntarily."

Lara smiled. From his stature, he was the alpha. "Well, I told this one here that I wanted only to talk."

The alpha took a deep breath, taking in her scent. He glared at her for a few moments and then said, "So, what are you?" He glanced at Carn. "He's human and not afraid, so you have faced beings like us before."

Lara replied, "We have. And we have killed many by our hands, but only those who deserved it."

The alpha pursed his lips. "So, Swords. I think you might have been responsible for the rogue werewolf near Diran?"

Lara nodded. "Aye."

The werewolf next to her growled, but did not move. It was probably one that had been part of that pack, but with the alpha present, he would not dare.

She could see the alpha waiting for her to explain what she was, and she added, "As for what I am, I'm a lycan, with an extra twist."

The man stepped forward, taking another sniff. "Smells like a vampire to me." He looked directly into her eyes. "From what I heard, that isn't possible."

Lara smirked. "Well, it is." She kept eye contact and stated, "So, can we talk?"

He sucked in air between his teeth as he looked her up and down. "You can." He turned to Carn. "But the human stays out here."

Carn tensed, but Lara glanced at him. "Understood." She could tell Carn did not like it, but he would stay alert and ready, if needed.

Leaving Carn outside, Lara followed the alpha into the house. Once in the hallway, the tall man asked, "So, what do you want to talk about?"

Lara looked up at him. "I would like some clarification."

He glanced back at her as they entered a lounge with four armchairs centred in the room. An entire wall was covered with full bookshelves and tucked in a corner was an intensive bar, more well-stocked than the average inn. A young man who had followed from the moment they entered stood by the door. The alpha gestured to the armchairs and asked, "Drink?"

She replied, "Aye, anything strong."

He nodded and walked over to the bar and poured a couple of drinks. He passed her one and then sat, gesturing to Lara to take the chair opposite. Lara slowly sat down and kept her eyes on the alpha. Taking a sip of her drink, she responded, "This is good."

"Not many can manage it."

Lara smiled, knowing he was trying to figure her out, and she was doing the same. She glanced around the room and said, "So, as I stated, I'm here to talk."

He nodded, taking a sip of his drink. "You mentioned you wanted clarification. On what?"

Lara took another sip. "As you know, I dealt with that rogue werewolf. But I wanted to know why the local lycans weren't keeping the residents safe, so I went to see their alpha." She studied him as she spoke, seeing his neck muscle twitch when she mentioned the lycans. Seems she had hit a nerve, more than killing a fellow werewolf, even if he was a rogue. She continued. "And what he told me was rather interesting."

The alpha raised an eyebrow and took a sip of his drink. He was leaning back in his chair, looking relaxed, except for the tense neck muscles. "You're here to find out if what he told you is true?"

"Aye. And after the fact of talking to another source, I had conflicting information."

"I see. So, what do you want to know?"

"Dray's daughter, I picked up her scent as soon as I got here. I'm thinking, with the security being relaxed, that she's here of her own accord."

The alpha smiled. "So, I'm guessing Dray told you something else?"

"He did. And I would like to hear what his daughter has to say."

"Understood." He looked up and nodded to the young man who was standing in the doorway. The man left. A few moments later Lara picked up the lycan scent and a young woman, probably in her early twenties, entered the room and stated, "You wanted to see me, Orthur."

Lara studied the dark-haired woman. She could see the resemblance to Dray, and she could also tell she was not a captive. Her heart rate was relaxed, and she looked unharmed.

Orthur smiled. "It seems this lady here would like to talk to you."

The girl turned her attention to Lara. "What do you want to know?"

"I'm Lara. I just want to know why you're here."

"I'm Raia, and may I ask why?"

Lara focused on her grey eyes. "I spoke to your papa." The girl instantly tensed, and Lara quickly added, "I'm not collaborating with him. I was wanting to know why your papa's pack wasn't protecting the residents outside of Shadefall."

The girl sighed, taking a seat between the two. "My papa doesn't care about anyone outside of the city. What did he tell you?"

"Well, I got the impression he didn't keep to the standard ethics of a lycan alpha." Lara glanced at Orthur and stated, "He told me he was letting the werewolves run loose outside of Shadefall as they knew which werewolf pack was holding you captive. He claimed they had ambushed you, and killed all but you. The deal was, they would tell him where you were being held, if he let them do what they wanted. Yet it seemed they weren't being very forthcoming with their information."

Raia cursed, as did Orthur. The alpha snapped, "I knew he was up to something."

Lara responded, "He's making it very clear to his pack, that whoever is holding his daughter is the enemy."

Raia added. "I hate my papa. But it wouldn't be his doing. That's Tomlin's conniving." She studied Lara. "Are you here to take me back?"

Lara shook her head. "Nay. Like I told you, I'm not working for your papa. When I spoke to him, he thought I was going to find you and bring you back home. I believe he doesn't want his pack to think he's weak. But still, my instinct was telling me something was off. I then talked to a werewolf, a loner. He gave me conflicting information. So, I needed to find out for myself. I also feel there's a power struggle between your papa and his brother, Tomlin." She gazed at the young woman. "Can you tell me why you're here? And why do you think Tomlin's involved?"

Raia sighed. "The connection with Tomlin is that Orthur's pack rescued me from his men."

"Can I ask how that came about?"

Raia folded her arms, looking tense. "I never agreed with my papa's ways. I wanted the pack to protect all humans and non-humans, not just in Shadefall, but the surrounding villages, too. I found out about a rogue werewolf pack and that someone had spotted them near Diran. While I was looking into all of this, I found out that Tomlin wanted the werewolves to cause trouble outside of Shadefall. I believed he was going to use it against my papa; to prove he was weak, and not fit to be alpha. Even though Tomlin doesn't care about anything outside of Shadefall, like my papa, he would end the werewolves and use that to position himself to take over. So, I needed to act, and put a stop to all of it. I had done some investigating myself, and found out about Orthur's pack here. From what I had learned, if my papa wouldn't do anything, Orthur would. I had a witch send a message to Orthur asking to meet. Of course, Tomlin had found out, and sent a few members of the pack that are loyal to him, to stop me. I had taken a couple of pack members that were loyal to my papa, but who, like me, believed we should honour our traditions. Tomlin's men ambushed us, and their orders were to kill us all. Then there wouldn't be anything, or anyone, to stop him from taking over when the time came. Luckily, I was close to the meeting point, and Orthur's pack, which had been waiting for me. They came to my rescue. None but me, and one of Tomlin's men who ran, survived. Orthur's men brought me here for my safety, and I have remained here ever since."

Lara nodded and responded, "When I saw your papa, Tomlin wasn't hiding his dislike and thoughts of taking over the pack. He also didn't like the fact I had taken out the rogue alpha near Diran."

Raia sighed, "Aye. He knows, with me out of the way, he can take over. My papa and I may not always get along, but the pack knows he would do anything to protect me. They knew to keep me safe, and do as he says. But Tomlin has always disliked me, and is using the fact my papa would do anything to protect me, to his advantage. Tomlin has a loyal band of lycans within the pack, and I have heard rumours he wants to fully take over. As soon as he can challenge my papa, he will. But I would still have control, too, and Tomlin wants it all for himself. And he will, once the loyalists on his side makes sure I'm taken care of. But I was never sure until the attack on me. They were all Tomlin's men. I know if Orthur's men hadn't been there, they would have killed me, and blamed it on the werewolves. That would have given Tomlin an opening to take over. My papa wouldn't have been focused, and Tomlin could have beaten him. The fact I had escaped changed Tomlin's plans slightly, but the outcome, I know, will be the same. I need to let my papa know what Tomlin has planned, but feel he won't believe me."

Lara's father had told her years ago that, even if he were challenged and lost, she would still have most of the control with the pack, just by being the firstborn. Of course, they were not a large pack, so Lara never really thought about it being an issue. It was in all the old books, and was something that had been set in lycan law centuries before. With them having such strong family values, the children of the alpha would be next in line. If a challenger won the fight, they would have to share the pack's responsibilities with the eldest offspring. To most packs, the law was never an issue, but for one's like Dray's, that did not adhere to tradition, it seemed Tomlin was willing to bend the rules in his favour.

"From what I saw, your papa seemed to be aware of what Tomlin was feeling, but seemed confident he could be kept in check."

"Aye, he would. Tomlin has tried before and failed. But I don't think my papa realises how many are now loyal to Tomlin."

Lara nodded. Orthur stated, "So what now? If you're not working for Dray, why come all this way?"

Lara regarded him. "I'm from a long line of lycans, and I know their laws well. What Dray and Tomlin are up to is against that. I wanted to see why."

"And now that you do?"

Lara shrugged. "I won't interfere any further. I was concerned for the people outside of Shadefall and wondered why Drays' pack weren't being the protectors they should be. I killed a lycan alpha many years ago, as he wasn't following the true lycan laws." She studied Orthur. "I have nay quarrel with werewolves either, but I will kill them if they're harming innocents."

Orthur said, "And I thank you for dealing with that rogue. Most of his pack dispersed. Some returned here with mine that I had sent to spy on them. I informed them if they would accept me as their alpha and keep to my rules, they could stay. From what I could find out from them, they knew they didn't have to worry about the lycans."

Lara asked, "Did they work with Tomlin?"

"All they would say is their alpha made some deal with him. Of course, some of them didn't like that idea, but were loyal to their alpha."

Lara nodded. "I see."

He studied Lara and added, "I know that lycans and werewolves haven't always got on, but our core ethics are the same."

Lara looked at him. It seemed the rogue wolves were not doing his bidding as they had chosen to join the other alpha's pack. Everything she had read of werewolves was of them being rogues, and not having any ethics. But looking at this pack, they seemed to go against those reports. "You differ from other werewolf packs I have come across." She paused, finishing her drink. "I think if Tomlin isn't dealt with, I can see trouble coming to your pack."

"Aye, I agree." He paused for a moment and then said, "As you are Swords, could I ask you something?"

Lara looked at him and shook her head. "I don't do contracts like that, if you want Tomlin dealt with. But if he crosses me, that's a different matter."

Orthur nodded. "Understood. But knowing you're an ally would be useful."

Lara said, "As long as you keep those ethics, then we will be." Lara paused and studied him. "Surprised you aren't repulsed by what I am. Most are."

"You *are* rare, and though some of my pack will think differently, I only see a Sword with good ethics, and that is all that matters to me."

Lara nodded. "Then I will be on my way."

Orthur's lips curled slightly upwards. "Next time you pass this way, you'll both be welcome."

Lara stood and nodded to Raia. "I hope you can sort out your papa's pack. But be warned, Tomlin's going to take it over as soon as the opportunity arrives. I suggest you do something before then."

Raia asked, "Can't I convince you to deal with him?"

Lara shook her head. "This is politics. Like I said, unless innocents are harmed, or he crosses with me, I stay away. But if you need me for other concerns, Roclus's inn is a good place to leave word. I pass that way often."

The young girl nodded her thanks. Lara and Orthur left the lounge, and he led the way out of the house and back out into the clearing. There, leaning against a tree trunk, his eyes constantly on the house was Carn. He stood straight as soon as Lara emerged. The werewolf standing nearby also turned.

Orthur stated, "Show them the primary route through the wood. They are allies, and are welcome here whenever they pass."

The werewolf nodded and pointed towards the path snaking through the trees. Lara nodded her goodbye to Orthur and then walked with Carn and the other werewolf onto the path.

As they walked back out of the wood, Carn asked, "So?"

Lara glanced at him. "Seems the werewolf was correct. Tomlin tried to kill Dray's daughter, Raia, but alpha's, name's Orthur, men rescued her. She was on her way to making a deal with the werewolves so they could work together. Of course, Tomlin wants Drays' pack, but needs Raia gone so he can have full control."

Carn nodded, glancing back at the werewolf. "He looked like he would do anything for power. Dray wasn't all squeaky clean either."

"Nay. Raia knew a truce with the werewolves would help."

"I'm surprised they didn't hire us."

Lara laughed. "Oh, they did, but we aren't contract killers. I did say though, if Tomlin crosses us, we'll deal with him."

"Aye. That's true."

The werewolf stopped at the edge of the trees and nodded a good day to them both. They then walked back to the inn and found a table to have something to drink and eat. Carn gazed at Lara as they waited for their order. "So, what now?"

Lara took a sip of her drink as soon as the barmaid put it down. "As nay other contracts have come up yet, we could start sorting that cabin out?"

Carn smiled and nodded to the barmaid when she placed down his order. "I like that plan." He took a mouthful of food and then added once he had swallowed. "Then still do the contracts, but we will have a permanent base."

"Less sleeping under the sky."

Carn looked distant. "Ahhh, but some of those were good nights."

Lara smiled, remembering some very well. She leant towards him. "Think it's time to go to the room."

Carn raised his eyebrow and quickly finished his ale, leaving the rest of his food. The two then headed quickly to their room.

As soon as they entered Lara's room, she pulled Carn close, kissing him passionately. With his arms around her, Lara directed him towards the bed, not letting their embrace end. When they stopped at the bed, Lara pushed Carn backwards onto it. He gazed up at her as Lara undressed. She smirked and threw her clothes to the floor. Carn began pulling off his clothes when Lara stopped him. She gazed at him as she finished undressing him. As she pulled off his black trousers, she raised an eyebrow as she glanced at his growing groin. Discarding the clothing, Lara started kissing his thighs. Carn closed his eyes in ecstasy. When he felt her lips envelop his phallus, he groaned in pleasure. She seemed to have a magical touch, caressing him in the right places to make his body betray him. Her hands brushed his thighs softly as her mouth moved up and down. Carn lost control of his body, his thighs tensing as his hips lifted slightly, her warm mouth so welcoming.

Lara paused and glanced up, seeing Carn's features full of satisfaction. She then moved her lips across his stomach and chest. Capturing his lips with her own. Her body leant against his, their groins touching. Lara moved into position, straddling him. Guiding his phallus inside her, Lara gazed down at Carn as their hips moved in unison. He grabbed her breasts, feeling his body tighten, strumming. Lara's body also betrayed her. As both came to orgasm together.

CHAPTER 30

THEY HAD STOPPED at Roclus's after travelling back from Silver Wood via Derlin. It was nice to see familiar faces again, and they had their usual rooms and table near the back of the inn. Lara took in the scents, and it was good to see the place busy once more. They were stopping here before continuing across the country to Red Wood in the northeast, which was a bit out of their way. Both Carn and she agreed it would be best to avoid the coastal city of Shadefall, not wanting to cause any unnecessary trouble. They both decided to not take on any new contracts until they built the cabin, but had stopped at Roclus' in case any had been left and to leave a note with Roclus about their plans. Their plan gave them a much needed break, as they had been working non-stop since Barberium. Lara glanced at Carn as he finished his meal, knowing the rest would help him more than it would for herself.

The scent of a lycan and a werewolf broke Lara's thoughts. She looked up to see who had entered the inn to find Raia and the young man from the pack at Silver Wood. Both looked exhausted and concerned. As soon as Raia picked up Lara's scent, they walked briskly over to them. Lara stiffened, as well as Carn, his meal forgotten.

Lara gestured for them to sit as she asked, "Something's wrong. What happened?"

Raia looked around the inn and lent forward. "News hasn't reached this far yet, but everyone at Silver Wood has been slaughtered."

Lara leant forward, her face mirroring her concern. "The village?"

Raia nodded. "The pack went to investigate as soon as they heard the screams. But it was already too late."

Lara took a breath, taking in what had happened. "Who did it? A rival pack?"

The young man studied them and stated, bitterness in his voice, "Nay. It was Tomlin and his trusted men. But we think he's going to spread rumours it was werewolves."

Lara's eyes widened; Carn leaned forward. "Are you sure?"

Raia nodded. "Aye. When I went down to the village, I picked up his scent. This will help in making his leadership appear strong."

Lara asked, already knowing the answer. "How?"

Raia responded, "He thinks you must rule on fear, and believes that's how he can become alpha. He'll say my papa isn't doing anything, and had allowed this to happen. And his men will back him all the way. His close, core men who are as corrupt as he, and would have helped him at Silver Wood. They will ensure any that have doubts, won't for long."

Lara sighed and nodded. "Aye, makes sense. Add in the fact, humans can't tell the difference between us, except someone who has faced werewolves or lycans before. He'll even have the city of Shadefall behind him."

Raia agreed. "If you saw what they did to the village . . . How lycans could kill like that, I'll never understand."

"I can. If those that follow him are loyal, they'll do anything. Where's Orthur?"

"I convinced him to wait and help clear the village. I told him he needed to calm down and focus on what needed to be done. Then, as soon as he was busy with the pack, giving orders to clear the village, I had Jon come with me to find you as quickly as we could. But I fear Orthur will already be tracking Tomlin in the Old Wood. He won't be thinking clearly, and I believe that Tomlin may set a trap. With Orthur out of the way, Tomlin will have nothing to stop him once my papa is dead."

Lara nodded and glanced at Carn when he asked, "What do you want us to do?"

Raia looked at them both. "To find Tomlin. Orthur's out for revenge. I need someone to look at this clear-headed and find Tomlin, then deal with him. I need to continue on to Shadefall to talk to my papa and try to end this before things escalates."

"We'll head to Old Wood and track Tomlin. How many days ahead are they?"

"Only a day. When I convinced Orthur to wait, we left straight away. But I know that he will soon turn his sights on Tomlin with what he did. We gained good time as we ran here in wolf form, so we are well ahead of them. Tomlin and his men had horses, from the tracks I could see. Yet those tracks were not heading south either. They seemed purposely confusing. I know he's planning to face Orthur in the forest. I think Orthur and his men will have gone in wolf form, as in their anger they would be compelled to change in response to their rage. They will also be faster and stronger that way. But, as I said, I think Tomlin wants to face Orthur, so it could be a trap. I didn't have time to investigate all the tracks I found, as I wanted to get to you as quickly as we could. I also need to get to Shadefall before word reaches them, and get my papa to see what needs to be done; before it's too late."

Lara scratched her chin. "That forest is dense, so it would be hard to ride fast on horses, and it's easy to lose tracks. So it makes sense that Tomlin may give Orthur and his men the run-around. You may be right that he's going to set up an ambush. I don't know your papa's brother well, but know he'll want to make sure Orthur's pack is dealt with so no one can deny the story he will spread. I think Laycain is on your side with leaving so quickly. Tomlin wouldn't have expected anyone to leave so soon, so you would have missed the ambush."

Carn added. "Heading from here, we should cross their paths. Maybe distract Tomlin, so Orthur gets an advantage."

"Agreed," responded Lara.

Jon added. "Orthur's an excellent tracker."

Lara replied, "Maybe, but if Raia says he's out for revenge, he may not think as clearly." She studied the two. "Be careful when you get to Shadefall. Tomlin may still have men there."

Raia smiled. "Don't worry, I know ways into the city that Tomlin doesn't know about."

Lara nodded and turned to Carn. "Nay, time to lose. We should get moving."

He agreed. "I'll get our things from the room."

Lara got to her feet. "I'll get the horses." She turned to Raia. "Do you need food and rest? We've paid for two rooms, so you may as well use them."

Raia smiled. "Thank you, but we need to get to Shadefall as soon as we can. I dare not delay."

She nodded, knowing how far lycans could run. But even then, they would need some rest. "Just make sure you aren't too exhausted when you reach the city."

"Don't worry." Raia turned to the young werewolf and smiled. "Jon has my back."

Lara nodded, seeing some chemistry between them. "Well, take care. We'll continue to Shadefall once the situation has been resolved."

Raia nodded and the two left. Lara went up to Roclus and told him they had to leave and would not be needing the rooms. She then headed out to the stables to get the horses ready.

It was not long before they were riding into Old Wood. It was already nightfall, but in the forest's denseness, it made no difference. They took the same route they had taken when they travelled to Silver Wood, all those days before. Carn glanced at Lara as they rode. "Do you think they may come across that creature?"

Lara shrugged. "They may. If so, we'll have much less to deal with."

Carn nodded, looking ahead. The forest was even darker with the density of the trees, but let Lara lead, as she could see clearly in the low light. They could not ride very fast, but having been this way before, they knew the best route.

They had not been riding for long when Lara picked up shouting, then a yelp and a roar. Lara instantly knew that Orthur had come across the creature. She glanced at Carn. "Orthur and his men need help."

Carn nodded, both jumping from their horses. They could move quicker on foot. They ran through the trees, hearing more growls and yelps ahead, but as they weaved through the wood, they came to a clearing to find their route blocked by Tomlin and five of his men.

The leader turned to them and smiled coldly. "I can't let you help them. That creature is saving us the job of killing those werewolves."

Both Carn and Lara drew their swords. It seemed they had to deal with the lycans first, and hoped Orthur and his men could hold on and deal with the creature themselves. Tomlin's men drew their swords, split up, and ran at Lara and Carn, drawing them away from each other.

Carn parried the lycan's sword. He had to work hard but he had fought creatures who had been just as fast, and could keep up well enough. His opponent may have had speed, but not the experience with a sword, unlike Carn. Soon the lycan was down, bleeding out. He glanced across to see Lara fighting four of the lycans; it seemed they were aware she was more of a threat than he was. Carn wondered where Tomlin was. He saw movement out of the corner of his eye, and he turned to see the leader. Carn cursed. It looked like he was going to have to face Tomlin on his own. Carn took a firm hold of his sword, his body protesting after fighting the one lycan, but he had to do it.

Tomlin gave him a sly smile and threw down his sword. Carn swallowed. That was not good. *What is he doing?*

Then Tomlin unbuttoned his shirt and snarled. "As you like to feck a lycan, let's see if you can fight one in wolf form."

Carn cursed. It was hard fighting them as a human, but in wolf form was when they were at their strongest. Carn took a deep breath, gripping his sword. Tomlin changed just as fast as Lara could. Carn pulled one of his daggers free and threw it as the lycan started running at him as he changed. Tomlin dodged the dagger and pounced as he took full wolf form. Carn sidestepped and parried the wolf's claws. Tomlin landed on all fours with ease, and turned to face Carn again, snarling with his menacing wolf teeth. Carn took a breath, holding his sword, keeping his eyes firmly on the large brown wolf. Tomlin ran at him again. Carn went to move as Tomlin pounced, but the Sword misjudged and cried out in pain as the wolf's claws slashed across him brutally.

Carn felt the excruciating pain in his shoulder, a tingling sensation in his arm, and then the loss of grip on his sword. He staggered back, already knowing the wound would be life changing. He fell to his knees, feeling dizzy from the loss of blood pouring from his wound. Tomlin turned, skidding on the forest floor, and snarled, ready to run at Carn again and to make the fatal blow.

Having dealt with the other lycans, Lara ran over, pushing Tomlin out of the way, sending the wolf flying. She ran over to Carn as he struggled to get back up, his arm limp at his side, his shredded shirt and jerkin covered in blood. Lara studied his shoulder. The wound was brutal; she could even see the white of his bone. She cupped his cheek in her hand and whispered, "Don't leave me."

Carn smiled softly through his pain as he staggered back, dropping to the floor, his features pale. Lara turned to Tomlin, and the large brown wolf snarled at her. Lara started unbuckling her belt. "This fight is between us, Tomlin. Wolf to wolf."

He growled and stood his ground, watching Lara as she quickly stripped; she saw a werewolf run towards Carn. Lara picked up his scent on the breeze. It was Orthur. It seemed they had dealt with the creature. Lara turned back to Tomlin, as Orthur returned to human form to help Carn. Lara turned into her wolf form, ready to face Tomlin. The lycan charged at her, and Lara jumped to one side with ease, landing on all fours. Facing him, she made her wolf body as big as she could. Tomlin was an enormous wolf, almost as big as an alpha. That did not faze Lara, she had faced alphas before; and won. Lara growled at him, she would not let him intimidate her. Tomlin growled back and ran at her. Lara stepped to the side, dodging him. Then she jumped, turning her body to clamp her jaw down on his neck as he passed her, and ripped at his flesh. He yelped in pain; he may have been bigger, but he was not as fast as Lara. Tomlin stopped and turned back towards her. He snarled, then ran at the two men on the ground. Orthur was unaware as he focused on Carn's shoulder, packing the wound with moss to stem the bleeding.

Lara ran at Tomlin, knocking him out of the way. She growled at him, standing between him and the two men. She lunged at him again, slashing her claws across his back as he dodged. Yet Lara was quick. She spun around and sunk her teeth deep into his neck again, and made the fatal move, snapping his neck. As Tomlin's wolf form convulsed and turned back to human, Lara trotted over to Carn.

The Sword looked very pale. Orthur had bandaged his shoulder roughly by using Carn's shirt and moss from the forest floor. But blood was already soaking through. Lara quickly changed back to human form and knelt by Carn, studying him with concern. She looked up at Orthur, whose features also looked grave. "He needs a healer. *Urgently.*"

Lara nodded, sensing Carn's heartbeat had slowed and his breathing shallow. Her stomach twisted. She could not lose him now. "We need to get him to Roclus's inn." She pointed back the way they had come. "Our horses are that way."

Orthur nodded, turning to two of his men standing nearby, still in werewolf form. He snapped at them, "Find the horses."

They ran off as Lara stood and pulled on her clothes as she asked, "What happened? I heard wolf cries."

He looked at her as he grabbed Tomlin's clothes that he had discarded earlier. He checked on Carn and said, "Some creature back there, never seen one before, killed one of my pack, but we soon dealt with it." He turned to Carn, who was now barely conscious due to blood loss. "We'll get him on a horse and get him to the inn. I just hope he'll make it."

Lara knelt beside Carn, studying him. "He's too stubborn not to."

Orthur smiled and ordered one of his men to pick Carn up when the two returned with Carn's and Lara's horses. The man obeyed and carefully placed Carn on Lara's horse as she climbed up behind him to keep the barely conscious man in the saddle. Orthur climbed onto Carn's and turned to the two werewolves. "Take Ligh back to the manor and bury him. Once Carn is settled, I will return and we'll mourn our lost comrade."

The werewolves nodded and ran back towards where the creature was located. Lara glanced at Orthur. "I'm sorry you had to face that thing without our help, but Tomlin was blocking our way." She paused and then asked as they trotted as fast as they could back towards Roclus's inn. "Did you see the nest?"

"Aye. Have you seen that creature before?"

She nodded. "We came across it on the way to Silver Wood. I said to Carn we would need to come back and kill it. Wish I had done so then."

Orthur smiled softly. "It's not your fault, but mine. It wasn't on any major route, so had avoided humans for many a year. I shouldn't have forced my pack after Tomlin. I knew this wood was dangerous but, in my rage, I wasn't thinking clearly."

Lara nodded, looking at Carn when he groaned. "Thank you for coming to his aid."

Orthur nodded as they reached the edge of the woods and could pick up speed. With no moon, it was pitch black, but not to their wolf eyes. "I could hear the fight and we came as soon as we could. I could smell Carn's blood and knew something was wrong."

When they reached Roclus's inn, Carn was fully unconscious. Lara jumped down and, with Orthur's help, pulled Carn gently from the horse. She half-carried and half-dragged him into the inn. The sight of a man half covered in blood made the few people still up in the inn at the late hour stop what they were doing, and the barmaid gasped in shock. Roclus, on seeing Lara and the wounded Carn, ran from behind the counter. "By the gods, quick, bring him in 'ere." As he headed to the rear rooms, he shouted back to the people in the inn. "Someone get Scarlett. NOW!"

Orthur helped Lara get Carn into the back room as Roclus cleared the way for them. Lara asked, as she carefully laid Carn on the bed, "Who's Scarlett?"

Roclus looked at her as he lit the candles, in the almost pitch black back room. "She's a healer, doesn't live far from 'ere. Her cottage is to the south."

Lara nodded, having never seen or picked up the woman's scent. That meant she was a witch who was also a healer, as she had to be using a sort of shielding spell. It was a good defense when the rogue werewolves had been around. Lara turned her attention back to Carn as he muttered softly. "Must help Lar . . . "

He was already getting a fever. She studied the blood-soaked makeshift bandages and looked up at Roclus. "I need hot water and clean cloths. I need to do something while we wait for the healer."

The innkeeper nodded, his features looking grave, and ran from the room. Orthur stood to one side, unsure what to do. Lara gently whispered to Carn, unaware of the werewolf. "Don't leave me. I love you too much."

As she removed the bandages and moss, the blood oozed and Lara could feel her vampire side being pulled towards it. She took a deep breath, trying to focus. She could not let the vampire side rear its ugly head. Roclus came back with the water and cloths and gave Lara a grave look. "Ya don't look well, lass."

Lara clenched her fists, she could do it. Then a hand squeezed her shoulder gently and Orthur stated softly, "Let me."

Lara reluctantly stood, having to pull her eyes from the blood, and whispered, "I need some air."

Orthur nodded and started tending to Carn's wound. The innkeeper almost retched when he saw the torn flesh and the exposed muscle and bone. Lara dashed from the room. As soon as she was far enough, she could regain control.

CHAPTER 31

LARA SAT OUTSIDE the inn, the cool night air helping her regain control. She cursed under her breath. Even in his hour of need, she could not help the man she loved without that other side of her trying to gain control. She wiped away a stray tear, praying to Laycain that Carn pulled through. She just could not lose him. She was not ready to. She chided herself for not having fallen in love with a lycan. That wound would have healed by now. She sighed, wiping the tears that were now flowing more freely. If Orthur had not been there, she may have lost Carn in the forest. She just hoped the healer called Scarlett arrived quickly.

She felt like she had been sitting outside for hours, but dawn was still a good way off. She looked up, then she saw the man from the inn running towards the building, a tall red-haired woman with him. From the scent, it had to be Scarlett, her name was aptly chosen. The man ran in, yet Scarlett paused, studying Lara with disdain. Lara wiped her eyes and pointed inside. "You need to go to the back room. Please save him."

She studied her; her slender features were now neutral. "I will do what I can."

As Scarlett entered, Roclus was at the door and said, "She will save your papa, Lara."

The woman glanced back, slight confusion on her features, before rushing to the back of the inn. Lara knew the witch had sensed what she was and, of course, the truth as it related to Carn. Maybe not that they were lovers, but they were not father and daughter. Lara got to her feet. She had to be at Carn's side and entered the inn once more. As she reached the back room, Orthur was leaving, looking annoyed and stated, as the door shut behind him of its own accord. "The witch threw me out, saying she didn't want my kind in there."

Lara sighed, looking towards the room. "Well, she won't like me in there then."

Orthur placed a hand on her shoulder and whispered. "Carn's strong. He'll make it."

Lara's eyes lingered on the door. "He *has* to."

Orthur took her arm softly and directed her away from the room. "Come, let her do her work."

Lara reluctantly went with him back to the almost deserted inn. Only Roclus was still up, and looking concerned.

It was dawn before there was anything from the witch about Carn. Lara had been pacing the inn for hours, unable to relax, making Orthur and Roclus nervous. They had both asked her to sit and have a drink, but she was too tense with needing to know if Carn would make it. Then Scarlett entered the inn from the back room and Lara froze on the spot, almost at mid-pace. She turned to the woman and asked nervously. "Well?"

Scarlett studied Lara coolly, glancing at Orthur, who sat behind her. "So, a lycan did this?"

Lara replied, "Aye, but I killed him."

Scarlett nodded slowly, not taking her eyes off Lara. "And you are Carn's *daughter*?" the witch's voice had an edge of scepticism on the last word.

Lara again nodded. "Will he be alright?"

The woman pursed her lips, glaring at Lara with suspicion. "Aye, in time. But . . ."

Lara's stomach twisted. "But?"

"He sustained severe damage to his shoulder, some of his muscles and tendons badly torn. Because of this, he may struggle to use a sword again."

Lara nodded, feeling numb. "Oh."

Scarlett turned towards the back room. "Come, you can see him now." She paused. "The wound has been cleaned and covered, so there isn't much blood now, which I believed affected you earlier."

Lara nodded and followed the woman into the back room. The smell of herbs and incense overwhelmed her senses as soon as she entered it. Once alone, Scarlett asked, her voice cold. "So, what is your relationship with this man? He is most definitely not your papa."

Lara studied the pale sleeping Carn for a few moments. His shoulder bandaged well and then dragged her eyes away to focus on Scarlett. "So, you know what I am. I can reassure you I'm nay danger to you or anyone here. As for Carn, we love each other greatly."

Scarlett responded. "And the werewolf in the inn?"

"Again, nay threat. He's a client, and a friend."

Scarlett pursed her lips and studied the sleeping Carn. "He's strong. Few would have survived that injury."

Lara smiled softly, looking across at Carn lovingly. "He's too stubborn."

The woman regarded her, but her features still mirrored the caution she felt. "I can see you love him, and I'm gathering you have been close for a long time?"

"Aye, a very long time."

Scarlett nodded, silently checked Carn's shoulder, then turned back to Lara. "There's nay more I can do. The wound needs to heal, and he needs to rest." She pointed to a medium-sized jar of green paste off to the side. "I have made enough ointment to last a few weeks. Make sure you reapply after you wash the wound daily. Ensure the wound is left open until dry. Then add the ointment and recover with clean bandages."

Lara nodded. She took Scarlett's hand in hers; the woman stiffening at the touch. But Lara did not let go and stated, "Thank you."

Scarlett relaxed slightly; then fully once Lara let her hand go. The woman nodded, then turned and left. Lara watched her leave and then turned back to the sleeping Carn. She focused on his pale features before turning her attention to his bandaged shoulder. Lara wondered how he would react, knowing he may never use a sword again. Her eyes strayed to his greying hair and lined features. Then again, he was at an age, and they had been talking about putting their swords up, finding somewhere to settle down, and spend their nights sleeping indoors. It seemed they would be pulling the retirement plan further forward than they had thought. Then again, with the amount of coin they had earnt over the years, they did not need to work. It was time to build that cabin in the woods, and just have time together.

CHAPTER 32

CARN SLOWLY WOKE, his body feeling heavy. As he became aware of his surroundings, he could feel a dull throbbing ache in his shoulder. It surprised him at how little it hurt, despite his expectations. Opening his eyes, it took him a few moments in the room's darkness to make out where he was. He could not remember getting to a bed, then again everything was hazy since he faced Tomlin. He remembered the agonizing pain as the lycan's claws sliced into his shoulder and muscles, scraping his bone. That feeling resonated through his entire body. He had never known such pain. Then he vaguely remembered the shocked look on Lara's and Orthur's faces and knew that it had to be severe. By Rosh, it felt bad, the tearing and the burning, his entire arm going numb. He remembered his grip going on his sword as soon as the claws sliced through the skin and muscle. At that moment, he just knew it was not a flesh wound. The agony was so much it hit him like a brick wall, knocking him to his knees. He remembered Lara telling him not to leave her, and he would not, even as he felt the blood pouring from the wound. His vision kept blurring, but he remembered her facing Tomlin. He could not remember if she won or not, he had been so dizzy. Everything was so hazy. Then he remembered Orthur. The werewolf had said something, but he found it hard to focus, and knew it had to be the pain and loss of blood. He felt sick remembering all the blood. There had been so much. Then there was nothing, he must have fallen unconscious. It amazed him he was still alive. Carn sighed. He slowly focused on his surroundings, feeling a hand holding his. He was too weak to sit up, and turned his head slowly, his neck stiff. He smiled softly, making out Lara, her head resting on her arm, her hand holding his. *How long has she been there? How long have I been out?*

Carn turned slightly as he moved his good arm over to wake Lara, and winced at the twinge of pain. He gently squeezed her shoulder, not wanting to startle her. He felt her move slightly, then sat up. In the low light, he saw her features fill with relief and she smiled at him. He croaked, realising how dry his mouth was. "Hey, sleepy. How long have I been out?"

Lara rubbed her eyes, glancing across at the window and then focusing on his eyes. "About two days."

He tried to sit up and cursed at the movement when a sharp pain stabbed through his shoulder. Lara quickly stood and helped him sit up. He looked at the shoulder, already knowing the answer, but still asked, "How bad?"

Lara softly smiled, her features unable to hide the sadness she felt. She glanced down for a moment and squeezed his hand as she found the best way to tell him. "You may struggle to use a sword."

He nodded, feeling forlorn. He already knew what the answer would be, but hearing it still shocked him. "I expected as much." He looked back up at her, his mouth feeling like it was filled with sand. "Can I have some water?"

Lara nodded, only just realising that he would be thirsty, and passed him a mug filled with water. He took it with his uninjured hand and had a sip, noticing his hand was shaking. Slowly, everything sank in. He passed her the mug back, and she studied him, kissing him on the lips. "I was so worried I'd lose you."

Carn gazed at her and cupped her cheek in his hand with his good arm. He dared not try to move the wounded one, as it made the pain so much worse. "You could never lose me. I'm too stubborn."

Lara's eyes closed for a moment, savouring the gesture. Then she chuckled softly and gazed at him. "I know."

Carn sighed, his eyes lost in the depths of her green. "Well, seems the retirement plans have come earlier than expected."

Her full lips curled upwards slightly. "We'll build that cabin in that clearing we found in Red Wood."

"Aye. As long as I have you, I'm happy."

Lara smiled and kissed him passionately, stopping when he winced in pain. "Sorry."

He tried to shrug, realising the gesture was not a good idea. He then pulled her towards him, wanting the kiss to continue. When they parted, he studied her and asked, "So you want to stay with an old, retired, one-armed Sword?"

Lara gazed at him with affection. "Till the end of time."

He chuckled and regarded her. He did not care if he never raised a sword again if he had her. He struggled to sit up more, trying to only use his good arm, but the movement still aggravated the shoulder and he winced. Lara moved around the bed to help him sit up more, trying not to cause him any pain. Carn hated that he felt so helpless, but he would not be staying in bed for days. He would have to get out, otherwise he would go stir-crazy.

Lara sat on the side of the bed, holding his hand and studying him warmly. "We'll soon get you up and about."

Carn smiled softly, and squeezed her hand. He wanted to thank Orthur for helping him. "Is Orthur here?"

Lara shook her head. "Nay, he headed back to Silver Wood as soon as he knew you would make it."

"I just wanted to thank him."

"I thanked him, and he said once things were taken care of at Silver Wood, he would come back to check on you." She paused and smiled. "His exact words were to make sure you weren't bouncing off the walls and sending me and Roclus mad at your incessant moaning."

Carn raised his eyebrows, feigning hurt, and gasped. "Really!"

Lara laughed and squeezed his hand. "I'm only teasing. He wanted to come back and see you were alright. He said you fought well against the lycans."

Carn smiled. "Well, I have had some practice over the years." He leant to get the water, realising he was trying to use the injured shoulder again; he would have to get used to not using his dominant arm for a while. As Lara passed him the water, he added, "What happened to him in the woods? Was it that creature?"

Lara nodded. "Aye. I spoke to Orthur yester morn before he left, and he told me everything that had happened. He lost one of his pack to it, but with them all being in werewolf form, they soon cornered and killed it. He told me about the nest. It had remains going back years, seems it had become the apex predator in the forest. But I feel, when food ran out, it would have ventured towards one of the towns."

Carn took another sip of water. Talking to Lara had made him forget about the pain and heaviness of his body. "Nay wonder the forest had such a reputation."

"Aye. I wish we had dealt with it when we came across it. Then there wouldn't have been any casualties."

Carn sighed, squeezing her hand. "We weren't to know." He suddenly felt extremely tired and leant back a little, not wanting to make it too evident and make Lara worry. When he felt unwell, he took a deep breath and kept focused. He added. "Anyway, if it wasn't for Tomlin, we would have killed that creature in the next few weeks."

Carn felt a more constant ache developing in his shoulder, reminding him that his Sword days were behind him. He sighed and closed his eyes for a moment as Lara stated, "Aye, we would have dealt with it."

Carn nodded and whispered, "It wouldn't have known what had hit it." His eyes were half open as he leaned his head against the wall. He felt exhausted. He gently squeezed Lara's hand, making sure she was still there. "So, the cabin, do you want it to face south or west?"

Lara squeezed his hand and replied, her voice sounding so distant. "South, I think."

Carn smiled. "Humm." Then added, more like a whisper. "Think I'll just rest for a while."

Lara smiled softly as Carn's features relaxed and he fell asleep. He looked exhausted and so pale. But he was on the mend; it would just take time for him to heal. Knowing he needed a lot more rest, Lara left the room to stretch her legs. The main inn was empty, the inn almost silent in the early hours. Walking over to the bar, Lara poured herself a drink and stood by the smouldering fire, savouring the alcohol. She was glad Carn was going to be alright. He had taken the news well about his arm, yet, she could tell in his voice and features that he already knew. Then again, he would have known the moment he lost the grip of his sword. Every Sword knew what their limitations were.

She sat down in the chair near the fire. She had thought she was going to lose Carn when she saw his injury in the forest. And Lara just would not have been able to continue without him. She studied the smouldering embers of the fire and sighed. She was reminded that the day would come when she would outlive Carn, and she dreaded it. She wanted to make sure she spent as many moments with him as she could. At least he was on the mend, and they would have some years left together. Yet, being in his fifties, the years of being a Sword and the injuries, especially the ones from demons, were taking their toll upon his body. Maybe it was a good thing he had been injured; it would make them rest and change their lifestyle, giving them as many years as they could.

Lara sighed again and closed her eyes for a moment. If Scarlett had not reached the inn and helped, then the outcome would have been so different. She shook her head, telling herself to stop thinking about what could have happened and look towards the future again. The past was done; she had dealt with Tomlin, and Carn was on the mend. They would still have many years together. They could lead a quiet life, and if anyone came knocking on their door, she would deal with them.

CHAPTER 33

IT HAD BEEN a few days later when Raia stopped at the inn on the way to Silver Wood. The inn was not too busy, and she found Carn and Lara sitting at a table near the back. Carn was eating a plate of meat and potatoes, and Lara was chatting with him. It seemed he had finally had enough of being cooped up in the back room and wanted to be around some other people. He looked pale and drained, but was in good spirits. Both looked up when Raia reached their table.

Lara gestured for the young woman to sit. "It's good to see you. So, tell me, what happened with your papa?"

Raia studied the two, her eyes lingering on Carn's shoulder. Even though covered by his grey shirt, the bandages could still be seen. "First, it's good to see you up and well, Carn." She glanced between the two. "And thank you for dealing with Tomlin."

Lara and Carn nodded; the latter stated as he took a sip of ale. "Well, nay, more Sword contracts for me, but glad Tomlin and his men can nay longer cause any trouble. What of your papa?"

Raia sighed. "It was hard work, but I have convinced him to protect more than just Shadefall. I feel things are looking positive."

Lara inquired, "Did you get into any more trouble?"

"Aye, at first." Nodded Raia. "Some of Tomlin's men tried to stop me. But with Jon's help, we dealt with them. I may look small, but my wolf is formidable."

Lara smiled, knowing being the next in line, Raia would nearly have the strength of an alpha. Raia continued, "I told my papa everything, and he asked for his forgiveness for believing his brother. He understands what he was doing was wrong, and wants to be a better alpha, with me at his side." She paused. "I threatened him as well. Told him he protect Shadefall and beyond, or I would challenge him. Papa knows that I would have the backing of most of the pack as well now that Tomlin has gone, and his men."

Lara raised her eyebrows. "Good for you."

Raia smiled, then sighed. "I wish I had been forceful with him sooner, then Tomlin wouldn't have got the power he had, and maybe Silver Wood would . . ."

Lara placed a hand on hers. "Don't think that. Tomlin was a menace. He probably saw you as more than a threat, and would have killed you the first moment he could."

Raia nodded. "Well, we're now protecting everything up to Derlin, and the same distance east, west, and along the coastline. Papa has even given me more responsibility than I asked for, and we'll work equally."

"A good lycan pack." Lara asked, "What about Jon?"

Raia responded. "Back at Silver Wood, helping get everything back on its feet. We have an alliance with Orthur now."

Lara nodded, studying the young woman. "What I meant was you seemed close to Jon."

Raia smiled. "We're good friends."

Carn chuckled and muttered. "Looked more than that."

Lara nodded and took Raia's hand. "Tell me the truth. Was there anything more?"

The young woman gazed at her for a moment. "Nay, we're friends and nothing more." She studied Lara, who eyed her disapprovingly and then sighed. "Alright there was something, but we ended it."

Carn stated, eyeing the two. "I knew it."

Lara glanced at him, rolling her eyes, and then turned back to Raia. "Just keep it as a friendship. Both your papa and Orthur are traditionalists. If you and Jon became more than friends, it will cause a rift."

Raia smiled softly. "I know. That's why we parted as friends, knowing we have to look at the greater good."

Lara nodded, studying the young girl. She had a sensible head on her shoulders and she would make a good alpha one day.

Raia took a sip of her ale and studied the two. "So, what now for you both?"

Carn glanced at Lara and then stated, "Retirement."

Lara agreed, "Aye. We have decided that it's time to put up our swords."

Raia gazed at them both. "But there will always be a need for an excellent Sword and you, Lara, could still fight."

She smiled. "Aye, but I'm older than I look, and think it's time."

Raia nodded. "I hope you will both be happy."

Carn glanced at Lara. "Aye, we will."

Lara smiled at him, wanting to kiss Carn, but they had to keep the father-and-daughter act going while in the main inn. Raia leant forward. "Does anyone know about you two?"

Lara shook her head and Carn stated, "Nay. And we want to keep it that way. We are papa and daughter, but once alone . . ."

Raia nodded, glancing around the room. "Understandable."

Lara took a sip of her drink and regarded the young woman. "So, are you going back to Shadefall?"

Raia shook her head. "Nay, not yet. I'm making a patrol of the area. See where we may need to place some of the pack, and then onto Silver Wood and rebuild with them."

Lara nodded. "A good plan."

They continued to talk for a while longer before Carn made his excuses to leave, feeling tired. His strength was returning, but he was still tiring quicker than he would normally. The two lycans chatted for a while longer, having a drink. Lara told Raia about her time travelling the land, and the history of her lycan heritage.

Carn returned to the back room and slumped on the bed. Now alone, he let his exhaustion take hold. He was trying to be strong for Lara, but his body ached and his shoulder was agony. He glanced at it and sighed. The pain ran deep, he was sure he could still feel the claw marks in his bones. He leaned back against the wall, sitting on the bed, letting his body rest. He closed his eyes for a moment. It had only been a few days, but could not help but wonder how much longer was he going to feel so exhausted. He sighed. He had to let his body heal, and that meant to rest. Something that he had always found hard to do. *But I'll just closed my eyes for a little while.*

Carn snapped awake, the pain in his shoulder sharpening his senses. He glanced across at the window. It was still light outside, so he could not have nodded off for long. He moved off the bed, wincing when he used his injured shoulder. He took a deep breath and glanced around the room. His eyes focused on his sword leaning against the wall. Getting to his feet, he strolled over to it. He grabbed the sword with his good arm. Studying the worn, but decorative scabbard. He had had his sword for years; it was part of him. He took a hold of the leather hilt and pulled it free. For a few moments, his wounded arm clasped the long sword. Carn felt the sword in his hand, feeling the familiar weight. Maybe he would be alright. Then his arm shook, his grip weakened, and the sword clattered to the floor. Carn slumped back onto the bed, glaring at his hand as it shook uncontrollably. "Feck!"

He buried his head in his hands. He had known that his Sword days were over, but to feel the sword fall from his hand, unable to stop it, hit him like a hammer. His days as a Sword were done.

Carn felt a gentle hand on his arm. He slowly looked up to see Lara crouched before him. She smiled softly and glanced at the sword on the floor. "Give it time."

Carn smirked, flexing his hand as it shook. "Time? My arms fecked, Lara."

She sat beside him, taking his shaking hand in hers. She gazed at him. "Remember when we fought that ghoul a few years ago?"

Carn frowned. "What has this –"

Lara answered, cutting him off. "The ghoul slashed your forearm, remember?" Carn nodded, studying her. Lara continued, "You swapped your sword to your other hand, without a second thought, and sliced that fecker's head off."

"So?"

Lara sighed. "So, you are a formidable Sword, Carn. The best I have ever seen. Aye, your arm may be fecked, but you're just as strong a Sword with your other arm. Give it time and you could still wield a sword with expertise if you ever wanted to."

He gazed at her with sad eyes and smiled softly. She always knew what to say, and when he needed to hear it. He gently cupped her cheek in his hand and he kissed her gently. "I love you, Lara."

She smiled softly and kissed him again. "You can get through this. And I will be with you every step of the way."

CHAPTER 34

CARN FOCUSED ON Lara's head as it rested on his chest, his fingers playing with her brown hair. It had been a couple of weeks and his shoulder was almost healed. On the outside, the skin was still pink and there were going to be scars. Yet internally the muscles were still painful and the strength had not fully returned to his arm. But after weeks of recovering, he had had enough of being treated as an invalid and needed to get out of these four walls before he went stir-crazy. He whispered. "I've been thinking."

Lara turned slightly so she could focus on his features from where she lay against him. "About what?"

Carn gazed at her green eyes. "I think it's time to leave."

Lara leant her chin on his chest, studying him. "To Red Wood?"

Carn shook his head, Lara sitting up with more curiosity in her features. "Nay. I had been thinking; before all of this . . ." He glanced at his shoulder. "You wanted to go to Ra to look up information about that creature."

She nodded. "Aye, but there is nay need now. It's dead."

Carn pulled himself up into a seated position, wincing slightly. "True, but I think it still should be checked. If it hasn't been recorded, it needs to be."

Lara raised an eyebrow regarding him. She took his hand in hers. "There's more, isn't there?"

He smiled softly; she knew him too well. "Aye. I'm going stir crazy here, and I want to build that cabin. But if my Sword days are over, I just want one more ride. You know, across Lost Island, go to Ra, up to Silver Wood and then back to Red Wood."

"But we both agreed we would stop."

Carn nodded. "Aye, we did, and we have. But I feel like I just want to ride one last time. Nay contracts, just ride and see the land before we settle down for a while. But I feel if I don't do this, I'll get twitchy."

Lara smiled and leaned forward, kissing him. "Alright, one last ride." She raised an eyebrow. "And to be honest, I want to see if there's a record of that creature, as I know I will always wonder if I don't."

Carn chuckled, unable to pull his eyes away from hers. "I knew it. You love that library too much."

She smirked. "Well, my papa used to say I always had my head in a book. I blame him." She studied his shoulder. "Will you be alright riding?"

Carn was fed up with everyone asking, and snapped, "*As for my fecking shoulder, aye it hurts, but I'm not fecking dead.*" He sighed, realising his voice had sounded bitter, seeing the hurt in Lara's features. "Sorry. But I'm not an invalid. Aye, it was a close one, but I have had severe injuries before. There's still life in me yet, even with a fecked up shoulder."

Lara glanced away from his blue eyes. "Sorry. I don't want you to feel I'm treating you like an invalid, and I won't. But it *was* a close call and there were moments when I thought I would lose you."

Carn nodded, kissing her gently, cupping her face in his callused hands. "I know, and sorry I snapped. But I *will* be alright." He studied her lovingly. "Anyway, you can't get rid of me that easily, but you will lose me to boredom if we stay here much longer."

She eyed him. "You are one stubborn fecker."

Carn gasped, placing a hand on his chest, acting hurt. "Me? Stubborn?"

Lara chuckled. "Well, you are, but then again, so am I."

He kissed her. "That's true." He sighed and added, "I may not lift a sword again like I used to, but that doesn't mean I have to stop living."

Lara smiled softly. "Alright, you've made your point. We'll leave for Ra in the next couple of days."

He nodded and kissed her passionately, pulling her towards him, ignoring the pain in his shoulder. "So . . ."

Lara raised an eyebrow. Carn smiled and kissed her again; his shoulder would protest, but he was not about to give up sex with the woman he loved.

After making love, Lara dressed and left to check on the horses. Carn watched her leave and smiled softly, always feeling ecstatic after making love with her. He leant back, savouring the peace for a few moments, his shoulder a dull ache. Carn took a deep breath and climbed from the bed. Grabbing his shirt from the floor, he struggled to get on, his shoulder burning with pain. He cursed under his breath and glanced at it, seeing the hideous scar. Several covered his body, and all ached more than he would ever confess. Another to the list made little difference. He sighed, fastening the shirt. He needed more time to rest and heal, but could not keep sitting around for much longer. They would spend a lot of time in Red Wood when they built the cabin. Yet, things would be different there. They would not have to hide their feelings, where, on the road, they had to be careful. Carn donned his trousers, which had been discarded on the floor. He sat on the edge of the bed and pulled on his boots, cursing when a sharp, stabbing pain shot through his shoulder. He would put on a brave face, knowing that if Lara saw how much he was still in pain, she would insist they wait longer. Leaving the inn would help him mentally, and physically as well.

The visit to Ra would do them both some good. He was aware that her vampire side never liked staying in one place for too long. She would not admit it, but she had to be itching to travel again. Lara also loved that library, and books had always fascinated her. Carn saw a different side to her whenever she was there and did not want her to miss out on the opportunity to visit the place again. He sighed. They would still travel after they finished the cabin, but when they wanted to, and not for a contract.

Carn slowly stood, feeling a little dizzy. He placed his hand on the headboard and took a deep breath to regain his vision. He hated this and wanted to look as well as possible. Otherwise, everyone would keep fussing over him and that was making him crazy. Carn took a few more deep breaths, until he was feeling like he would not pass out, then he left the room. When he reached the main part of the inn, Roclus gave him a nod and a smile as Carn walked over to the counter.

The innkeeper stated, "Lara says ya well enough to travel. And 'ave to say, ya looking well."

Carn smiled broadly. "Aye. I want to get back on the road again and, to be honest, you can have your room back."

Roclus nodded. "Anything, my friend. I keep offering Lara a room, but she insists on sleeping on the floor in yours."

Carn smiled, glad for when the father-daughter act could end. He had been the one to insist on it, but now he just wanted to be Lara's lover again. "Aye. I have told her the same, but she wants to keep an eye on me."

"That daughter of yours has a good heart."

Carn replied, "Aye, that she does."

"So ya heading north?"

Carn nodded, taking the mug of water Roclus offered him. He leaned against the counter trying not look like he needed to sit down. "Aye."

The innkeeper smiled. "Well, there are always rooms here for ya both."

Carn lifted his mug in salute. "Thank you."

He turned when Lara came up beside him, placing a hand on his arm. "I have arranged with Roclus for food supplies. Horses are prepared and we can go in the next day or two."

Carn nodded, glad they would not have to stay too much longer. "That's good with me."

When the play acting ends, he would be happy. He knew it was just a means to an end. He had seen his fifty-sixth winter, and Lara looked twenty-one. Little did anyone know she was nearly sixty. He followed Lara to a nearby table and waited for the food he had ordered. He studied her as Lara told him about the horses. Although she looked like a young girl, when you studied her eyes, you could see an old soul in them; one he wanted to live out the rest of his life with. He felt a twinge of pain, not from his shoulder but, in his heart. One day he would be gone, and she would live on, for maybe hundreds of years. He had thought of this before, but somehow it seemed to hit harder now. Maybe it was the constant ache he now felt in his joints, making him realise he was getting old. Yet in his heart, he still felt in his thirties. Studying Lara as she talked, it was her that made him feel young at heart. She would outlive him, but he was going to savour every moment he had with her.

She frowned, studying him. "What are you thinking about?"

He smiled, taking a sip of his water, glancing at the barmaid when she placed his food down in front of him. He nodded thanks, and turned back to Lara. "Just about us, and the cabin."

"Aye, it'll be good for us."

Carn focused on her eyes. "Nay more hiding."

Lara smiled softly. "Aye."

Carn gazed at her for a few moments, wanting to kiss her passionately, but it would not be wise. Suddenly, he was not hungry. He wanted to hold Lara so badly he ached. He suddenly stood, raising an eyebrow. "I need some air."

Lara followed him out of the inn, and they walked to the barn. Once alone, Carn kissed her passionately. When they parted, he studied her and said, "Let's leave at dawn."

She nodded and melted in his arms when they curled around her. She leaned her head against his chest and whispered, "Aye. I just want it to be you and me."

Carn kissed the top of her head and smiled. "The same. Nay more acting. Let it just be us."

She looked up at him. He looked exhausted, and partly knew he needed more rest, but it was what Carn wanted, and she was not about to stop him.

CHAPTER 35

LEAVING THE INN behind at dawn, they headed to Derlin and then onto the city of Ra. It had been a while since they had been to the affluent capital, but when they visited, it always took their breath away. Ra was the largest city that they had ever been to and was the home of the royal family of the island. It was situated on a cliff top, overlooking an inlet from the sea. The River Ra cascaded down in an impressive waterfall to the inlet and the sea beyond. The royal castle stretched over the river, which made it look like the waterfall was falling from the palace itself. The city had impressive white marble walls all around. At the cliff tops there were smaller, ornate walls along any exposed cliffs. The low walls allowed the city folk to see the large dock below. Zigzagging, white, cobbled roads and well-worn paths led from the city to the docks and over to a fishing hamlet. At either end of the inlet, were two impressive watchtowers where there was always a regiment of the royal guard on duty. For over a hundred years, none had ever seen combat, and all hoped it remained that way for more to come.

Their principal objective when they reached the city was the royal library. It was situated to the south of the main square and looked out over the cliffs to the sea beyond. Lara had talked to Orthur about the creature before he had left. Even though dead, it would be useful to see if there was anything in the library, and if not, she could add her own and Orthur's accounts.

They entered the city via the main gates made of silver, which had a swirling design similar to what still could be seen on the city walls. They reminded Lara of Dalimor. The gates there were just as tall and as impressive, with carvings of eagles in flight across mountains. Lara wondered if it was the same in every city where there was a royal family residing. She looked up at the watchtowers above, making out the guards looking alert but also bored. Most people would not be able to see them from this height, but Lara's vision gave her the advantage. Riding side-by-side, Carn and Lara trotted at a steady pace to the inn near the centre which they had used several times before. The cobble streets were busy with travellers coming and going, market stalls had been set up to catch a quick trade or last-minute bargain. To the east were large barracks, walled off from the residents, the building was an impressive sight. Further in, and to the west, was the non-human quarter, which took up a large section of the city. When they reached the heart of Ra, there was another grand square, and down one of the side roads was the inn, The Malt House, they usually used.

Dismounting outside the inn, Carn and Lara took their belongings and let the stable boy take their horses to the stable behind. The two entered the large inn, and found it remarkably busy. Carn headed for the main counter while Lara looked for a table. After speaking to the innkeeper, Carn walked over to Lara, who was seated at a table near the back and sat opposite her, passing her a drink. He took a sip of his ale and stated, "Only one room left, not his best, but to be honest, all aren't bad."

Lara smiled and studied him. "Well, we only need the one, anyway."

He gave her a quick wink and smiled. "So, do you need me when you go to the library? I was going to get the horse's shoes looked at and then the supplies we may need for the cabin."

Lara gazed at him. "You always get fidgety when you go with me." She paused, giving him a sly smile. "And always asking if I have finished yet."

Carn turned down his lips, looking sad, then laughed. "You know me. I just need to keep active."

Lara raised an eyebrow. "Like that time in the ancient history section."

Carn blushed slightly, remembering the extra activity they got up to in the incredibly quiet section of the royal library. He gave her a sly smile. "Well, that's definitely more entertaining."

Lara chuckled, leaning forward. "You know, the main librarian gives me disapproving looks every time I go there now. I feel sure she knew what we were up to."

Carn took a big sip of his ale and responded, "I don't think we were the only ones to get up to something in that library. And she's been there so long that she has seen it all."

Lara had to agree that the elven librarian would have many a story to tell. She focused on the inn while Carn ate his food, which he devoured as soon as it arrived. She regarded everyone in the inn. Most were traders from human to dwarf. The rest were a mix; she spotted a few Swords and a couple trying to keep a low profile. She took in the scents, picking up the metallic ones of the dwarves and the earthy smell of a few elves dotted about. She even picked up a vampire one. Seeing a lone woman in the corner, Lara focused on her for a few moments, but she was alone. It was no concern to her if a vampire wanted a quiet drink. She then picked up a second vampire and watched him walking towards the woman and Lara raised an eyebrow. It had been some years, but it looked like Fashor. Lara smiled to herself, wondering when she would cross paths with the vampire again. She watched them for a moment and Fashor looked her way; he raised his glass to her, and she returned the favour. They did not need to exchange words. He cocked an eyebrow, focusing on Carn, and then turned away. Lara smiled and turned her attention back to Carn when he asked, "Someone you know?"

Lara nodded and smiled. "A vampire who was kind to me when I was first turned."

Carn nodded, glancing over, then turned back to Lara. "Do you want to go and talk?"

"Nay, he just nodded a greeting. We will cross paths again one day."

Carn nodded and focussed fully on her. "So, I know I won't need an early start in the morn, will you?"

"The library doesn't open till mid morn."

Carn smiled, raising an eyebrow, a mischievous glint in his eyes. "Good."

The two soon headed up to their room, knowing they were supposed to be father and daughter in public. But as the door to their room locked, they could be lovers once more.

It was mid-morning when Lara walked across the city to a large open square where the royal library was located. She had left Carn at the inn, as he was going to get the horses' shoes replaced and then look into the supplies. They would need some to build the cabin. She smiled to herself, it would be good to have a cabin. She fondly remembered the one that Derwyn and herself built all those years ago near Yarl. It had been good there, and the spot they had picked had been perfect. They could have lived there for as long as they wanted. Lara smiled softly, thinking about the spot in Red Wood that she and Carn had found. It would be perfect too. Even though they had to bring their plans forward after Carn's injury.

She reached the impressive building of the royal library; the doors were large and ornate. There was a carving of an open book in the centre, so when the doors were closed you could see the entire image. But at this time of the day, the doors were wide open, allowing anyone entry. Lara walked up to the main desk and smiled at the stern-looking female elf, who seemed as ancient as the books in the library itself. Lara felt a little guilty wondering if the woman knew about what she and Carn got up to in the ancient history section those years before. Yet she just smiled, admitting nothing. "I think I may have found a new demon and want to check the entries that are already here."

The elf studied her for a moment, then pulled a key from under the counter. "Here, but you can't remove any of the papers."

Lara nodded, knowing the rules all too well, having been in the vault of documents several times over the years. Taking the key, Lara walked across the vast library, which comprised of six large floors. In the main atrium, where the main desk was, she looked up to see the floors above, all full of bookshelves packed with every book imaginable. Walking to the far end, she stopped in front of a large oak door. Carved into the wood was a horned creature. It was the entrance to the main vault, which held all the records on demons that had ever been documented. There were books in the main part of the library, but to get hold of the oldest information, and to find everything that had ever been recorded, the vault was where to look. Inside was another locked door that held books on witchcraft and demonology. The key for that one was on the authority of the King only, as the library deemed them to be too dangerous.

Lara unlocked the main door and entered the room, closing it behind her. The air was stale and musty from being kept enclosed, and the fact some papers and books were so old. Lara would be here for some time as the older books had to be treated with great care so as not to damage them. She went to the desk she always used, and discovered it had papers scattered across it. It seemed she was not the only one who used this room for research. She looked around at all the shelves and wondered where to begin. Going by her instincts, she headed towards the back where the older volumes were kept.

After a few hours of going through various tomes and scrolls, it seemed the creature she had found in the forest had never been documented. Lara went to an unused desk and took out the worn, leather journal she was never without. She had included her own account of the demon and had added the information Orthur had shared with her. She took a seat and copied it down. Once it was all written out, she let the librarian know so it could be officially added to the archives. With all that done, Lara wandered around the library, glancing at the other books for a while, knowing she could happily stay there for days.

Once she had finished wandering around. Lara walked back through the city towards the inn when she picked up a familiar scent and could see Carn ahead. He was talking to a flower stall owner and Lara smiled, knowing exactly what he was doing. It seemed to be his thing to bring her lavender. At first, he thought it was a fragrance she had liked. It shocked Lara he could pick up the scent. Then when she finally told him, after they found each other again, why she smelt a little of lavender, Carn still insisted on buying her a small bunch now and then. Lara had to admit she did like it and had kept the first lot he had given her until they had disintegrated to dust. She had been so disheartened when the last gift he had given her had finally gone. But at least now she would always have more.

Lara walked up to Carn as he turned from the stall and he grinned. "I was just getting you a little something."

Lara smiled, taking the small bunch of lavender and sniffing it. "Thank you."

Carn studied her. "So, what did you find out?"

Lara sighed. "Not much. It seems they haven't any record."

"So, what now?"

Lara fell into step beside him as they walked across the city. "Well, I added mine and Orthur's account. If any more pop up, then at least there is a record."

Carn nodded and looked ahead at the city. "I've had the horses' shoes redone, and have got us a couple of decent axes."

She nodded, knowing they would help with the cabin building. She wondered if Carn would be alright with using an axe, but it was wise not to ask after that morning at the inn. He had hated being treated like an invalid, and she understood completely. She would see him now and then wince, but decided not to say anything. Letting him take the lead if he needed help or rest. Lara partly knew they should have stayed at Roclus's longer, but Carn needed to leave. She felt the need in her bones too, but hers was down to her vampire side wanting to move on. Yet Carn hated to be helpless. He had always been an active person, and one who could deal with anything. To suddenly be in the position of being weak, she could see why he felt so frustrated. Lara had to agree with him that the ride here had done them both some good.

They returned to the inn and Carn ordered food and drink, as Lara headed off to find a quiet table at the back. Carn came over and joined her, smiling. "So, head for Silver Wood?"

"Aye, it will be good to see Orthur. See how they are doing with the village."

Carn nodded. "I still find it hard to believe Tomlin would have done such a thing."

Lara shrugged. "We'll never fully know why, but his hatred was deep. He saw it as a way to get what he wanted."

The arrival of the food made Carn realise how hungry he was and drew his attention to it. Lara leaned back in her seat and studied the inn. No sign of Fashor. Maybe he was just passing through. She turned her attention back to Carn as he ate; it was good to see him almost back to his old self again. The wounded arm seemed to stay at his side more as she noticed he favoured his stronger shoulder. She wondered how much it was still hurting him, but he would never say. She focused on his face and the scar that trailed under his beard, realising how many he had all over his body. Some were from when they were apart, but she felt guilty for all the ones he had got while they fought side by side. Yet she knew he did not regret any of them. They had a good few years fighting side by side and it felt good knowing that old life was now in the past.

CHAPTER 36

WHEN THEY REACHED Silver Wood, it surprised them at the amount of activity in the village. There was no sign of the slaughter all those weeks before. Lara saw Orthur, and he strode over as the two dismounted. The alpha took Carn's arm and beamed. "Good to see you well."

Carn nodded and surveyed the village. "Looks like nothing happened."

Orthur smiled, looking around. "Aye. I had the pack move in with their families."

Lara frowned. "I didn't see any families at the house."

Orthur responded. "Nay, they lived further in the woods. But I think it made sense to have them take over the village. In time, others will come, but I want to ensure what happened isn't too well known. It could cause issues, and this village deserves to live again."

Lara nodded in agreement. The last thing his pack needed was a more negative opinion. Lara glanced towards the inn. "I'm hoping the inn has rooms."

Orthur nodded. "Aye, it does." He studied the two. "And nay hiding here, we all know what you are, Lara, and your relationship with Carn."

The two smiled, glad that at last, they did not have to do the father-daughter act. Orthur took hold of their horse's reins. "Come, let us have a drink."

They followed the alpha to the inn, and the three found a table while the innkeeper brought over drinks. Lara studied Orthur and said, "Raia told us of the alliance with the lycans."

Orthur replied, "Aye, with Raia in charge, we'll work with her pack. I'm weary of her papa, but I trust her."

Lara nodded, knowing it would take him time to trust Dray, but it was good news they would work together. She took a sip of her drink while Orthur turned to Carn. "How is the shoulder?"

Carn smiled, glancing at it. "Mending well. I want to thank you for helping me in the forest."

Orthur patted him on his good arm. "The least I could do. It was hit and miss if you would make it. I thank the Goddess Wolvina," he glanced towards Lara. "But Lara also said you were too stubborn to give up."

Carn chuckled, studying her lovingly. "Aye, that's true." He turned back to Orthur. "Goddess Wolvina?"

The alpha smiled. "Ahh, aye. All werewolves owe their lives to the goddess." He glanced at Lara. "As the lycans have the God Laycain, we have the Goddess Wolvina. She created us one eve to help protect the lands from vampires and demons." He paused, raising an eyebrow. "Even from lycans."

Lara said, "I had read something that you worshipped a goddess but never knew the name."

Orthur smiled. "Aye, it has been lost over the centuries with the werewolves born by the bite. But we teach the ones of pure blood of our origins."

Lara nodded and smiled. "I knew we were all alike in more than just family traditions."

Orthur studied them. "So, is it true you have both retired?"

The two nodded, and Carn smirked. "I ache too much."

Orthur chuckled. "My papa would say things like that, and he lived to one hundred and twenty."

Carn replied, "Well, hoping there are a good few years left in me yet."

Lara touched his hand. "There is, and I'm counting on many."

Orthur studied the two, both looking at each other lovingly, knowing they did not have to hide it anymore. He downed his drink. "I'll leave you both. I have pack business to deal with."

The two nodded but seemed unaware when he left. Carn breathed. "Shall we go to the room? I've had enough of people for a while."

Lara nodded. "Me too." Taking his hand and leading the way.

Once in their room, they kissed passionately. Lara unbuttoned Carn's jerkin blindly. He winced slightly as he pulled it off, but grabbed Lara, pulling her body against his. His hands slid to her belt, unbuckling it as he continued to kiss her. As it fell to the floor, his hand pulled her shirt free and roamed up her bare back. Lara's skin tingled at his touch. Lara pushed him gently towards the bed.

Carn's legs hit the side of it. He grabbed Lara around the waist and pulled her with him as he fell backwards onto it. Their embrace never broke. As Lara laid on top of Carn, she pulled up his shirt, trying to unthread the lace-up fastening. She cursed, pulling away from him. "I hate this fecking shirt."

He gazed up at her and chuckled. His hands went to hers and unfastened it in only a few moments. He raised an eyebrow as her firm breasts were exposed. "I have nay problems with yours."

Lara gazed at him from where she sat straddling him. She smirked and grabbed his shirt, ripping it open. Carn glanced down. "That was my favourite shirt."

Lara sucked her bottom lip and gazed at him. "Less talk."

Carn chuckled, grabbing her waist in his hands, then roamed up her body and cupped her breasts. He pulled himself up and sucked one of her nipples. He gazed up at her as his hands roamed back down to her waistband, his hand sliding down towards her groin, making her moan in pleasure. He whispered, "I love a woman who knows what she wants."

Lara moved her groin on his, making his trousers bulge. She smiled at him and slid her hand into his trousers, massaging his groin. Carn grunted in pleasure. Grabbing her around the waist, and flipped her round, so he was on top, ignoring the pain in his shoulder. He stood, pulling his trousers off and then hers. He gazed at her and smiled. Carn started placing gentle kisses across her breasts and then her torso towards her groin, eager for her familiar taste on his tongue once more.

He then moved back up to her, and Lara opened her legs for him to enter her. She felt him thrust hard, her loins shuddering in delight. Lara gazed up at him, her eyes lingering on the scars on his shoulder. Carn leaned forward, keeping his hips moving as he kissed her gently on the lips. Lara felt his arm shake. But before Carn realised it, Lara grabbed him and, using her strength, flipped him over so she was on top. Their connection never breaking. Lara smiled at him as she kept her hips moving. Carn gazed up at her, his features flushed as he reached orgasm. Lara felt her body buzzing with delight as she felt her own body about to orgasm as well. Soon they climaxed together and Lara fell into Carn's embrace as they both gasped, their bodies still connected, feeling each other throbbing with pleasure.

After a couple of days at Silver Wood, they continued on their journey, reaching Red Wood after a week. They knew where to go in the large forest to get to the clearing they had found all those years before, and it was still perfect. They built the cabin within a few weeks, even though it was hard for Carn to use his shoulder. It felt good to have a home they could call their own; it was simple, but they were happy. Lara could hunt and run whenever she wanted. Carn started hunting and grew vegetables in a garden by the cabin. He began training with his other arm and could soon use a sword again if he wished. They could live there for as many years as they had left together. And live as they wanted, and not by what others expected to see.

EPILOGUE

TEN YEARS LATER

ARN REGARDED THE three lycans and one human, with expert eyes, as they repeated the moves he had instructed them to do. They filled the open area to the side of the cabin with swooshing sounds from their swords. His blue eyes wandered towards Lara, who was showing a young girl how she could use her lycan strength to her advantage. Carn's lips curled up slightly, remembering that morning when Lara had been in his arms. He still found it amazing that they had been living in the cabin for over ten years now and it was the best thing they had ever done. To wake every morning with the woman he loved, he would not change it for anything. They had a vegetable patch to the rear, a stable for the horses and, for the last seven winters, the open space off the side of the cabin had become a training area. The cabin would get a little crowded with the recruits sleeping on the floor, but it was what they wanted.

Carn dragged his eyes from Lara and turned to Raia, realising she had said something to him. "Huh?"

The lycan alpha smiled, her eyes flicking to Lara and back to Carn. "I said, how are they doing?"

Carn regarded the thirty-year-old woman. Raia had taken over as alpha after her father's death a few winters back. With Carn's and Lara's reputation of being excellent trainers for the locals who wanted to become Swords, Raia had asked the two to help train the younger members of her pack.

He replied, "Well. They're quick learners."

Raia regarded his grey hair and beard. For a man having seen over sixty-five winters, he was still strikingly handsome. "They have told me you are a hard taskmaster."

He looked across at the trainees and said, "Aye. I think I should have given up my Sword contracts earlier than I did."

"Do you miss it?"

Carn shook his head and rotated his shoulder that had sustained a serious injury years before. "Nay. It was hard to adjust at first. Even when I took up some contracts after my injury. But soon realised I was just getting too old for it all."

Raia glanced across at Lara as she talked to the trainees. "Is Lara still taking them?"

He looked across at his lover of several decades. "Nay. She did her last contract last winter. Lara only did them when we needed extra coin. But with the fact we are now so sought after as trainers, we collect more coin with this than we ever did with contracts."

"So, you're both retired?"

Carn smiled at her. "Aye. Think we are."

Raia regarded Lara as she strolled over to them. Carn curled his arm around her waist and Lara said, "What's Carn been telling you?"

The alpha smirked. "I think you would know with your lycan hearing."

Lara chuckled, gazing up at Carn. "Aye, and we have retired. Think we won't have time with all the requests for training."

Raia responded, "Your reputations precedes you both."

Lara smiled. "Well, we must travel to Ore in the morn. We have a request to train the villagers there."

Raia nodded. "Aye, I have heard they have issues with a demon." She raised an eyebrow. "Maybe make some extra coin?"

Lara shook her head. "Nay, not for us now. I can recommend them a Sword. He was one of our first, and he's making good coin now."

"It's good that your training is giving us some well renowned Swords."

Lara gazed at her. "He was a natural, and now his reputation is preceding him."

Raia responded. "Then I will ensure I look out for him." She turned her attention back to the three young men and the girl. "As I'll need to leave soon, I could take the group back with me if you must travel to Ore in the morn."

Carn smiled. "Aye, that would be helpful. We intended to travel with them to the nearest inn, then go our separate ways. But if they leave now, then we can cut across the country."

Raia regarded the two. "You can then have some time together this eve."

Lara leaned against Carn and smiled. "Thank you. It has been a little awkward with everyone sleeping in the cabin."

Carn smirked. "We managed to this morn."

She looked up at him. "Aye, by making them do a dawn training run."

Raia laughed. "I now know why they say they have a lot of training runs."

The three burst out laughing. Raia then strolled over to the group, telling them to pack their things. Lara gazed up at Carn. "It will be good to have the cabin back to ourselves for a while."

He kissed her gently on the forehead and raised an eyebrow. "I have a few things in mind to keep us occupied."

Lara chuckled and looked across at the training area as Raia spoke to the small group. When Carn had suggested turning their skills to training, she had never realised how popular they would have become. But it seemed there was always a need to have well-trained Swords and, with their skills, they were natural teachers. She cherished Carn's embrace and, to have all this time with him, she would never change it.

Lara gazed at Carn, wondering how long they could keep up the training. Even though they had stopped their Sword contracts, it was in their blood and Lara knew Carn would want to do it till the day he could no longer lift a sword.

AJ Ashton

TWENTY YEARS LATER

The two had been well renowned trainers for over ten years. But it was then time to put their swords up above the mantle for good and have blissful years of retirement. One winter, a fever started spreading through the towns and villages. Lara had been unaffected, and thought with being in the woods that Carn would have been, too. Yet there was no escape. Carn caught the fever, and being in his mid-eighties, it seemed it was a fight the old Sword would not win.

Lara opened her eyes when she heard Carn's breathing becoming laboured. She studied his frail features; he looked so old as the fever took hold of his body. All the injuries he had endured over his lifetime had slowly caught up with him. For the last ten years, they had lived a quiet life at the cabin. Lara had still done the odd contract, but soon put up her sword to spend as much time as she could with Carn. Then Carn had developed a fever. At first, they had thought he would fight it off, but after the last few days, Lara realised it was something he could not beat. All she could do was sit by his side, nursing the best that she could, and wait.

She gently placed a cool, damp cloth on his forehead, trying to keep him as comfortable as possible. Lara focused on his features. The scar on his cheek was masked by his full, grey beard. Lara smiled softly, remembering he had let it grow before they had reunited, and he had claimed it made him look wiser. Lara had teased him about it for months. She gently traced her fingers over it, the beard still soft. Carn suddenly stirred and coughed, his chest wheezing more. From her senses, she knew it would not be long.

Carn's eyes focused on Lara and smiled softly, his withered hand cradling her cheek. "My love, I feel so cold."

Lara placed her hand over his and smiled softly, kissing him gently. "I'll get you more blankets."

He smiled and gazed at her. "You haven't aged a day since we met."

Lara smiled and studied him. In her soul, she was older, but to everyone who saw her, she was just a young woman. Yet she and Carn had been lovers for years. He had never said he was worried about her appearance, but she still remembered the act they would put on of father and daughter. But when alone, they were just two souls madly in love. She placed another blanket over Carn, tucking him in. He smiled and then coughed violently again, his chest rattling even more. She could sense his heart failing. Lara gently took his hand, tears welling in her eyes. Carn opened his eyes to look at her, but his gaze seemed distant, and he smiled softly and then whispered, "I see Iesha. She looks so happy."

Lara controlled her emotions as her heart broke. "You should go to her, my love."

He smiled; his eyes still distant. "She's with Isabel. They're calling to me."

Tears rolled freely down her cheeks as she squeezed Carn's cooling hand. "Go be with them. They have missed you so much."

Carn turned to her. He focused on her once more. He smiled and placed his free hand on her cheek, his thumb wiping away the stray tears. "Don't cry, my love."

Lara smiled, unable to trust her voice. Then his eyes became distant as he slowly took his last rattling breath. Carn's hand slipped from her cheek, and Lara crumpled onto his chest and cried.

Lara stood in front of the grave, tears rolling down her cheeks. Carn's sword planted firmly in the ground as a gravestone. She gently kissed her fingers and placed them on the newly dug earth. "One more candle has gone out in the sky. May your fallen ancestors lead you on your way."

She looked up at the sky and sighed, thinking about Derwyn. He would be in his late seventies and hoped he was fairing well. She took a deep breath and studied the grave.

"I'm going to head home. It's been so long, and I feel I need to set foot on Moonstar at least one more time."

Lara smiled softly, knowing there would not be an answer, but still felt good to have told him.

Will I ever be this way again?

She looked at the cabin. She would board it up and send word to Raia. If any of her pack wanted somewhere else to go, they could use it. The only condition would be that they tended to Carn's grave.

Lara took a deep breath, wondering if, in her long life, she would ever love again. Maybe. But for now, she just wanted to be on her own and mourn. Yet to see her homeland again it would be good for her, perhaps even travel to Lake Wood. She wondered if it would still be a small village. She smiled softly. She would go up to the woods and see if she could find her parent's graves. It would be good to know if the house was still standing. Someone may have been living in it. She would find out in a few years. That was how long she expected it would take her to get home, but then again, she had all the time in the world.

LARA WILL RETURN IN
OUTCAST THE RETURN
BOOK 3

After a hundred and forty years, Lara Tarrenfall returns to Moonstar, a land haunted by memories she cannot outrun. The echo of her soulmate Carn, the shadow of her brother Derwyn, and the lingering ache of a farewell to Ulric still weigh heavily on her immortal soul.

In the capital of Great Oak, Lara crosses paths with Evie Ranger, a sorceress of legend whose own past is steeped in power and peril. Their unlikely bond sparks a friendship that will shape the battles to come.

But Lara's journey takes her deeper still, to her childhood village of Lake Wood, where long buried secrets about her mother's death resurface, and a reunion she never dreamed possible awaits.

Her return, however, has not gone unnoticed. A dark enchantress rises, the vampire elite known as the Cleansers draw their blades, and Lara is thrust into a conflict against an enemy she never knew existed. To survive, she must call upon old allies and legendary Swords and face the terrible cost of immortality.

In the epic conclusion to The Tarrenfall Chronicles, Lara must confront the weight of her past, the fire of lost and rekindled love, and a darkness that threatens to claim her forever. Will she endure... or fall beneath the power that hunts her?

AUTHOR BIO

A J ASHTON was born in the 70's, in Derbyshire, UK. She still lives in the area, juggling a full-time job and being a mother.

From the age of seven, after seeing a rather famous sci-fi film, for the first time. Her creativeness to write was born. Inspired by a strong princess being rescued by a notorious smuggler. She wrote sci-fi, but her passion was soon drawn to fantasy. Where the world of Zentos was born.

Sign up for A J Ashton's monthly newsletter at
www.ajashton.com

For more information about the world of Zentos, visit my website for maps and a bestiary, which will be continually updated.
www.ajashton.com